THE STAMP *of* GLORY

THE STAMP *of* GLORY

A Novel of the Abolitionist Movement

Tim Stafford

THOMAS NELSON PUBLISHERS®
Nashville

Published in Association with the literary agency of Alive Communications, Inc., 1465
Kelly Johnson Blvd., Suite 320, Colorado Springs, CO 80920.

Note to Readers: Many of the characters in this novel are based on (and named after) real
historical persons who were crucial in the American abolitionist movement. Most of the
events described are, similarly, real and are told with as much historical accuracy as possible.

Scripture quotations are from the KING JAMES VERSION of the Holy Bible.

Published in Nashville, Tennessee, by Thomas Nelson, Inc.

Library of Congress Cataloging-in-Publication Data

Stafford, Tim.
    The stamp of glory : a novel of the abolitionist movement / Tim Stafford.
        p. cm.
    ISBN 0-7852-6905-3
    1. Antislavery movements—United States—History—19th century Fiction. 2. Slave
insurrections—United States—History—19th century—Fiction. 3. Afro-Americans—
History—19th century—Fiction. I. Title.
PS3569.T25S72   1999
813'.54—dc21
                                                                    99-33892
                                                                        CIP

Printed in the United States of America
1 2 3 4 5 6 QPV 05 04 03 02 01 00

To Nell Pope Herrod Stafford,
who brings me great joy.

Contents

Book IV: The Beginning of Blood

Book I
Youthful Hopes

Chapter 1
1824: Liberty to the Captives

In THE COLD, wet months of the winter of 1824, Martin Nichols withered and failed to eat. He showed no signs of disease, no fever or diarrhea, but the sickness cut into him like a north wind. He lost his taste for food, and his sparrowlike limbs grew daintier, his skin more like parchment. In this sickness old Black Mary, the keeper of the house and ruling mother for all the slaves, watched over Nichols night and day, spooning food into his mouth, wiping his chin. He lay like a doll in his mahogany bed, lost in its coarse, woven blankets. She would put one vast hand on the small of his back, lifting him upward toward the teaspoon she wielded in her other hand. When he utterly refused to eat, she occupied the kitchen, concocting delicacies to tempt him toward life. The house was filled with aromas then, as she stewed and spiced the venison with her best magic. Still he had no appetite and would only take a spoonful and then turn his head away. She told him sternly he must eat, but he did not.

Nichols was a planter near Triana, where the broad plain of the Tennessee River created bottomland for cotton. Nichols was old; his body had shrunk down to a frail, childlike frame with wrinkled, yellow skin stretched over the bones. Once he had been a strong, mean-souled Caesar, carving the plantation out of wilderness. Now his sons kept the farm without consulting him about it. Nobody paid much attention to the old man except the house slaves, some of whom were nearly as old as he was, and looked older. Nichols had brought them with him when he came from South Carolina twelve years before, when the country was opening up to settlement. They took their worth from that: the original settlers of north Alabama, Carolinians to the day they died. The head of the field hands said, those house servants don't know they are Negroes.

Nichols kept his bed by the window, so he could see every hint of life on the compound below. He watched the Negroes, mostly. You could rarely find his sons at home. They were out and about, riding and hunting and visiting their reckless friends. Nichols's daughter, too, was usually gone to Huntsville, where she could find society. Black Mary sat with the old man in his cold and forlorn room, unchanged since his wife had died, the French paper darkened with patches of creeping mildew. Mary listened as he pronounced doom on everything and everyone, particularly his sons.

"They're draining it," he said in a high, raspy voice, referring to the value of the land he had bought and partly cleared. "All the labor of my hands is draining away. Mark me, you'll be left with nothing." If you had overheard him you would have thought he expected Mary to feel the same alarm he did. But in reality she was only a slave, not someone he could treat with feelings, even if she did know and understand him more than any of his own flesh and blood.

Any time bad news had to be given the old man, his oldest son, Martin, Jr., would get Mary to tell it. Somehow she could get the old man to see the will of God in unpleasant matters. Nichols was a pious Methodist, though there was no Methodist church in Triana. He couldn't abide the Presbyterians or the Baptists, so went to no church at all. Yet he remained a Methodist, firmly.

Every day Nichols told Mary to send for the Methodist minister in Huntsville. *Go now, go now, get the preacher.* She said, right away, yessir, she would do it. He would hear her toiling down the stairs, breathing hard. Each step took half a minute; he would listen to the familiar squeak of each floorboard and grow furious knowing she could ignore his orders. After she had gone his mind would wander, however, and he forgot his need. The next day he would remember in a spasm of anxiety and ask again. She said the same thing, yessir, she would do it, right away.

In reality the minister had already come, riding into the yard on a frozen January morning, his nag's hooves making hard, metallic raps on the stiff ground. He had glanced at the old man with his practiced eye and knew he was not yet ready to go.

"When I'm needed, send word for me," he told Martin, Jr., and the young man understood. It was a day's ride to the plantation from town and back; the minister could not come until death was imminent.

The old slave Mary did not tell this to the old man; there was no need. "The preacher will come," she told him. "Don't you worry. He is a good man, that one. He will surely come."

Nichols was afraid to die, not that he doubted in the least that he would be united with his Savior when he awoke, but that he felt alone. None of his children had professed religion. He wanted to talk with someone who knew what he was talking about, and it would never have occurred to him that Mary qualified. He had that peculiar blindness of slaveholders: he would talk with Mary about his land, his children, his departed wife with an intimacy that no neighbor would ever gain, yet he thought of these conversations as no conversation at all, but more like thinking out loud to himself. He was, by his own accounting, quite alone at the end.

Mary noticed his cough in the late afternoon. A succulent fruitiness had replaced the ordinary dry hack, and when Mary put her hand to Nichols's forehead she found it warm and moist as a July afternoon. Mary sighed and shook her head. "What are we going to do with you?" she said, as though speaking to a child, and then turned to go downstairs.

She was not afraid of death, she had nursed it a great deal, and as far as she was concerned Martin Nichols was only one more puny man before the awesomeness of God. She was a Christian and, regardless of what she might think of Nichols's character, wanted to well guide him over the river. She could let go of this old man, to whom life had bound her, only when he was safe in the Savior's arms.

Descending the stairs she heard the rain hammering against the windows, as it had all afternoon. Martin the son was in the library, his feet up to the fire, his face sulky and mean. Even for him the weather was too wet, and being trapped inside left him restless and moody. Mary noted the squeezed lemons, the sugar, and the rum by the fire near his feet. All his father's threats and imprecations were no longer able to control his drinking in the house. She stood in the doorway, humming under her breath, waiting for some time before he noticed her.

"What's the matter?" he asked loudly. "Something wrong, Mary?"

"There is maybe," she said. "Your father has a bit of the fever."

Martin sat up in his chair. "So?" he said.

"You know, he is pretty weak, and sometimes when a man is puny the fever can take him quickly."

Martin picked up his glass, which was on the floor by his chair, and had a sip of its liquor. He was a strong, stocky man, thick waisted. His hair hung down long and uncombed onto his neck. "I'm sure you know how to treat a fever, Mary, as well as any doctor."

"Yes, Master Martin," she said. "I do. But your father wanted the preacher to come, you know."

He looked at her, scowling. "Mary, you don't expect me to go out in this weather!"

"No, Master," she said stubbornly, "I don't expect. I just thought you would want to know." She turned her large, thick body slowly, like a heavy ship tacking into the wind, and began out of the room.

"Mary," he said, and she stopped. "Did the fever just come on?"

"It just did," she said, turning back to him but not letting him see her eyes.

"Don't you think it might pass?"

"It might."

"Then let's wait a little longer. Even if I got to Huntsville in this rain, the preacher wouldn't come before the morning."

"The river might be up," she said.

"That's true," he said. "Then I'd be stuck there in town and no help to you either. Let's wait. I'll send Brady up to help you."

Brady was the youngest son. Ten years old, he ran wild on the plantation and had never gone to school. His mother had died at his birth, so Mary had raised him, if anyone had. He came upstairs and sat in a chair in the old man's room. He was towheaded and impatient like all the Nicholses. After Brady had bothered Mary with a dozen questions and kicked at the wall half a hundred times she sent him off to get the dinner bell for her. She said she would use it to call him if she needed him.

Mary sat by the sleeping old man, wiping his sweat with a cloth. The rain continued to pound. Late in the evening Martin came in, yawning. He turned up the light and looked closely at his father's sweat-beaded face, keeping his hands at his sides, not touching the old man. "He looks all right," he said. "He'll be fine, don't you think, Mary? Just a passing fever from this damp air."

She responded with a grunt that could pass for anything.

Martin sat down in the chair that Brady had used. "I'm going to go to bed, Mary. If anything happens in the night, you call me. If he's bad in the morning, I'll go get the preacher."

"If he goes that way, he won't need a preacher. Except for a funeral."

He scowled at her. "Listen to that rain. Now Mary, you can stop looking at me that way. I am not going out for an old man's whim. The preacher won't come now anyway. Methodist though he be, he is not a complete fool."

"The man said he would come when it was time."

"Well, how do you know it is time? Do you think I can go and say,

'Reverend, come on with me, let's swim the creek in this storm because an old black woman says it is time'? Do you think I can say that?"

Mary did not answer him. The rain sounded like sand being thrown violently against the house.

"Well, I am not going to say that. I am not going to ride to Huntsville in this rain in the dark. On a fool's errand."

"That's right," Mary said finally. "You get some sleep, Master." She had that ability, to go along with a master's authority yet reserve the judgment of her own mind.

This aggravated Martin, and he could not help himself; he still tried to win the argument. "If he is going to pass on, the preacher cannot stop it. Why does he want the preacher? The man has no power over life and death."

She grunted assent. "That's right. Your father just wanted to talk, you know."

"He can't talk anyway. Now can he?"

"No, Master. He hasn't got any talk in him just now."

Martin stood up and took a long, silent, clinical look at his father. "He looks all right to me," he said, and went out.

Mary dozed off and was awakened in the middle of the night by loud talking. At first she thought that someone had come into the room. Then she realized that the old man himself was proclaiming. He lay on his back, his eyes open but seeing something invisible. He was talking in English, but she could not follow his gibberish.

Putting a hand to his forehead she found him very warm. At her touch he shook his head, seemed to wake from his trance, and then darted his eyes about the room. He gradually focused on her, and his face grew sullen and snappish.

"You *will* burn the fire," he said. "Open a window. It's burning up in here."

"The room's not hot, Master," she said. "You've caught a fever."

He set his jaw. "Don't you talk back to me, you black beetle. You do what I say, or I'll have you whipped." His frail, stretched face had frightening command.

"Oh, yes, Master," she said and walked slowly around the bed to the window. Pausing with her hands on the window frame she looked at Nichols and saw that his eyes had closed. "The rain has stopped, Master," she said, "but the wind is blowing fierce. River might come up."

Nichols made no reply.

"You've been sleeping," she said, "since dinnertime. I've been right here with you. Master Martin came up to see how you were. So did Master Brady. They're sleeping now." When she saw that he had forgotten about the window she walked back around the bed and began to wipe his face. "This cloth cool enough, or should I get another one?" she asked.

He was sweating profusely and beginning to tremble. As she watched, his breath came faster, and she heard a catch, a slight gurgle, at the bottom of each one. Moving with quick and surprising grace, Mary plucked the dinner bell off the table and rang it four times. Then she pulled all the covers up to Nichols's neck, in order to sweat him. A low moan came from his throat.

Martin came in with just a pair of trousers pulled on, his bare, broad chest crowned with a dark golden haze of hair. "Is he worse?" he asked.

"He's coming to a crisis," Mary said.

"How soon?"

"I can't tell that, honey. Sometime before the morning. Sometime soon. I wish the preacher were here. That would give him a lot of comfort."

"I can't help that," he said curtly. "You'll just have to do the best you can."

Martin stood over his father, still not touching him. The old man looked like he had already gone, with his bloodless skin stretched tight over his face. The breathing grew more labored, leading to a spasm of loud choking and gasping. For an instant the old man's breathing stopped, and Martin held his breath with him.

Then the old man softly sucked in air again. The breathing grew steady, regular. Mary kept on wiping his face, and she was humming some tune.

She glanced up at Martin. "It's not yet, honey," she said. "It will take some time."

The rain was slashing at the windows again, as though trying to get in. Feeling cold, Martin told Mary to build a fire and watched her as she brought wood and skillfully blew the coals into a blaze. He put out a hand to feel his father's forehead and was startled by the heat.

Martin thought he should sit with his father, especially if the old man was finally dying. He had done so with his dog. Yet he was in many ways more intimate with his dog. Standing over this strange and vehement mask of his father, he could feel his own helplessness as though it sucked all the oxygen from the room. He would do no good; he would sit here hating it, begrudging his father his death. The old man did not want him. He wanted the preacher. The warmth and softness of his bed still clung to Martin's sleep-hungry memory.

"A lot to do tomorrow," he said at last. "I'd better get some sleep. You do whatever you can, Mary. Catherine, you stay and help her." He spoke to a slave girl who had silently appeared. "Anything you need, you just get it. Call me if it's . . . necessary."

"That's right," Mary said. "You sleep now, Master. I only wish that preacher was coming."

"Now shut up about that," he said, and went out.

Catherine, a lean, long-legged young woman, lay down by the fire and slept in a blanket, while Mary dozed in a chair next to the bed. She woke occasionally to put wood on and to check Nichols's breathing, but he slept quietly and might have seemed to recover except for the persisting fever.

Sometime in the early morning hours Mary got up and saw that his eyes were open, watching her.

"Sing for me," he said. "Sing 'Harvest Time.'"

She did so, in a low, dark voice. "Louder," he said, and she poured out the melancholy words of intense longing. When she was done she saw that he had closed his eyes, and she wondered whether he had gone back to sleep.

"Gates of Pearl," he croaked, and she sang that. He was quiet then, and she went to touch his cheek. It was still hot, hotter if possible. Yet his breathing was quiet, except for a slight muzziness when he breathed in.

"Is the preacher coming?" he asked without opening his eyes. When she did not answer, he repeated the question, then said, "I told you to have them call the preacher!"

"The river is up," she answered. "The preacher can't come."

She thought he would roar, but he remained silent. He opened one eye and looked at her. That one brown, staring eye seemed to be the only living part of his face, creased and yellow as it was. "Can't come, huh?" he said. "Did anybody go?"

"No, Master," she said. "Master Martin said he would go in the morning."

"Am I going to be alive in the morning?"

"Of course you are, honey. It's almost morning now," she said. She had not meant to say *honey*, but the word had slipped out. She had been with him since he was a boy. But he seemed not to notice.

"Mary, you tell me the truth. As God is your witness, will I be alive in the morning?"

"Only God knows these things."

He opened both eyes and looked at her fiercely. "Tell me," he hissed.

"You're asking me to tell what only the Lord knows. This fever is going to come to the crisis pretty soon, and then we'll know."

"You'll know what?"

"Whether this fever is going to kill you."

"And if it does, will the preacher make it in time to pray for me?"

"Maybe he won't," she conceded.

For a moment he was still, thinking of that. Then he said, weakly, "Sing for me. Keep singing."

"What do you want me to sing?"

"All the church music. Sing them all."

So she did, singing of Jesus and the Bible and heaven and most of all the judgment, one hymn after another. He seemed to be sleeping, but whenever she paused for long he opened his eyes and looked at her with outraged disapproval.

She noticed a slight tremor in his hand. She lifted it into her own, lightly holding its birdlike claw. While she sang "Servants of God" she felt the trembling increase. When the hymn was done she stood beside him, pulling the blankets over him. He said something, and she had to put her ear by his mouth to hear him repeat, "I'm cold."

She shook Catherine awake, took the blanket off her, and told her to build up the fire. Wrapping the extra blanket around the old man, she began to sing again. When Catherine had the fire blazing she squatted in front of it, her arms wrapped around her knees, swaying slightly.

The chills came on violently, and the old man's rasping breath grew louder, like the sound of a crosscut saw run slowly over an oaken board. Mary mopped at his brow, but he signaled for her to stop. "Pray," he gasped. "Pray for me."

His hands were jumping with the shakes, but she held her hand across his while she reminded God of all the great things she could think of from the Bible: Moses, and David fighting Goliath, and Jeremiah and the word like fire, and Ezekiel's bones, and Paul and Silas singing in prison. She could not read the Bible, but she had heard. She summoned all those men into the room to testify to the greatness and power of God.

The old man had his eyes closed, and though his hands and chin were still shaking violently, he seemed more at rest when she was done. In fact, a tight smile came on his lips, a little tan rosebud of a smile, like a private joke. He opened one eye again, a dark, staring eye in the colorless parchment of his face, and then both eyes. Slowly, unmistakably, he winked at her. He said something, words that came out in a cough she could not understand, setting off a fit of choking and gasping for air. When he had stopped strangling, though his breathing came harder and his face beaded with perspiration, she asked him to repeat it. The little smile came back on his lips. "You'll be free," he said in a voice so low it was barely audible on her ear next to his lips. "This morning." She heard it clearly. Then the smile disappeared, and he shut his eyes tightly, as though summoning all his strength for the battle.

She was suddenly wide awake and trembling ever so slightly herself. Could he be fooling? He was a cruel man, but at this time?

She sang again as she tended to him, a whole different species of song, about trumpets and Beulah Land and the Great Glad Day. He did not open his eyes again. His breathing grew gradually louder, his shaking more violent, until very early in the morning he began to spasm. Mary quietly told Catherine to wake the boys. Sister was gone, in Huntsville.

When Martin and Brady and Thomas, the middle son, came in, Mary released the old man's hand. "You can talk to him," she said as they held back. "He might hear you yet."

But none of them said anything, nor did they come near. The only sound was the old man's heavy, staggering breath. It was an awful, sickening interlude that seemed to go on eternally.

Finally Thomas said, "Good-bye, Daddy," and turned quickly away from the bed. He was the most talkative of the three, a young man full of himself and his opinions, but even he was quiet in the face of what stretched before them.

"Listen to that rain come down," Brady said. He was the only one with a shirt on. A soft, gray suspicion of morning came from the window, lighting three young, magnificent torsos, strengthened by riding and running and fighting, three potent young men standing around a shape that must once have looked like theirs.

The old man's body lurched. The low, long death rattle came out. By the time Thomas had reached his father's side the breathing had stopped.

After a long minute Martin reached over to close the old man's eyes. "I wish I'd had a chance to say good-bye when he could hear me," he said. "Did he say anything, Mary? Any last words?"

"No, Master," she said. "He was comfortable, I believe, and he didn't say much. I was just singing hymns for him."

James Birney's carriage rolled into the Nicholses' yard, shuddering to a halt by the front door. Birney looked around with bemusement. This was not what he thought of as the planter's life. The house had a brick first story, to which an ugly second story of wood had been added in a makeshift fashion, as had two unmatched wings made from rough-sawn planks. There were no gardens, no fruit trees, only mud and weeds. From behind the house several slave women and a swarm of children watched him carefully.

At one side of the yard was a long mound of red dirt, as yet unmarked: old Nichols's grave. Next to it was a marble cross, which Birney had never noticed; that would be Mrs. Nichols's grave. Three or four simple wooden crosses marked the burial places of slaves.

A black man dressed in shapeless, dirty clothing came jogging out of a sagging shed that served as the carriage house. He moved with a little trot that seemed a child's imitation of a pony's gait but propelled him more slowly than a long-legged stroll would have. He was already talking to the horses, not to Birney. "Hey, boy, hey, you are a fine looker, a fine looker. I'll have you for breakfast, I will." Birney saluted the man and got out of the carriage. Before he had reached the house the black man had begun unharnessing the horses, talking to them all the while in a high singsong.

In the parlor Birney found the four Nichols children, all in their Sunday best and looking irritable and uncomfortable. They stared at him, dismayed.

"Are you all right?" Martin, the oldest, asked.

"Just muddy," Birney said, "and I received a small cut on my leg. I am sorry to delay you, but I will have to clean myself."

He had suffered an accident while maneuvering his team through a muddy backwater; the lead horse's rein caught on a stump, and Birney had been forced into the water to untangle him. Fortunately he had brought another suit in his bag.

He was taken to a bedroom upstairs where servants brought water and soap and scooped up his muddy clothes. An ancient black woman, broad as a schooner, attended to him. Birney recognized her, though he did not know her name.

"You came to read the will?" she asked in a deep, slow voice.

He knew what was in her mind and loathed it. It would be in all of the slaves' minds. Some would be sold. All would have new masters. A slave knew no time so fearful as the death of a master. Often enough they would be divided regardless of family; even a mother and her children might be torn apart.

Birney was quite sure that he alone knew what was in the will, for Nichols had worked it out with him secretively, demanding that he tell no one. "I've been troubled by the old man, by old John Wesley's writings," Nichols had explained. "He always wrote that it was evil, did you know that? I'm a Methodist." He had stopped at that, musing on the all-important fact of Methodism.

"It's my family," Nichols went on. "My boys. It stains them all, you know, even if they're good boys, which mine certainly aren't. Both those older boys are with the nigger wenches already. I can't keep them away, when they see every white man in the county followed around by little nappy-headed copies of himself."

Birney had found the conversation distasteful in the extreme. What old Nichols said was unfortunately true. There were mixed-race slaves on every plantation, and with some it was disgracefully obvious that the master or his sons had made dark imitations of themselves.

"Do you have children here?" Birney asked the old black woman kindly. That would be her great anxiety, to be sold away from her children.

"Yes, Master," she said. "I have six children. And two more dead."

"They're all here?"

"Yes sir, thank the Lord. Master Nichols kept us together; he wouldn't sell any. Some of my grandchildren live away. George, my oldest, married a girl from the Fanchers'. He has three children there who look just like him."

The Fanchers lived downriver several miles. It was common for slaves to marry from other plantations, but they suffered most when a master died, for the new master might live at too great a distance for the couple to be together. Often the master insisted that they take new partners, whom they could breed with freely. There was no profit in having slaves married to someone too far distant to comfortably reproduce.

"It might be Master Fancher would sell that girl," Mary ventured, not looking at Birney. "If you were looking for a good worker you could depend on my George."

Birney was kind enough not to laugh at her. He felt sorry for her, but also repulsed by her plea. Birney did not care for servants who presumed on him. He was an impeccably honest man who tried to behave honorably toward his own slaves, but he did not see it as his duty to care for other people's. "No, Mary," he said, "I don't need any more servants. I have too many mouths to feed already."

Mary helped him to put on his boots, and she held a mirror while he straightened himself. Just as he was leaving she gripped his arm. "Did Master do what he said?" she asked in an urgent, low voice. When he did not answer, she swiftly let go of his arm and looked down at her feet.

"I don't know what your master said to you," he said coldly. "But you'll know soon enough what he did."

It was common enough for slave owners to promise servants that they would be given freedom, although they often failed to act on their promises. Nichols had told Birney that he had made no such promises, but he must have done so to this poor woman. Perhaps he had said it and then forgotten, but this old black woman had treasured the word in her heart ever since. What a pity, Birney thought, that any human creature should be born a slave.

The reading of Martin Nichols's last will and testament took place in the library, a small, shabby, plastered room with only a few worn Methodist volumes on the hand-hewn wooden shelves. A fire had been built, but it barely warmed the damp and drafty room. There was no carpet to cover the plank floor. Birney sat at a small, carved French wooden table, his papers before him. The four children took seats, none close to Birney or near to each other.

Cecilia would be most apt to fly off and storm dreadfully, Birney guessed. Or else Martin, who had not dressed or shaved for the occasion. Martin drank too much and had none of his father's religion to ballast against barbarism. Brady, just a child, would not understand much. He would monkey the others. Thomas, Birney could not judge. The young man was intelligent, but not sensible.

The will began with a prologue Nichols had dictated, testifying to his lifelong faith in God and warning his children to follow in this path. The children's stiff, wary appearances quickly degenerated into slouches and bored expressions. They had heard the old man's religion countless times.

Birney paused, cleared his throat, and went on to read the division of property. Cecilia, known as Sis, inherited all the china, cutlery, crystal, and linens. She also received a horse and carriage of her choice from the stock on hand, and a sum of one thousand dollars. The rest of the plantation— land, stock, buildings—was to be divided between the three brothers, except that Brady, the youngest, was to have his share held in trust by Martin, Jr., until Brady reached the age of twenty-one. The land was not to be sold or divided for twenty years, though by common agreement one of the brothers could buy out the share of another.

The sting came at the tail end. "In the fear of God, the Almighty," Birney read, glancing curiously up at the four, "and believing it wrong for one man to hold the life of another, I have suffered the injuries of slavery my whole life. I have seen the unchristian effects of this institution on my own self, on my family, and on my nation. I am determined not to pass these evils beyond my generation. I want for my children to learn righteous living, which was impossible for me. Therefore I hereby declare all slaves which I own, ninety-seven in number, as well as their children present and future, free forever."

Birney glanced up to see the impact on his audience. It did not seem that they understood, for they stared ahead without expression.

He finished the reading, outlining the legal proceedings for making the slaves free. As he began gathering his papers, Thomas stood up in confusion. The news had filtered its way into his head. "Let me see that," he demanded, grabbing at the will and staring at it. "Crazy old man," he said. "The land's no good without slaves."

"I'm not going to give up Catherine," Sis said loudly and self-righteously. "I don't care about the field hands, but the house servants can't just go off. They're members of our family."

Martin rolled his eyes at his sister's stupidity. He took the papers out of his brother's hand and turned quietly and seriously to Birney. "You drew these up?" he asked. Martin sat down and began to read them for himself.

"What a ridiculous thing," Cecilia was telling Brady. "It can't possibly succeed. I don't believe Daddy could have done it. Someone put him up to it."

Birney gradually became aware of noises coming from the kitchen. Then Martin heard them, too, and one by one all four children lifted their heads and listened.

"Sounds like shouting," Thomas said. "Something going on." He got to his feet and hurried out, and a few moments later they heard his voice, angrily rising. He came back with his face rigid and blotched with red.

"What happened?" Brady asked in his high child's voice.

"Nothing," Thomas told him.

"Come on, Tommy, tell me."

"It's nothing, I said."

"It's not nothing, we all heard it, and we heard you shouting."

"The slaves in the kitchen," Thomas said. "They were celebrating. They thought they were free niggers already."

"Well, I hope you licked them good," Cecilia said.

"How did they know?" Martin asked.

Thomas shrugged. His white skin was flushed, his nostrils slightly flared. "I suppose someone was spying on us here," he said. "Unless Mr. Birney had spread the news beforehand."

Thomas strode over to Birney and poked a finger in his chest. "You managed this, didn't you? My father couldn't have done this unless you helped him. You were the great mechanic turning the wheels; all he had to do was to say yes."

"Be quiet, Tommy," Martin said.

"I'm not going to be quiet," he said, poking his finger in Birney's face. "Look what you've done. You think you've done those niggers a favor?"

"They seem to think so," Birney said coolly.

"That's because they don't know a blessed thing. They've spent their whole lives never thinking about what to do in the morning. Somebody told them. Somebody fed them."

"Somebody bought and sold them," Birney countered.

"Not these niggers," Thomas shouted. "We take care of them. Now nobody will take care of them, and they'll wander around like half-wits until they starve or hang. Meanwhile this plantation will go to ruin too. You can't raise cotton without slaves. It can't be done, it's not economical."

"You may be right about all that," Birney said with strained courtesy. "You will note that when I gave up my plantation here I sold my slaves to a good master rather than to set them free. But you are quite wrong about my role with your father. He wanted these people freed. At my urging he provided something to help them make a start, because I was concerned about just what you mention. Otherwise it was completely his idea. I merely executed his will."

"If you hadn't, he couldn't have found another lawyer in Alabama to do it," Thomas shot back.

Thomas wandered out of the house, onto the veranda. Birney would stay for dinner—that was mere courtesy on the frontier, regardless of the hard words they had passed—and Thomas wanted never to see him again.

The land could not be divided for twenty years. Thomas was condemned to work in harness with his older brother, and worse, without slaves. To buy or rent new slaves would cost cash, which only the New Orleans factors could lend. Thomas had read enough and listened enough to know that once the factors had you in their debt, they had your cotton forever. He would never be able to bypass them and go directly to Manchester with his bales.

He felt tight and hot, as though he were squeezed between two iron plates. He would be forty years old before he could even begin to work his scheme. Impossible to wait that long. Impossible to work Martin's way.

He ambled to the stable and in its dark, warm depths found Charles, the slave with the pony trot, asleep in a corner. Thomas kicked at the small, crumpled body with a boot toe. "Saddle Briar," he said when Charles jumped up. While Charles did so, Thomas paced in the yard, not even joking with Charles as he usually did.

Behind the house he saw a skinny black girl hanging Birney's clothing on a line. The sight filled him with loathing, as it called to memory the unpleasant scene he had just endured, and the Negroes he had found with their mouths open in celebration. They must have washed Birney's soiled garments as though they were angels' wings.

Down the lane of cedars and into the forest, Thomas rode under the vast, spreading trees that kept the ground in darkness all summer. Cleared ground was still sketchy even in this rich river plain. He passed by a crew of blacks, laboring with axes. Would they know the news already? It made him sick to think so. He would like to bash their heads.

But no, he thought, if they knew they would be beyond the foreman's control; they'd be dancing and singing, not swinging their axes. Unless swinging at the foreman's head.

As he came nearer the river, the large trees were fewer and the path he followed grew sandy, working its way through a tangle of vines and scrub. The horse was walking, but Thomas kept urging it forward with his knees until he climbed a small rise into a thicket and suddenly overlooked the Tennessee River—vast, brown, a plain the color of mud, dotted with moving debris. No boats, no buildings, no human life was visible. For

Thomas it was a giant and quieting relief to look out over the river's hugeness.

The Tennessee gave the widest view he ever got. Everything else in his life was hemmed in—by trees, by his family and circumstances. Now, he thought bitterly, he was hemmed in for life.

Of all the Nichols children Thomas had waited with the greatest anxiety to receive his inheritance. His temper was excitable, voluble, easily inflated by triumph and quickly angered by frustration. A handsome twenty-two-year-old, he had white skin and copper hair, with delicate, boyish features that made some women want to mother him, though he was really far too restless to be mothered.

Just the way a boy in Connecticut might fool with machinery, Thomas was inclined toward notions about growing and selling cotton. As a small boy he had made himself a nuisance to the overseers, following the slaves into the fields when they chopped weeds from the new pale plants, brandishing a toy whip that an uncle had presented one Christmas. He had even learned figures just so he could calculate each day's yield. His father had no use for this; he could tell at a glance whether the harvest was strong, without subjecting his mind to paper squiggles. He always dismissed Thomas's interest in cotton as nonsense, which had the effect of strengthening it in Thomas.

Alabama was an ideal environment for wild, romantic preoccupations, to the few so inclined. Thomas was so inclined. Living among people who knew little about books or the world, Thomas's mind could range free, inventing elaborated philosophies and opinions without anyone to contradict him or even to care much what he thought. If he had been raised in Boston or Baltimore somebody would have scoffed or scolded him out of half his ideas, but here he grew free of any such nurturing.

He thought the current system for bringing cotton to market was ruinous to planters, a view that was common along the Tennessee. Planters ragged on the bankers and traders and factors who were stealing from them at every turn. Like farmers everywhere they turned instantly from complaints about their losses to bragging of their latest improvements—buildings and cleared lands and slave populations—without seeing any irony. They were cautious men, rooted in what they knew, and Thomas believed that their caution was wrecking them. He had the idea that he would ship and sell cotton directly to Manchester, bypassing the cotton factors in New Orleans. From reading newspapers he had got enough information to sound knowledgeable, and he spent long hours drawing lists of figures that proved his scheme practical.

But he had not been able to convince his father. The old man was not about to bet his land against the New Orleans factors, who extended credit, bought supplies, and gave advice, conducting all kinds of business that the Nichols family knew nothing about, regardless of newspapers.

So, like many frustrated sons, Thomas had waited, filling his time. He had been bored, and restless, and dissolute. Now it looked as though he would be restless forever.

He sat on his horse for some time watching the water move; then he wheeled and started back on the path.

When he reached a wide stretch he struck the horse and began to gallop, even though the path was rough and there was some risk he might damage the horse. He was headed back, but not to the house. Looking at the river he had thought of a familiar relief to his frustration. He was going to visit Catherine.

The slave cabins stood in a line fifty yards behind the house, small, rudimentary buildings with a hard-packed bare yard in front. A cluster of women stood by a fire, heating a large kettle. They glanced at Thomas with a look that seemed hostile to him, though it was actually empty, all feeling masked. Two tiny, skinny boys ran toward him, laughing, perhaps to beg or to hold his horse. A word from one of the women halted them, and their laughter evaporated.

They know, he thought, *they are looking at me with contempt. I would whip them all.*

He got down from his mount and stood impatiently, holding the reins. "Well?" he said. "Is someone of you going to take this horse?"

After the swiftest and most minute exchange of glances, one of the women came over. She was stooped and small, her lined face looking older than she could possibly be, since he knew she had birthed a baby within the year. He felt momentarily ashamed as he turned away from her.

The door to Catherine's cabin was made of three hand-hewn slabs of pine, pegged together. A latchstring of dirty cord hung out of a hole; hands had polished the rough wood all around it to a dark shine. He pulled on the cord, feeling the wooden latch lift inside the door. He pushed the door open without knocking.

Catherine was seated on the bed, reading, or pretending to read as though she had not known he had come. She was just a girl, really. Her face was narrow and small, with deeply hooded eyes and a wide, heavy mouth. Her body, leaning over the book, was lithe and spare. She was beautiful, though he did not think of her so, since she was African. He took a seat on the only other furniture in the room, a chair. She was reading the book he had given her, a primer.

"I came to give you your lesson," he said.

She glanced at him and did not return his smile. For a moment he saw that soft hesitation, that vulnerability that so excited him, and then it vanished. Her face closed.

"I'm a free woman now," she said archly.

He had not anticipated that; the master keeps from himself the slave's resentment.

He turned his head in disgust and spat toward the corner. "Free or not, you want to learn to read, don't you?" he said. He had been teaching her, which was not yet contrary to Alabama law but was certainly considered foolhardy. Slaves did not need to read, and if they read, the ideas they consumed could not be easily controlled. Knowledge was power, the planters knew that. He had enjoyed the rebellion implicit in teaching her, to say nothing of the closeness of her breathing as she sat by him sharing the book. He had known other slaves before Catherine, but somehow the reading had made her more a woman, less an object of mere lust, which disgusted him when he was done with it.

"I want to read," she said.

"Well?" he said. His desire for her, dampened for a moment by her mention of freedom, returned. He put out one hand and touched her knee.

She would not look at him. He had liked not only her beauty but the bold way she stared into his face, when other slaves (apart from Mary) would only look at the ground and mumble. He stood up and took her chin, moving her face toward him, but a swift glance was all he caught before she averted her eyes.

He angrily grabbed her wrist. "You're not a free woman, not yet. You got a paper proving you're free? You belong to me."

She tugged, briefly, then let her arm go limp. She had her chin down on her chest, keeping not just her eyes but her whole face from him. He held her face between his hands and forced the head to look up into his eyes. Again he received just a glance, an angry and frightened glance, before her eyes were averted.

"You belong to me," he whispered fiercely, and kissed her, hard, on the lips.

When Thomas opened Catherine's door again he was momentarily disoriented. Here, just beyond the door, was a public place with children playing and women washing. Talking ceased before him as surely as if he were the angel of death. None of the women looked up; they continued their business as though he were invisible. One woman had a long stick; she was pushing clothes down into the boiling pot while the others squatted on their haunches around the fire. Only the children stared his way, and even they were silent. Thomas got his horse from where it was tied to a post, mounted, and threw the animal into a canter.

He did not go to the house but down the lane and away from it; still he could not face Birney. He sat straight in his saddle, moving rhythmically with the horse, reliving in his mind his moments with Catherine. He had enjoyed himself; he had asserted himself. A slave owner had this privilege, to act the master.

He urged the horse to a gallop and gave himself to the sensation of speed. The vegetation along the road became a blur. Eventually he slowed to a trot, then a walk.

He had forced her. Never before had Thomas done that; she had always been willing. For all his pride Thomas did not like the thought of forcing her. It spoiled the reassuring value of the act: was he really desired, was he really by nature the master, or was it only violence that made him so?

Teaching her letters had made their relations seem pleasant, almost equal. Of course, had he thought about it from her point of view he would have known that she had never been in a position to choose; no slave could disobey without the risk of paying dearly. Still he had paid her, in a currency she wanted, the alphabet. But he had not thought of it as payment. It was pleasure to him. Now the hint of doubt came in: had it not been pleasure to her?

He discarded the thought. *It's the freedom,* he thought. *It confuses them. Now she doesn't know who she is or what she wants.*

He cursed his father. Before this Catherine had been very agreeable and had profited from it too. Learning her letters, learning how the white man thought, could keep her in the house and out of the fields. Now, who knew where she might end up?

I'll leave, he said to himself suddenly. *I can't stand it here.* He could not endure twenty years with his brother, raising cotton just to sell it through the factors, in the same old way.

Where would he go? His whole lifetime had been spent anticipating his ascendance here, on this land. South Carolina was a distant memory; he had left there when he was ten.

As the horse walked through the dead winter fields, rusted and wrecked and colorless, Thomas formed a plan. He would sell out his land to his brother. Never mind that they had no cash; his brother could borrow some and pay more yearly from the cotton profits. He, Thomas, would not ignobly quibble over the price; he would accept any reasonable payment. Then he would go, immediately, to New Orleans, to catch a ship for South Carolina. He had an uncle there. He would go into some sort of business, to make money, until he could come back to buy up land and begin his work beholden to no one.

He considered what would be said. He remembered how they had gossiped about Birney, when he lost his land. That had been quite a comedown, from a planter to a law man. But Thomas resolved himself. Money would answer the talk. They said you could grub fortunes in trade, though you had to sacrifice the dignity of life on the land. Well, he would do it. His stomach turned from it, but it would be the brave thing. Immediately he wheeled his horse and headed back to the house, to talk to his brother.

Chapter 2
1829: Finney in New York City

IN NOVEMBER of 1829 Charles Finney arrived in New York City, making as much news as the arrival of the actress Jenny Lund from England, or (nearly) the visit of Charles Dickens. The older, conservative pastors of New England had tried to stop Finney's advance; even Lyman Beecher, an activist himself, called a meeting to oppose him. Finney's style was too denunciatory, they charged. His methods seemed designed to force God's hand. But that was exactly the reason why businessmen invited him to New York. In their faith as in their trade, they could not bear to sit still and wait for events. They sought an instrument to make God's work evident on earth.

Hubert Hamilton went to hear. He was the dandy, sardonic clerk who worked beside Thomas Nichols at Bradgett and Castle, the dry goods wholesaler. Hamilton was always one to follow a crowd; he could find entertainment in a drunk Irish mob as though it were a circus parade. Nichols expected to be amused by Hamilton's wry description of the revival, but that was not what he got.

"It's not what you think," Hamilton said about Finney, his voice unusually somber and his eyes taking on an unprecedented dull, waxen seriousness. "It's not what you think at all."

Nichols was not about to go see a preacher. He looked on religion as the sum of his boyhood's inferior excesses: ignorant, emotional, taking no account of science or rationality, its leading men wearing patched pants, muddy boots, and having half their teeth.

Hamilton could not be dissuaded, though. He was the last man Nichols would have thought vulnerable to preaching, yet he seemed stunned as if by a beating. After he had urged and almost begged Nichols for three straight days to attend a meeting, Nichols agreed for the sake of friendship.

He was sorry as soon as he got to the church. All around them in the balcony (Nichols wanted to be as far from the dais as possible) sat working men in stained and shapeless clothes, their bodies acrid and overripe. They were just the sort of people to fall into derangement. Nichols braced himself for the rising, mumbling noise of madness, for the moment when the first man thumps down to his knees and then his stomach, for the high, strange chanting voice of the preacher urging them to "give to Jesus, Jesus, Jesus. Give to Jesus." He knew these all too well.

The service began in an orderly way. There were prayers and hymns, all commonplace, even if there seemed to be an extraordinary concentration under the calm surface. Then a tall young man with a high forehead stood and began talking. Involuntarily, Nichols was drawn into the man's plain, sensible words. He had been listening with interest for some time when he began to wonder why the fellow talked so long. He nudged Hamilton to ask who he was.

"That's Finney!" Hamilton whispered loudly.

It was that surprising air of reasonableness that stuck into Nichols. Here was a man who talked sense, who understood that you had to prove things. He talked like a lawyer, which Nichols understood he had been before he was called to preach. He would have been a very effective man of business, Nichols thought, a comment that had become his highest praise since coming to New York.

Finney's text was a verse from Ecclesiastes: "One sinner destroyeth much good." He painted a picture of the American individualist, who claimed that his life was his own and no one else's. Then he used illustrations to prove that the claim was nonsense. He started with the master of a canal boat who, in defiance of the law, exceeded three miles an hour on the canal and set up a wake that eroded the bank, which led to the degeneration of the canal, and ultimately contributed to the destruction of the whole prosperous valley. It was a very right case for Finney, coming as he did from the Erie Canal and knowing a good deal about how it had transformed the economy of the region.

"What would be your verdict?" Finney asked the congregation, in that lawyer's voice, as though they really were a jury and would decide. "The boat's master would tell me to mind my own affairs, since he knew well enough right from wrong and it was no one's business but his own. What would be your verdict?"

Then Finney spoke of an engineer who produced faulty plans for a bridge, which collapsed under the weight of a hay wagon and killed the farmer hauling hay. He told of a schoolmaster who neglected his own studies and kept his job by charming the parents; and he traced how his impoverished teaching affected half a dozen of his students. Finney told of a drunkard who said his drinking was no concern of anybody else's; then Finney described his wife and children, dirty, threadbare, hungry.

Finney described a minister who knew well enough about God's warnings to sinners, but thought stern preaching would upset his elders and so stayed with reading tried-and-true sermons that were elegant and learned and inoffensive. Finney did a good imitation of the minister, peering into his text, that made them all laugh.

Until this point Finney had spoken quite calmly, but as he described the minister's trial before God his eye swept over the congregation like an eagle's. Nichols now sat transfixed, heart hammering, holding his breath as he heard the minister claim a decent life and heard God's scorn as he blew away his claims like a hot wind among so many dry leaves.

"You say that you have no reason to change your ways, to give in to God and confess your sins. You say that you don't care for the meddling of ministers and professional busybodies. You say your life is yours, that this is a free country. You'll plan your life in the way that suits yourself. You'll rely on your abilities to make a name for yourself. You'll do great good things, you say. You'll make your godless pile of money. But what will you say when you stand before his awesome, holy presence and hear him say, 'Today, you fool, your life is required of you'?"

Afterward, Hamilton wanted to talk as they walked home, but Nichols heard him like the buzzing of a mosquito in his ear. He was listening intently to the high, fine voice of Charles Finney. Halfway back to the boardinghouse it occurred to him for the first time that he had seen no emotion. The audience had listened in paralyzed silence. No one had moaned, even.

He tried arguing with Finney's voice. He, Thomas Nichols, had no quarrel with his maker, nor his maker with him. Nichols was not a guilt-stricken person; all his life he had felt quite pleased with himself. In the year since he had come to New York his spirit had soared with ambitious happiness, as he had mastered his way in the chaos and noise of business. Yet something in Finney's eye had seemed to see, without possibility of contradiction, another light by which his soul must be judged. Something in Nichols's own soul was caught by that contention, as surely as though he were a moth pinned to a board. He had no answer to Finney's assurance that his life and ambition had no more intrinsic worth than a handful of cinders.

———————

The conversion of Thomas Nichols into a successful Yankee man of business had been prepared, it seemed, by every event in his past. Through his dreaming about the cotton system, he had learned to apply his imagination in commerce. Through his failure in Charleston—he had lost his entire stake—he had shed his terror of losing. Even his father's freeing of the slaves had taught him to rely only on himself, not on any inherited advantage. All events had conspired to break him free from traditional habits of mind, to make him think not so much of defined roles in society, as to run after any chance at success. At Bradgett and Castle he was caught up in the invigorating, enthralling race of progress, using his quickness of mind for money.

The firm sold cotton goods, and the main room showed hundreds of samples, each bolt of cloth in its own carefully labeled niche, the polished wooden cubbyholes reaching up into the lofty darkness of the ceiling. A vast mahogany counter stretched across the front of the room, manned by ten or fifteen clerks in coats and collars showing samples to customers or marking in ledgers. The whole affair spoke of money, money studied carefully, money changing hands rapidly, money carefully saved and well spent on the very best fixtures.

Hubert Hamilton had been the first to take him in hand and explain the system. Business was conducted by invariable rules, Hamilton explained, but you would make a mistake to focus only on the rules. Behind the rules—and this was the key, he said—were no fixed principles. "The old men who launched this place didn't say, 'Such and such is my business. Such and such is my rule for setting a price.' They said, 'My business is making money, and I'll sell anything and try anything to do it.' That's the secret of Yankee business in this age. Why, there's a man in Boston who's made a fortune selling ice in the West Indies, do you know that? Ice to the darkies. Why, they didn't even know what it was at first. He had to give it away until they knew what to do with it. Now they can't live without it! The man cuts it off the ponds at Boston and carries it south on clipper ships. Do you know what ice is? It's water and cold winters! He sells them water and cold winters! Now that's the Yankee spirit."

When Nichols entered the warm, uproarious noise of Bradgett and Castle's main room, he was reminded of bees when they hive: their dark swarm without fixed shape, ranging the land ominously, randomly searching for a place to make honey. So it was with Yankees seeking profit.

He had not been many months clerking before he began, with Hamilton, to dream of making their own firm. "We'd advertise your Southern connection," Hamilton said, for Nichols had developed an expertise at selling to Southern traders. They came in squint-eyed and suspicious, certain they would be cheated, until he set them at ease.

"No, no," Nichols said. "Southern people wouldn't trust the place if they knew it was run by an Alabama fellow. They'd be sure the goods were poor. What they want is a good, strict Yankee firm with a Southern fellow to wait on them and wink at them and give them a better deal on the sly."

"Fine," Hamilton said. "I'll own it, and you can be my clerk."

In the summer evenings Nichols often walked through the streets of New York just to see what buildings were for rent. His old dream—of returning to Alabama to revolutionize the cotton trade—was replaced by a shinier, distinctively Yankee vision. He need own no land; he could live by his wits.

He was boarding with a widow, Mrs. Frasier, and her three young children. He went there directly after hearing Finney for the third straight night. The bell rang for supper and he went wordlessly to the dining room. Something was wrong with him. He could barely sit still in his chair or look at the children. The aroma of cooked food came over him suddenly; he felt nauseated by its dense smell. The girl, who was about ten, was talking to her brother in a piercing, womanish voice that made him want to grab her small, round body and shake it. He frightened himself with these impulses.

For three nights he had gone, against his own good judgment, to hear Finney flay him. He did not sleep well afterward; he argued with Finney in bed and thought of the argument all day. He knew that religion was nonsense. He had seen it in nauseating quantities as a boy, unseemly emotions and pretentious morality, stuff that could make you sick. These arguments would not stick to Finney, though—he did not seem to speak of religion. He spoke of the plain facts of human life, of the direction of a soul, of one's messy failure to live before God as one ought. And Finney seemed to see, as though it were real as a stone building, the possibility of choosing a right life, of active benevolence toward your fellowman. He made you want to be good, and ashamed to be bad.

Mrs. Frasier, the widow, was a warm, ample woman who always had a timid look on her face. Thomas often feared that her brown eyes would fill up with tears when he spoke to her. Tonight, as every night, she surveyed the children to think of who should offer grace. She asked Tommy, the older boy, to lead them.

She had asked Nichols to pray once when he first came—he had declined the honor. Now he felt suddenly and irrationally enraged by her action. He was being treated like a child—actually beneath a child.

"Let me pray," he said fiercely.

Mrs. Frasier lifted her head and stared at him. "All right," she said. "Tommy, let Mr. Nichols lead us."

He did not know what he was doing. What came into his thoughts was anger—blank, raw, swirling, unshaped, like the white leaking out of a boiling cracked egg. He realized that the family were waiting for him in silence, but fury so filled his mind that he got out half a sentence and stopped. His imagination filled with the disgusting memory of camp meetings, men lolling on the ground, in the mud, their eyes open, their great soft mouths sobbing. That was praying.

"Heavenly almighty, mighty God, we beseech thee our blessings on this hour . . ." In a few phrases he ran through his stock of pious language. He stopped short, then started up again. "The cares of all mankind are upon thee . . ." He did not know what he was saying, he was just trying wildly to make it sound like a prayer.

"Remember this thy servant Finney . . ." A burst of words suddenly. "Shut up the mouth of the man, shut up these words of ignorance . . ." Nichols opened his eyes, jolted that such sounds had emerged, yet feeling oddly satisfied. It was freakish, to look around the table while Mrs. Frasier and her children had their eyes tightly closed.

Mrs. Frasier seemed to be trembling. After a moment of silence she opened her eyes to look pleadingly at him. Cocky as a parrot, he stared back.

"I must pray for you," she said through tears. "I must." She got up from her chair and began to kneel beside it.

"No," Nichols said in a hurry. "No! I want to go to my room now. I won't want any supper." He got up and hurried out, feeling ashamed and alarmed, knowing that he had lost control of himself, regretting that he had ever heard of Charles Finney.

In his room he lay full length on the bed, staring up. What was wrong with him? He had not been right since the first night he had heard Finney. He had lost the happiness that had preoccupied him from the day he came to New York.

He got off the bed and lay down again on the floor. The solidity of the boards under his back seemed to provide comfort, reminding him of a stable and predictable world of materiality. Yet when he relaxed his thoughts for even a moment the blank, pure hatred reentered. He could not let himself slip into the vaporous atmosphere of religion, to carry him who knows where.

He lay still until he heard the children shuffle to bed, the streets grow silent. Then he stood and began to pace, his footsteps making the floor shudder. He walked in a narrow rectangle, the length of the room from the door to the window, along the wall by the window, then back to the door. Past midnight he threw himself on the bed, fully clothed, but only for a few minutes. Then he began to pace again. He tried to think sensibly, but every time his thoughts turned into panic and anger directed against Finney.

Near dawn, a gray light seeped back into the room, and he felt calmer. The bed, the table, the walls were again solid, stable shapes. He thought that he would be able to regain himself, that the nightmare was ending. He was seated on the edge of the bed, contemplating his weariness, when a terrible pressure came on him, pressing his heart, his lungs, his head. He fell to the floor, onto his hands and knees. "You will repent," a voice in his head seemed to boom, "You will repent *now!*"

At Bradgett and Castle, Hubert Hamilton told him that an inquirer's meeting had been announced for that night. "I don't know, I might go, I might not," Hamilton said. "I would like the chance to talk to Finney."

Half a dozen times Nichols resolved to go; half a dozen times he swore he would not. At noontime he walked the crowded streets, rather than talk. Hamilton was looking at him mutely, with eyes of prayerful concern. Nichols hated that. It seemed like betrayal that Hamilton was no longer the cheerful, skeptical friend he needed to keep his mental balance.

As Nichols walked the colorless streets, gray from winter and solid with brick and stone, he saw more than ever the dirt and drunkenness, the crudeness and the lack of brotherly concern. He even saw a drunkard, splayed out full length on a sidewalk near a tavern, where pedestrians had to step over him. Finney had described just such a scene, accusing them all of not caring for their brothers. Nichols watched for some minutes and saw a dozen men walk across the unmoving body. He was appalled at himself, both that he had never bothered with such scenes before and that he was giving them so much attention now. He thought of crossing the street and shaking the man awake, but what would he do then? He could not bring himself to it. He wished to simply forget what he saw and to forget Finney and to return to his previous happiness.

That thought helped him resolve not to go to the meeting, and he stayed firm for much of the afternoon. By closing time, however, he knew that against his best judgment he would attend. Why? Was he responsible that men were drunk? Was it his concern to lift such a man from the street? New York was full of good Christians, and they did not come along.

Hamilton had given the address where the meeting would take place. Nichols walked by it, a private home in a quiet street near the Bowery. The house was stone, two-storied, with a garden in front and painted shutters at the windows—a home that spoke of comfortable peace. Inside there must be a family, nice furniture in the sitting room, a supper cooking. Nichols did not dare to stop, lest someone inside might be watching his movements. He looked at the house sidelong from under his hat.

In the next street, walking almost blind, he found himself in an open market. Business was wrapping up for the day—the stalls' owners standing over their potatoes and turnips with bleak expressions, merely waiting to go home. There were geese, fat and imperious though imprisoned in their tight cages made from sticks. Thomas stopped and gazed blankly at these.

How did they stay so white in such a dirty place? Ambling on he saw apples displayed in a cart, and bought a dozen, thinking he could bring them home as an apology to Mrs. Frasier. Biting into one he was surprised by its juicy flavor, and he ate it down in a hurry. He was hungry, he realized. Of course, he had not eaten since the morning. He bit into another apple, made it disappear in great chunks, then another and another. After four his appetite suddenly ceased, and a cloying aftertaste remained, so that he wanted to spit up into the gutter.

Suddenly then, for no reason that he understood then or even later, he realized he would go to the meeting.

The home was just as he had imagined it: spacious, simple, and homely, with a carpet on the parlor floor and mahogany furniture. He was met wordlessly at the door by a black servant and ushered into the parlor. About a dozen men and women were present, seated solemnly in a variety of straight-backed chairs facing the stove. Aside from a few whispers, the room was quiet.

More people came in behind Nichols after he was seated. Then Finney came in and stood in front of the stove. He welcomed them all, speaking frankly in a friendly manner about the purpose of the meeting. His manner alone quieted Nichols's worst anxieties. Finney seemed quite human: fiercely focused, perhaps, but extremely this-worldly. He described the decision that lay before them and dealt with several of the most ready objections. Then he began to circulate among them, counseling with one at a time.

Nichols looked at his hands, he looked at his feet. The room was quiet, except for low, muffled sighs coming from somewhere behind him. Glancing back he saw that Finney was kneeling with a man. They spoke so quietly that Nichols could not hear their words, but he saw the man shake his head violently at one point, saying repeatedly, "No, no, no, no."

Finally Finney was with Nichols, speaking to him. Finney had oversized, pale blue eyes that didn't blink but looked—with what expression? Sadness?—into Nichols's soul. "Have you never given your heart to God?" Finney asked, as directly and plainly as a man might ask what woolens were in stock.

He found himself telling of his childhood religion. Finney pressed him: was not the real reason for his atheism a deep and penetrating sinfulness? Did he not love his sins, want to treasure them and keep them safe from God? "Don't you know the stench of your soul fills up this room? That even if no one else can, God smells it, and hates its vile odor?"

Nichols's mind was not muddled; if anything it was more alert than normal. Talking to Finney was like having your soul pulled out of your body and held up for examination. He was quite aware of every word that Finney said, of Finney's stern, staring eyes, even of stirrings and mutterings from elsewhere in the room as people moved around. Yet another part of his mind operated by quite different principles. The rational part of his mind attended to the sensations of this other side, which was filled with panicky fears, with loathings, with phantasms. He found with surprise that he could no longer talk. He choked, he sobbed, he could not control his tongue to speak, and yet he was quite clear, quite in control in his mind.

Nichols began to taste the apples in his mouth, cloying, metallic. He tried to burp, even while listening to Finney. There was pressure in his abdomen, but he could not gain relief.

"Go ahead, say it." Finney's voice cut through to Nichols's consciousness. "Say what you are. God knows it all too well."

At Finney's fine, ringing voice he knew instantly the truth he had to say. He was terrified to do it. He was frightened of being, as it were, naked in this room, and even more afraid that even as he said it, before the words were out of his mouth, he would be judged, thrown down, consigned to darkness, burned up to ashes. His rational mind attended to this fear but could not calm it, could not even communicate with it.

Also he was not sure he could speak at all. He was nauseous. He wanted terribly to relieve himself of the dizzying sense of sickness, the oversweet taste of rotting apples in his mouth.

The words came out, with an upthrusting effort, then in a rush. "I am a sinner. Wretched and worthless. God have mercy on me. God have mercy." As he coughed it up he thought that the plea was useless; God could not stoop so low as to have mercy. He seemed to hang suspended over infinite darkness, terrified, cringing like a child afraid to be drowned. He looked at Finney's face, concentrating on his eyes. His nausea increased. For one lucid instant of horror he knew that he could not fight the turbidity another instant, that his stomach was coming up. Then vomit like hot pitch scalded through the channel of his throat, out between his teeth, his torso spasming to make a perfect channel for the refuse. He tasted the burning, acrid gruel of half-digested apples on his lips. It splashed everywhere, on his shabby suit, on the floor. He was humiliated, horrified at what he had done. "Oh God, help me," he groaned.

Then his soul was suddenly, instantly swept quiet. At that moment, kneeling limply in the vomit at Finney's feet, he knew that something astonishing had occurred. Later he would realize it was the sensation of being saved.

Nichols knelt at his chair, harboring the peace and silence. He had never known how turbulent his soul had been until this moment, until the restless chatter was quiet. He contemplated the stillness, and he tried to pray, though his words never lasted more than a sentence.

Finney had dismissed the meeting. Nichols had no wish to leave. He stood and wiped his face with his handkerchief. He still tasted the vomit.

Finney spoke to him, talking normally, asking him not about the quietness in his soul—he seemed to know all about that—but about his line of work. "I want you to meet someone," he said, and led him through the chairs to the entry hall. A group of men were talking by the stairway. They turned to Finney as he approached.

"I wanted you to meet one of the men who was hopefully converted this evening," Finney said. "Especially you, Lewis, since this young man, Mr. Nichols, is in a career very like yours immediately across Hanover Square."

Nichols found himself looking into the small hazel eyes and delicate features of Lewis Tappan. He knew him instantly. Tappan and his brother Arthur were famous, the most successful silk traders in New York. More to the point, he and Lewis had met on Nichols's first day in New York, at Mrs. Fairbanks's boardinghouse. Tappan had commandeered the parlor for a prayer meeting; Nichols, incensed, had stormed at him. He had so hated piety; why had he hated it? Now he could only stare. The eyes of his soul were so intensely focused inward, on the quiet of his soul, that he had temporarily lost the ability to respond to anything outside himself.

He realized that Tappan did not remember him, had quite forgotten their quarrel. He talked amicably of affairs, of prices from London, of the banks, a conversation that Nichols found he could manage only with great effort, while the main portion of his mind remained far away, bathing in the stillness.

"Are you quite content with Bradgett and Castle?" Tappan was asking.

Ordinarily Nichols would have answered with some pleasantry. But in his present state of mind he had forgotten completely how to lie. "No," he blurted out. "I've been very restless."

Tappan bobbed his head knowingly. "Sharp practices?" he asked, and did not wait for an answer. "My brother and I would like to have a man like yourself to work with us. Would you be interested in discussing such a thing?"

Nichols could not answer. Tappan took his hesitation for doubt. "I won't pretend that we pay our clerks overly generously," he said. "But there is no better way to begin a career in business. Many men have gone on from clerking with us to considerable careers." He hesitated and cocked his head at Nichols. "Perhaps you are still too new to New York to know the reputation of Tappan Brothers."

"No, I do, I certainly do," Nichols answered. "I pass by your store every day."

"Well then, come by and talk to my brother," Tappan said. "There is a great deal we could do together for God's kingdom."

Chapter 3
1830: Free People of Color

EVERY TIME that Martin Nichols heard from his brother Thomas in New York, he got drunk. The letters did not come often, because Martin did not answer them, but Thomas would write every few months, mainly with the purpose of urging his brother to give his life to Jesus. Martin generally spent that day in the parlor, a green bottle of whiskey on the table beside him. He drank until all the liquor was gone, and then fell into bed. Maybe Martin got drunk to prove to himself that he was beyond all possibilities of religion, or maybe he did it to make himself forget the contrast between his brother's success and his own looming failure.

Even in the first years after he got his father's land, when Martin worked hard and drank less, he lost money. Cotton prices were unsatisfactory, and without the free labor of slaves his expenses were high. Each year his debt grew with the cotton factor in New Orleans.

Increasingly now Martin neglected the plantation. His cotton looked spotty and overgrown with rank grass. Sometimes the seed went in late. Martin, too, seemed to spoil. His powerful frame became dumpy, as though he wore a sack of corn under his shirt. In February the factor, Mr. Enoch Barstow, came upriver bringing bad news about London prices. He could advance no more credit, he said, until Martin paid part of his debt. After that Martin was drunk for three days. Then, still smelling sweetly of corn whiskey, he went to his brother-in-law to ask for money.

Frederick Barnes sat in his paneled library, blond and neat, offering Martin no whiskey though a decanter of the soft, brown liquid was visible on the table behind him. Barnes had married Cecilia two years before and had seemed by the magnet of his person to pull her up and out of her rude, mother-deprived upbringing; now the two of them had airs far above Martin. Barnes greeted Martin cordially, as though seeing him in the office were completely ordinary. He listened to the whole story without saying a word. Then he volunteered to buy Martin's land—all of it. "At least it will remain in the family," he said in an offhand way.

Martin Nichols scowled. "I might sell some of the land to clear my debts, if that's your interest," he said. "But I would throw myself in the river before I would sell all of it."

"That's not a sensible thing to say, Martin." Barnes's tranquillity was profound. "You'll end up selling the land piece by piece, which is a sorry thing. You haven't got slaves, and you don't have the money to buy slaves, so you're going to keep on losing money until all the land is broken up and you don't have a thing left. You should get out now. You'll have enough money from the sale to invest in a business in town or to do whatever you want."

"What I want," said Martin, lowering his head like an ox about to charge, "is money to plant cotton this spring."

"Well," Barnes said with a cool wave, "talk to Mr. Waugh at the bank."

By that time you could not buy a drink in town because James Birney was mayor and had passed a law against liquor. As everyone knew, Birney had been converted at the Presbyterian Church, and his religion had made him more moral than ever, if that were possible. Martin thought he had never hated the man more than at this moment, when he needed a drink. He kicked around the courthouse for an hour or so, talking to anyone who would listen to him complain about his brother-in-law, and about Birney, and about Negroes. He then rode steaming all the way home. Cecilia heard he stayed drunk for a week. He was hardheaded to a degree that his brother-in-law had probably underestimated. When he emerged he had figured out a plan to his satisfaction.

He would manage without money, he decided. He had seed from last year's crop. His blacks, free though they might be by law, would work whether he paid them or not, because they had no choice. They knew nothing but the Nichols plantation and its cotton, and certainly no one else in Triana would offer them work. His little brother Brady could go to Sis's house to live; Martin would have only his own mouth to fill. He did not seriously try to figure out how he would survive or what the blacks would eat until he had a crop in. He simply thought he could plant cotton, and somehow that magical crop would provide his salvation and the land's too.

Shortly after the planting a windy storm from the south brought three days of heavy rain, washing gullies in the fields and drowning nearly everything. Martin had no more seed and no money to get some. He went to see his brother-in-law again. His face had a dark yellow complexion, like old mustard. He looked sick. He did not offer his hand when he came into the office. He plunked down in a carved cherry chair and kicked at the Turkish carpet with his boot heel.

"I need money," Nichols said in a belligerent voice. "I have no seed to plant." He never even looked at Barnes.

"All right," Barnes said, after a long period of silence. "But you'll have to sign some papers."

"You'll get your money," Nichols said. "Nobody ever lost money from me."

"Yes," said Barnes, "but you will have to sign some papers."

Barnes went to see James Birney to draw up a contract. When the papers were ready he sent one of his servants to find Nichols. He was discovered, after a search, by Huntsville's big spring, the marvel that had attracted settlers in the first place, where water from the roots of the hills gushed out in an eternal flow. It was a placid, unpeopled place, ringed by high grass and shrubbery, with a red pathway worn into the bank. Nichols was staring at the waterworks as if he were drunk, though he didn't smell of whiskey. Perhaps he knew, or sensed anyway, the implications of what he was about to do.

He signed the papers without reading them, and Barnes accompanied him to the bank to get $150. The banker counted out fifteen gold coins on the counter. Nichols slid them across the counter and into his pocket. Then, as an afterthought, he took one out, slapped it down and asked for it to be changed. Without a word he left the bank, unhitched his horse, and rode off.

He got the cotton in, and this time it grew, but he had no money to feed his blacks. Martin had some fat on his middle to live off of, but those people were thin already.

Two of the families just disappeared. The other Negroes said they didn't know where they had gone, though it was a good guess they had decided to take their chances and go somewhere, maybe north, rather than starve. How far they got, and whether they ever reached safety, was impossible to say. It was dangerous for black people to travel, because the only semblance of protection they had was in the people who knew them. The families who left were all ignorant men and women, raised as slaves, who had never set foot farther than Huntsville. All they had was a piece of paper (which they could not read) saying they were free, and that was of severely limited value. Neither family was ever heard of again. Possibly a passing slave trader caught them and took them to Natchez or New Orleans.

The rest remained. Nichols could do what he liked with those Negroes, for free persons of color were less protected than slaves, being nobody's property. He would have killed them if they had refused him somehow. No white man would have testified against another white man for hurting a Negro even had he chanced to know something about it.

You can only get so much field work out of hungry people, though; at some point their hunger overcomes whatever fear you can generate. The men and boys were out nights chasing possum or anything else they might consume, and the women went grubbing in the woods, digging up things they knew to eat. They were too weary and weak to work worth a penny. Slaves on nearby plantations said that they stole, and there were rumors of juju rites on a sandbar in the river. The neighbors complained among themselves. They had never liked the Nicholses. The Nicholses didn't like them. None of them offered to help Martin Nichols out, and he wouldn't have accepted if they had.

By July the Nichols blacks weren't even pretending to work. They would be gone when Martin came to get them in the morning. He'd go stamping and shouting around their empty houses, and if by luck he found some and got them to the field, they would disappear under the green canopy of cotton the first time he turned his back.

Martin himself was living on whiskey, which he had made himself and stored in better times. The fields looked moth-eaten, spotty, and uneven rather than smooth and dark and dense as a field of cotton should appear. Little green caterpillars an inch long came and ate the plants. Still, there was something to harvest, had there been anybody to do the picking.

The $150 was supposed to be repaid, without interest, in five installments through the harvest. Nichols made the first two payments by selling the little cotton he got picked to a speculator in town; he paid the third and fourth installments by selling his remaining cotton in the fields, unpicked, to one of his neighbors who calculated he had enough slaves to get the cotton in. That was the end, of course. Nichols had no more cotton to sell.

So it came that James Birney went to serve papers on Martin Nichols. A lesser messenger would have done, but Barnes thought his brother-in-law should receive the news with some wrappings of dignity. Frederick Barnes's aim was not to steal his brother-in-law's land but to keep the property intact and in the family, and to deliver his brother-in-law from a situation that was clearly impossible. The papers called for Barnes to gain title to all the land, for which he would pay a fair market price as well as clear all debts. Considering how much Nichols owed to the factor Barstow, it was not a bargain for Barnes.

Birney rode out on his chestnut mare, having just the afternoon to make the trip. He was leaving the next day for the eastern seaboard. The new university in Tuscaloosa had commissioned him to look for a president and some faculty. He carried letters of introduction from Henry Clay and Governor Moore.

First, however, he had to deliver papers to a drunken planter.

Birney found the old house more dilapidated than he had guessed possible. A single, muddy trail led from the kitchen to the barn through waist-high weeds. The front door was faced with pink dust.

A black woman dressed in a faded velvet gown answered the door. Birney thought he remembered her from better times. Her beauty had been stolen by hunger; cheekbones stood out from her face like hatchet blades. She told Birney, boldly, he thought, that Master Nichols had gone out. She made a nod toward the parlor. "You can sit there, Master. He might be back soon."

Birney said he would look around. He was not about to sit in this dirty parlor waited on by Nichols's black mistress. He went to the barn and found Nichols there, currying his horse. It gave Birney a shock, for white men of any substance did not care for their horses.

The barn was dark and still cool from the night. It did not smell right; there was no clean scent of hay. Though Birney coughed slightly, Nichols did not seem to know he was there. He continued with his stroking of the horse, working slowly, his head almost leaning against the horse's flanks. When Nichols turned toward him, Birney saw his eyes, which had in them the look of a man in a knife fight when he realizes he will lose.

Birney coughed again. "I have brought some papers," he said. "And a letter from your brother Thomas, which your sister asked me to carry to you."

"What do the papers say?" Nichols asked.

"They're court papers claiming title to this property."

For just a second Nichols seemed startled, as though he heard an unexpected wind in the trees outside. Then he returned to his brushing.

"Frederick Barnes asked me to arrange for the two of you to meet about the arrangements," Birney added. "Any time that is convenient with you."

"Will these papers hold up in court, Mr. Birney?"

"Yes."

"You drew them?"

"I did."

Nichols dropped the curry brush and did not stoop to pick it up. He ran his thick, stubby fingers through his auburn hair. "All right, Mr. Birney, leave them there."

"Leave them where?"

"Anywhere you please."

Birney looked around for a table, a stand, anywhere to put papers. He finally used the edge of an old feeding trough. "What about meeting Mr. Barnes?" he asked.

"Get off of my land," Nichols said, and turned toward Birney, glaring at him with red eyes and doubling his fists by his side as though to pummel him. Birney was no coward; he held his ground while Nichols walked forward to three feet in front of him. He stood there, six inches shorter, his eyes in deep, red-lined sockets. "I'll give you five minutes to be off my property," he said, "and then I get a gun, and you'll be carried off."

Chapter 4
1830: Catherine to Huntsville

ON THE BARNESES' moving day a procession of six wagons set out from Huntsville, packed high with furniture and carpets and everything a modern household would need. In one of the wagons the household help, a dozen well-dressed slaves, sat on the dining room chairs making noise like a treeful of crows. About twenty field hands trudged on foot behind the last wagon, shackled together by a chain that attached to each of their right legs. Ordinarily this precaution would not have been necessary, but about half of these slaves were new, bought in New Orleans. There being no telling what such slaves might do, Barnes thought it best to chain them for the journey. They soon fell far behind the last wagon, with only an overseer on horseback to accompany them.

Cecilia, in her carriage at the head of the procession, could not quit talking to the maid she had brought with her. She remarked happily on every familiar landmark they passed—the squatter farm, the swampy creek where her brothers had fished, the dark forest so much reduced in size and fearfulness now that she was older. Before her marriage Cecilia had found Triana dreadfully dull. Now that she was a full-grown woman, however, with a child on the way, she adored the lordliness of a plantation. The Barneses would keep their house in town but make Triana their country estate.

They had waited until October to move, when the crops were in and they could use their blacks to refurbish the house and grounds. It had been, thankfully, a dry autumn. The roads were passable.

Martin had already left Triana, packing his few things in an old wagon and selling the family furniture to his sister. At Barnes's request a Mr. Pow had hired Martin as an overseer. Pow did not allow liquor, and to Cecilia's surprise her brother had accepted that stipulation. He had a house and a manservant and a cook of his own. Cecilia thought he should be grateful. Martin did not see it so, however. He still would not exchange a word with Barnes nor with her.

Cecilia's carriage arrived at the old house far in front of the wagons. She coasted from room to room, clucking at the dirt, worrying over the scratched floors, telling her maidservant where the items of furniture must go and which of the old things would be moved to the servants' rooms. From an upstairs window she saw a black child standing in the middle of the overgrown, muddy yard, staring up at her. "You there! Boy!" she shouted. "You go down to the cabins and get Catherine to come up here. Tell her I want to see her."

When Catherine arrived twenty minutes later, Cecilia was aggravated to find her so thin. "I want you to be here with me in the house," she said. "Just as in old times."

Catherine did not respond.

"What do you want?" Cecilia asked a trifle impatiently. "You can have my old dresses."

Catherine spoke in a plain, matter-of-fact way, as though mentioning tomorrow's weather. "You know I am a free woman now."

Cecilia was annoyed. "Yes, I do remember that idiocy. I can pay you. What, I don't know. What do you want?"

Catherine looked hard at her. "Five dollars a month," she said. "Besides my food and clothes and place to bed."

Cecilia knew nothing about money, but she said that was all right and set Catherine to work. She would get the money somewhere, from her clothing money if need be. The wagons arrived shortly thereafter, and soon she was ordering the house Negroes to hurry and to be careful as they carried her carpets and furniture and portraits in over the rutted yard. Already she could imagine the splendor when the garden was newly planted, the house repainted, and the interior walls papered with the new styles. She had even thought of adding a ballroom in the rear.

Frederick arrived on horseback. He sat up very straight on his mount, looking every inch the planter except that he was so short. He would not have chosen Triana for his estate, it being farther from Huntsville than he preferred, but he had acceded to his wife's wishes and had no regrets. The land was fine. His first concern was to see that his desk was placed by a window in the library, with its papers safely under lock and key. His second concern was to talk to the free blacks on the place.

He might have walked to the slave quarters, but he chose to ride on his stallion, accompanied by his overseer, a small, joking man known as Mort. Still seated on his horse, Barnes had Mort gather all the blacks. He barely looked at them while they straggled out of their homes: old men in rags, coughing and shuffling; younger men with powerful torsos exposed but whose skin was dull, whose hair was uncombed, and who stared down at the soil underfoot; boys and girls, skinny and quick, full of life, the younger ones more than half naked; all, it seemed, with snot running down under their noses; old women who looked at Barnes with baleful expressions, as though he were Satan about to tempt them to sacrifice their children to demons; younger women, thin as knives, with black inquisitive eyes and babies tied on their hips. There were about seventy-five people in all. The old people's coughs and the babies' wails made a constant background noise.

"Is everyone here?" Barnes asked.

No one answered.

He scanned them all. "Everybody needs to hear this. Are all of the former servants of Mr. Martin Nichols, Sr., here? Anybody missing?"

"My mama is not here." A little mulatto boy had said it. He stood on the edge of the gathering, as though estranged from the group; and he wore trousers and a shirt that were clean and had no gaps or tears.

"Where is your mama?" Barnes asked. "Who knows where this child's mother is?"

"She is up at the big house," one of the young women said in a low voice. "She is helping Miss Sissy."

"Who is that? Catherine?" Barnes asked. There was a general muttering of yes, it was Catherine. "You go and get her," he said, pointing to a young man. "You tell her I don't want her in my house, and she is to come immediately. And you come back too. Now run, don't walk."

Barnes had anticipated the problem. His wife was attached to Catherine; she had been her playmate as a child. Cecilia wanted Catherine to nurse her baby when it came. He had insisted, however, that he would not permit Cecilia to keep free servants. This was a principle with him; free blacks were dangerous, as they tended to be shiftless and drunken and would stir up unrest among the slaves.

Catherine came sullenly, trailing behind the boy who had fetched her. Her thinness exaggerated her deep eyes.

Barnes only glanced at her. "Now is everyone here? I want you to know that I am the new master. I own this land. You may stay on my land only if you surrender your liberty and serve me as a bondservant. If so you will be fed and cared for, providing that you obey. My man Mort"—he gestured slightly, with his chin, toward the overseer, and Mort grinned broadly as though he had been complimented—"has papers drawn up to make it all proper.

"If you will not serve me then you must be gone from this estate today. I have new people who will be glad to have your place."

The gathering did not move or murmur, but it seemed as though a wind blew through them. One tiny old woman, built like a stunted tree, finally spoke. "These are our houses," she said. "Master Birney paid for them with the money Master left."

"You may take your houses," Barnes said. "But be sure they are off my land by tonight."

When Frederick Barnes had gone away from the slave cabins, the black children played, shrieking in high-pitched joy, ignorant of their tragedy. The men sat on their haunches, folded down, immobile, unable to speak, looking off into the trees. Even the women were silent for a time. They were beyond demonstrations of sorrow. Their possibilities were so few, and so utterly unknown to them, that they could not find a way to talk them out. Many had been born here, most had spent their lives here; many had never, in fact, crossed the property line of the Nichols plantation except to go, in a company, to camp meeting before Master Nichols had died.

In a more settled place they might have been hopeful of fending for themselves as free people of color, but even the town of Huntsville was almost a legend to them. Only a few had ever been there. You cannot exaggerate, hardly, how little knowledge of the world outside the plantation they had. You could take a four-year-old and put him down on the streets of Chicago, and he would be better equipped. Inside the Nichols property lines they were clever and cunning, but beyond its borders they were lost. They had no maps, nor any idea how to read a map, nor even an idea where they were, except in something called Alabama or America, and probably very few of them had any idea that one of those was geographically within the other. They only knew north, where the polar star hung over a land of freedom. That seemed as far off and unreachable as the star itself.

They thought, naturally, of James Birney, who had negotiated their freedom, but Catherine told them (she knew somehow) that he was gone on a long journey. Barnes must have calculated on that, of course. Apart from Birney they did not believe they could expect help from anyone anywhere in the world.

They chose, therefore, the way that nearly anyone would under those circumstances: they did nothing. All the choices were bad, so they chose none, hoping that something would turn up. The mothers wandered off after their children. The men sat and spat in the dust, and then two of the young ones made a fight, and they cheered them on as they smashed each other.

You must remember that while they had been free for six years their freedom was a legal fiction. They had worked as hard or harder than ever at the same tasks they had done when they were slaves, and they had not even been fed let alone paid. Gut instinct made them cleave to the legal fiction of freedom but, practically, Barnes's coming could only improve their lot. He would treat them as valuable pieces of property. They would at least eat.

That evening a young man who had gotten some knowledge of religion gathered them together and preached to them, and they sang songs of glory. The new slaves brought from Huntsville joined in, cautiously. They had kept themselves apart all day, like watchers at somebody else's funeral, but they joined in the service. Those who had belonged to Barnes for some time said that he was not cruel, which encouraged the free people to a degree.

Nothing happened the next day, but the following day Mort, the overseer, came with a table that he set up in the yard, and some papers. Some signed, and some refused to sign and were run off, and others, seeing the choices, went into the woods and hid, still hoping that something might turn up. In the long run, more than half the blacks were absorbed back into Barnes's corp of slaves. Some never signed but were simply allowed back and their lack of papers forgotten. Some camped by the river and then, one day, were gone without anyone knowing when or how they left. Perhaps they caught a riverboat that needed help for poling. Perhaps they were kidnapped and carried downriver to sell. Others disappeared immediately, setting off for St. Louis or Nashville or some other name they had heard. Nobody ever knew what became of them, and how would they? None of them could write, nor could they have said where the Nichols plantation was to someone trying to address a letter.

Catherine Nichols missed all this, because on the very day that Barnes came she packed her things and departed. She had been with Cecilia at the big house when the boy came telling that Master Barnes was gathering the blacks. To Catherine's surprise Cecilia had instantly broken down crying. "He'll be a good master, Cathy," she had said. "You won't be sorry."

"Sorry for what?" Catherine had asked, and Sis had told her that Mr. Barnes wouldn't abide free Negroes.

"I don't care what he will abide or won't abide," Catherine had said. "I am a free woman." She had sense enough to know that she could not talk that way to just any white woman, but to Cecilia she related almost as though to an equal.

Catherine did not think for a minute of signing away her freedom. Black Mary had transmitted great inner dignity, and Catherine had inherited the feeling if not the faith behind it. Freedom was not, to her, a gift from Master Nichols.

Besides, Catherine had been a white man's mistress since she was fourteen. She had always had her way with men, black or white. Her self-possession was the kind you see in a beautiful young woman who has been the center of attention since she came of age and thinks she always will be. Master Thomas had taught her to read, had given her dresses, had treated her well. She had thought all white people, all Nicholses at any rate, were inhuman and mean-hearted, so this had surprised her. She had been mute, overwhelmed at first. But she had learned to talk to him, to please him, finally to get what she wanted from him. At times she had flaunted the privileges that came as a white man's woman.

Then the father died, and all the meanings seemed to change. Thomas left, she had her child, and she had seen how it was. She realized freedom was not enough; you could not eat freedom. So she looked for her chance with Martin, the brother. She cut her eyes at him and dangled herself before him, and before long he sent word that she should come to the big house.

He was different, that brother: rough, plain, not given to talk. No matter. He would buy her trifles in the first few years, when he had money. Later there was no money, but she had grown accustomed to her position. At any rate it had been better than the slave cabins.

Now that time was over, and she had a child to keep, but she never thought of surrendering her freedom. She set out from the slave quarters in the afternoon, carrying her clothes in a bundle. She had beautiful clothes given her by her men. They were her only possessions, and they were much more to her than possessions. They were her treasure. Her son, who was nearly six years old, walked by her side, holding her hand. He had her large, dark eyes, but his skin was brown and his hair sandy colored. Sometimes she looked at him and saw in a flash the face of that Thomas Nichols who had gone. The child made her proud. He chattered continuously, pointing out squirrels and telling her the names of flowers they saw along the road. He would jerk on her hand for attention if he thought she was not listening.

"Where will we sleep tonight, Mama?" he asked. "Mama, I'm talking, where will we sleep?"

When they had gone about a mile and were beyond the plantation boundaries, they saw a squatter's cabin near the road. "Is that where we sleep, Mama? Who lives there?"

"No, not there, Tommy."

"I'm tired, Mama. Why don't we stay here?"

"We don't know these people, Tommy. We have to get to Huntsville."

"Who do we know in Huntsville? Mama, I'm talking to you."

Catherine told him to be quiet, they had a long walk, and he would see when they got there. "Be quiet," she said. "You need your strength."

Not long after they passed the squatter's cabin Tommy began laughing and pulling on one end of her bundle of clothes, and before she knew it he had pulled one of her dresses into the mud. She had to stop and tie the bundle again, and she could not get it to stay tightly together. She had to be constantly checking it and pushing loose ends back in.

She cajoled Tommy along. He stopped chattering; his steps became short and wandering. He pulled at her hand to make her stop and rest; and after they had stopped for a while by the stripped and dying cotton fields he would not get up, so she carried him thrown over her shoulder. She told him she would carry him as far as the big oak tree, and then he would have to walk again. But he only went a short distance before he wanted to rest, and so she picked him up and held him over one shoulder while clutching her bundle of clothing. She could not walk that way without resting at times.

"You lie still," she said to Tommy, because he was squirming around to see. "If you can't lie still you will have to walk."

She would mark progress by some landmark, usually a tree, that she would sight far down the road; when she reached it she would take a rest. The rests grew longer, and the landmarks grew nearer. She made Tommy walk, but never for long. He had given up asking questions. He did not fall asleep but carried a dark expression on his face, as though angry.

Catherine had no idea how far Huntsville might be except she knew someone could walk there in a day. She had heard stories of it; it seemed familiar to her, as heaven does to the devout, but there was no detail in her mind. She only knew that the road she took was the road to Huntsville.

The light began fading. She thought she had come an immense way; she kept hoping, every time the road came to a bend, that she might glimpse the town. Finally, when the dark had come down so she could not see the road, she found a thicket near a creek. She wrapped her precious dresses around her son so he could sleep warmly, then curled next to him, shivering. She had been hungry but now felt merely empty and blank. Tommy begged her for some food, and shouted at her that he must have food, then cried and fell asleep, hungry though he was.

Catherine lay restlessly, forcing herself to lie still so as not to wake the child. She had not seen a soul since leaving Triana. It was certainly the longest she had ever been alone. At times, lying there, the wideness of the world seemed too much, and she had to make herself be quiet. She could not afford to panic. She thought of what Black Mary would have done. Black Mary would have sung. So she tried to sing, softly, in her throat, but she had never made the songs her own, and she could not remember words. Finally her mind relaxed and gave up her thoughts. They went swirling up, like the sparks in a fire, turning into dreams.

The morning found them wet and hungry. The thicket of brush dripped with dew, Catherine felt stiff and huffy, and Tommy cried until she slapped him. He said he wanted to go home, and she said he had no more home, that Mr. Barnes had stolen it away from him. Tommy said he would kill Mr. Barnes, and Catherine felt a chill go through her. She told him sharply not to talk that way, to hush. She held him close to warm him, but he would not be comforted. Finally she made up her mind that the best thing was to walk, to get on to Huntsville. The sun did not appear—cold, heavy clouds had settled in—but walking eventually unstiffened and warmed her limbs.

As they proceeded they found more and more trails leading off the road and signs that horses had passed recently, even this morning. Tommy cheered up and began to run ahead of her.

Their road struck another road. Judging by the ruts, it was far more traveled. She was not sure which way to turn, to the right or the left, so she sat down on a tree stump and let Tommy chase after snakes in the grass. Soon enough she heard the rattle of a wagon and got to her feet. She stood by the side of the road with her head down until the wagon was nearly to her, and then looked up to see a white man, a squatter, dressed in shapeless, nut-colored homespun clothing. He had a cloth hat on his head, pulled down almost to his eyes.

She did not say anything; she glanced at him then looked down again. She willed him to stop, and he did, pulling the mule up short.

"Well, who do you belong to?" he asked, looking her over. "I haven't seen you before."

She still did not look up, but smiled so he could see. "I'm going to Huntsville, but I don't know the way," she said.

"Well," he said, and paused to think. "I'm going that way. Why don't you get on up here in the wagon?" He patted the seat beside him.

She straightened up, turned her back on him, and called loudly. "You! Tommy! Come right now, this man is giving us a ride."

The man hesitated, swore, shook the reins. The harness squeaked as the mule leaned forward; the man clucked his tongue, and the mule swung into a trot. Tommy came up and looked after the wagon, which was already fifty yards down the road and halfway behind a rise so only the man's shoulders and hat were visible.

"Why didn't he wait?" Tommy said. "You said to come."

"I guess he didn't want both of us," Catherine said. She was pleased with herself. She had gotten the information she wanted and no trouble.

Huntsville was a town of five thousand, looking like any one of a hundred raw, western towns. The roads were mud, the best buildings were red brick and white clapboard, and dark log cabins slumped behind them and filled the poorer sections. Flies rose up from the street whenever anyone passed, for the mud was mostly horse manure, beaten into a thick, chocolate paste. Dogs lay in the street. You saw few women, white or black, for it was men who roamed outside the home. There were nearly as many black men as white, and you saw them more, the blacks being visible holding horses at the blacksmith's, or digging, or carrying, or standing with the wagon while their masters talked inside.

The town was nothing extraordinary at all, except for the hills. Huntsville rested just above the floodplain of the Tennessee River, hemmed in by spurs from heavily wooded mountains that rose to the north. These muted the town's crude energy and countered the featureless, deadly plain that began where the town stopped. In the summer you could stand at the courthouse and look out over that plain and think of all the cotton to be grown and all the blacks toiling under the steaming sun. If you turned to look at the mountains, however, you felt their cool creeks and green shade.

Below the town's center, just at the border between the plain and the hills, was a large pond with many paths leading down its steep sides to the water. This was a spring, famous throughout the state of Alabama for its sweet, infinite water. It was by this spring that Harriet Long found Catherine and her son Thomas just at twilight.

"Who do you belong to?" Harriet asked in a blunt, almost hostile voice. She was a short, heavyset black woman, twenty years old, although she looked closer to forty. "Somebody new move to town?"

Catherine ignored her. Catherine had been crying and did not want to show it; furthermore, she did not answer to ugly black women.

"I asked, who do you belong to?" Harriet said.

Tommy was in Catherine's lap; she had her arms wrapped around him, and he began to whimper. Catherine told him sharply to be quiet.

"The child is hungry. Why don't you feed him?"

Tommy began sobbing, and when Catherine squeezed him in her arms, he would not be still but thrashed against her.

Harriet squatted down on her haunches and for a few minutes studied Catherine. "You're in trouble," she announced. She glanced around, then asked more softly, "Are you running?"

"No," Catherine exploded. "Who ever heard of someone around here running?"

"I've heard of it," Harriet said.

"I don't have to run," Catherine said. "I'm a free woman. I've been free for six years."

Harriet's face, which had remained hard and suspicious, showed unwilling surprise. "Is that so? Where are you from?"

"Nichols's plantation."

"Oh, yes." Harriet had heard about the freed slaves there. "Well," she said finally, "I am free myself."

Catherine looked up, taking the woman in again. She had never seen a free person of color before, apart from those who, like herself, had never really been free.

"Well," Harriet said. She used the word to fill gaps in her conversation, for she was not a quick talker. She got up on her feet, and Catherine saw that she had in her hand a large, square tin with leather straps attached to it. "You come home with me, and we'll see if we can feed that child something." She went down to the water, balancing on a stone that had been placed a foot from its bank, and stooped to fill the tin. She lifted it, dripping, and in one smooth movement swung the weight onto her back, with the leather strap over her forehead as a tumpline. "Well come on," she said. "You can't sleep here."

She went a few feet before she suddenly swung around and glared at Catherine. "You stay away from my husband," she said fiercely.

She then leaned her head in the direction she was going. "Well, come on. I'll feed you."

Their path did not climb up to the streets of the town but wandered along through thickets on the slope of the hill. Harriet Long moved more quickly than looked possible, considering her build and her load. In something under a mile they came into a clearing with a small log cabin. Two children came running out of the front door, a slender girl of about four and a boy of about two toddling just behind. When they saw Catherine they jerked to a stop as though they had reached the end of a chain, and turned and tumbled over each other back inside. Harriet did not speak or slow down but pushed open the front door, leading the way inside. She set down her water in the corner and pointed at a bed that took up much of the room.

"Sit there," she said. "Rest while I cook."

The cabin was almost completely dark, for it had only one window with a scraped animal skin tacked across it. At one wall was a clay fireplace, where Harriet knelt and blew on the coals until she had a fire; then, with the shadows from the flames dancing behind her, she slapped something into a cast-iron spider, something that sizzled and soon smelled intolerably delicious. She was making johnnycake.

The two children peeked out of the shadows and Tommy, seeing their eyes, chased after them, out the door. Catherine was left to watch Harriet stir the batter into the pan and set it onto the fire like a baby in its cradle. When Harriet was done she stood up, stretched her back, and came to sit on the bed next to Catherine.

"Well," Harriet said. "You haven't told me your name. I am Harriet Long. I bought myself, and I am buying Obadiah. And I will buy my children, too. Who are you?"

"How do you get money to buy people?" Catherine asked.

"Well, I take in laundry from the hotel and from boarders at Mrs. Shadows's. I used to belong to Mrs. Shadows, and she let me keep the money I got for the laundry. She is a good lady. What do you call yourself?"

"My name is Catherine. This lady, would she have any extra laundry do you think?"

There was a silence, and then Harriet Long spoke slowly. "Catherine, you haven't eaten my food yet. Don't be fast to take my living."

Despite that, they were soon talking. Catherine had been through the most astonishing day of her life, and even though she had no vocabulary for what she had seen, she tried to tell about it. The principal fact that stood out to her was expressed in the word *straight*.

Nothing at Triana was straight, except the boards of the big house. The paths were not straight, nor the borders of the fields, nor the river and the trees: everything followed the contours God gave it. Here, in this town, stores were crowded together as though their builders could not get enough straight into one structure so put a dozen back to back. And the wooden shelves on which white people walked along the street were straight, and so were the roads that stretched straight as the river was flat, far down and away until ending in a hill or a forest. And so many white people! And so many big houses! Catherine wanted to tell it all to Harriet, who kept laughing in a low chortle.

Harriet was glad to hear the conversation of a young woman her age. Free black people were scarce and lived most carefully. Harriet concerned herself every day with not being noticed. Slave owners did not like their servants associating with her; her existence as a free person with black skin could only be disturbing. A few other free people of color lived around Huntsville, mostly out of town. They did not associate publicly. If Catherine had met Harriet in town, Harriet would not have spoken to her.

It was quite dark when the door creaked and Obadiah entered. Catherine was aware of Harriet watching her closely, so she kept her head low, not looking at him. Obadiah spoke to her as though completely unsurprised to find a guest. He took a three-legged stool and sat by the fire; soon he was nodding into sleep. Catherine saw with amusement that he was supremely ugly: a small, berrylike head with tiny eyes sunk into sockets deep as two tin cups; a nose that seemed to have been smashed against his face by God's own fist.

But when Harriet served up the johnnycake she treated Obadiah better than the richest white man in his own dining room. Tommy, who was leaning on Harriet's knee, reached out to grab a piece of cake and got his hand slapped hard. Obadiah silently munched his cake and was offered more, and yet more, before the rest of them could eat a bite. He nodded off to sleep again on his stool while the children and the two mothers crowded around the pan, eating as fast as they could stuff it down. When the cake was gone Catherine felt sick; it was the first food she had eaten since leaving Triana.

The children were put in the bed and fell asleep. Obadiah awoke from his nap.

"Bring me a cup of water," he said, and Harriet scuttled to the tin in the corner with remarkable speed. He gradually drank it down, then motioned Catherine to come close to him. In the firelight his face looked uglier than ever, though she did see a fine set of teeth.

"So, my dear," he said. "How did you come to my house?" He listened thoughtfully, nodding and saying yes, yes as she told him. He did not look at Catherine but into the fire, which surprised her. Ordinarily men could not help themselves looking at her.

She told him how she had arrived in the town shortly after noon, when everything was quiet for the lunch hour. This is not what she told Obadiah; she had no idea what a lunch hour was, but it is what he inferred when she told him of the blacks eating from their buckets behind the stores. Tommy had put up a fuss; he was so hungry that he looked pale; she had to hold him tight and put her hand over his lips to make him be quiet. Disoriented by the straightness, by the multitudes of white people, and by the walls of buildings, she had walked through the town, up the hill past the churches, then back down to Madison Street. Never had she imagined such a commotion. She stood in the street until almost run over by horses. On the sidewalk she had been told to get out of the way by a store owner. Tommy had stopped crying; he had worn a dark, surly, silent expression on his face, an expression she had not seen before yesterday, an expression that made her feel as though she did not know her own child's mind.

Catherine knew how to speak with one white person, but here were so many that she could not break them down into individual personalities. Here was not one door but a hundred, not ten windows but a thousand— a matrix of doors and windows that she did not know how to penetrate. For the first time in her life she was genuinely bewildered and frightened.

She had wished to think, to sit and catch her bearings, but she had to eat; she could not let her child go a second day without food. So blindly she had entered a building, a general store as it turned out, though even that was a concept beyond her experience. A white face had asked what she wanted and when she said *work* had sent her out again. She had gone into another door, leaving Thomas beside the door outside, warning him not to move. She had not stopped thinking of him, worrying about him for a single instant while she looked at the floor and moved her lips saying, *I would like to work. I am a good worker,* and was told no and felt chilled just by the sound of the voice. She had gone to houses, too, where she never saw the white lady but was told rudely to get along by the slaves themselves. Blindly, doggedly, she had gone on, in and out of doors, but without her skill, without that female clever seductiveness that she used to gain control. She had no skill because she was afraid and had her mind pulled back into herself, instead of poking outward into the minds of the white faces. At the end of the day when the businesses closed she had knocked on a door and, when it opened, had been struck casually, with the back of a hand, and told to get away.

She had given up then, had walked blindly down toward the plain, and had discovered the spring. She and Tommy had not drunk water since they sipped from a branch outside Huntsville in the morning. She had put her head down into the water and drunk deeply, and for a time it filled her stomach. Then she met Harriet Long.

Listening to Catherine's story, Obadiah had a silent laugh that welled up inside until he shook. "I'm not laughing at your hurt, honey. I am laughing for all us poor Negroes," he said. "Oh, we are a sorry lot." Catherine was offended at first but shortly realized he meant no harm. She noticed Harriet's face watching him with a mixture of adoration and mean, animal protection. Catherine dropped her eyes off the man.

Obadiah asked for another cup of water, which he sucked on in silence.

"We cannot help her," Harriet blurted out. "We have nothing to spare, Obadiah. If we don't buy you God forgive us, for we might as well kill those little ones. Don't think about helping her."

"We might help her without spending money," Obadiah said mildly.

"Food costs money, Obadiah."

"We can raise more food."

"No," she said.

He closed his deep, wrinkled eyes, then opened them and turned to Catherine. "You say you don't know anyone in Huntsville. Even someone who knows your old master?"

Catherine could only see those mobs of white, blank faces, none of them known, none of them seeming even human. She was about to say no when a meteor struck her. "Mr. Birney," she said. A second later her hopes sagged. "But he is gone on a trip."

"He is a good man," Obadiah said. "But he is gone. Still perhaps his wife will remember about the Nichols slaves."

That is how the next day Catherine found herself on the back step talking to Agatha Birney. She was a slight, quiet woman who seemed exhausted. Catherine was trying all she could to find a way to get to her, to work her. She told her story while Mrs. Birney patted her hair and seemed distracted.

Tommy began to squirm. Catherine had not wanted to bring him, but Harriet Long had insisted on it; she did not trust him alone in her house, she said.

Agatha Birney looked on the little mulatto boy with distress. "Is this your boy?" she asked. She had caught from her husband a deep disgust for the mixing of blood. Catherine noticed the look and felt anger rise, but she pushed the feeling down and kept talking, using all the strength and sugar she had.

Finally Mrs. Birney grew agitated and said, without looking at Catherine, "All right, you can come. Come tomorrow, and we'll see what you can do. Good-bye."

Chapter 5
1831: Prayer Meeting

THE NEW MAN that was Thomas Nichols began to pull apart, Nichols felt, when he first saw Ruth Van Ingen stand up to pray in Joel Parker's Free Church. Never before had he witnessed a woman speaking in public; women, in his experience, had human substance only in the privacy of a home. The shock of seeing a woman thus exposed had something to do with his unraveling, but it was more than that. The trouble was that his precious new life, constructed (he believed) on the religious principles, had no space in it to accommodate the aching glory of a female. Ruth, when he saw her, broke up his neat surface like a spring flood shattering the ice on a river.

What she did had nothing brazen or coarse about it. She was fair, and small, and her skin almost translucent. Nichols was seated near her across the center aisle, and he saw clearly the bright peach color like a morning sun spread on her cheek. Her low voice trembled. Yet she stood to pray clearly and calmly and bravely. He had heard of women praying in Finney's revivals, but he had never seen it. Her delicate embarrassment and her daring stuck in him as surely as a barbed hook.

He did not see her as an eligible partner, or a winsome lady, or in terms of any generality. He saw just her, unexpected and lovely as a lost continent pushing up from beneath the jade surf.

His gaze kept straying back to her. Once, by accident, their eyes locked, and he hurriedly looked away. He could not concentrate and did not even know what passed in the service. After the closing benediction he stepped quickly into the aisle and, without looking around him, worked his way out of the church. The whole time he was feeling her presence behind.

At the next prayer meeting he took a pew in the very rear, where he could barely see her. He knew her by the straw-blond hair, a few strands of which escaped her hat and decorated her neck with lazy spirals. He remembered not a single word of what was said in the service. For that he was deeply disturbed. He thought it could not be godliness that would distract him from his prayers. It was lust, surely, however disguised.

He had thought his conversion so complete he would never desire a woman again. Before he had gone with prostitutes whenever he had the money, but since his wonderful day that was gone completely. If he thought of women at all he imagined he would someday marry, an idea that was vague and domestic to him, almost sexless. He had been happy to be free from passion.

This distraction from a woman, this lust, this agitation—he asked God to take it away from his heart, to make his mind true again, but he suspected that he was not praying from faith. He did not altogether want thoughts of Ruth Van Ingen to die away.

For several weeks he made a point of coming to prayers at the last minute and sitting in the back, as far from her as he could manage. Once he went through the whole evening without seeing her—a triumph, he thought, of self-control, only it left him miserable with doubt. Had she been present? Was she ill? Perhaps terribly ill?

Sometimes he quit struggling and gave himself entirely to spying on her. He saw the gracious way she had of slowly nodding when she talked, saw the whiteness of her hands and the pure straw-yellow of her hair. He grew miserable with love, distracted at work, sleepless at night, and worst of all, sexually tempted.

Late one night he was walking home from a meeting of the Tract Society, when he wandered through the poor streets near Five Points.

Among the scattered trash, detritus of a busy market day, he saw two women arm in arm, dark-featured, laughing. Standing under the hissing street lamp, their faces sharply visible, they looked like ordinary young women except for the way they openly laughed together, embracing, inviting attention. Both wore shining linen dresses, he noticed with his usual eye for clothes. One noticed him looking and smiled, then tilted her head toward a house, gesturing for him to go with her. He quickly looked ahead, then walked away from the street as though pursued. He had done nothing, but he was terribly shaken.

He could not stop thinking of what it would have been to enter that house. It was a sickening testimony to his unredeemed, carnal nature that he even imagined it. He had not yielded, but only because of shame and fear. Was this the way of a new creature, remade in God's eternal image? He knew it was not.

Still he could not help himself. The next night he found himself pulled back to Five Points. He walked the street staring furtively at every woman decent and indecent until one, whether a whore or not he could not tell in the brief instant their eyes made contact, looked back at him. With burning shame and fear he averted his eyes. He was terrified to be seen by another Christian, though really his outward appearance was so stern, so moral, so disapproving no one would have guessed at his mushlike heart. Fortunately the night grew late, the streets became deserted, and he returned to his boardinghouse, his feelings sunk.

Of course, Nichols still remembered how he once would have scorned this humorless, rigid person he had become. How he and Martin would have mocked, and laughed! That only made his misery worse—he felt both contemptible and risible.

He made himself stay off Five Points, shying away like a dog that has been kicked. But the mere fact that he wanted to return was enough to cast his soul into hell, he knew. He could control, barely, where he went, but he could not control his thoughts.

Until that time somebody from Huntsville would hardly have recognized Thomas Nichols. Was this the roughneck Nichols boy, the dreamer whom people expected would end up dead or in Texas? At twenty-nine years old he worked long hours at the Tappan Brothers store and long hours in the evenings with various benevolent causes, leaving barely time to eat and sleep. Before his conversion he had thought of nothing but money; now he thought of it hardly at all (yet thanks to God had more prospects than he had ever dreamed of). Before he had shirked hard work, doing it only for the money it brought; now he loved the busy hours he spent being useful. He sought no glory for himself; he was merely thankful to be caught up in good works. Disinterested benevolence, Finney's highest ideal, was planted in his soul.

With a convert's impulsive generosity he told of his salvation to everyone he knew. The widow, Mrs. Frasier, wept, frightening her children again. Hubert Hamilton offered up his solemn congratulations. Nichols told the clerks at Bradgett and Castle, who acted disinterested. He wrote to both of his brothers and to his sister.

Cecilia was the one to finally respond. He received the letter not long after his fright in Five Points. Sissy made no mention of his conversion nor of Reverend Finney. She offered routine congratulations on how well he was doing in business; she supposed he was rich by now and would come back to home carried in his own riverboat or in a chariot or whatever people used in New York.

You are not the only one doing well, she wrote.

You know Frederick and I are back in Triana at last, and you will never recognize the old home when you see it. A happy, peaceful home at last, and we have Abner our beautiful child here to be master himself some day.

The whole house is painted blue and the garden planted with bulbs from Holland, very rare beautiful ones. Not even Mr. Birney has so many, and you know his garden. The slaves are mostly back in their place, too, the very ones that Daddy set free. They have come back because Mr. Barnes said he would not tolerate them unless they were proper slaves, and only then would he take care of them. They were so thin it was a sin to look at them. Except Catherine and her child. She would not come back but went to Huntsville with Tommy, and I hear she works for Agatha Birney. I thought she was very ungrateful. I wanted her to stay in the house, and Mr. Barnes was very agreeable, but he said she cannot be free.

Strangely, until the letter came, he had not thought of Catherine. When he had vomited up his sin not one single thought of her had entered his mind. He read Cecilia's letter with a shudder of horror; how could he have repented and never thought of this past? It was a fearsome thing to remember that wasted time; even the memory seemed to hold a threat of return to meanness and chaos.

His body had the memory of Catherine, skin and scent. Once he had begun to recall, he could not control his mind from ranging far into his past with her. Somehow—he hated this—those thoughts tangled with the blond delicacy of Ruth Van Ingen. He would think of one and then, help-lessly, think of the other.

He cried out to God for relief from this horrible confusion. He wanted only to be pure and simple again. Why must he be caught in this web of lustful delusions? He wished that he had never seen Miss Ruth Van Ingen. And yet he did not wish it.

———

He was with Lewis Tappan one soft spring evening, when the setting sun turned the sky pink behind the dark buildings. The two of them hurried from the store to one of their reform meetings. "I hope you will not mind," Lewis said with his crisp Connecticut voice, "if we stop off for a moment at the home of Mr. Heusden. I need some papers that are there." Tappan led him to a very elegant home on Galen Street, where a servant introduced them to a luxurious parlor.

The room was dense with furniture, draperies, cushions, brass lamps. There was even a small black carving of an elephant on a side table. Nichols looked around with some alarm and interest. Reform-minded Christians usually kept simple homes.

"Rather ostentatious, I would say," Lewis said stuffily after the servant had left them. Lewis scowled at an elegantly carved mirror on one of the papered parlor walls. "What is the use of all this ornamentation, I would like to know. We need a mirror to straighten our hats or to brush our hair." He brushed at his hair with one hand.

A tall, spare, gray-haired gentleman entered and was introduced as Mr. Heusden. The man wore a thin gray mustache on his flat upper lip, a mustache that Thomas remembered from somewhere. Then with a jolt it came to him: This was Ruth's father! No, he then thought quickly, this was the man who accompanied Ruth to church, the man Thomas had always assumed was her father.

Mr. Heusden was speaking to him. Thomas nodded, even though he had been too preoccupied to take in the words. Lewis said, yes, that would be fine, it would be on their way. Mr. Heusden went out of the room, and Thomas inquired where he had gone. "To call her, I suppose," Lewis said.

Before Thomas could think what that meant, she was there. She opened her mouth and said something—he supposed it was, "How do you do?" She extended her hand—a white, almost fleshless hand, with the blue lines showing under the skin. He took it in his own fingers and felt it, cool and waxy. He thought, in the instant that he touched her, that he felt a slight tremor—or was it his own trembling? She gave not the slightest sign that she had ever seen him before, but she was so pleasant, so demure, so tender with her eyes, that he could not help thinking it was for him.

In a moment they were out of the door, he and Tappan and Ruth Van Ingen with them. He did not know where they were going or why she was with them. He did not dare ask.

Tappan inquired politely about Miss Van Ingen's health, and then, walking quickly with his short, powerful legs, concentrated on something else. Thomas heard their shoes clattering on the stones of the street. The silence was unbearable. What was she thinking of? Did she even notice him? Where were they going, and why?

She spoke to him. It was the only time he had heard her voice, except in that first public prayer. It sounded low and throaty, almost hoarse. She asked him whether he worked with Mr. Tappan. He said yes, and then tried to think what else to say. Surely *yes* was not enough.

"Mr. Nichols has become the chief secretary in our store," Tappan said, stepping in. "We rely on him in all things. And he is active in the benevolent societies, Miss. We are on our way to a reform meeting now. We quite often attend together. Together at business and together in the Lord!" he said jovially, panting slightly from the exertion of talking while walking so quickly.

Miss Van Ingen asked which society they would attend. Tappan had not anticipated the question and was embarrassed. He coughed. A man would not discuss the subject with a woman other than his wife.

"It is called the Magdalen Society," Thomas threw in before he thought. "It offers help to young women who have come into the city and have strayed."

Then for a moment Thomas's mind was paralyzed. Miss Van Ingen kept silent. The reference to prostitution was offensive to her, surely. He had spoken without thinking, invidiously. He wanted to kneel on the pavement and beg forgiveness; he wanted to seize his lips and tear them off before her. But of course he merely continued walking and felt his face burn.

She spoke, and her low, hoarse voice came like the sound of a soft, southerly breeze in the upper limbs of a forest. "You have a pleasant voice," she said. "May I ask where you are from?"

He sat through the Magdalen Society meeting barely able to attend to business, so filled were his thoughts with Ruth Van Ingen. Afterward he walked the New York streets until early in the morning, jubilant, whistling, greeting the lowliest worker with a hearty hello. He even strolled through Five Points, simply to prove to himself that there was nothing but light in his soul, that temptation had vanished. Not once while he was with Ruth had he felt anything but purity and delight, the most elevated feelings.

After that marvelous night it was easy to speak with her. He escorted her home from church once, a distance of nearly a mile, along with her uncle and two younger cousins. He learned that she was an orphan, taken in by her uncle; that she had lived in New York all her life; that she loved to read the Bible and had considered becoming a missionary in the Sandwich Islands. This last bit of knowledge alarmed Thomas, at the same time as it filled him with respect for her.

One Wednesday afternoon the Tappan warehouse was its usual slam-bang, hustling tumult, but Thomas's thoughts were with Miss Ruth Van Ingen. A few more hours and he would be with her. He had asked her to walk with him to the prayer meeting. She would slip her hand inside his arm—he could almost feel, already, her slight pressure there, inside the crook of his elbow. She would speak in her low, melodic, husky voice, so low it seemed almost to vibrate. For the first time they would be alone together in the anonymity of the street.

Thomas spoke bitingly to two young clerks who had crabbed the ledger, and then felt sorry for his meanness. He was impatient to escape.

Upstairs, on the third floor, having seen to the lifting of a crate by rope and pulley up to storage, he paused by the door to Bethel. This was a simple room that the Tappans kept as a prayer chapel. Nichols had other matters to attend to but he paused, drawn by the holiness of the place. It was a bare room, lined with plain benches on a clean, golden, waxed floor. Looking around to see that he was really alone, he knelt by one of the benches. His soul was hungry to pray. He could not be selfish; he must seek God's will, even if it might mean she would leave for the Sandwich Islands. He prayed, out loud, for "a certain young woman." After he had completed his prayers he remained kneeling for a few minutes, happy in his own frame of mind, mingling religion and love.

Near closing time, while he was at the front desk looking over the last, straggling customers, he saw a familiar figure walk in the door: Charles Finney. Finney surveyed the room with his famous, staring eyes. He was undeniably handsome, tall, proud, and completely unconscious of self. Nichols hurried to greet him, wondering whether Finney remembered him, hoping that he did. Finney did, of course, reaching out his hands in a hard clasp, greeting him with real love.

In the eighteen months since Nichols's conversion, Finney had preached in Utica, Rochester, Buffalo, and Auburn, with results that were reported and pondered everywhere. The Rochester meetings had, by their feverous example, spawned revivals up and down the country. A great awakening seemed to have begun. All over America church membership was leaping, crime and drunkenness deflating, the upward spiral of American hopes fastening on God. Finney was at the heart of it all.

Finney circulated to every clerk in the Tappan store, shaking hands with them and speaking earnestly. Nichols led him to Arthur Tappan's tiny cubicle, and then—seeing there was nowhere in the cubicle to sit, for Arthur kept only one chair—upstairs to Bethel. Arthur and Lewis and half a dozen clerks followed. Arthur solemnly asked Finney for a summary of his activities, "what God has done through you and around you since we last met."

Finney said he had been resting at his father-in-law's home in Whitesboro. "In Rochester they said I had consumption, that I would never recover, that I must stop my labors. The doctors told me I was done for. But I said to the physicians, 'Gentlemen, God has called me, and I must go on. If I die, let me die while leading others to life. Who can say whether this present opportunity will continue beyond this week, this month, this year?' The truth is that my case is special. For years doctors have been informing me that I will die, but as soon as I get some rest I am all right. As you can see!"

He did look well. He gladly launched into accounts of each of the New York towns he had visited. He mentioned people they knew (for everyone passed through the Tappan store), he told wonderful accounts of salvation, he described astonishing changes, such as the elimination of drinking to such an extent that tavern owners along the Erie Canal closed their doors for lack of business.

"Rochester was most amazing," he said. "Quite unprecedented. I had never seen such a work of God. On New Year's Eve I asked Theodore Weld—you know him?—to preach for temperance. Three hours he spoke, and then people stayed on to testify and commit themselves and to form committees on the spot. They wouldn't go home. Next day, on the street in front of the biggest grocer in the city they rolled out casks of liquor and broke them up with an ax. They had whiskey running in the street. Yes, hundreds of gallons of whiskey in the gutters! For a time they say the canal was twenty proof.

"Within a week you couldn't buy a drink in Rochester. You can't today. The people are not merely converted there, they are *reforming* their *society*. I have seen many lives converted, but never have I seen an entire *city* transformed by the gospel."

A clerk came in to tell Arthur Tappan that it was closing time and they had bolted the door. Tappan nodded and let Finney's stories continue: amazing narratives of families converted, infidels brought to their knees in the fear of God, drunkards sobered, scoffers humbled. Forty-five minutes later the same clerk came in and said that some of the clerks would like to go home. Arthur asked Nichols whether he would see to it, and reluctantly he got up to help secure the books and cash and see the clerks out the door. Then he hurried back upstairs.

Finney was talking about the Oneida Institute, energetically boosting the place for Lewis Tappan, whose oldest boys needed a school. "You'll find it marvelously inexpensive," he said, knowing that would impress Tappan. "It runs on the manual labor principle, so the students work on the farm and earn enough to pay most of the expenses. The remaining cost is $5.50 a term."

"That is certainly a good price, if they offer a good education," Tappan said.

"Oh, I think quite good," said Finney. "They work hard with their bodies, they work hard with their studies, but they labor most of all with the spirit. It is a place where the soul is fed as much as the mind. The most influential student is Theodore Weld."

"The man who spoke at Rochester," said Lewis. "He is a student? I had heard of him as a temperance lecturer. You know that my brother"—he nodded toward Arthur—"has offered nonalcoholic wine for sale to churches for their communion. We have thought of contacting Mr. Weld."

"He is undoubtedly the most powerful young man in the west," Finney said. "Anyone who knows him will say so. Converted at Utica in our revival there in 1826. At the time he was a great enemy of the revival, determined to oppose me. He found me in a grocery store and abused me in front of a large crowd. Then God got a hold on him. I did nothing, I merely told him, 'Cough it up, Mr. Weld, cough it up!' The next day he stood up before the whole congregation at our meetings and confessed his sin. What a victory for the Lord was won that day! If you send your boys to Oneida, they will fall under his influence, for he is the real leader there—more even than the principal. Weld could have his choice of some of the best churches in our state, but he insists on finishing his education before he will be a pastor. I would consider his presence reason enough to send my boys there."

"I want them exposed to real gospel life," Tappan mused.

"Then by all means Oneida. It is a serious place. By the way, Weld tells me that he has heard from Captain Stuart. You know him, the Scottish gentleman who was so active in our revivals? He is in England now and has thrown himself totally into the cause of the slave. Weld says he is lecturing and writing on the subject there."

"I know Britain shows renewed interest in that cause," Lewis said, for he kept in close correspondence with several British reform societies. "I had not known that Captain Stuart was involved."

"What do they want to do now?" Nichols asked before he thought to restrain himself. The subject irritated him. A year ago Arthur Tappan had given money to a dapper, talkative young man named William Garrison, who talked more claptrap about slavery than anyone ever had. The Tappans had bailed him out of jail in Baltimore and helped him launch a newspaper in Boston that was full of antislavery agitation. It annoyed Nichols that Northerners might tamper with something they could not understand.

"Apparently some in Parliament want to abolish slavery in the colonies," Tappan answered, "such as Jamaica."

"It must come," Finney said. "One cannot think that under God's rule one man will own another. Is Wilberforce involved?"

"I am afraid he is too feeble to be active," Tappan said. "But they say he is an encouragement."

Suddenly, while Thomas Nichols was still feeling irritation at statements that seemed so irresponsible, his ears stopped hearing the conversation. Ruth! He pulled out his watch and saw that he was already late.

He wanted immediately to flee. Yet he did not feel that he could leave in an unseemly way. Nichols waited for what seemed to be an hour, though his watch said merely five minutes. There came a pause in the talk. Nichols stood compulsively, said that he had an urgent appointment, shook hands around, looked full in the face of Finney, and hurried out. He kept his composure until he was down one full flight of stairs, and then he ran.

She was extremely small, he realized. Nichols was holding his hymnbook down low so she could read. They were standing together in church services, singing. Her size and delicacy filled him with an unutterable thrill of protectiveness.

Coming to her home in a cab, an extravagance he never allowed himself, he still arrived a half hour past the time he had promised. He apologized profusely for being late. When he stammered out the reason, she was quite bowled over. To be with Finney! For her it was too wonderful. "I could never have blamed you if you had stayed with him all evening and forgotten about me!" she said.

To be sure he was pleased to tell every detail of how Finney had looked and what he had said. Thomas talked while they rode in the cab—another extravagance!—to the prayer meeting.

The First Free Presbyterian Church was another of Lewis Tappan's reform programs. The pews were not rented out—thus the name "free"— so the poor could worship on equal terms. Joel Parker had come from Rochester as pastor and had been so successful that in February they moved into the vast Masonic Hall on Broadway. It was in this aging arena, dingy and ornate, that the prayer meeting went on.

Grave, orderly, slow-moving, the church's services moved Nichols like the deliberate power of a great river. Full-throated hymns vibrated the pews; prayers were heartfelt and long. The people, respectable and otherwise, were drawn together by this deep drama: the worship of almighty God, the visible conversion of souls. It was so Methodist, in one sense, allowing Thomas to recapture the emotions of his boyhood religion—he felt far more positive about that now than he had before his conversion—but it allowed no hint of unseemly ranting, keeping all that passion bottled up.

This night Ruth's physical closeness did not distract from his spiritual ardor. Just the opposite: as they went into prayers, kneeling at their places, he found himself intensely moved. Tears began to flow, and joy filled his chest so he could not breathe. Tears! He was so glad for this evidence of true life. He was ever so tenderly aware of Ruth by his side, of her small- ness, of the careless brush of her arm against his own.

While they knelt a dry, gray, old man's voice prayed for the conver- sion of the city—picturing before God the lost, the desperate, the deceived. Compassion for the world spilled into Thomas's heart, filled it so it flowed over. Images appeared in his mind's eye: memories of New York's crowded streets, and its poor quarters, and its careless immorality. He thought of Five Points and the shaming lust he had endured. The place was filled with the shadow of darkness. Oh, to help it! Then his thoughts moved to his brothers and sister and the Alabama home they had grown in. Ruth could never have known such meanness; she could never imagine the selfish spirit of his boyhood. *Oh, God,* he prayed, *I am so thankful to be redeemed.* The tears rolled down Thomas's cheeks and drew his soul nearer to the small, fragile source of goodness next to him.

The dry voice carried on, calling on the Lord's mercy for New York and its oppressed, but Thomas had stopped hearing. Catherine had entered his mind. He could see her, could picture her face with its heavy eyelids and long jaw. He tried desperately to put the thought away. Catherine was a shame he did not want to encounter again, even in memory. *Oh, God, no, please, while Ruth is so near.* Then he realized that he was not feeling lust, he was simply remembering. Catherine was not a succubus, she was a woman, as real as this one on his arm. She was a human being whom he had used for his own pleasures and then deserted. She was a mother with a child. He was not drawn to her flesh anymore, he was heavy with her spirit and with his own saddening history.

Suddenly he saw how the cause against slavery could entice men. This insight came to him like a flash of silver water between dark trees. That something could be done to save those vast, helpless heaps of black humanity—to help Catherine and all her kin. That the abused and subhuman might become, somehow, truly free. This was a titanic thought. It would take a Finney. It would take a movement of God.

Thomas rarely opened his mouth at prayer meetings, but no matter. He would speak. The impulse was on him to pray for the slaves. He would show that his thoughts of Catherine were not lustful, but transformed. The figure at his side inspired him. When the dry, gray voice was done, Thomas stood. For a moment he peeked about him at the bowed bodies, devout and still. He opened his mouth, and a solid voice came out. He spoke about his concern for the poor and needy, and especially those most abused of all, those who could not control their own lives, our brothers and sisters in slavery.

Thomas knew well enough that the prayer would rankle some. Southerners objected fiercely to any criticism of the Southern way of life. He did himself. Others might be unhappy that a controversial subject had been introduced into prayers. They wanted no divisive politics in a prayer meeting, people said. Nonetheless Thomas felt that he had been moved by a true inspiration of the Spirit. He felt for the moment immune to sin.

Ruth was quiet as they walked toward her home. "Are you tired?" he asked. Some doubt about her feelings had crept in, because of her silence.

"No," she said quietly. "I am only thinking about your prayer. I have never known one of the poor creatures."

They walked on while Nichols wondered what to say. Had he distressed her? At every street corner they came into the hissing yellow light of a street lamp, swarming with moths; then as they strolled on, the pavement grew dark again, and Ruth held his arm more tightly.

"I grew up with slaves," he said. "That was ordinary in Alabama. A slave nursed me. She ran our house after my mother had died. Black Mary, we called her. A very godly woman."

"No wonder you pray for them," Ruth said. "Do you feel for them very deeply?"

He did not know how to answer. He had never thought to pray for them, never, not once.

"What has happened to those slave people? Do they ever write to you?" Ruth looked up at him with the most melancholy sympathy.

He almost laughed at her question but caught himself. How little Northerners understood of the blacks. "They cannot write, nor read," he said. "My brothers and my sister sometimes tell me a little news of them.

Many of them have left the plantation. My father freed all the slaves when he died, so many have gone. Except Mary, who is dead and buried at home. She was already old when I was born."

"Isn't it wonderful that they are no longer slaves? That your father freed them! You sound so somber."

Thomas thought of explaining all that had happened. It was too much. "Their lives may still be very hard, though," was all he said. The inspiration that had led him to pray was gone out of memory.

She had already asked him to come in to her home, and so he sat in the parlor, his hands on his knees, talking with her aunt and uncle. Gradually his spirits lifted. His past was over, after all. This, here, now, was the life God had given to him.

Mr. Heusden had a quiet, head-nodding way of listening—that was surely where Ruth had learned her habit. He stumbled over his words but managed, in a gentle, bumbling way, to find out all about Thomas's life and prospects. He seemed especially interested in knowing what responsibilities Thomas carried with the Tappan brothers. Midway in the conversation Thomas had the illuminating thought that although Mr. Heusden sweetly seemed to know nothing, he was in fact well informed.

Mr. Heusden made a very good living manufacturing lanterns. He had no children of his own. Still, Thomas was unprepared for Mr. Heusden's broad hints when he spoke of his need for a young partner who could take on the business.

When Thomas said good night to Ruth, she gave him a small, proprietary smile. After he was out the door and walking home, elation filled him up to bursting. She was his; she loved him. He was sure of it.

Book II
Reading the Signs

Chapter 6
1831: Nat Turner's Rebellion

He saw the sun go out. He could read the Bible and tell its significances, he had dreamed of white spirits and black spirits at battle, and he knew for a fact that God had appointed him as the Moses of his people. Until he saw the sun go out, however, Nat Turner did not know that the time had come to strike.

Of course they all saw it: the ghostly darkness at midday, the crescent lights scattered like paper ornaments in the shadows of the trees, and two Negroes struck blind by looking. Even the white people seemed frightened by the rising darkness, though they made like they knew all about it and were amused by the Africans and their superstitions. They all saw it, but only he, Nat Turner, could read the signs and tell that the time had come.

He was well regarded in that quiet, rural district of Virginia, by whites as well as blacks. Whites would sometimes ask his thoughts on religious questions and listen with a half-mocking smile to his answers. White slave owners encouraged their servants to attend his meetings, for he set a good example of honesty and hard work. They never guessed, none of them, that the Lord had selected him for the work of vengeance.

He chose seven to fight, though they were not the only ones who believed. Not a man with black skin in Southampton County did not know the Reverend Nat Turner and believe in his powers. Seven came on a moonless night, August 21, not because more would not have come but because these were the ones Turner had chosen. Seven was a holy number; they were chosen people, he said, like Gideon's band sent to smite the Midianites.

They made their final plans in total darkness, in a little clearing in the woods. The air was still and hot, with no breeze yet from the ocean. Turner said they could not slap at mosquitoes, for fear of the noise. As they walked silently out of the woods on the path to Travis's home they were covered by small, black, feasting monsters.

Travis was the man who had bought Turner. He lived in a small, lonely house. He was not an especially bad man; he only had the misfortune to think he could own God's instrument. One of the men got a ladder out of the barn; with a soft smack it hit the side of the house, and Turner climbed stealthily to an upper window. He raised it, put his head inside, then his shoulders, then, with a neat kick, dragged his legs behind him. He got off the floor and sneaked down the stairs, found the key, and opened the door for the others.

They shuffled in, breathing strangely because they were terrified. Would they really destroy God's enemies? Would they really be free and as rich as kings? Turner took an ax from one of their hands. He knew he could not hesitate, or they might all lose nerve and run. He led the way up the stairs. Someone behind him tripped and fell on another; they cried out, briefly, and then made more noise as they untangled and got to their feet again. Turner heard Travis call out, he heard the bed creak as Travis got up, heard his bare feet pad across the floor. There came the man, a pale shadow standing in his nightshirt, exclaiming, "What the . . . ?" Turner did not hesitate. From the head of the stairs he raised the ax and smashed it into the man's side. Travis staggered, his arms flying up in surprise. Turner raised the ax and brought it down on his head. It made a dull, soft thud, exactly like killing a pig. Travis never spoke a word.

The children were killed in their beds, except one who hid underneath her cot and had to be pulled out by her hair before being hacked with a machete until she was still. Travis's wife tried to run out; they stopped her easily, and she screamed frightful, wordless, tooth-aching shrieks until they made her silent forever.

Turner lit a lamp and inspected each of the bodies. The others were frightened and stirred by the light. What they had done in the dark showed clearly—they had killed white people. The light showed also the blood on their clothes and arms and feet, though Turner quoted from the Bible that blood must be shed. "Now we are all new," he said. "We are God's army baptized in the blood of the wicked." They ate some food—some bread and a meat pie that Mrs. Travis had locked into a cupboard, and drank some water—and then Turner led them out.

The dawn had come. Soft shapes of trees showed against a pinkish sky. "We are going to free our people," Turner said to his army. "We will be as rich as white men. We are marching to Jerusalem as the Lord's army, and we must kill everyone who stands in our way."

Southampton County was a sparsely populated tidal plain in southeastern Virginia. Jerusalem was the county seat, twenty miles from the Travis house. Turner led his band that way, collecting volunteers as he went, until he had a mob of drunken, giddy black men who killed nearly every white person they encountered. Traders who accidentally drove up on them were dragged out of their wagons and dispatched; children and women were axed; farmers were chased through their own fields until they were caught and shot. Turner's men killed nearly sixty people, catching most of them by surprise.

By the second day, the alarm had spread. They found farms hastily deserted, food still on the table. Near Jerusalem the militia waited, augmented by every able-bodied white man in the county. Turner's army panicked and ran.

The white men scoured that county. If they found a black man who looked sideways, they were suspicious, and if they were suspicious, one of them was likely to kill the man while the others looked on. They hunted Africans with dogs, ran them day and night, and generally slaughtered them where they found them.

They needed two months to catch Turner, tracking him into the swamps and forests. He was given a trial and hanged, along with seventeen others. By that time he was the most famous man in Virginia. White people looked differently at their slaves after that—especially those slaves who, like Turner, loved to read the Bible.

Chapter 7
1832: Longing for Freedom

CATHERINE NICHOLS picked up the yellowed newspaper in the shrubs by the Birney house, where it had evidently blown off the veranda. With the automatic deception of a slave she surreptitiously tucked the newspaper into the front of her dress and carried it home. Catherine was always looking for something to read. She felt her knowledge of letters made her superior to other people, and she wanted to exercise the skill, to keep it current and also to demonstrate it before Harriet Long, who could not even sign her name.

She had stayed very late ironing clothes for Sunday morning and walked home in the dark. Taking off her dress to lie down in her corner bed, she rediscovered the damp, folded wad of paper. When she went by the fire and read a few lines she felt quite suddenly awake.

"What is that you've got?" Harriet Long asked. She always had her eye on Catherine, had not trusted her, particularly with her husband but really with anything, even though she had shared her home and food for more than a year.

"A newspaper," Catherine answered.

"Where did you get a newspaper? These are bad times for black people to be reading," Harriet said. They had heard about Turner, despite the white people's attempts to keep it from them. Word spread from mouth to mouth, out of sight and hearing of the white master.

"Nobody knows what I read here," Catherine said. "I found this paper in the bushes by Mr. Birney's house."

"How do you know what they know? How do you know nobody saw you pick up that paper? All they have to do is come here and find that paper. Then where will we be?"

"There is nothing in the law to say I can't read. I am a free woman."

Harriet sniffed. "Well," she said. "Well, you may read the newspaper, but you can't read the times. Who do you think is going to care what the law says?"

"Mr. Birney would help me," Catherine said. She still did not know how to move Birney, for he seemed so righteous as to have not a single crack where a female could get leverage. She was reasonably sure, though, that he was fair. She had doubted it severely, as she would for any white man, but she had watched him enough to be convinced.

"Well. How big do you think that man is?"

"He was mayor of this city. He must be pretty big."

"Then why aren't you still at Triana? Why are those Triana Negroes back slaving for Mr. Barnes? You think that man is big enough to stop all the ugly white people in this county? Or even one?"

Obadiah was lying full length by the fire, a bed for his two sleeping children sprawled across him. "You are right, Harriet," he suddenly interposed with a quiet but authoritative voice. "Mr. Birney cannot protect us. But why should we be free if we always act like slaves?" He shut his eyes, as though to muster strength. It was a long speech for him. "It is a good thing to read," he continued. "Free people ought to read. I pray to God my children will read."

Harriet bristled but held her peace. She never contradicted Obadiah.

"Catherine," Obadiah said in a voice so soft they could barely hear, "are you finding something interesting in that paper? Why don't you read it to us?"

She read it out loud, and that is how they learned that there were white people in the North who wanted to end slavery. The paper denounced them as fanatics and anarchists. It said they should attend to the evils of their own states, whose workers were treated far worse than any Southern slaves. But the newspaper's denunciations went through their minds like water. The one fact that held their interest was that someone, a white person, was speaking against slavery in words whose strength they could only guess from the vigor with which they were denounced.

"Well," said Harriet, when they had listened to every word. "Mr. Garrison must be a big man."

Early the next morning, in a cold mist, Catherine set off to meet her son. Thomas was seven years old, and Mr. Birney had arranged for him to work in the house of a cooper at Parker's Bend. He got room and board and twenty-five cents a week, which Mr. Birney collected. For helping Mrs. Birney, mostly doing laundry, Catherine was paid two dollars. She gave a dollar and a quarter to the Longs, and tried to save the rest. For what, she was not sure.

Catherine saw Thomas only once a week. To meet him she usually followed hidden paths through woods and along creeks, but this day the wet and muck were so profound she made up her mind to chance the road. She had on one of her beautiful dresses, a blue silk, and worried that the mud and drooping brambles of the paths might spoil it. A cape she had made from old sacking covered up her dress, not only to keep off the rain but to keep envious eyes away. The surest way to trouble was by giving the impression that you were proud. A lot of white women did not possess a dress like Catherine's.

As she walked she thought about the newspaper she had read. It was not that she had any hopes. She would have scoffed if another African had told her that slavery could ever cease. Her own single-hearted ambition was somehow to be taken as a house servant, by the Birneys or someone, and to live in that soft, white luxury and still to be able to say, I am a free woman.

Yet how amazing that white people were discussing slavery, talking its evils. The very idea was tempting, like whiskey. She could not remember much she had read, only the pleasure of it. She wished she had kept the paper. She had said she would hide it somewhere in the woods, but Obadiah had said no. He had made her burn it and stir the coals to be sure it was all consumed.

The hour was too early for churchgoers and too raw for pleasure riders. Fog hung around the tops of the trees and dripped heavily onto the road. The air smelled occasionally of smoke. Several times she thought she saw Thomas coming and hurried her step, but the figure disappeared, or developed into a tree stump, or became a fold in the land. She began to be anxious for him. He could not leave the farm until he had milked both cows, and it might easily be that one of the cows had balked, or that the master had kept Thomas for some other chore. But naturally, as a mother, she thought of other possibilities: that he had fallen sick, that he was injured, that perhaps he had been caught up in a white man's anger.

She walked as fast as she could now. The mist had turned into tiny, individual droplets of rain, which weighed down her cape. She came over a hump that gave a view of the road another half mile ahead. Scanning it for sign of him, she found nothing. He had always met her before this stretch. She was almost running now, her heavy cape swinging and sloshing at her sides.

She heard him. He cried out to her, and she whirled around. "Thomas!" she shouted, thinking he was hurt, and he sang out again in a voice unmistakably cheerful. He was sitting in a thick, spreading branch of a tree twenty yards back from the road. He was dangling his legs and looking pleased with himself.

"What are you doing up there?" She was angry at once for the fear he had put her through. "Get out of there this moment," she said crossly. "We have a way to go, and you have made me walk a mile too far. What are you doing up there?"

"It began to rain," he said.

"It is raining on me. Come down. We want to go to church."

Then she was sorry, because she saw him only once a week, and he was still a small boy dressed in tow sack, barefoot, and he looked as skinny as a walking stick. He was the only thing that belonged to her, apart from her dresses. "You're so dirty some rain can't help do you good," she said, seeing where the drops had streaked the dust on his face. "Why don't you wash?"

"Boys don't wash," he said.

They walked back to the town in the spitting rain. Catherine asked questions, but Tommy did not answer much. Whatever he had been doing and thinking had passed through him like a bird's song and was gone forever. Now was nearly all he knew, and she was left without much to treasure in her heart. She lived for these few Sunday hours, when she had him.

On the outskirts of town she helped him change into the clothes she guarded throughout the week. He had outgrown them, but she had added a strip of cloth to the cuffs. He complained that the shirt pinched. She told him never to mind, he couldn't wear a tow sack to church. Truthfully black children rarely attended church, but she had only this time to be near him.

They sat in the balcony with other Negroes, most of them house slaves to the solemn white Presbyterians worshiping below. Thomas loved church and sat mesmerized throughout. He rarely did sit so still at any other time. Catherine occupied herself watching him, his black, bright eyes unwavering on Reverend Doctor Allan.

She could never keep her mind with Dr. Allan for long. She did learn a good deal about fashion, surveying the white women in the congregation below. By now the clothes she had brought from Triana looked old, like a maiden aunt's. It was one reason she wanted to be a house servant again: to angle her way into more.

After the service the balcony emptied out onto a back alley, where the various slaves mingled. On a fine day this served as the African society ball, the brown girls cutting the black boys, the house slaves from the finer families condescending to those from lesser households. Today, though, with rain still spraying from heaven, one small, crowded, dripping porch held the only shelter. Most of the worshipers stood only a few moments, calculating the rain, and then scuttled off toward home.

Catherine was putting on her cape when she felt a tall presence at her elbow. It was a thin, intensely black, lantern-jawed servant from Frederick Barnes's house in town, Robert.

"Hello, Miss Cathy," he said. "How are you today?"

"Damp," she said. "And how are you?"

He spoke in a low voice, looking out into the rain so that it would not be obvious to anyone that he was speaking to her at all. "The Reverend Princewell is here," he said. "He stayed in my house last night." Princewell was a black Baptist preacher, who traveled irregularly through the area, preaching where he could. People said Princewell was full of the Holy Ghost. Catherine had been to a memorable meeting where he had proved it true. The man sang and prayed and preached like a thunderstorm.

"We are going to have church today," Robert said.

"Where is that?"

"In Mr. Rutter's barn. Mr. Rutter said he would keep any trouble away." Rutter was a wheelwright who had a small farm. He was a religious man, a professing Baptist who had given Robert a Bible. Catherine knew this because Robert had offered it to her on loan, since he could not read.

Her first thought was elation: they would have a place to go from the rain, Thomas would be happy, they could hear the black man preach and sing. She almost said yes, but suddenly felt the meaning of Robert's invitation. He was a widowed man. His wife had died from fever a year ago. She had sensed it before, but now she knew to a certainty: he would ask her to marry him.

Catherine was suddenly short of breath, not because she was surprised—she always instinctively assumed every man wanted her—but because she wanted so much to go that way. Robert was a good man, a slim tall man, and she would be safe. She could perhaps be in the Barnes's house, and

Cecilia might give her dresses and favors. She wanted to have a man, as she had not since leaving Triana.

But Robert was a slave, and she was a free woman. "You say hi to God for me," she said. "Say hi to Reverend too."

"You can come," he said, shock and hurt slipping into his voice.

"No," she said lightly. "I have things to do."

She could not marry a slave, she told herself as she led Thomas by the hand through the back paths to the cabin. As a free woman she might be worse off than many slaves, certainly worse off than Robert, but if she married a slave she would be tied to him just as Harriet was to Obadiah. She would be shackled, and so would be her children. She had considered it and decided, fiercely: she must not tie knots into the slave world.

She surveyed the sky for cracks of blue, thinking perhaps they could stay out of doors instead of returning to the Longs' cabin. If they went there, Thomas would play with Harriet's children rather than be with his mother. Catherine was jealous of every minute. But the clouds still piled high, dense and heavy with rain. She continued on the pathway, pulling Thomas by the hand and thinking of the slave Robert. She would have liked to go to that church.

She heard a scuffling on the path ahead of her. A branch got hastily knocked out of the way, and the Longs appeared. Catherine saw Obadiah's eyes, staring wide and fearful out of that small, wrinkled head. He carried his youngest child Samuel in his arms, and Harriet was close behind, one hand gripping Susan's forearm. They took in Catherine and Thomas at a glance and did not even slow. "Come on," Obadiah said sharply. "There's trouble." He said it in a way that allowed no contradiction.

Catherine was a contrary person, who needed explanations. "Where are you going?" she began to ask, but Obadiah had already disappeared in the trees. It took her only a moment to see what she must do. She jerked on

Thomas's arm and began running back the way she had come, following Obadiah and Harriet.

They did not go far before coming up on Obadiah, who had stopped before a creek clogged with leaves and light-brown sugary silt. He was carefully putting his feet in the water. "Do what I do," Obadiah said, and he walked gingerly upstream. "Try not to leave sign," he said.

They followed. A hundred yards up Obadiah got out and walked around on the bank, telling them to stay in the water; then he led them another fifty yards through the creek and got out again, scuffling in the mud before softly stealing back into the water. The third time he got out they had reached a spot where the creek was hidden in a fold of the land. They got out and scrambled up and over the steep bank, into some heavy brush. A hundred yards on, Obadiah disappeared under the drooping branches of a large cedar tree. Following, they found him in a small clearing, invisible from outside, snug almost as a cave.

Obadiah seemed calm now, though his black marble eyes shifted around them while he talked. He had gone to church alone, he said softly to Catherine, Harriet staying home with the children. At church his cousin Harold had slipped into a seat next to him and whispered that there would be trouble, to get on home and get his family out of his house. Harold belonged to a planter named Arnold, known as a dangerous man.

On the way he saw Arnold and two other white men. "Fortunately," he said quietly, "I saw them before they saw me." Arnold was on a horse, the other two men on foot, following the road that ran near to the cabin. Obadiah had taken back paths, running, to reach the house before they did.

"They didn't have any dogs," he said.

"You don't know they were going to our house," Harriet said. "That road goes lots of places."

Obadiah considered that for a moment, then spoke in a voice as still as a cold winter sky. "I heard them talk."

"What did they say?" Catherine asked.

He glanced at the children and did not answer.

The cedar sheltered them from mist, but the earth underfoot was heavy and wet, and now that they were motionless, they felt its chill. Little Samuel began to whimper. Harriet held him tight and told him to be quiet, because the white men would hear him. They sat silently for the longest time, staring, shivering.

Catherine grew bored. She wondered how long Obadiah would have them sit here in the cold before letting them return to the warm house.

Then Obadiah lifted his hand to silence them. They heard one rock scraping another, and then the murmur of a human voice. Branches rubbed together, footsteps scraped, occasional words came to them muffled by the wind and heavy air. Obadiah lowered his head onto his knees and clasped his hands together. Catherine reached out a hand to Thomas, clutching at his wrist, putting a finger to her lips. She saw tears in his eyes, and her fear grew that he would not be able to stand the tension and would sob. She prayed like Obadiah, to whatever God might be, that her son would stay silent.

Now they heard bodies pushing through brush; there were long pauses as the men evidently hesitated, taking stock of their direction.

"Niggers might be miles gone by now," a man's voice said, quite clearly and close.

"They're here," another said, close to the first. "Keep going. They have children. They're not going to go far."

"Well, they might," said the first voice. "Nigger children love to run."

The footsteps passed nearby, perhaps thirty yards away. Obadiah had his eyes shut, and his mouth was moving soundlessly.

"Why is Obadiah talking?" Thomas asked, before Catherine could get her hand clapped over his mouth to smother the sound. Absolute fear sang through her like a spear of lightning. She was sure the men must have heard. But half a minute passed, and not a sound answered. She squeezed Thomas's torso but kept her hand over his mouth though he struggled against her. Her heart hammered.

"They could be anywhere in this brush," said the first voice, perhaps nearer. "We're missing the fun at Rutter's. Don't you want to see that nigger preacher sweat?"

"Shut up," said the second voice. He seemed to be almost on top of them, he was so close. Catherine's eyes strained the gray-blue walls of hanging cedar branches, thinking she would see a piece of the man.

Then it began to rain. For just an instant they felt a hush of anticipation, as the first huge drops splashed, and they heard the swelling breath of heavy rain on the woods; and then, before they could think, the rain was pounding through their clothes. This time it was not tiny droplets; the darkness above emptied itself inside out.

"I'm going," the first voice shouted. "Come on." They heard his body pushing through the bushes, and then, after half a minute's hesitation, the other man following. In very short order they could hear them no more, for the pounding of the heavens swallowed up the sound of their feet.

———

Each adult held a child in what little shelter his or her body could offer from the rain. Obadiah had his eyes still closed and was praying; his whole face was shining black with the rain. Harriet had a grim set to her mouth; her thick body hunched over the baby Samuel as though daring anyone to touch him.

They waited perhaps an hour. They did not risk taking a pathway back to the house but pushed blindly through the viny undergrowth of the soaking forest. When they reached the clearing they stayed in hiding for a long time, watching, until Obadiah went alone, opened the door, and signaled the rest of them to come. The cabin was dry and dark inside, a relief to their skin, but as their eyes grew accustomed to the light they saw the wreckage. Ashes and smoking coals from the fireplace were scattered over the floor, the bed's legs had been broken so it lay spavined, clothes and broken dishes and pots and spoons had been thrown around. Little Susan began to cry and ask her mother who had done it. Obadiah took her in his arms and held her while Harriet stooped over, picking things up and putting them in order.

Suddenly Catherine had a notion. She ran to the corner where she kept her box. "My dresses!" she cried. "My dresses!"

She rampaged through the cabin, blindly throwing aside blankets and clothes. She found her two working dresses, but the fine ones that she had brought from Triana were gone.

When all hope was extinguished she sat down on the edge of the bed. Its weakened legs shifted under her weight and dropped her four inches, so she landed with a jolt. She cursed the bed, then jammed her hands over her eyes. She did not cry. A cold, pure anger filled her—anger for her helplessness and for her son to see her so.

Harriet came and knelt before her. Catherine knew she was there but did not take her hands from her eyes. She did not want to see Harriet. She wanted the whole world destroyed.

"You need to go out of this place," Harriet said in a hard, insistent voice. "What is keeping you here? You should take that boy today and go."

"Sure," she said, still not looking. "You want me to go, I'll go. You don't owe me."

"No," warned Obadiah sternly, and then more softly, "she doesn't mean that."

"She means it!" Catherine shouted, taking her hands away in order to see Obadiah, in order to fight him with her eyes. What she saw instead was Harriet, with a queer, twisted expression. Harriet's face was not that daily, hard, oaken, angry surface. Something else had come into her eyes. Catherine stared at her, caught off balance like someone who has pushed hard on a wall and found that it falls down at a touch.

"I can't go," Harriet said. "I cannot leave Obadiah. But I promise you, Catherine, the day this husband and these children are free, we will go north. We will not stay here. What is keeping you here? You haven't got a thing. Nothing. Now you don't even have your dresses. And I tell you Catherine, you will not get more dresses. They give dresses to slaves, not to free people."

"What do you know about north?" Catherine said. "I was born here, I know these people. I can live here."

"You can live here as a slave. You can't as a free woman."

"I'm managing." The hostility between the two women had returned, mercy replaced by scorn.

"You almost didn't today," Harriet said. "You listen. You can stay with us so long as you pay, because I want every penny to buy my family. I'm not saying this for me. I'm saying this for you. There is no room in this country for a free black woman. You should go."

"I can't go," Catherine said. "This is my home."

Chapter 8

1832: Weld's Second Conversion

THEODORE WELD rode into Hudson, Ohio, on a hulking, sagging, slow-footed gray, the third horse he had worn down since starting north from Alabama in July. It was October now, and even in the clear, late, honeyed sunshine Weld was glad for his thick shag coat. A tall man, he showed deep-set eyes and shaggy, dark hair under his fur cap. Those eyes looked but did not see. He was deep in thought, rocking back and forth, humming and staring, so abstracted and brooding that someone coming on him might have taken him for a madman or a criminal. Periodically he flapped his arms against his sides, to make the blood go.

Weld stopped for direction at a tannery on the creek. It was a poor place, one low-roofed, two-room house and a collection of work sheds. Everything was painfully neat: not one stray leaf marred the clipped grass. Inside a tidy white outbuilding Weld found a muscled man with gray hair and a stutter. His stringy arms were bare, and he was sweating at his work, hauling stinking, dripping hides out of a dark, wooden tank. He paused reluctantly to listen while Weld introduced himself and confided that he hoped to offer temperance lectures at the college.

"I am a college trustee," the tanner volunteered. He looked Weld over, seeming to think whether he should help him or get a gun to shoot him. "What church are you belonging to?"

Weld told him he was a Presbyterian.

"You had better go up and see Charles Storrs," he said finally. "President of the college. You go up the road, turn to your north at the general store, and watch for a big house with columns across from the college." Then without so much as a "good day," he turned his back and returned to his work, plunging his arms deep into the tank.

This severity did not trouble Weld. The tanner was just the type of Yankee he understood. When you had convinced such a man of something, he would never swerve from it.

For the better part of a year Weld had been traveling to remote western towns in the Mississippi Valley, giving reform lectures to anyone who would hear. That partly explains the gladness he felt in reaching Hudson, a small, ambitious Yankee town in the Western Reserve. A kind of nervous tension fell out of him like a sigh—he had returned to familiar ground.

The village looked as neat as a Sunday suit. How was that possible, in a place cut out of the wilderness just twenty-five years before? Every pin was in place, the fences freshly whitewashed, the sidewalks swept. Most impressive of all was a three-story stone building known as South Hall, or simply The College—a certain sign of the town's ambitions, for a college could make a town.

Weld had no difficulty in arranging temperance lectures. Here on the frontier no one knew his name; he was not the glorious (or notorious) Theodore Weld. Here everything was frank and manly, people listened with an open mind, he did not have to contend with the shadows of vanity and reputation. He met the reform-minded teachers at the college, and instantly they recognized their like-mindedness. Professor Beriah Green offered him lodging.

Out walking that night, as was his custom, Weld felt as though a weight was off his shoulders, that he had found kindred. The yellow moon rose like a lamp through the woods as he thought over his long journey. Dozens of towns, thousands of curious faces and active minds. How many miles of track he had traveled!

A year ago, while Weld was still a student at the Oneida Institute, Lewis Tappan had gotten him to travel down to New York City, to participate in discussions about a possible antislavery society. Several times Weld had appeared at the Tappan breakfast table dressed in his western butternut clothing and fur hat, carrying a small satchel. He and Tappan developed an ongoing argument, Tappan maintaining that New York, the crossroads of trade, must be the nerve center of reform, Weld advocating the frontier where everything was open and unclogged with traditional habits. Anyway, he was too rough for the city, Weld told Tappan; he could never succeed where fancy dress and fine manners prevailed.

Weld thought he had not exactly won the argument, but he had at least convinced Tappan that he could never change. Lewis got his brother Arthur to fund a new organization, The Society for the Promotion of Manual Labor, and hired Weld as its first and only worker. Weld's assignment—his own idea—was to travel throughout the West lecturing on the manual labor principle of education, and to investigate a site for a reform-minded, manual-labor seminary. In the West the kingdom of God could be building without the impediments of history and hierarchy.

Two nights later Weld, President Storrs, Green, and a Yale graduate named Elizur Wright, professor of mathematics, gathered at President Storrs's home. They were young—Wright and Weld in their twenties, Green and Storrs in their thirties. They sat in the parlor, Storrs with a bowl of nuts in his lap, which he cracked using a clever device, painted red and blue to look like a soldier. The professors wanted to hear all about Weld's travels, showing particular interest in his plans for Lane Seminary. In Cincinnati Weld had found a fledgling Presbyterian seminary that was willing to adopt manual labor, especially if the Tappans might provide financial support. Somehow the Lane trustees had convinced Lyman Beecher to leave Boston and come as president; Weld promised to bring a raft of students from Oneida.

Weld started to explain manual labor, but he didn't go far—the others' remarks soon showed their familiarity with the cause. Manual labor was based on the scientific premise that a blend of bodily work and study gave the ideal conditions for learning. Students operated farms and workshops while they studied; their produce was sold to sponsor the school. Thus education could be available to all, not merely to those who had inherited wealth. Of course everyone knew that education was crucial to an enlightened democracy; and manual labor schools offered the right kind of education, countering the forces of reaction and privilege.

President Storrs, an affable man with twin whiskers down the sides of his face, cracked his nuts and cautioned that the Hudson trustees would resist a manual labor program. "Because they don't remember anything like it when they were in school," he said with a grin. "The educational process must follow as precisely as possible the very pages of the texts that they remember—or misremember."

"Yes, they have a very definite idea of education," Green said. He was an energetic type, his hands always rubbing at his beard. "They aim to make gentlemen who believe the same stuff they did."

They spoke as men who already understood each other, who could say a few words and expect the others to fill in a whole world. The atmosphere put Weld in mind of the Holy Band, with whom he had followed Finney and helped in the revivals: all so confident of God's hand, so matter-of-fact, so natural.

"We ought to tell you, also, that we are at an awkward time," Wright said, looking at Weld with a cocky half-smile. "The townspeople are already on guard against us, due to the hullabaloo I started about slavery."

"Oh?" Weld said. With all the hundreds of conversations he had pursued in the past year, covering every aspect of reform imaginable, he had barely spoken of slavery. Only with James Birney in Huntsville had he found a deeply felt concern.

Wright explained that he had scandalized the town with a newspaper series criticizing the colonizationists as adding to the slave's burdens. Weld was even more surprised. "But why oppose the colonizationists?" he asked. "Surely they are the only friends that the slave has."

"We believe they are the slave's worst enemies."

"You are joking, surely."

The professor of mathematics leaned back and looked over Weld with evident pleasure. "Not at all," he said. "I am deadly serious. If we are ever to put an end to slavery, we will have to put an end to the Colonization Society first. I can explain it to you, if you will bear with me."

"All right," said Weld. "I would be very interested."

"Follow me, then," he said. Wright wore a waspish smile on his narrow face. "How many slaves are there in the United States?"

"I don't know," Weld said.

"Approximately three million, from the last census," Wright said snappishly. "And multiplying fast. At the Revolution there were fewer than two million."

"Yes," Weld said. "When I traveled in Alabama that was the chief concern, that blacks were coming into the state so fast they would soon outnumber the whites."

"Quite. Supposing that those three million slaves were to increase merely 100,000 in number over the next five years. That is approximately one-third the rate they are presently increasing. What would be the monetary value of the increase? Approximately."

Weld said that from what he had seen in Alabama and Kentucky, a healthy slave could be priced anywhere from $300 to $1,000.

"So if we take a figure of $500—that would be fair, would it not?—the increased value of slaveholders' property would be $50 million. That is what it would cost to purchase the increase in slaves, not considering the expense of sending them to the colony in Liberia, and not even attempting to lessen their numbers. Mind you, we are leaving the three million alone. Do you think there is any prospect that fifty million dollars could be raised for the cause over the next five years?"

Weld was regarded as the most effective fund-raiser in Finney's circle. He said thoughtfully that it was impossible. Merely to raise $20,000 for Lane Seminary was daunting.

"How much money has the American Colonization Society raised for this purpose in its nearly twenty years of existence?" Wright asked.

"I don't know," Weld said.

"Well then, how many slaves have been sent to the colony in Liberia? A hundred? Perhaps as many as a thousand? What are the prospects of their freeing 100,000 over the next five years?"

Weld admitted that it was impossible. "I think you may be approaching their plans too narrowly, however. I believe that the colonizers hope to convince the slaveholders themselves that the blacks are a menace to them, so that they will voluntarily free their slaves and send them away."

"Yes, that is what they say, and it hardly sounds as though they were friends of the African if they call him a menace. Do you know that the free blacks who are offered opportunity to go to Liberia nearly always refuse? They say they were born in this country, and they consider it their home. Still, suppose that the slaveholders were willing to free their slaves in great number. The freed slaves would have to be sent, and the cost must be, say, $100 per slave for a transatlantic passage. That would be $300 million for three million slaves. Is it likely the slaveholders will provide that much? Is it likely they will relinquish over a billion dollars in personal property? Or, tell me, is it not far more likely that the American Colonization Society is a way for slaveholders to delude conscientious people that something is being done, to lull to sleep the consciences of those who might speak forthrightly against slavery?"

Weld's immediate thought was of his friend James Birney. Weld had so urged him to accept a position as agent for the colonizationists.

"You believe the society is a fraud, then?" Weld asked.

"Not exactly a fraud. It is more like a drunkard who promises to taper off his drinking by gradual measures," Wright answered. "He may actually believe that he will do so."

"Surely some of the society members are sincere! I know a man in Alabama who is very active in the society. I hardly know a more genuine man in the world."

Wright admitted that the society had deluded some excellent people. "But most of them want to be deluded. It's in their interest to pursue a program that can never actually change anything. They can then congratulate themselves on their purity, without the nuisance of real reform. Slavery is like a snake that has wound its coils not only around the slaveholders, but around our entire nation. The manufacturers of the North sell their products in the South, the lenders provide credit to the planters, and more and more the two halves of our nation are seamlessly bound together. Without slavery the Southern states would have no income to pay for Northern goods, nor would Southern nobility be able to live luxuriously off the sweat of other men. They would have to become Yankees and compete with their brothers in Massachusetts!"

The whole room, terribly solemn to that point, broke into laughter.

Beriah Green spoke up, bouncing in his chair as he did so. "Even here in the Western Reserve there is a terrible fear of disrupting domestic tranquillity. As soon as Brother Wright published his views, the ministers, yes the *ministers*, of the area tried to silence him. They tell us that such views are too outrageous. They claim we are stirring up violence. Of course, they threaten the violence."

"Without intending it they prove my point," Wright said dryly. "The colonizationists are tolerable because everyone knows they will never accomplish anything. If they really succeeded in ending the evil of slavery they would foul all the cozy, convenient relationships men have set up at the expense of other men's freedom."

Weld got up and took a new chair nearer to Wright. His eyes had a gleam in them now. "There is great fear of the blacks," he said earnestly. "I don't say that the fear is justified, but it is genuine. People fear that if colored men were set free to roam the country they would be violent and uncontrollable. The colonizationists have a plan to remove the problem of free blacks."

"A thoroughly impractical plan!" Wright said.

"Perhaps so, though they might make a strong argument with you. At least plausibly they have a plan!"

"But not a righteous plan!" Wright said. "They say they are friends to the black man, but they do not even treat him as a man. They want to buy him up and send him to a country he has never seen, against his will. Just how is that different from the original slave traders, who brought them to *this* country against their will?"

Charles Storrs, who was the most cautious of the three, put in a word. "At least when they go back to Africa they are free men. That is different."

"Well, yes, as you would be a free man if I bound you and carried you off to Africa and left you there. I do not know that you would like such freedom!"

Weld hardly slept that night. He had a pallet in Green's attic, where a strong smell of dust and wood sap from the shingles penetrated his nose. He liked being there, tucked under the eaves, seeing the moonlight sifting through cracks in the roof. He could think.

Colonization pretended to be serious reform, but it was really at heart an excuse to avoid reform. Why had he never seen it before? It was exactly parallel to the reasons men give for not coming to the Savior, those reasons he had heard so often in so many meetings. Men sound sincerely dedicated to self-improvement, but their schemes are all an excuse because they will not surrender to the Savior. Of course colonization was such an excuse. How else could it be so earnestly supported by slaveholders themselves? How else could it seem so reasonable while accomplishing nothing? Could sin be transformed by gradual measures?

Did not sin require complete repentance and renewal of life? Weld had no doubt that slavery was sin—he had never doubted that it could only be understood in moral terms.

He felt something close to nausea when he thought of James Birney, the lawyer whom he had met and lodged with in Huntsville, Alabama. That was a noble man, all the more precious because so unexpected in that place. Elegant, stately, grave—Birney was just the opposite of a wild western man, Weld thought—Birney had spoken with stinging words of his distress with slave society. He wanted to escape to the North, though it would mean leaving everything behind. Then, on the last day before Weld left Huntsville, a letter had come from Ralph Gurley, president of the American Colonization Society.

Birney had called Weld privately into his office to show the creamy letter scratched in spidery black ink. "What shall I do?" he had asked. It seemed strange to see this sober, dignified man so unmanned. Gurley asked Birney to become a society agent in the Southwest, to travel through the raw country between Alabama and Louisiana. To Weld's mind the offer seemed God's provision, quail from heaven. Birney could remain in the South. With his great reputation and his understanding of Southern society he might impel the movement forward.

Had he pushed the man into a false position, oh, that would be intolerable for Birney—one true man in a society deluded by luxury and pride.

Weld thought with some revulsion of Reverend Doctor William Allan, Birney's pastor. Allan was a talkative, middle-aged man with a good deal of soft, fuzzy hair on his face. He looked something like a possum, with a pointed chin and a sly grin. Excepting Birney, he was the best-educated man in Huntsville. Allan was always looking for intellectual companionship and for news of the world; neither appeared much. When Weld came to his door he had seized on him as would a puppy on a stick, gleefully establishing whom they knew in common, principally Presbyterian ministers. And he did not politely steer around slavery. He had asked, almost eagerly, what Weld thought of the institution, now that he had seen it firsthand.

"Really, my reactions or any man's matter very little," Weld had said with painful caution. "Do you think that God approves of your holding other men captive?"

Allan smiled, then laughed, then stroked his soft brown mustache. "You come to the point," he said. "And you ask a difficult question. Let me put it back to you. Did God approve of Abraham holding Hagar in slavery? Did he agree with the apostle Paul when he sent the slave Onesimus back to his master Philemon?"

"The people in the Bible were no more perfect than we are," Weld answered, "but the Lord Christ told us to love our neighbor as ourselves. Surely that makes a clear path through the thickets."

"Clear, perhaps. I take it to mean that I should treat my servants kindly, to watch out for their best interests."

Weld sat forward. "Surely, if you were a slave, you would consider it in your best interests to be released, not merely held captive with kindness."

Allan looked reproachfully at Weld for a moment, then turned toward the doorway. "Jimmy," he called. "Jimmy, come here."

A small, young black man walked in cautiously, as though on tiptoe, and stood in the doorway. He had tiny eyes, with dark rings around them.

"Come near us, Jimmy, we want to talk with you."

Jimmy came hesitantly forward.

"Jimmy was born in this house, weren't you, Jimmy? His father and mother have been with our family since Mrs. Allan and I were married. Jimmy, Mr. Weld and I were talking about slavery. What do you think: if you could be free tomorrow, would you like that?"

Jimmy looked down. "No use to think about that, Master," he said.

"Just for our sakes think about it, and tell us what you think," Dr. Allan said in a kindly manner.

Jimmy sneaked a glance at the two men, hoping for some clue to their motives. Finally he said, "I guess that would be fine."

"What would you do with yourself, Jimmy, if you were free?"

"I don't know, Master." Agitated, he seemed to shrink into a darker color. "I don't think about such things."

"Well, think now, Jimmy. It's all right. Nobody will hold your answer against you. Think: if you were a free man, where would you go? What would you do?"

Jimmy couldn't help himself, he smiled, then quickly killed the smile. "I guess I would get married, and I'd get a horse to ride."

"How would you get money to live?"

Jimmy said he didn't know, he guessed he would hire himself out.

"Who do you think might hire you, Jimmy? Mr. Barnes?"

Jimmy gave a slight start. "Oh, no, Master. Mr. Barnes doesn't hire. He won't have a free Negro around."

"Then who? Come on now, answer me," Allan insisted. Jimmy began to look frightened, his small head almost retreating into his neck.

"I don't know, Master," Jimmy said stubbornly. Then, after a pause, "Are you going to free me?"

Allan laughed. "Well, who knows what I might do? Mr. Weld thinks I should. But Jimmy, I am not so sure that would be a kindness to you."

"No, Master."

With a flick of his hand Allan sent Jimmy away, then looked at Weld with a long, significant expression. He sighed and said, "We have these people in our care. They are a fact and a living responsibility. Here in Alabama they are nearly as numerous as we, and we cannot simply release them to roam the countryside at will.

"Can you imagine Jimmy as a free man? And take it as true from me: he is one of the more intelligent of the Negroes. There are exceptions, but as a group they are incapable of discipline. Leave them to themselves, and they will dance and drink and fight and fornicate. You heard Jimmy, he wants a horse and a wife. He has no more idea how to get them or how to care for them than he would an elephant. So what can we do with these people? The Northern states will not take them, will they? Would you take three million slaves into the North?"

"No," Weld agreed. "Most Northerners share your opinion of blacks."

"Well, then, how can you criticize our approach to their welfare?"

"I do not speak as a Northerner," Weld said. "I speak as a follower of the blessed Savior. What is impossible with men is possible with God." After a brief pause he went on. "But I notice that you call Negroes men. Do you agree that they are human beings like ourselves?"

"Yes, of course."

"What do you say is the chief end of man?"

Allan gave a small, sly smile before quoting from the catechism that every Presbyterian knew. "The chief end of man is to glorify God, and enjoy him forever."

"Yes. And how do you teach your people that someone glorifies God?"

"By obeying him in all that he commands, I would say."

"Would you agree with me, however, that obedience must be freely given? There is no value in observance that is coerced, as when, for example, someone is required to attend church services. If he is there only to avoid a whipping, that is not glorifying to God in the sense that you mean it, is it?"

Allan pulled at his mustache and agreed that it was not.

"Then tell me: do you believe it possible for a slave to glorify God while he is in slavery?" Weld was following a chain of questions he had learned from Charles Stuart, his old friend who was now active in the British anti-slavery crusade. "He cannot *choose* to do anything good, because he has not been given the freedom to choose. He cannot serve his neighbor, or even his master, because service is not his to give. The essence of his humanity, that he is a free moral agent, able to choose to glorify God, has been stolen from him."

Allan leaned back in his chair, his face beaming with his delight in having a worthy partner in debate. As Weld lay in his attic remembering that smile, he thought that it never occurred to Allan that he might lose the argument, or change his behavior if he did.

"I think you exaggerate the servant's loss of agency," Allan answered. "Doesn't the apostle Paul command that servants obey with singleness of heart? I might make my servants obey me, by beating them if necessary, but I cannot make them obedient at heart. That kind of obedience is theirs to give or to withhold."

"True," Weld said. "Your slaves may be blameless if they serve cheerfully. It is *your* blame that concerns me. Dear brother, by force, you keep a fellow human being from glorifying God most fully. Jimmy *might* freely choose to serve his neighbor, he *might* practice disinterested benevolence, he *might* be a perfect example of godliness, but he cannot. You have stolen his right to do good, his very right to be a man. He can only do good if you command it. I do not even mention the practices of some slaveholders, refusing to allow their slaves to read the Scriptures, refusing them permission to attend church services, putting males and females into promiscuous living quarters for the purpose of breeding. I am sure you do not do such things. Yet merely holding a man as property is enough. *His* real dignity as a child of the Holy One has been stolen away."

It was a striking contrast, as Weld remembered it: his own disturbed, haunted mind, on the one hand, and Allan's happy, busy pleasure in the discussion.

"Perhaps Jimmy has lost some moral agency," Allan said dryly, "though really I find it hard to imagine him becoming a better man if I freed him. Even so I protest that I am not to blame. If you say it would have been better had Jimmy's forebears never come to America, I will not argue. I wish we had never seen the blacks. My problem is what to do with the situation as it is, not what it might have been if no slaver had ever taken Jimmy's grandfather from Africa. I did not choose to have slaves; my wife brought them into the marriage. Now what must I do with them? I could sell them, but that would merely transfer what you consider my immorality to someone else, who might be a crueler man than I. I could set them free, but they would cause intolerable trouble, and very likely end by going hungry. By the way, I am not speaking theoretically. A planter here named Nichols set his slaves free ten years ago or so, and that is just what happened. Not a one of them has been anything but dirty and troublesome, and most of them ended up signing themselves into slavery again because it was a better life. The Negroes may talk about being free, but when it comes to it they know what is best for them."

Weld took a long draw of lemonade. Dusk had come down, and the room was so dark he saw only a dark lump where Allan sat. The pastor called out. "Jimmy! You, Jimmy! Come bring us a light!" The two men held their conversation while the small black man came in to light the lantern.

It was typical of Weld that his voice was calm and patient, like a parent persuading a child. "Consider another case," he said. "Suppose that someone in your congregation inherits a business that sells whiskey. He might claim that the great sin lies with his uncle who started the business, or with the legislature allowing whiskey to be sold. If he stops selling it himself, somebody else will sell the same stuff, and his children will suffer because the business will fail. He sees no gain in stopping the sale of liquor, and much trouble. I *do* see a clear gain, however: a gain for the salvation of his soul and that of his family. I suspect you agree: the clear path is for him to break all connection with the practice, no matter what it may cost him, and no matter the cost for society. It is the same with slavery. If it is evil, a Christian must break from it and do all he can to help others break from it. Anything less is sin."

Allan looked at Weld, smiled, then laughed, shook his head. "You are relentless. If slavery is wrong, why do you think the Scriptures condone it? At least, they do not speak against it."

"The slavery in the Scriptures is a different institution from our own. Your ownership is eternal, while theirs was for a limited term. The patriarchs' servants had rights as human beings, while yours possess none but what you decide to give them. If they marry, you can dissolve the marriage, in contradiction to the law of God, and separate a mother from her children. You can buy them or sell them like so much stuff. You can kill them with work, if you like, or brand them like cattle."

"No," Allan said, "actually it is illegal to mistreat a slave."

"In this county, has anyone ever been prosecuted for it?"

Allan was silent.

"And is that," Weld continued, "because you do not know of a master who mistreats his slaves?"

Allan laughed. "You have me there," he said, showing on his face the pleasure of a good argument, though there was some ruefulness.

"I would add this point," Weld said, his fervor showing in his deep eyes. "Can anyone imagine our Savior as a slaveholder?"

———————

Weld had such qualities of concentration that while he remembered this conversation he felt nothing of the place where he rested. He only knew a powerful excitement. He thought again of Birney. To trap a man like Birney in a time-serving, fake reform was evil of the first rank. The case must be made clear, so such men could never be deceived again.

Weld could already see himself dashing the colonization argument to bits. He could outline here and now the case he would make, that the slaves must be freed immediately, without repayment, for Christian reasons.

He also saw—and this caused his mind to buzz—that this view of slavery would be unpopular in the extreme, most especially with the solid and respectable citizens, the ministers and the merchants who were the backbone of reform. It would trouble the careful, principled, thrifty men. They all claimed to be distressed over slavery, but they did not want, as Wright put it, to upset the applecart. He could not even feel sure of the Tappans.

A true, immediate abolition of slavery, such as the professors advocated, must change the whole nation in all its relations. For slavery was the bedrock sin—not the stealing of a man's goods, or his wife, or his honor, but his very humanity. What a dam this sin must hold against the breaking out of the freedom of the sons of God. To destroy this sin must bring more than the light of a few candles, it must begin the dawn. And oh, how the enemies of the Lord would hate it.

In the middle of the night Weld got up quietly and went out of the house, walking far into the country among the rolling fields where wheat and corn had grown and now left a low stubble. The moon was nearly full, and its yellow light filled the chill air. Weld continued to argue the issue, the electricity of pure excitement filling his chest. The thought of turning the world upside down, the only weight at the end of a long lever, filled him with elation. He walked fast, his strides gulping the ground, and then began to skip, seeing his enormous shadow flying into the air in front of him and speeding to the ground again. Going down a slight incline, he broke into a run and went on at full speed for at least a hundred yards before stopping.

"What will Finney think?" he asked himself as he panted. "What will my father say?"

He knew what his father's view would be. He would want to know when and how he would complete his education. Ludovicus Weld was already frustrated that his son had taken so long to advance. He had spat out brief but forceful words against this year's detour.

"But I will continue my education," Weld said. It struck him that Lane Seminary was on the very border of the South. You could almost throw a stone across the river and hit a slave. Or a slaveholder. Had he not seen slaves in coffles at the Cincinnati wharf? "I will go to Lane and make it the training place for the most fanatical group of reformers who ever lived in this country."

Chapter 9
1833: Cholera at Lane Seminary

THEODORE WELD saw from the beginning that the plague was providential, a testing brought by God. If death must be the means of Lane Seminary's transformation, then so be it. He was ready not merely to fight the cholera but to show, in death as in life, absolute love.

They had heard reports all summer as Philadelphia and New York were decimated. In September cholera swept the streets of Cincinnati. Through the fall and winter nearly a thousand died, and one out of every six families loaded up and left. Streets fell silent, some houses deserted, others occupied by people who feared to go out.

Lane Seminary, high into the leafy wilderness of Walnut Hills, out of sight of the city and the river, had been free from the plague. The students saw it as a work of God, protecting them in their enclave away from the world. Then one July morning William Brow reported twitching in his gut, and they knew that what they had dreaded had appeared, that the testing had begun.

By breakfast Weld had organized the students into a Board of Health. They worked through the morning removing anything rotten, food scraps, and high-grown grass—whatever might contribute to bad air. Some were assigned to mop the stairs and hallways with a reeking disinfectant, and others took reports on premonitory symptoms. William Brow stayed in his bed, tended by several volunteers, but did not grow sick.

The weather had turned hot, the unhealthy, dense humidity of the river coating them with perspiration, and mosquitoes hovering around with unearthly keening. Morning came with no new cases. At morning prayers they looked at each other with a knowing cheerfulness, not willing to say it out loud, but thinking that they had escaped the cholera.

At breakfast, Alexander Burr sat staring at his mush. Burr was a Virginian, and very much admired. After gazing into his bowl a long time he finally rose to go to his room. He had not gone halfway across the dining room when he staggered and caught himself on a chair. "Oh God!" he called loudly, startling the room. Weld was beside him in a moment, putting one arm around him and almost carrying him out, down the hallway and to his room.

Soon that room was crowded with students, who came pushing in from curiosity or the desire to help. Weld had stripped off Burr's trousers, and Burr lay awkwardly under a sheet with a basin beneath him. The violent diarrhea had begun, a stench filled the room, and Burr's guts were cramping painfully.

Nevertheless he weakly drew Weld near. "I am not afraid," he said in Weld's ear. "I could not ask for a more wonderful place, than here surrounded by this powerful band of brothers."

Weld caught his hand. "We will stay near you," he said.

Daylight hurt Burr's eyes, so they covered his window with a blanket nailed to the window frame. Yet even in the obscurity his face grew obviously stretched and gaunt, his eyes sunken. Weld fed him medicines, put on poultices, bathed him.

Word of Burr's faith was passed to those in the hallway outside. Students were ushered inside, a few at a time, to witness Burr's drama, even though they knew that people attending cholera patients often themselves take sick. The cholera had changed his appearance; his skull stood out from under his stretched skin. To look in his face was terrible, but that hollow-eyed, sunken-cheeked death's head and its staring eyes managed to encourage everyone who came in. His voice was soft, clear, and almost unearthly. He asked each student to promise to be strong in prayer, to never neglect the pursuit of holiness, to give their lives to save sinners. Burr spoke of the cross, of Jesus' suffering there.

Students emerged weeping. The conversation, they said, was the closest thing to seeing Jesus himself. That only increased the dilemma of those who waited anxiously outside, wanting every detail yet afraid to enter.

At about midnight the final spasms began, terrible, uncontrollable convulsions in Burr's feet and legs, sometimes his back. Weld's hand on his body could feel the muscles writhing beneath the skin.

There were periods, however, when the spasms paused and Burr could speak. "Just think," he said to Weld in one such interval, "just think, Brother Weld, how much more difficult for our Savior, to die with only thieves for company."

Burr lifted up on one elbow. "Yes, I feel I am ready to die. Am I wrong to say so, Brother Weld? I am not afraid. It is not a terrible thing to die, for those who are in the Lord."

To the touch he was clammy. Weld found it hard to look in his face, and yet it was the greatest privilege, he thought, to be near a man so good as he made his passage into God's presence.

"My dear brother," Burr said to him, "it is all but over. I have no more breath to speak. Go and rest. Let the others care for me now." But Weld only felt a kind of golden exaltation, that in the privacy of Burr's ordinary room the most holy work was being carried out.

It grew very late. Others went to bed from exhaustion; the room and the hallway outside were quiet. Burr's breath was very slight now; his chest, which had heaved earlier, moved imperceptibly. He still vomited, but in the most serene way—a slight cough, a turning of the head, and a trickle. Weld was bending over him, holding a rag to his lips. That close, he did not see the death's mask, but only the eyes that looked out of the face in a staring rapture. Soft, brown eyes, they were, beautiful and serious.

"Dear brother," Burr rasped, for his voice was weak. "Dear brother, I feel as if I am beginning to die. Don't you think that I am?"

Weld saw only the eyes now, looking sweetly into his own. "Yes, my dear brother," he said. He found that he was squeezing the rag tightly with both hands, and made his fingers relax. "Your Father calls you."

"Yes, he calls me." Burr spoke slowly, as though distracted. "Yes, I am beginning to die." His eyes jiggled, as though something else had entered his view. "Oh, blessed be God, I am beginning to live."

For a few moments Weld waited, and then he realized he would hear no more. The soul had departed. The eyes, still staring, had no life behind them.

Weld put the rag on the floor and with both hands gently touched the eyes and closed their lids. Now the body was asleep. Something like a rush of rain pushed through Weld's chest. "Oh, blessed, blessed, blessed," he cried loudly, like a death wail, "blessed are the dead who die in the Lord!"

He went out of the room. The hall was dark; evidently all were asleep. He must tell someone. Those last words. "Oh, blessed be God, I am beginning to live." Weld almost wondered if he had imagined them, imagined the man who had died with such tenderness in his eyes and tongue. In the dark hallway and the sheer night silence it seemed possible he was emerging from a dream, that behind him was not a saint's body but only his own rumpled bed.

Weld went back to the room, looked at the body, a solid and unmistakable lump, then caught up the lamp. He marched down the dark corridor, looking for another human being. He climbed the stairs to the second floor. At the end of the hall he saw shadows moving in a rectangle of lamplight that fell from a doorway. Weld walked there quickly, put his head inside. It was another student's room, another sickroom. A figure on the bed was thrashing from side to side, moaning softly. The smell of excrement was overpowering. James Thome, a Kentuckian, was seated on a chair by the bed, holding a basin in his lap. Weld's old friend Henry Stanton got up out of a chair in the far corner of the room, coming over to Weld. His face was a mask of weariness, so much that Weld caught his arm in pity. The room, with its stink and trauma, utterly erased the ecstasy Weld had borne.

Stanton told him the sick student was Hopeful Turner, an Ohioan who had entered the school's literary department. "He developed the disease only three hours ago," Stanton said. "The spasms have been almost constant."

Weld began telling about Burr's death. Stanton and Thome did not react with the jubilation Weld expected. Stanton looked down at his feet, as though embarrassed.

"I tell you honestly," Weld said, "that I have never seen such beauty in a human face." He spoke urgently, trying to transmit what he had seen.

"Mr. Turner has not done so well," Stanton said.

"He was very afraid," Thome added in his soft, Kentuckian voice. "Screaming afraid. And now, as you see, he is beyond conversation."

"His hope did not sustain him," Stanton said, with deadly seriousness.

Turner died in the early morning, only eight hours after his sickness began. Stanton tried to put a good face on it to the other students, but Weld stopped him. He told the truth in all its grimness: hope had not sustained the man, he had died in apparent torment. By that time three other men fought the cholera, and twenty more were confined to their rooms worrying over symptoms they feared might be the end.

It fell to about fifteen to care for the sick, the all-night watching, the waiting, the applying of medicine, and the constant cleaning. Weld was the soul. He went for forty-eight hours without sleep yet did not even seem to notice. He had come to the seminary with a reputation, but now the students felt his Christian greatness. He would give his life for them.

He conveyed to them that the battle was not with flesh and blood, with vomit and filth, with miasma and bad air, but with the demons of despair and fear that afflicted those who walked through the valley of the shadow of death. It was at this point that greatness must be won. It was here that the final test of a man's strength could be witnessed. Here words were nothing: it was a test of power.

For ten days Weld never slept more than in snatches on the floor of someone's room. He ate only when food was put into his hands. He changed his clothes just once, when an afflicted student exploded excrement all over his trousers. Yet the farther Weld went toward exhaustion, the more extreme his circumstances, the simpler and more patient he seemed to become. He said nothing of himself, but as the siege went on the others more and more turned toward him.

About one hundred men had come to Lane, the largest theological class in the nation. This was a city on a hill, but they did not plan to stay on the hill. Lane students planned to descend and transform the surrounding lowland culture—the whole Mississippi Valley, which is to say the West. The famous Lyman Beecher had arrived as president. With his unforgettable, apelike body, his incessant whirling energy, Beecher put away all lingering questions about the future of the new institution.

Weld, though, more even than Beecher, seemed to be the epitome of leadership. The Lane trustees had offered him a teaching position, but he turned them down to remain a student. That was typical of him: he wouldn't write anything for publication, he protested if one of his letters got into print, he wouldn't speak at anyone's convention. He feared the heady egoism, which he knew must be purged away to make him truly good.

Battling with the invisible enemy, Weld was submerging himself to serve others. If people admired him for this there was no danger of egoism. He could freely lose himself in straining the bounds of his nature.

On the sixth day of the crisis Henry Stanton found Weld in the kitchen, an outbuilding once a classroom in the former school. Now it had a sand floor and a large cookstove, in addition to a fireplace with hooks where various kettles hung into the fire. The place was a muddle of young men running into each other. Weld saw Stanton come in, saw that he was anxious to talk, but continued consulting with the kitchen chief, a small, youngish student known as Brother Fletcher.

"It's George," Stanton said when he finally got Weld to listen. His broad, intelligent face seemed flattened by sorrow and fatigue.

A rain shower had cooled the day; they had to pick their way single file along the muddy path. When they reached the steps of the hall, Weld put out a hand to Stanton's elbow.

"When did it begin?" Weld asked.

"Just now. I knew you would want to see him at once."

Weld nodded. "How is he?" he asked gently.

Stanton understood that he did not refer to physical symptoms. At eighteen, George Stanton was one of the youngest students in the school, a muscular, bullet-headed blond. Only a few knew it, but he was not a believer. He had described it all to Weld on their trip down the river.

They had come to Lane, the two brothers and Weld, in the spring melt. At the headwaters of French Creek they bought a boat for twelve dollars and floated it down to the Allegheny, and thence all the way to Pittsburgh. Nothing beats a river float for loafing. They had made themselves comfortable on their bundles and spent the days reading out loud, singing hymns, praying, and talking their dreams. At the meeting of rivers they sold the boat and took a steamboat down the Ohio, sleeping on deck and cutting wood on the banks to pay for their passage. Most of all, and especially as they drew near to Cincinnati, they talked about Lane and the fire they planned to light there. And George had told of his unbelief.

He had been fifteen when Finney came to Rochester, converting his brother and turning the town upside down. Somehow he had not been converted himself. A thin string of doubt and self-watching always held him back from tears and full repentance. As one revival after another shook the town he had gone to the anxious seat a dozen times, had asked for prayers, had attended inquiry meetings, had watched friends and family members emerge with the glow of faith, and sometimes he had been on the very edge of conversion, but he had always pulled back with further questions, hesitations, pleas for more understanding. After a time his self rose up and asserted its pride. He came to believe that his mind was more searching than them all.

He had gone so far as to write out a creed of unbelief, which he showed Weld. It was not a settled position—otherwise he would not have followed his brother to Lane—but he was all the more aggressive for that. He liked to argue and get the better of people. George had been brought up surrounded by God-fearing Calvinism and never met a real skeptic except in a book, so his newly discovered materialism seemed quite potent to him—an all-purpose solvent to dissolve anything but the here and now.

They had argued it all the way down the river. Weld never grew impatient. George could not shock him with impiety; neither did he seem to shake Weld's faith in the slightest. Weld appeared to have heard every argument George made and had an answer that, if it did not convince George, did strike him with its sheer confidence.

George had seen the epidemic as a grand counter-opportunity to carry on the argument. He wanted to show Weld that the fear of hell was sheer invention, that the wrestlings with angels in death passages were sheer imagination. Had Weld seen anything that could not be explained by common sense? George stuck by Weld, worked by his side not so much to help the sick as to argue.

One could almost imagine angels and demons hovering over their souls as they talked into the night while watching over the sick. The darkness of the night, the drama of life and death, and the sheer reality of suffering created an extreme atmosphere. Perhaps this environment conspired against George. It is hard to be a materialist under such circumstances. He told Weld cheerfully on the fifth day of the plague that he could not see his way out of a difficulty Weld had introduced to his mind. George was quite buoyant about it, however. "Don't you start crowing over me. I'm just a little stuck right now, but it won't last. I'll find my way along, and give you an answer in a couple of days. Just wait! You'll see!" He cast off a laugh. Weld laughed too. He had inherited Finney's confidence that almost anyone could be brought to salvation through the proper means.

Now, from his bed, George looked up wanly at Weld. His usual enthusiasm was utterly gone. His eyes looked wary, hurt. He had his lips slightly parted, as though he had difficulty getting a breath. He fought his way up on one elbow and said to Weld, "Don't think you have the advantage of me now." He tried to grin, but it was more a grimace.

The doctor came from Cincinnati after suppertime. He looked at George all over and asked what remedies they were applying. When they told all they had done he said that should be right, just keep it up.

Henry Stanton and Weld followed the doctor into the hall. They asked him what to expect. He was a short, round man who bunched his full gray beard in his hands. He spoke in an ordinary voice, too loud. "I have attended at more than a hundred cases," he said, "and I have never seen any more desperate than this one."

"Do you mean," Henry Stanton asked softly, "that he may die?"

"Yes," the doctor snapped. "He will certainly die. He cannot possibly recover."

"This is the man's brother," Weld said softly to the doctor.

"It makes no difference, the man will die," the doctor said. "Now I must get on."

"How long do we have?" Weld asked.

The doctor pursed his lips and considered for a moment. "Two hours," he said. "Perhaps three. Not more than that."

Of course the world of revivals always stressed that one could be taken at any moment, that men had no time to spare. Weld was an expert at breaking the back of resistance by stressing this point, so that the anxious could throw in their sins and be converted. He knew how to warn against waiting for tomorrow. Yet with George he had always been patient, willing to excuse the delays.

"We must tell him!" Stanton said. "It is the only possibility."

"He will think we are trying to frighten him into repentance," Weld said. "Let him!"

When they returned to the room, George had his mouth agape. He seemed unable to catch his breath and had lost strength as they watched him. Weld kneeled on the floor and put his face near to him.

"George, can you hear me? Please listen. We have spoken to the doctor. He says that he has never seen a worse case than yours. He says it is impossible for you to live. You have only a few hours, not more than three, and possibly less. You must die, and then face the eternal one. It is not too late for you."

George interrupted him with a hoarse refusal. The words came out of the face like a voice from a shipwreck. "No. Don't, Brother Weld. I've made up my mind. You must leave me alone. I am going to try my experiment. I am right, I know it. It will be over, nothing to weep for."

Weld bowed his head slowly for an instant, then went on. "If you will confess yourself to Christ, he will forgive you in an instant. He can save to the uttermost. He *will* save to the uttermost, and you will this very day be in Paradise with him."

"Stop it!" George ordered. His voice was a croak. "Leave me alone! I am determined to try my experiment!" And he turned his head away.

Weld sat by George, bathing him with a moist cloth. Henry watched from across the room. He was normally the most matter-of-fact person, energetic and indefatigable, but he seemed quite stuck to his chair. When Weld tried to talk with George again, George actually hit out at Weld, though his arm was so weak it was almost a caress. "Leave me alone!" he said. "Let me die in peace!"

Over the next two hours Weld sometimes tried, gently and carefully, to speak to George. Sometimes he would sing, sometimes pray. George would not react until Weld began to talk of the Savior. Then he would look so demonically angry Weld felt a small, revulsive fear. Weld never changed his tone, only pleaded with him the urgency of the situation. He could be reconciled with God while there was still time. George stared off somewhere.

"You will see the one who made you, George, perhaps within the hour. What will you plead? How will you face his anger?"

"Stop it! Stop it!" At this weak screaming his brother Henry half ran, half fell across the room. He was weeping, and he put his head down to George's neck to let the tears fall there. "George," he moaned, "George, please listen, won't you listen to your brother?"

"NO!" George said. "Let me alone, I want you to let me go in peace!"

"What will I tell our poor mother?" Henry wailed.

"Leave me alone!"

Weld had stood up while Henry went to his knees beside the bed. For a moment he was dizzy. His lack of food and sleep was telling. Looking away from the bed, where brother struggled with brother, he thought for the first time that he must rest. Weld doubted that George could maintain this demoniacal energy for long. He must die soon. He would be damned.

Weld was chilled by this cold assessment. He wanted to get away. He wanted to be alone, perhaps to sleep for a little while. When he let this thought come in, it grew up to become a desperate physical hunger.

Weld let himself out the door and trudged up the stairs to the fourth floor. He had no light but could feel his way well enough. He knocked on a door and entered. He was going to awaken one of his Oneida brethren, Sereno Streeter, to tell him that Henry Stanton needed help. Just as he reached down to shake Streeter awake Weld heard his name called. The sound came in the window, a hoarse voice far away.

Down he ran, hammering the hallway planks with his heavy footsteps, racing down the dark stairs three at a time. When he reached the first floor he could hear George clearly, calling his name. "Weld! Weld! Weld!"

The call continued even after he had raced into the room and seized George's arms. George had a look of sheer terror in his eyes, he was calling out for Weld as a child cries when he is frightened by a dream. George at first did not realize Weld had come. When he did, he seized Weld's shoulders, with a strength Weld thought had long since gone. "Dear— Dear Weld, I'll hear you now. Tell me, I'll hear you, is there an eternal hell? Give me the arguments, show me your proofs, I'm ready to hear. Oh, to be damned! To be damned! I can't see! A light. Bring me a light. I cannot see. A light, oh save me. No, never, never, never, never—" he began to thrash

back and forth as he said the word with ever-increasing vehemence—
"never never NEVER NEVER NEVER NEVER! NEVER!"

His tongue stopped, and for an instant he looked at Weld, or through
Weld, with a look of utter exhausted dread. Then before Weld's eyes the
look blinked out of his face. George Stanton had died.

Chapter 10
1833: New York Antislavery Society

So now he would become an abolitionist, Thomas Nichols thought as he walked briskly home with his new assignment. He would gain the contempt of every white man in New York. Ruth would demand to know why he had to do it, and he would be unable to explain.

Arthur Tappan had dropped the arrangements in his lap: make plans for a meeting to form an antislavery society. He could not resent it. That the Tappans trusted him with their business and their benevolence—it was his pride. And the brothers were never intimidated by public opinion—he took pride in that too. But this. To form a society specifically to benefit Negroes and to raise up the impossible issue of slavery. He knew very well what would be felt.

He found Ruth in the bedroom with her fingers in Rebecca's mouth, feeling for a tooth. Bekka was a fair, fat baby, limp and placid. He watched Ruth as she stroked the child's thin hair. Ruth was quite as beautiful as she had been when he married her, slight and blond to an almost dazzling extent. He perceived her very differently, though: no longer as fragile and delicate, but as strong and stubborn, steel wire.

"We heard some news from London today," he said. He spoke in an offhand way, knowing she would think it was merely business. "A pilot got it off the *Black Swan* before she docked. The brothers had posted a reward for the first to bring the news. Five pounds."

"And what was so important in London?" she asked in her low voice, all the while holding the baby by the hands and bouncing her.

"The Parliament has outlawed slavery in the colonies, such as Jamaica. There will be quite an outburst about it. Lewis and Arthur both think we should move ahead and found an antislavery society here. They asked me to make the arrangements for a meeting."

She will not understand why I must do this, he thought. *She cannot understand the debt I owe the Tappans.*

"I should be quite busy for the next week," he said.

She seemed not to hear. "Come here, Bekbek," she said, holding out her arms for the toddling child. He was relieved and then immediately disappointed at her reaction.

"You surprise me," he heard himself say. "I thought surely you would be angry."

"Why?" she asked, not taking her eyes off the child whose two hands she was holding aloft, steering her steps across the room.

"I know you don't like me to be gone. I would not have chosen this task, darling, but Mr. Tappan simply handed it to me." He put a hand to her cheek, wishing that she would give him her attention and sympathy.

"Oh, that's all right," she said. "Bekka and I will manage. Won't we, Bekka?" She smiled fondly at the child, seeming not to notice him.

———————

They called the meeting for October 2, putting notices in several newspapers and posting bills in the streets. Their announcement was quickly countered by James Watson Webb, editor of the bombastic *Courier and Enquirer;* by Ralph Gurley, head of the American Colonization Society; and by *OTHER SOUTHRONS.* Their counterflyers urged all interested parties to join the meeting at Clinton Hall and shout down the "leaders in the crusade against the white people of the United States."

Nichols saw the notices posted on Broadway and brooded no more on the wisdom of the society. He was a natural fighter. If someone said you could not do a thing, he would do it.

The morning of the event Lewis Tappan summoned him to Arthur's cubicle. Arthur had his hands folded neatly on his desk, a glass of water and some crackers by his elbow. His small, delicate face looked weary and in pain. "I am sorry to tell you both that the trustees of Clinton Hall have removed their permission for our meeting this evening," Arthur said tonelessly. "They feel it is likely there will be incidents."

"They didn't!" Lewis exploded. "You gave money to build that hall!"

"Yes," Arthur said. "I believe I was the largest contributor. Nevertheless I was outvoted. I am afraid there is no possibility that we can persuade them otherwise."

"Can we get another place?" Thomas asked.

"It is too late," Arthur said. "The interested parties would not receive word in time."

"Why not send personal word to all that we know might come?" Lewis suggested. "We could move to the Chatham Street Chapel. Mr. Nichols could pass by Clinton Hall to see whether there be any sympathizers trying to get in." He clapped his hands, suddenly jubilant. "I see it is for the best, Arthur. Our enemies will think they have us defeated, and while they are crowing we will be meeting. We may not have all our forces there, but we will not have the opposition either. It will be a coup."

Nichols spent much of his day dispatching messengers to various locations in the city. By late afternoon he could go over the list with Lewis Tappan and see that most of the names had been checked off. He went home for an early supper.

Ruth sat with him while he ate chipped beef and boiled potatoes. She looked pale and languidly drew designs on the table with her finger as they talked.

"Are you all right, my love?" he asked. "You look tired. I hope you can sleep tonight."

She said nothing but dipped her finger in his cup to continue her designs. "Is the baby well?"

She blushed. "Yes," she said. "Tommy, I have some news. I will be giving birth again."

"When will it come?" He counted quickly. "April?"

"About then," she said. "Aren't you glad?"

"Yes, of course I am," he said, blushing.

She burst into tears. "Oh, Tommy, please stay home tonight."

He felt suddenly cold toward her. She had been like this when the first child was expected, and they had had terrible quarrels. "There's nothing to be afraid of," he said.

"There is, and you know it. Martha told me today"—Martha was the Irish girl they hired to help—"that men are going with guns and knives."

"You were the one who encouraged me in this cause," he said. "Remember, when I prayed for the slaves? And when the word came from England you said nothing to make me think you were worried. They won't find us there in any case. We moved the meeting, didn't you hear me?"

"Don't go," she said, taking his hand. "They don't need you tonight. You've done your work."

"This is just how you were when I was working on the chapel. I cannot always stay with you. The Tappans depend on me."

"To do what?" she asked. "What do they need you for tonight?"

He answered reluctantly. "I am to go to Clinton Hall to see whether I recognize any of our people and inform them of the changed location."

Ruth put her hand over her mouth.

"I am not known to any of our enemies," he added hurriedly, "so there will be no danger."

How could he know? she asked. Didn't the Tappans' enemies watch to see who came and went from the store? Thomas told her she was being silly; there would be nothing he couldn't manage.

The first lamps of the evening were being lit as he approached Clinton Hall. A solid crowd silently pushed forward against the door to the hall. Friend or foe? Nichols climbed up onto a pushcart so he could see. A hand suddenly gripped his elbow. Thomas jerked it away, whirling, ready to fight. Below him was the smiling, ironic face of Hubert Hamilton.

He had seen Hubert only once since leaving Bradgett and Castle. "How are you? How are you? Are you still with those gloomy old men?" He jumped down and happily pumped Hubert's hand.

"No," said Hubert, who was impeccably dressed in a blue jacket with a rose in the lapel. "I've gone into politics. It's the same business, though: skin them all you can. A fellow I met was working for the Democrats, and he said he could get me on."

"Doing what?" Nichols wanted to know.

"Oh, whatever the bosses say to do, or whatever trouble I can dream up by myself. Just like selling: you've got to churn, churn, churn. What about you? You're still with the holiness crowd? They're the ones causing all this stir, you know." Though Hubert had been among the first to be impressed by Finney, he had never quite been converted.

Nichols saw, out of one eye, a paving stone go hurtling up from the crowd. It smashed into a Clinton Hall window, and glass shattered, tinkling down. A man with a pike began wedging up the pavement near them. As fast as he did it the stones were seized by eager hands and lobbed toward the building. Most bounced off the brick with a dull thud, but occasionally a window was hit, to jubilant acclaim.

Hubert asked what had brought him to Clinton Hall. "Oh, I came just to see if I saw anybody I knew," Nichols said, barely truthfully. "What's going on?"

"Looks like nothing," Hubert said. "The place is closed up. I guess the nigger lovers were scared off. Too bad, we could have had fun. You know anything about what your boss is up to?"

Before he could answer a fight broke out in the crowd, and a cheering circle of men rapidly surrounded it. One thickset, olive-skinned man with a bandage on his head tackled his opponent, succeeding in tripping him to the ground. Seizing his hair, he began pounding his head on the pavement.

"This isn't going so well," Hubert said with a grimace. "I better change the music." He jumped up on the pushcart and began yelling for attention. He got it, partly, and instantly began to harangue the crowd. "What did you come here for, men? Are you here to cheer for Arthur Tappan?" He got a lukewarm *no* in response. "What about Mr. Garrison, would you like to carry him around on your shoulders for letting His Majesty know that Americans consider their country as upright as a Philadelphia whore?" There was some laughter, and a chorus of *nos*. Arthur Tappan had helped send Garrison to London, where he had made a speech widely considered insulting to America. The newspapers had reported it.

"How would you like to carry Mr. Garrison, then?"

"By his neck," someone shouted, to a chorus of approval.

"Till he be dead," said another with a high-pitched voice.

"Then what could you boys be doing here?" said Hubert, his hands on his hips, obviously enjoying his chance to perform. "Didn't you know that Tappan and Garrison were going to lead an abolitionie meeting here tonight?"

At this moment Nichols glimpsed someone familiar—a young face directly under a streetlight, a man intensely interested in the proceedings. After an effort Nichols placed him: it was William Lloyd Garrison himself.

It could not be he. He should be in England still, or Boston. But yes, it was Garrison. Nichols watched him intently, wanting to hustle him away from the light, yet afraid to draw any attention to him. Probably no one would recognize the man. He must have just arrived from England.

"Let us proceed to Tammany Hall! [Cheers!] We can make resolutions of our own! [Cheers!] We can show the abolitionies what white men believe! [Cheers!] Come on!" Hubert jumped down from the pushcart, and, seizing Thomas's arm, began striding fast toward Tammany Hall.

Hubert began to shout out a political song. He looked at Nichols with an idiot grin, singing an asinine lyric at the top of his lungs.

The song was joined by the men around and behind them. Nichols turned his head, trying to see Garrison, but he could see only shapes of heads and hats moving behind them.

———————

Fifty men or so, including a few interested Negro ministers, all in suits, all carrying hats, assembled in the lecture room of the vast Chatham Street Chapel. At a few minutes after 7:30, Lewis Tappan had the street door locked. They prayed most solemnly, and then proceeded to resolve that a new society be formed. Divided into committees, they began to write a simple constitution and nominate officers.

Partway along they heard shouts from the street, then loud, metallic hammerings on the gate. They proceeded without minding. Arthur Tappan was elected president. Elizur Wright was named corresponding secretary.

The din from the street grew louder. Occasionally one voice would rise above the others, though they could not make out any words. Then one, single, high-pitched voice rang out clearly: "Ten thousand dollars for Arthur Tappan," the voice sang. "Ten thousand dollars for his skin!"

Arthur Tappan maintained his sober dignity, sitting upright with his small, intelligent head at attention. A committee was appointed to publish the news of their proceedings in the newspapers. Then, with a benediction, they adjourned.

For a few moments they stood in uncertainty, listening to shouts from outside. All the members were highly respectable. They were not men accustomed to mobs.

"I would suggest," Lewis Tappan said, "that we need a diversion. I would further suggest that the best diversion would be to let the mob inside. Let me give the key to our gate"—he held it up—"to our janitor."

He pointed at the man, a short, grizzled fellow standing attentively at the door, almost mummified in a heavy coat. "While we leave by the back door, he can let the mob in by the front. They pour in, we pour out—and all will be well."

"What if they break up the building?" someone asked.

"Better that than break our heads," Lewis said, his eyes gleaming.

———————

Thomas Nichols stood at the back of the surging, drunken crowd outside the chapel. He had followed Hubert to Tammany Hall; he had sat next to him in a front-row seat while several speakers made incendiary speeches about defending the greatness of American democracy by keeping its racial purity. Surreptitiously he had looked for Garrison but saw only red, whiskey-fed eyes and faces. When shouts from the back of the hall said that the abolitionists were at Chatham Street Chapel, Nichols had taken the opportunity to jump up and push out the back of the hall with the mob. The mass of men had broken into a mad, shouting rush when they reached the street, and he had rushed with them. At first he had thought he would slip into a side street. Then, realizing that he was anonymous in the darkness and confusion, he continued to the chapel.

The mob milled around the locked front gate. No one seemed prepared to destroy the building, which was after all a church, even if a church converted from a music hall for Charles Finney's preaching. Suddenly the crowd pressed forward, baying deeply. The gate had broken open. They were going in. Thomas pushed ahead with the rest. No one knew the inside of the chapel like he did, for he had overseen the refurbishing on behalf of the Tappans. He might be able to get to the meeting first and help them find a way to escape. At any rate he could fight, if it came to that.

He slipped up the stairs, two flights, and then down a long, pitch-black corridor to the lecture room. He found it dark and empty, though the stove was still hot, and he thought he could almost smell their bodily presence.

Disappointed, breathing heavily, Nichols tried to think where his comrades could be. From below him in the building he heard muffled shouts and hammering feet.

After Lewis Tappan handed the key to the janitor, telling him to let in the mob, he led the abolitionists toward the back of the building. They clambered down three flights of stairs to a cellar, then reached a subterranean rear entrance. The nearest light did not reach there; they felt their way along a damp brick wall. The cold, musty scent of rat droppings filled their mouths and throats.

The door was locked. Tappan jiggled the handle with dismay, realizing that the proper key was on the ring he had given the janitor.

They heard the mob surge into the building overhead. Footsteps sounded just above their heads. Crowded together in the dark corridor, they lost hold of their dignity. Some of the group began running back up the stairs to the top of the building, despite Lewis's call to wait.

"Come," he said calmly to those who were left, "there is another way."

About a dozen followed him, including his brother Arthur. They had no light, so felt their way down a hallway, then up a steep set of narrow stairs. Lewis stopped at a curtained doorway. A dim light could be seen on the other side.

"Move quickly and silently," Lewis said. "All ready?" He pushed back the curtain and stepped through.

The others followed, finding themselves on the stage of the main sanctuary. In the center aisle, toward the back of the vast space, a lantern could be seen jigging forward in someone's hand. Its light dimly illuminated two tiers of balconies rising toward the highest darkness.

"Who is that?" A call came from the floor. The abolitionists ignored the question, moving on. Lewis led the way up a short set of stairs to a door, which he began to unlock.

"Come on, boys!" The call was answered by short whoops and the sound of feet on floorboards. Lewis fumbled his keys, dropping them on the floor with a clatter.

―――――――――

Thomas Nichols had crept back down the stairs, sure his comrades must be gone. He hoped to see that no one broke up the building or set it on fire. It was, after all, his handiwork.

Near the door inside the main hall stood a huddle of rioters. By their lantern he could see their well-made broadcloth, their smooth faces. These were respectable men, who stared at him suspiciously as he approached. None of their faces were recognizable to him, but he wondered for a moment whether they knew his. He thought about turning around but knew that would betray his fear. Instead he marched up to them as though on business.

Someone shouted a challenge from another part of the hall. "Who is that?" For a moment Thomas thought it was directed at him. Then he saw the rioters' eyes turned away from him to look across the auditorium. His eye caught movement; he saw a line of men on the platform and realized instantly who it was. Hardly anyone but he and Lewis Tappan could know that there was a door leading outside from behind the choir.

"Come on, boys!" It was the same voice, drawing attention to Tappan and the other abolitionists.

Thomas stepped forward, put his hand firmly around the wrist of the lantern holder, leaned over and blew hard toward the flame. Instantly the hall was dark. The lantern holder grabbed at him for an instant, but he wrenched free and then moved two steps to his left and into one of the pew slips. The hall was full of clamor. They were calling for light. Thomas slipped slowly and silently between the pews to the side aisle, feeling his way in the darkness while shouts of confusion and consternation rang through the room. Finding his way to the main entrance he quickly walked out. No one paid him any attention; the street was all but deserted. As soon as he had made it to a quiet side street, he ran.

"Tell me," Ruth said in her warm contralto, "why you are doing this." She held their sleeping child in her arms and was herself wrapped in heavy, woolen nightclothes, but the mulish expression on her pale, slender face was wide awake. Thomas looked at her warily, remembering that he had once thought her compliant and tender.

He had come home at midnight, brimming full of the story. She listened to his telling, Bekka in her arms, but some point buried deep in her blue eyes conveyed her doubts even while she quietly listened.

At first Thomas was too full of the fight to mind. After leaving the chapel he had gone to Lewis Tappan's home, where they joined their two sides to make the full story. Together they had walked through the dark, filthy streets to the newspaper office. The morning's newspaper would tell the full account of the founding of the New York Antislavery Society. They had outwitted the mob.

Again and again, to everyone he met, he related the story of blowing out the lamp. Now, to Ruth, he told it again, with undiminished excitement, except he noted that pinprick in her eyes. Then she asked, no demanded, to know why he was doing it.

Thomas actually blushed at her question, his freckled white skin showing his confusion. "Of course I am doing it out of conviction," he said.

"I had the belief that your views regarding slavery were indistinct," she said. "You have never said that you thought it could be abolished. Has something changed your opinion?"

Thomas was quick with his emotions, not with his thoughts. He dreaded these sessions when she demanded his reasons and he could not explain to her satisfaction.

"I must know," she said, when he did not answer. "If you are to put your life in danger I must be sure that it is truly from conscience." From her small and fragile frame, from her small birdlike head, so much insistence.

"But you out of everyone have been sympathetic to the slave," he said to her.

"Yes," she said. "But this is past sympathy. It is one thing to pray for the slave and something very different to form a society in favor of immediate abolition. This is too extreme. People will not stand for it."

"This is the North," he said.

She gave a quick and impatient shake to her head. "People despise the blacks," she said. "They say you want to amalgamate the races."

"There has been no such talk," he said. "The question is enslavement."

He was at a loss: angered by the way she had ruined his jubilation, frustrated, too, that she asked him for a product of his mind that he could not produce. He was not sure of his thoughts regarding the abolition of slavery.

"Tommy," she said softly but with just as much resolve, "I am truly and deeply sorry that I have not shared in your work recently. When we were married I thought we would dwell together like twin souls. But now I am afraid we are grown separated. I have the children and the home, you have the great outside world. I want to share in your life. But I must understand why you are willing to do this. Who do you think will suffer if you are injured or killed? Or even if your reputation is ruined? Do you think of your children?"

Already, he noted, she was the mother of two in her own mind.

"You probably cannot understand what I feel toward the Tappans," he said to her. "You do not know what it is to be without a friend, without God, without any future. I owe them all that I am. You cannot grasp that, but you ought to respect that."

"So is it for the Tappans?" she asked. "Is it that you cannot refuse them?"

He pictured the many reform causes that swirled in and out of the Tappan store. Most of the Tappans' friends did not support abolition, in fact. He could say no.

He could not sleep, though Ruth dropped off instantly and completely, cozy and limp as a child against him. A dozen times his mind marched to Tappany Hall. A hundred times he reached his hand to grasp the hand that held the lantern, and leaning toward it, blew it out.

Why could Ruth not be glad? He had come home safely, triumphant. Why could she not be glad? She was stubborn, a strong and stubborn woman. He had been foolish and naive to think her so tender. A man was always fooling himself about women.

He found himself thinking about Catherine, his slave mistress from so long ago. Had it not been the same? When he wanted solace she would not give it; she proclaimed that she was a free woman. The bitterest day of his life, and he had borne it alone. It was, he knew, a terrible thing he had done to her, it was all a terrible state of life he had lived, but he would not, even in that sinful state, have been so ignoble except that on that miserable day she thought only of herself, only of her freedom.

To think of her made him recoil with pain and revulsion. So much guilt and misery were wrapped up in her memory. He had been a different self then, before Christ. Tonight, forsaken as he was, it seemed to make no difference. Before salvation, or after; black or white, crude or cultured: they were women.

Some moments with Catherine he could still recall vividly—the colors, skins, smells. Then he felt shame to the point of agony that such sensual thoughts still lived in him—he, who had so much to be grateful for in Ruth and his daughter and another child yet to come. Dear God, the very memories of that woman made him want to justify what could never be excused: his sin with her. What was wrong with him?

He got out of bed and went down to the parlor, to sit beside the dull embers of the fire. This was the wrong choice, as something about the low warmth from the goneaway fire reminded him of the close warmth of Catherine's cabin. Those memories again. Nichols fell to his knees and begged the Lord to purify his mind. He prayed long and hard for divine aid in forcing lewd thoughts from his mind. Yet though the carnal images were kept at bay, no light entered to replace them. He must not think of her!

It was all sin, he realized, nothing but sin. All of a sudden it came to him why he was plagued and the Lord had not provided relief. Slavery was sin! Not just his life, not just his adulterous evil with Catherine, but slavery itself that gave a master such power over women, over men, too, to sin to such a degree. Not merely had he sinned against Catherine, he had owned her and thought her to be his own property. He had taken from her the right to refuse his lust, to retain her dignity and purity. He had done it, but slavery had done it. He had done it as part of slavery. He had thought to exterminate a portion of God's creation, to make it serve his agency instead of its own; and still in this nation of freedom it was held as law that God's creatures made with a dark skin had no right to choose, no right to refuse, no status of moral agency before a God who demanded that his people choose the right.

It was exactly what the immediatists had said all along, but he had not grasped it. Slavery is sin. He had argued in his mind about Abraham's slaves, and Onesimus and Philemon—the Bible questions, whether Scripture actually opposed the institution or accepted it. He had seen slavery with the mind and not the heart.

Did he yet harbor a splinter, perhaps even a log, of the sin? He had never repented it. He could never confess these things. He leaned over in his chair, agonized and ashamed, and tried to think how Finney would treat his case. The idea that came to mind was benevolence. Finney always emphasized the way benevolence came to the fore in the converted man or woman.

This realization came: antislavery was exactly his call. He had been led by the Tappans, but by God surely, into the one hospital that could cure his sickness. There it lay before him, though he had not looked for it. He was called to practice benevolence for the slave, and by doing this to purge his life of every remnant of sin and shame. Catherine was the emblem of a sin that ensnared the whole nation of the United States and kept it from its divine destiny. He felt tears start up again and actually run down his cheeks, and he was glad! Surely the Lord was in this place. Surely the ground was holy.

In the morning Nichols lingered over breakfast. Ruth sat with the baby in her lap, feeding spoonfuls of mush into Bekka's mouth. Nichols wanted to talk, but a shyness had come over him. In the night, when he had made his realization, the insight had seemed to blaze. Now he remembered the way Ruth had probed and questioned, and he feared that if he told her what he had seen she would ask questions until it all came undone in confusion. And anyway, he could never tell her about Catherine.

Nichols put out a finger to Bekka and felt for teeth in the warm pulp of her gums. He commented on the two fine, sharp chisels protruding through, but broke off when he realized that he was avoiding what he wanted to say and that Ruth was not listening anyway.

"What I do not understand," Ruth said suddenly, as though she were taking up a subject they had been talking of all morning, "is why you must free the slaves immediately. They have been in bonds for a hundred years. Will ten or twenty more be so great a difference?" Ruth spoke calmly, but great emotion seemed to lie under her words. Evidently she was not done with the subject any more than he.

She glanced at Thomas and went on with her thought. "I don't see what you would do with three millions of blacks if somehow they were all freed tomorrow. Surely they would be a menace to themselves as well as the rest of us. It seems to me that the Colonization Society, which good Christians support in the North as well as the South, have a positive approach. They will free the blacks and send them to Africa, which is their proper home and where they can do some good."

"My dear," Thomas said, "do you not remember when we talked of this with Mr. Weld? It was here in this very room."

She said that she did not remember. Probably she had been busy with the kitchen, and at any rate she had not taken the issue too seriously at that time.

Nichols could remember very well. Weld had come back to New York from his year in the West, and all he talked was immediate abolition. Weld was a severe, shaggy fellow, his hair in knots and his clothes with the look of a drayman's. He seemed like a staring idiot when he nodded and hummed while thinking to himself. When he turned his attention on you, though, it was unforgettable: he had the deepest, tenderest feeling for the lowliest person. Nichols had met him at the store and wanted to talk to him forever. Everybody felt that. When Weld got up to speak, they said he was the greatest convincer in America, excepting Charles Finney. Some people did not even except Charles Finney.

"Yes," Nichols told Ruth. "He talked to us. I am surprised you could forget it. I asked him just what you have asked, should we not support the Colonization Society? He said that the Colonization Society was the worst enemy of society, for they drugged the conscience."

Weld had made him get a pen and scratch out the figures to prove his case. He could still remember the numbers. If there were three million slaves in America today, where only two million were present at the founding of the nation, would it not be reasonable to suppose they would increase at least 100,000 in number of the next five years? And suppose those slaves were valued at an average cost of $500. How much money would be required to free slaves and send them to settle in Africa to *merely hold the numbers of Africans in check*? Did Mr. Nichols consider it probable that the Colonization Society could procure contributions of fifty millions of dollars in the next five years? Would it not exceed by fifty times the money contributed to all the benevolent societies?

"The sum of it," Nichols said as he relayed this conversation to Ruth, "is that the Colonization Society has no more real intention of freeing the slaves than has a drunkard of giving up liquor."

Ruth was flustered. Her own uncle, she pointed out, was a member, and hadn't the Tappan brothers themselves once supported the society?

"Of course there are a lot of sincere and well-meaning people taken in by it. Surely, though, nobody is going to keep on with it once they see it for what it is."

Nichols thought he spoke well, but Ruth was still looking at him with a tight mouth and doubtful eyes. "It may be you are right, that colonization is impractical. I don't see why, still, we want the slaves all freed at once. What would they do? I don't think you can hire them for clerks."

"I suppose most of them would continue to do what they do now. They are laborers on plantations or else they are household help. They would do what free laborers do here, they would work and take their pay."

She stared at him doubtfully.

"No one is advocating freeing the slaves overnight," Nichols said. "The point of immediatism is that the decision must be made completely, immediately, and irrevocably. Then we can discuss as brothers how the decision might be carried out. As it is, the slave owners will find fault with any and every scheme we might advance for freeing the slaves, with the result that nothing can be done at all. Reform is always impracticable until you make up your mind to repent of sin."

"I don't see that anything will be done the way matters are now."

"But who knows what can be done? Ruth, who could have foreseen my salvation? If Finney had thought of the likelihood of my reform, would he have bothered to come to New York?"

When he said it, he suddenly remembered that he had intended to speak of his own sin. The shame of Catherine, and of his feelings remembering her last night, were still green.

"We have never much spoken about my life in Alabama, before I came to New York," he said, choosing his words carefully, sounding stiff but unable to help that. "I do not like to speak of it; I want my days of carnal living to be forgotten just as God in Christ has forgiven them in his eternal mercy. I must simply tell you, however, that there are slaves to whom I owe a debt. I sinned against them. If I have opportunity to win some kind of redemption and reverse the curse of sin through this cause, I must."

She stared at him, searching him with her eyes. "Thank you," she said quietly. "That is what I must know. Tell me about those slaves. What do you owe them?"

He blushed to the roots of his copper hair. "I never can tell you," he said miserably. "You must simply believe me."

She still stared at him with narrowed eyes hard as a merchant's. "I cannot see why you would hide something you did so long ago, before you even knew the Savior. You can at least tell me their names."

They were just nameless colored people, and he had no idea whether he had *ever* known their names. "There was Mary, whom I have told you about. And a woman named Catherine. And . . . many others. Many."

"Who was this Catherine?"

"Just a woman who served in the house. And . . . I taught her to read."

Ruth's eyes broke off their hardness for a moment, as though she was confused by this information. "So, then, one of them can write."

"I suppose, yes, she could."

"But you told me that none of them could write to you."

For a moment he felt raw panic. "Yes," he said after he got his bearings, "Catherine could write a little, but she left the plantation, and I never knew where she went."

To his relief Ruth dropped her questions. She silently took up a spoon and began to delicately convey food into the baby's mouth. He was surprised to see tiny pearls in the corners of her eyes.

"What is the matter?" he asked.

"Nothing," Ruth said. "Only that I am afraid for you."

"Oh, don't," Thomas said. "No one will be hurt."

Chapter 11
1834: New York Riots

N ICHOLS SAT UP, stupid from sleep. The room was almost dark, and he could not at first remember where he was. He heard distant, droning voices. Ruth, he realized gradually, was talking to someone in the entryway. In dim light he saw it was Arthur Tappan, his bowler held in both his hands across his heart. Arthur had never been in their house before. Thomas would not have thought that he knew its location.

"I came to beg some armor," Tappan said with an apologetic smile. "Would you have an old scarf or somesuch I can put on to cover my face?"

"Certainly, sir," he said, struggling to his feet. "Whatever I have. What . . . what is going on?"

"The mob," Arthur said simply. "They have attacked my brother's home, quite seriously. He is not there, and I am afraid that they will destroy it unless the authorities move quickly. But I consider it unwise to go in that vicinity without some disguise. Since your home is not far I thought I might inconvenience you." Always decorous, Arthur gave a little bow.

Thomas partly listened while Arthur soberly described for Ruth the fragmentary reports he had from a clerk: that the mob was roaming the town, had broken down the door of Lewis's house, had smashed out all the windows. The police were standing by.

"Why don't you go with Mr. Tappan?" Ruth said to Thomas. "Two is better than one."

"I would not wish him to leave you and the children alone," Arthur Tappan said. "These are trying times."

"No, no," Ruth said. "I have given him up to the cause of the slave. You go, Thomas. The mob does not know our house."

Not so long ago he would have eagerly done it. Now, however, a paralyzing weight came onto his chest. Perhaps he was not completely awake. He did not wish to leave Ruth. He was afraid. Ruth brought his jacket, and a large, loose hat for Arthur to pull down over his eyes. "I would give you a scarf, too," she said to Arthur, "only it is so hot."

"Bring it," Arthur said.

They went out into the warm evening, Tappan hurrying as he pumped his short arms and Nichols following reluctantly. Deep shadows had claimed the streets. Thomas did not see how Arthur Tappan could endure the heat, wrapped as he was in a thick woolen scarf. Bands of men ran up and down, sometimes passing them with a clatter, sometimes running in the opposite way. If they saw anything odd about a short, round man wrapped to his ears in wool, they made no sign of it.

They heard and felt the mob on Rose Street before they saw it. A large bonfire was blazing in the street, with a crowd of exulting faces lit orange by its light. Some men were shirtless, sweating profusely. Up and down in front of Lewis Tappan's house rode a man in military dress mounted on a huge, prancing white stallion. He would canter up the street, halt, rear, and shout out some slogan. The mob roared in response. Lewis's house, lit by the fire, was a gap-toothed shell, the door and windows broken out. Occasionally a face would appear at a window to throw something out into the garden. Others on the ground would seize whatever object came out—Thomas watched a chest of drawers, two mattresses, a drop-leaf table come crashing down—and drag it to the bonfire, where it was thrown on with a shout.

"What are they shouting?" Tappan asked, leaning up to Thomas Nichols's ear.

Nichols listened to a rhythmic chant that had broken out in the hundreds of men jamming the street. He put his mouth to Arthur's ear. "They are shouting, 'Give us Arthur Tappan.'"

A sly smile broke over Arthur's small mouth. "They should investigate more carefully before they riot," he said. "Surely it is well known this is Lewis's house?"

Chapter 12

1835: Amos Dresser in Nashville

AMOS DRESSER awoke with the sun in his eyes, his mouth dry as felt, his head hammering. When he tried to turn, the pain made him weak. It seemed to have radiated from his back to every part of his body and especially his head.

"Do you need water?"

He tried to see who was behind the low, melodic female voice, but his head would not move. It had turned wooden. He had to catch his breath from the pain.

"Lie still," she said with a commanding voice. "You have a lot to do today. You will need your rest."

"Who are you?" he asked.

"Nobody you need to know," she said.

"I want to call you by your name," he said.

"Mrs. Leaven calls me 'girl'," she said.

He managed to turn over to see her. He was a Yankee; he had not detected from her voice that she was black. She was thin, dark, with eyes sunk into her face like painted wooden balls, with cheeks like hatchet blades. "I do need some water," he said to this strange, hardened face.

She poured some from a pitcher, helped him sit up and drink. Meanwhile she was talking. "We've got to hurry, Mr. Dresser. You have got a lot to do today. We have got to dress those wounds and figure a way to get you out of town."

He remembered then that his penalty, beyond the twenty lashes, had been to leave town in twenty-four hours. "I can't travel," he said. "I'm not up to it."

"You've got to go," she said. "Better yet, you have got to disappear. Men might be watching for you."

He looked at her, disbelieving, but she stared back in dead seriousness, those lids sliding down over her eyeballs like a crocodile's. "You don't have to believe me, Mr. Dresser, but it might profit you to think about how you got into all this trouble."

It was very unlike Catherine Nichols to extend herself to help a stranger, particularly a white man. Truthfully, she was curious. Ever since she had read a newspaper denouncing Garrison and the abolitionists, she had wanted to see one. When word spread in town that the mayor had captured one, had found him with papers proving he was stirring up the Negroes to revolt, she had felt her interest stirred. When the abolitionist was brought beaten and bloody to the very house where she lived and worked as a cook, she felt the most lively interest. This morning, after cooking breakfast, she had sneaked upstairs. Certainly it was dangerous to do so, but Catherine had all her life exhibited a disregard for danger.

She had been in Nashville for two years, after a long and wandering trip from Huntsville. She first had stopped at a crossroads where she caught on as a cook for a white man whose wife had died. After three months he began to look at her in the way that men do. She and Tommy went out the upstairs window in the middle of the night, walked as far as they could, then hid in the woods all day. She had had enough of getting pulled into white people's plans.

She hid even though she had not taken anything except some food.

Guilt or innocence would not make any difference with an angry white man. She and Tommy slept in the thickets by day and traveled by night until they reached Nashville, where she found work, a population of free blacks, and even a job for Tommy at the stables. They were able to live together, sharing the cabin behind Mrs. Leaven's house with three slave women. They even had a bed.

She told none of this to Dresser as she dressed his wounds. He was such a fool that if they caught him he would tell whatever they asked. They would surely ask whether he had talked to any black people. Instead she asked him questions about abolitionists, while she coaxed off his sticky, blood-soaked shirt, bathed his back, and told him to be still when he moaned. He explained about Lane and Oberlin, and told what he knew about Boston and New York, the headquarters of the new antislavery society. She did not take much of this in, as she had no real concept of geography.

He asked her how she knew about abolition. She saw no harm in telling him that she had read it in a Southern newspaper.

"So you can read?" he said with surprise. "At Cumminsville we have got schools to teach Negroes, and I never saw one who already knew, except one or two of the ministers."

"What kind of people go to these schools of yours?"

"Black people," he said.

"I mean how do they pay?"

"The schools are free. Most of the black people are saving up to buy other family members, so they don't have money for schools."

"Then they are free blacks," Catherine said.

"Yes."

Then she knew that she had to get to that place. She had tended north with a vague thought of reaching the far-off place of freedom, but never before could she imagine a specific benefit.

Once she had wanted clothes and the prestige and power a woman could get through the company of men. Now she had transferred her ambitions to Tommy. She wanted her son to prosper. He was ten years old, a tall, thin, talkative boy with no taste for work and too much taste for conversation. He might make a preacher, she thought, but she had enough vision to see that unless he could get schooling he would only preach to the ignorant. She doubted that would suit him.

When she asked where "Comeville" was, Dresser told her Cumminsville was near Cincinnati. She had, she thought, heard of that place. He said she would find it if she went north through Kentucky. She would have to cross the Ohio River. "Just get to Cincinnati and ask for Cumminsville, and when you get to Cumminsville ask anybody," he said.

Dresser was one of the Lane rebels, so-called, who had followed Theodore Weld out of the school after the trustees banned their antislavery society. A less rebellious soul never lived than Amos Dresser. Everybody liked him, though they sometimes privately laughed at him. He had a white, pudgy body with almost albino skin and a pink, half-formed face that looked to be waking from a long afternoon nap. Not a dash of skepticism had been included in his makeup, which was a necessary explanation for why he was found in Nashville, Tennessee, in August 1835.

He had gone south with a case of Bibles to sell, driving a flimsy, yellow-painted, one-horse trap he had got on loan from an old pot mender in Cincinnati. Dresser needed money to pay fees at Oberlin, the new school the students had settled on after being ousted at Lane. Dresser chose to go south for the simple reason that there were few of the Bible and mission societies so common in the North, and a great many families lacking a Bible. Dresser never thought of danger; how could he find trouble selling Bibles?

Yet he knew perfectly well that even in New York a mob had held the city streets for three days, destroying churches and Negro houses and burning every stick in Lewis Tappan's house down to the windowsills and doors. He knew that William Garrison had been dragged through the streets of Boston with a noose around his neck. He knew that in Charleston, South Carolina, men had broken into the post office and dragged off sacks of mail from New York—mainly containing antislavery newspapers flying out of the Tappan brothers' presses. He knew that a crowd of three thousand had, the next night, gathered to burn those papers and to string up effigies of Arthur Tappan and William Garrison. He knew that in several places in the South fifty thousand dollars was offered for the delivery of Arthur Tappan's body. (With the shade of a smile Tappan had said, "If that sum is deposited in a New York bank, I may possibly think of giving myself up.") Dresser knew that in Mississippi, this very summer, vigilance committees had lynched a number of Northerners and Negroes on rumors of a slave insurrection.

He had left his trap with the blacksmith for repairs. The workmen, while removing Dresser's trunk, dropped it. The lock popped open, and his precious cargo of Bibles spilled. So did some old abolitionist newspapers he had used to wrap the Bibles. The workmen, already suspicious because he was a Northerner, carried the papers to their foreman, who proceeded to the mayor's office, who sent the city officer to arrest him.

He who was so innocent, so painfully truthful, was questioned and requestioned until he was dizzy. He was held in a dusty office until the evening, then put on trial where a packed-in audience of farmers and workmen observed him from behind a rope, like onlookers at a fair. Yet that was not the worst. Seated before Dresser, on the dais, were respectable men, two he recognized from the Presbyterian Church. He had taken the Lord's Supper from their hands on Sunday. Yet their eyes did not contact his when he searched for a sign of recognition. The mayor, an intelligent thirtyish man with long sideburns, was very anxious to understand why Lane Seminary had expelled Dresser, yet somehow could not be made to understand that the students had withdrawn. The mayor spoke of Arthur Tappan and William Garrison as though Dresser must know them, despite Dresser's repeated clarification that he had never met or corresponded with either of them. Why could the mayor not understand?

Near midnight the mayor told him to stand. "Now, Mr. Dresser," he said, holding on to his lapels as he spoke, "I cannot think that any doubt remains of your sympathies with those who would gladly cause violent overthrow of our way of life. Yet we will give you a time for your own defense."

God helped him. His mind grew clearer, and he thought he saw what he had to say. He let out a great sigh before he began. "Gentlemen, I can't hide from you that I believe slavery to be inconsistent with the gospel of Jesus Christ. For the gospel tells us to love our neighbor as ourselves, and if the black man is my neighbor I cannot enslave him unless I would myself like to be enslaved. I know it offends you for me to say it, but I must tell you the truth, that the state of slavery is a constant offense against God." He stopped for a minute to think, and therefore heard the utter silence he had provoked.

"Even so, I consider that the emancipation of the slaves would be a benefit to the master as well as the servant." There were some catcalls from the crowd in the back, behind the rope.

"I beg you to understand that I have had very little interaction at all with slaves," Dresser said apologetically. "Living in the North all my life, I really have had few such opportunities. The times I have talked casually with a slave about his condition I have always urged him to follow the Bible's instructions, to be quiet, patient, and submissive. My whole policy is to return good for evil. I believe that is the Bible's policy. These antislavery publications I have never given to a slave, nor did I intend to do so. After all, I don't think many of them can read."

How could they fail to see that he meant no harm, had caused no disruption? Somehow they had not understood. The sentence was pronounced: twenty lashes.

They led him down the stairs and out into the plaza. The crowd pushed around him, jostling for position. Dust clouded up and darkened the moon, which was nearly full, pouring down light the color of a fish belly. Store buildings around the square stuck up their fronts like paper cutouts.

"Mr. Broughton," the mayor said, "remove the criminal's shirt."

Under the brim of his hat the city officer's face was invisible, shielded from the moonlight. He unbuttoned Dresser's shirt, his hands moving clumsily in the fastenings.

A hoarse voice shouted from the crowd: "I move that we let Mr. Dresser go." Everyone heard the call, and it seemed to Dresser that they stopped moving, stopped talking and jostling, to see what would happen.

Another voice: "I second the motion."

Then came a snarling swarm of reaction: curses, shouts of "No!" In the commotion Dresser was pushed to his knees. Officer Broughton tested a heavy cowhide whip in his hand. Then he brought it hissing down. The wound did not seem to be on Dresser's back, but in his head, like a wasp stinging the brain. The pain radiated up and down, in and out. Again Broughton struck. Now the audience was still. The only sound was the hissing and slashing of the whip, as it found its mark on Dresser's flesh. Dresser made no response except a little, deep-chested grunt every time the whip struck.

Broughton threw down the whip. The penalty was complete. Then from deep in Dresser's soul came an impulse of gratitude, that the worst was over, that he had endured, that he had kept his testimony. He began involuntarily to pray aloud. "Oh God, my God, Savior of the helpless, of the poor and needy, praise be to Thee for protecting Thy child and enabling him to endure . . ."

For a moment the crowd listened, fascinated. Then someone shouted, "Stop his praying!" and cursed God. There were shouts of outrage, an angry hubbub of dissent. Officer Broughton led him out of all that and back to his boardinghouse. Dresser could not remember going to bed; he remembered no more until he woke up in the sun with his back stuck to the sheets.

At noon meal the boarders were agog that the abolitionist was in the house. "He's got to be out by tonight," Catherine overheard one of them say, "or they'll come in and get him out."

She was sent out to buy potatoes for the evening meal and saw a wagon on the street across from the house, with three men in overalls and no apparent business. This was as she had suspected.

Mrs. Leaven was very upset that she had an abolitionist in the house. She went upstairs to talk with him in midmorning, and again after the noon meal. "He's ruined those sheets with his blood," she said. "He will have to pay for all that."

In the afternoon, before the supper preparations began, Catherine slipped up to his room again. She did not knock but entered silently, then shut and locked the door. He was still lying on his face. "It's me again," she said softly. "Listen closely because I can only be here for a minute."

He groaned.

"I said to listen," she said testily.

"I can't move," he said. "I am sick. Please tell Mrs. Leaven that I cannot move while I have this fever."

"Now you listen," she hissed. "Fever or no fever there are men waiting outside to tar and feather you, maybe worse. I am going to help you. If they catch me they will kill me. Do you hear?"

He was silent.

"Now," she said. "In five minutes you get up, go to the door, and call out. Somebody will come. It might be me, might not. It doesn't matter. Tell them to have your horse hitched to your carriage. Somebody will have to go get your carriage. Send to Mrs. Leaven that you will be departing in one hour; could she have your bill prepared. After that get dressed the best you can. Open the shades so people can see you putting on your tie or whatever. Then watch to see when your trap comes. You can see it out this window.

"When it comes, put on your hat, walk out the door, close the door behind you, and walk down the *back* stairs. Not the front stairs, the back stairs. At the bottom of those stairs is a door that leads to the cellar. Go right down there as quiet as you can. And wait for me. Do you hear?"

He moaned.

"Do you *hear*?"

"Yes," he said. "But I can't do it. I am burning with fever."

"You have to do it," she said. "You can do it because you have to. Remember, wait five minutes, then call for somebody. All right?"

"All right," he said after a moment of silence. He was still facedown on the bed. "Should I bring my valise?"

"Don't bring anything," she said, "except the clothes you put on and any money you've got."

She went back to the kitchen and set to making biscuits. She had a girl peeling potatoes. Catherine felt queer; it was a strange thing to talk to a white man that way. It seemed an eternity before she heard a weak cry from upstairs. She waited, let him repeat it. Then she said to the potato girl, "One of the guests is calling. Go see what it is."

While the girl was gone, she went to the bread box and took out a loaf of bread. She had an empty flour sack by the stove. She put the bread inside, then put it back by the stove.

When the girl came back she seemed tentative and confused. "What's the matter with you?" Catherine asked. "What did he want?"

"The man looks sick," the girl said. "He says he wants to leave and to get his carriage and his bill ready."

"Well then," Catherine said, "go tell Mrs. Leaven. When did he say he is going?"

"He never did say. He wants his bill ready," she said.

"So go and tell the missus."

A few minutes later Mrs. Leaven came bustling in. "Thank heavens he is leaving," she said. "I have to get his bill ready. You attend to supper without me. Can you have your boy go down to the square to fetch the man's cart? Tommy can get the horse out of the stable, can't he?"

This was exactly what Catherine had hoped. She called Tommy, took him outside and told him to go slowly. She hardly needed to say it. When he had a horse under his rear, he was sure to stretch the time. Then she worked at her biscuits until she saw Mrs. Leaven go into her office. As soon as she had disappeared in that door, Catherine picked up the flour sack, went to the back hallway, and climbed quietly up the back stairs. At the landing she paused to listen, then moved catlike up to the third floor where Mrs. Leaven stayed. Catherine had no business here; if she were caught she would have no explanation.

She opened Mrs. Leaven's door. Inside she found an elegant parlor she had heard of but never seen. Crossing the room she opened the door to Mrs. Leaven's boudoir. Quickly she rummaged through her closet. She wanted clothes that would not soon be missed. At the very back she found a long, spreading dress, dark blue in color, somewhat old-fashioned. All Mrs. Leaven's dresses were somewhat out of fashion, but this one more so.

The hat was harder to find. Not wanting anything to draw attention she settled on a plain, gray bonnet.

Both the dress and the hat she stuffed into the flour sack. Six quick steps and she was across the parlor, out the door, closing it silently behind her. She thought suddenly that she had not closed Mrs. Leaven's closet and froze for a moment. Should she go back? In the instant she considered, she heard footsteps on the front stairs.

Down the back stairs she crept. Just before the first landing she stopped to listen. Around the corner, quite near, a door closed. Catherine held her breath. Had someone gone into a room or come out? She waited and heard nothing. Finally, deciding that the hallway was empty, she turned the corner. Directly by her, not five feet away, was Mrs. Leaven, her back turned, looking down the hallway toward Dresser's room.

Catherine moved as silently as she could, one step at a time, watching her feet. She could not look at Mrs. Leaven to see whether she might turn; she had to keep watch on her feet to make sure they kept soundless until she was around the corner of the landing, out of sight again.

In a moment she was back in the kitchen with her sack of clothes and bread, which she put by the stove. She returned to her biscuits. What happened if Mrs. Leaven stayed in the hallway when that abolition man came out? The plan would be gone. God help her if they asked Dresser which black people he had talked to.

By now, she thought, Tommy would be gone with the horse. By now he would be collecting the carriage. She had her hands full of the flour as she rolled out biscuits. *Dear God*, she thought, *let him go slow with that horse. And bring that lady downstairs.*

She no sooner thought it than she heard the heavy, slow creak of steps descending the front stairs. A few moments later Mrs. Leaven put her head in the kitchen door. "No Tommy?" she said. "What's keeping him?"

"Ma'am, you know how a boy is with a horse," she said. "He's probably parading it around town."

"Next time I'll send someone else," Mrs. Leaven grumbled.

"Tommy is a good boy. He'll come."

There was a flaw in her plan that she could not get around: she could not see or hear when the carriage parked in front of the house. She could only wait and listen. After what seemed too long, she heard a door softly open and close again—the cellar.

"Rose," she said to the potato girl, "you go and see if Mrs. Leaven needs any help. That man must be about ready to leave. Don't bother her; just stand there and see if she gives you anything to do."

As soon as Rose was gone Catherine picked up her sack, turned the corner to the cellar stairs, and went down. "It's me," she said in the dimness.

"I don't know if I can do it," Dresser said. She had not seen him at first; her eyes found him where he stood in the middle of the floor with his shoulders hunched over.

"You've got to do it, if you want to live through this day." She could not see his face; the cellar was too dark. "And just in case you didn't know it, I might not live through this day either if they catch you and know I helped you."

She pulled the clothes out of the sack. "Here," she said. "You put these on over your suit."

"These are women's clothes," he said.

"You think I don't know that?" she said. "Put the dress on while I talk." She began to help him spread it over his head while she continued. "You are going to go out the back door when I say it's okay. You go straight out the back door, not hurrying, not looking around, and get out to the alley. There is a gate in the fence. You go out there and turn to your right. Right, you hear? You don't hurry, you hear? You walk along, don't greet anybody, don't look around, until you come to a stream. It's about half a mile. You go down into that streambed when nobody is watching you, hide there in the bushes until it is dark, then take these clothes off and bury them, walk out of town and keep going. Stay off the roads in the daytime until you get away from here. They will surely be looking for you."

Her eyes were accustomed to the dark now, and she could see his face. He was moving very slowly to put the dress on; every effort cost him pain. He reached out a hand to steady himself and caught on to her sleeve. When he realized he had touched her he jerked his hand away.

"It's all right, Mr. Dresser, I won't hurt you."

She put the hat on his head, smiling at him. "You look like a seventeen-year-old girl," she said. "Very pretty. This dress doesn't flatter you, though."

"What is your name?" he asked.

"You don't need to know that," she replied.

"What will you do if they catch me?"

"If they catch you, I hope I'll be gone."

"If a Mr. Amos Dresser lives around here, he must be living underground, because I *know* all the people who live on the top of the ground, and he is not one of them."

Catherine had stopped to ask directions from a heavyset black man who was sitting on top of a tree stump. Someone with a keen eye might have seen the female beauty that was once so green in her, but otherwise

Catherine was a bone-thin, sunk-eyed, long-angled black woman with a rag on her head and a flour sack dress on her body.

"I was told back there that Comeville was this way," she said.

"Maybe yes, but I never heard of a place called Comeville."

"Then what is this place?"

"This is no place."

"Then what is the name of the place nearest to here?"

"A little down this road you come to Cumminsville."

"That's the place I mean."

"Well, you should say it if you mean it," he said. "Where are you coming from?"

"From Alabama," she said, meaning to impress him.

"You running?" he asked. "With that boy, too?"

"No, not running. I am a free woman, and my son is free. If you don't know where Amos Dresser is, do you know a school for black people? He told me there was a school." She had not wanted to say anything about that, because she was afraid to be laughed at.

But the black man did not laugh at the thought of a school for black people, and as soon as she saw that, she knew that in crossing the river she had done something.

He took her to the school in the Methodist church, where Phebe Mathews was laboring with a disorderly classroom full of ignorant women and children and a few men. They were sharing slates, two students for each small copy board. They had no desks. Tommy hung on to Catherine's arm, his head tilted forward.

When the lesson was done and the students set to work, Miss Mathews pushed back her chestnut hair and came to speak to them. "Do you want to learn to read?" she asked. She had a soft, warm voice, clear and beautiful as sweet running water, a voice much bigger than her birdlike frame.

"No, ma'am," Catherine answered. "I can read already. I want Tommy to learn." She pushed him forward.

Mathews got down on her knees to look Tommy in the face. This so surprised him that he backed away into Catherine's skirt. Tears started in Mathews's eyes, and she put a hand on his shoulder. "Dear child," she said, "don't be afraid. Do you not know that Jesus loves you, loves you as his own darling boy, and that you will always be treated kindly here, because this is the home for Jesus' children?"

Tommy peeked out at this strange, frail woman.

"Would you like to come to school here and learn how you can become one of Jesus' own beloved ones?"

"Yes, he'll come," Catherine said, "if I can get work to feed us."

"You are new to Cincinnati?" Phebe asked, still from her knees. "How did you hear of the school?"

"A man in Nashville told me about it. Named Amos Dresser."

A stab of recognition and alarm ran through Mathews's face. She got up from her knees. "Amos Dresser?"

"Yes. Is he not all right?"

"Oh, yes, yes." Phebe put her arms out and held Catherine at arm's length, looking up into her face. "Did you see him whipped?" She said it in a whisper.

"I didn't see him whipped, but I saw him afterward. I dressed the wounds."

Mathews's eyes half closed. Then she straightened herself and assumed a businesslike face. "Come," she said. "Please come right away. We must go tell the others. Oh! To think!"

Chapter 13
1836: Angelina Grimké

ANGELINA GRIMKÉ sat on a low platform, studying her hand as it rested on the heavy wooden carving on the arm of the uncomfortable chair, aware even though she could not bear to watch them, that over three hundred women were squeezing quietly into the plain, sober church lecture room. These seemed almost reverent, looking up at her as though she were a god.

Just a month ago she had come to New York, with its easeless, whirling motion. Just a month ago she had attended the training of the Seventy, those daring men selected by the American Anti-Slavery Society to go out to every place spreading the word of immediate abolition. Just a month ago she had first encountered extraordinary men like William Garrison and Theodore Weld. It was all dizzying. This, however, was the most dizzying of all.

Angelina was thirty but did not look it. People found themselves drawn into her eyes when she spoke, for she was lively and yet genteel, cultured in the best way of a young Southern woman. She wore the most severe clothing, ugly plain Quaker dress and bonnet. Yet people would look at her, and sometimes even crudely mention her marital prospects, as though they still thought her a flighty girl. She made every effort to elevate the spiritual over the physical, but sometimes it seemed impossible in this world.

Her sister, sitting near her, might have been mistaken for her mother, she looked so much more worn. Sarah was a dull, tired spinster, who sucked on her pencil so that a small gray spot was usually visible on her lower lip. Sarah had relented from her opposition to Angelina's speaking. In fact, she had agreed to speak herself.

It seemed that all the women of New York were anxious to attend a meeting where two ladies from a refined Southern family would speak on behalf of the slave. Word had traveled first among Presbyterian ladies, then Methodists, and even Baptists. Ultimately it was judged impossible to fit everyone in a mere parlor, so they asked for and were given the meeting room of a Baptist church.

Some of the men had spoken up against this. A meeting in a church had a different character from a gathering at home, they said. It might become a "Fanny Wright" affair, the stately Gerrit Smith said, and damage the reputation of the cause. (He was referring to a freethinking Englishwoman who had crusaded for women's rights eight years before, and had ended up advocating free love and birth control. She was mentioned whenever the worst possibilities of female independence were considered.) The young and more daring men working in the antislavery office, however—Weld, Henry Stanton, Elizur Wright—urged the women to go on, and they did.

Reverend Ludlow opened in prayer. Reverend Dunbar, the Baptist minister, introduced Angelina. Then the two men left, it being improper for them to listen to a woman speak. Angelina felt, for a moment, great fear. The faces spread before her just as she had imagined. After thirty years as a nuisance and a gadfly to her family and everyone else, Angelina had somehow landed among people who saw her in an utterly different light. Proof: they would come to hear her talk in the church—she whom her family had treated as a mosquito, negligible and nettlesome.

She opened her mouth, and from the vibrant living sound of her own voice drew courage. "What is slavery?" she asked. She had heard Theodore Weld address that question just weeks before, during the Seventy's training. He spoke with thrilling moral rigor, defining the nature of the institution and proving it unchristian. He never mentioned his own heroism, though others at the meetings said he had faced down violent crowds and converted town after town to abolition. He taught the Seventy how to go out and do as he had done, anticipating every argument they might hear and every threat they might bear.

As Angelina had prepared her remarks she had found his advice less useful than she expected, however. When she spoke of slavery, it was not theoretical. She spoke of people she knew and events she had seen. So she did now, talking of her own slaves by name, and telling how slavery's immorality disturbed her more and more deeply until she was forced to leave her home. The further she went in such simple and direct talk, the more she caught fire. She forgot her nerves and spoke as though needing to drain herself of the thoughts that had so long possessed her.

She was done before she knew. Forty-five minutes seemed to have escaped like smoke in a wind. She wandered from the podium and sat down, wavering in mind, unable to think. She had done nothing yet she was exhausted. Sarah got up and spoke on the Bible argument, while Angelina sat blind in her heavy, wooden seat, still displayed before all eyes like a moth in someone's collection.

They sat in the Tappan parlor afterward, with chairs pulled up around a full-blazing fire, drinking from a pitcher of springwater and eating from a tray of the Graham cracker Weld urged on everyone as a formula for health. Julia Tappan, Lewis's daughter, described the women's meeting, telling laughingly what Angelina had not known: that a man had tried to get into the meeting to hear them. "Imagine," Julia said with a little shriek in her voice. "Mr. Ludlow had to almost force him to leave, he was so determined to hear the sisters from Carolina."

"The ridiculous object is not the curious man," Theodore Weld said abruptly, "but those who must shoulder him out for fear he might hear a woman."

"Come, I am sure they were concerned that our movement not gain the wrong reputation," Lewis Tappan said. "Suppose that the Antislavery Society were to be charged with promoting promiscuous assemblies."

"What thou callest promiscuous assemblies are what we Quakers normally pursue," Sarah said. "I do not believe thou wouldst find them filled with scandal."

"Well, perhaps you Quakers can manage it, but the average New Yorker doesn't believe a woman should be lording it over a man," Tappan said.

"There is no lording," Weld said. "Brother Lewis, how can it be lording if Miss Grimké tells of slavery in the Carolinas and I listen to her?"

"I tell you, Theodore, the controversy certainly would be there. Within a month no one would speak of us as opposing slavery; they would tell about our promiscuous assemblies and the scandalous women who hitch up their skirts to tell men what they should do. Soon we would have no more movement."

"I doubt it," Weld said. "The theory of dominating women is much more controversial than the reality. When people see a few poor fellows like myself listening peacefully to Miss Grimké they will not see any harm in it."

"Well, Miss Grimké, would you like to speak to the men?" Julia asked playfully of Angelina.

"I do not know what it would be like to speak to men," Angelina answered very soberly, "but I assure thee that I would not like to have a poor fellow like Mr. Weld in my audience. I could not speak."

They all laughed, though she had not intended humor. "There, you see?" Lewis Tappan boomed as he stood up and turned his backside to the fire. "The idea is inefficient in practice. Miss Grimké does not want to speak before men; in fact she says she could not."

Angelina thought to herself that the question was considerably more complex than that, but as the others seemed happy to leave it there, she did, in part because she really did not know how she would react if men were to come to their meetings. Later, when she was standing alone in a kind of stupor, not near the fire or talking to anyone, Weld wandered over and stood near her, though facing ninety degrees away and not saying anything. She supposed he had come near out of politeness.

She saw with concern what could not be noticed across a room: that the rims of skin circling his eyes were wrinkled and red. They said he had been mobbed at Troy, that he had attempted to carry on abolitionist meetings for weeks but had been violently opposed and then removed from the city. He had lost his voice, perhaps ruined his lungs.

Lowering her eyes to keep from showing her dismay, she asked the first thing to come into her mind, how he had become an abolitionist. He told her about a colored boy who had been in his class in school. "He was so teased and picked on, by the teacher as well as the students, and I felt so sorry for him, that I asked the teacher for permission to sit on the bench next to him. I thought that I would draw off some of the jibes to myself, but instead they stopped completely when the other boys saw what I had done. I have thought of myself as an abolitionist ever since," Weld said. Angelina thought he spoke mechanically, as though he had told this story many times and only did it again out of politeness.

Angelina considered telling him about the slave Kitty, whom she had adopted and tried to help, but she held her tongue. She would rather listen to Weld than to speak herself. She was still a stranger among these kind and noble people, because they were from the North and she the South, because they had an education and wide experience that she knew nothing of. Nevertheless, these were her people now, their land her land, and their task also hers. She no longer felt tired. She felt, in fact, a giddy leap of delight at the thought of where she stood.

If she felt a speck of unhappiness, it was not over any of these things, but over the tall, distant man who stood by chance next to her: Theodore Weld. She had never been so drawn to a man, with an attraction not physical or gross but with pure spiritual rays of love, and even more than love.

"You must speak a great deal more," Weld said to her suddenly, not looking at her but across the room as though he were angry. "And to every kind of audience, I don't care what sex."

She was startled by this outburst, and uncharacteristically did not answer.

"Of all the abolitionists, you alone—and Birney too—can speak as a Southerner, who knew slavery from birth, who has seen its terrible nature and knows the sufferings of our African brothers and sisters. You can do more good than any of us, perhaps than all of us put together."

"For a woman to speak . . . ," she began.

"You simply must do it," he interrupted sternly. "If it is discussed as theory, men's fears will be aroused. But they will not fear *you* if they hear you."

She could not help smiling. "You do not think I am fearful, then?"

He did not see her smile, but answered seriously, "No, not fearful to men. To the slaveholders and their sympathizers, yes."

He stood for a few moments, looking across the room, and then abruptly walked away without excusing himself.

So it must be, she thought. *We can join together in the cause. And that is enough. It must be enough.*

Book III
The Long Battle

Chapter 14

1838: Frederick Bailey Flees Baltimore

THE TWO MEN sat in an ancient, sweat-stained hack, parked in an alley just across from the Baltimore station. Isaac Rolls was a short man with a sweet, round chocolate face. Frederick Bailey was just the opposite: tall and powerful, glowering eyes, nose like a hatchet blade splitting his face. He must have had some Indian blood, for he had the fixed face of a chief, all plates and corners.

"Fred, don't do that." Rolls put a small, pudgy hand onto Bailey's, trying to stop its trembling. "They might see."

Out the end of the alley, cabs pulled up, disgorging passengers and luggage for the train of cars going to Wilmington. Bailey could not join them yet. If he went to the ticket window his papers would be scrutinized, and he would surely be caught. His papers described a sailor with a very different appearance from his.

"Not much longer," Rolls answered. He sat with his legs splayed apart, his whip trailing lazily from a hand set across one knee, humming a soft, melodyless rhythm. "We have to wait for the very last whistle. See, there are too many passengers still coming."

Yes, the cabs visible between two spanking-new brick buildings were still jostling for precedence. Bailey watched while these inched forward, discharged their passengers, and were gone. Then there was only one last carriage, wheeling up so fast it raised the dust. A woman with a parasol scurried toward the train. One loud, drawn-out hoot blasted over them.

Rolls slowly sat up. "Ready?" he said, and smiled.

Rolls shook the reins, and the horse pulled them into the hazy sun of a September day. With excruciating slowness he navigated the passage along the train. Porters stood with their carts, chatting. A few passengers were taking their last fresh air. A conductor shouted at Rolls to hurry; he paid no mind.

Toward the front of the train, where the stinging cinders and smoke were most troublesome, sat the colored cars. Rolls pulled up the horse beside one, said, "This is your car," and gave Frederick Bailey not a look. Bailey had hardly leaped into the crowded, jostling car when the train lurched, slammed its couplings, lurched again, and began to pull out of the station.

Bailey wore a coarse red shirt, a sailor's bandanna loosely knotted around his neck, and a flat, wide-brimmed hat on his head. He had never been to sea, had never sailed the smallest craft, but he knew ships from stem to stern because he worked in the Baltimore shipyards as a caulker. He had seen enough sailors to imitate them; Bailey, who had the gift of the tongue, could mimic anyone.

Sailors, even black sailors, were well regarded in Baltimore. They were the toughest, bravest men in the port. If any black man could move out of Baltimore without being questioned, a sailor could.

Bailey squeezed his way through the car, crowded with other black working men. Out the window he caught a glimpse of a familiar roadway, with horse and wagon waiting for the train's passage. He made himself look away. Straining to see the last of the city might give him away.

If he was caught he would surely be sold South, if not killed on the spot. Frederick Bailey was running. When he thought of that, when he imagined himself free, he almost made himself dizzy.

He could see the look on Hugh Auld's face when his property failed to appear at the house that night. Auld would ask the cook had she seen Freddy. He would inquire tomorrow morning at the docks, had anyone seen him. No, no one. Then the suspicion would grow in his heart, and he would think to look for Bailey's things and find them all gone. How he would rage! He would blame it on his softhearted wife, for teaching the nigger to read so long ago when he was a child. He would vow to catch him, a slave worth, what, a thousand dollars? Or more?

Maybe, Bailey thought with a sense of extraordinary exhilaration, *maybe I will write Auld to explain that he was the one who gave me the final determination to escape, when he took away what little dignity I had. Oh yes, I will write and tell him that he created his own loss.* For until a few weeks ago, Hugh Auld had let Bailey manage himself, boarding in a Negro house, finding his own work, and handing over three dollars every Saturday night. Then one Saturday Bailey had been delayed at work and had nevertheless gone off with some friends to a camp meeting without first visiting Master Auld and giving over the money. After a weekend of revival Bailey had brought his money to his master, but Auld had been furious, had made him move back into the house and give over every cent that he earned. Bailey was about twenty years old now—he did not know his age exactly—and having tasted some independence he hated to come back into the house he had known since he was a child.

All these thoughts passed through Bailey's mind as he stood watching the passing scenery. They were out of Baltimore now. How he wished the train would go faster! Then he heard the door slam at one end of the cars, and he saw the conductor come in.

He had been told everything he must do. Every word, every contingency had been rehearsed with him a hundred times, because he had never been on a train before, had never been on a journey alone more than a few miles from Baltimore. One misstep and he would arouse suspicion, and then it was very unlikely he would escape. There was constant vigilance against escaping slaves. To catch one was an act of patriotism, and the financial rewards could also be generous.

The conductor was a big man with a long, flaring mustache. As he worked his way slowly through the car, checking tickets and papers, he shouted at some of the men to hurry, if they were slow to produce their tickets. "Get out of my way," he snarled at one small yellow man when he could not move to let him pass, and he shoved the man so hard he lost his balance and landed in the lap of another passenger.

Bailey's blood was pounding. He concentrated everything on his hands, not to tremble, and on his face, to seem normal, strong, proud as a sailor would. How could guilt not show on his face?

Then the conductor was on him. "Sir, I got on too late to buy my ticket," Bailey said, holding out the coin he had ready.

"I suppose you have your freedman's papers, then," the conductor said, gruffly.

"I never carry my freedman's papers to sea, sir," Bailey said, putting all his dignity and just a touch of offense into his tone. He reached into his bag and pulled out his seaman's paper, with the forged date. They were authentic; the blue American eagle at the top of the paper showed that. But they were for another sailor.

The conductor barely looked them over. "You're all right," he said, and took Bailey's money. In a moment he had moved on, and Bailey stood, stunned, amazed.

Surely everyone in the car could see that he had lied; surely the guilt was evident. He had been prepared, if he were caught, to fight. It would be pointless, surely, but he had decided some years before never to back down again. He found his hands were trembling, and when he willed them to stop, they would not cooperate. He shoved them into his pockets and hoped no one could see his trousers vibrating as though in a stiff breeze.

———————

At Havre de Grace the line ended, and Bailey followed the crowd onto a ferry that would cross the Susquehanna River. The day was warm, and by now the sun was high; the crying of seagulls bit through the air. On the pier were the usual boys fishing, as tranquil as dogs in the sun. Bailey was beginning to relax. He was still in slave territory, but he had begun to turn his mind to the unknowns of a new life.

A blow struck him in the back. A voice said, "Bailey!" He spun around and found a black deckhand, dressed in rags the color of dust. "What are you doing here?" the deckhand asked. "I never expected to see *you* so far from Baltimore. Where are you going?"

"Hello, Joe," Bailey said in a low voice. He and Joe had grown up together around the Baltimore docks. "How have you been?"

"When did you become a sailor, Freddy? I never knew you had any sailor in you. Last I saw you, you worked on the docks!"

It was all Bailey could do to keep his arms at his sides. He wanted to put his hands on Joe's throat, to stifle him, to make him be quiet. Joe spoke in a normal, friendly voice, but Bailey was terrified someone would hear. White people were strolling by them as they stood on the deck. Any one of them might overhear and grow suspicious.

"Yes, well, the Lord puts us in many strange places, don't you find? I never thought I would see you here either."

Joe was terribly curious. He wanted to know where Frederick was shipping out from, what ship, who was the captain. He acted as though he knew all about every ship in the Atlantic Ocean. Bailey did not say much, except that he was on his way to Wilmington. "Joe, oh Joe," Bailey rolled out the name, putting on a smile. "You can't expect a sailor to tell you everything. But how is your mother?"

Joe said his mother was fine, said that he knew just about every man who sailed out of Wilmington. "Tell me the ship's name, and I'll tell you the sailors," he said. "Just try me and see."

Bailey shook his head, took Joe's hand, and said, "I've got to go on now, Joe." He sauntered away to the farthest corner of the boat. He found himself trembling again.

———————

At Wilmington a painted sign on the ticket office announced the steamers going up the Delaware to Philadelphia. Bailey was more thankful than he had ever been to know how to read. It might save his life, to avoid asking directions.

Sophia Auld had given him a start as a little boy. Hugh Auld had put a sudden end to that, telling his young, pretty wife that you don't teach niggers, for it would only make them proud and unfit for service. Ever after, however, Bailey had taken every scrap of newspaper he could find and worked it half to death. Later, he sat by the hour with an old black man, Uncle Lawson, who had him read the Bible to him.

Hugh Auld had ordered him to keep away from Lawson. He knew Lawson could only cause trouble in a boy like Bailey. As indeed, he had.

The wonderful Lord had told him, Lawson said, that Bailey would be a great preacher. Bailey said that was impossible: he was a slave. Lawson quoted from the Bible. "'Ask and it shall be given to you,'" he said. "If you want liberty, ask the Lord for it, *in faith*, and he will give it to you!"

After many years of praying since that day, Bailey had stopped asking for liberty. He was taking it. But the very idea that he might be free had first appeared when he sat singing and praying and reading with that stooped old man.

———————

Philadelphia was huge, confusing, filled with white people. He had names of Quakers who might help him, but he did not know how to find them. To ask anyone was to risk betrayal. He was bewildered when he thought of Anna, his intended, a free woman he had courted in Baltimore. How could she find her way through all the maze he had taken? She could not read. She might be lost. She might be kidnapped into slavery.

Bailey took a ferry up the Delaware to Trenton. There he found the night train of cars to New York. One last ferry at daybreak, and he was in New York City. He walked in a dazed, punch-drunk condition, trying to make his mind understand that this was the North he had long heard about, where no man could be a slave.

Everyone was white. Who, he wondered, did the work? Then he remembered what he had heard, that white people worked like Negroes in the North. On the great, wide strip of Broadway, he came upon a work crew, repairing the street, and they all were white. Digging with picks, and not a black man among them! Here, finally, in the cool September air, dazed from lack of food and sleep, he felt he was a free man. Surely this was another world, where the white man repaired streets.

Then he saw Allender's Jake. It might have been a mistake, a merely similar appearance, except that Jake had the same wandering gait he had always had, one foot turned in, the other describing an arc that made one think, at every step, he was wheeling to the right. Bailey had heard Jake was free. He almost ran to catch up to him, giddy with happiness. He was free, Jake was free, and by some miracle they had found each other in this bewildering vast city.

At first Allender's Jake pretended that he did not even remember Bailey. Then he said gruffly, "I'm not Jake anymore. They call me William Dixon here. And I can't talk to you. You're running, aren't you? Don't talk to anyone. Especially not to other niggers, you hear? They get paid three or four dollars for every runaway they spot."

"I don't know anyone," Bailey said in astonishment.

"I'm telling you, stay away from other Negroes. Don't, I mean *don't*, go to any colored boardinghouses. They caught me there, and I came this close to being sent back to slavery. It would happen to you in a second. They'll look for you there. Stay away from the docks, too. They'll know you'll go there and look for work."

"They are here? So . . . far?"

"Yes, they are here. New York is the worst place in the world for slave catchers."

Late the next day, hungry and exhausted after spending the night behind a warehouse, Bailey gave up the hope that some miracle would save him. He would have to try someone.

After many hesitations, he approached a black sailor who seemed to have an honest face. The man took him home and fed him, gave him a bed for the night, and the next day took him to David Ruggles, head of the New York Vigilance Committee. Ruggles, a white man, said he had been right not to speak to anyone, but that he now need have no fear. He put him with a black family and helped him compose a plan.

Bailey wrote to Anna, telling her to come. A few days thereafter she arrived safely. The two were married by a black Presbyterian minister, himself a Maryland runaway. To elude capture, Bailey took the new name of Johnson.

That same day Ruggles took him and Anna to board a ship for New Bedford, Massachusetts. As the whaling capital of New England, New Bedford should afford plenty of work to a ship's caulker. A small but strong antislavery society operated there.

Johnson, Bailey found soon after arriving, was a very common name in New Bedford. In fact the antislavery family that first welcomed him was named Johnson. As it happened they were reading aloud a novel by Sir Walter Scott. That book offered the noble Scottish name of Douglass. Frederick Bailey, free at last, changed his name a second time. He became a free black man named Frederick Douglass.

Chapter 15
1839: New York Runaway

As soon as Thomas Nichols opened the heavy wooden door to the antislavery offices, the familiar atmosphere flooded over him: the smell of ink in crowded, grimy offices; passages blocked by packages of newspapers and tracts; plaster walls with proof sheets and memoranda tacked everywhere; and men, young men, rushing at each other with letters and papers. You could barely move through the rooms, so many extra chairs and ink-stained desks filled them.

At one time, while still working for the Tappans, Nichols had seriously contemplated offering his services to the society. Since the Tappan bankruptcy, though, when he had taken over Mr. Heusden's business, Nichols had changed in his feelings. He felt that he, as a successful businessman, was sometimes viewed by the society in the same way a pigeon is looked at by a house cat.

Yet still, when he entered the offices, the old tingle returned. He was barely inside the door when Theodore Weld came rambling past on his way out. An oversize shag coat swallowed him up, might have wrapped around his gaunt figure twice. Nichols felt a flood of warm feelings. Here, at least, was a man who never asked for anything. Nichols grabbed at Weld's hands and pumped them.

"Theodore, Brother Theodore, I have not seen you since your marriage. All is well, I would imagine? I have not been able to tell you what great"—Nichols hesitated, groping for the word—"*strength* I found in *American Slavery As It Is*. What a volume! It brought to mind so many things I have seen . . ."

That very remarkable book had been published by the society over the summer. Much of its text was compiled from Southern newspapers: advertisements for runaways, descriptions of slaves for sale, short news items— all proving in the factual prose of the slaveholders' own press that slavery was an institution separating mothers from their children, mutilating the disobedient, encouraging immorality. *American Slavery As It Is* was making an amazing impact. Northerners who had never known slavery firsthand, and who doubted the abolitionists' sensational descriptions, now had proof that slavery was an American monster. It was powerfully clever, to have found such proof in the same Southern press that denounced abolitionist claims as mere exaggerations.

Weld scowled at Nichols as though trying hard to remember who he was. "I must say," he stammered, "that my wife and her sister contributed much of the labor. They slogged through thousands of dreary newspapers to find the items cited."

"And your wife and her sister are well?"

Weld drew a deep breath, as though sampling the first clean air he had inhaled for weeks. "We expect a child any day," he said.

Nichols clapped him on the back, feeling genuinely pleased. "What a child this will be!" he said. "Conceived in reform! A prince of abolition!" It was a silly thing to say, but he found it impossible to think of Weld's marriage as anything less than royal. Angelina Grimké was the most talked-of woman in America. She and her sister had created scandals in New York and Boston by allowing men to attend their very interesting lectures on the true nature of slavery. Clergy had denounced them for it. And now, Angelina had married the most mobbed man in America. It was the match of the century.

Nichols found James Birney in a back office, huddled with Lewis Tappan. Birney had summoned Nichols, sending a note with a hint of urgency in it. Nichols hoped it was not another wearying appeal for funds.

He knew it was not when he saw a deep black Negro man, straight, tall, and thin as a fence rail, watching everything closely from a chair in the corner. They shook hands all around, Birney introducing the black man as Robert Barnes. He had encountered Barnes, a runaway slave, while attending to his late father's affairs in Kentucky. Birney had brought him safely out of the South. "Robert posed as my manservant. I knew that if anyone recognized me it would be awkward in the extreme, either for Robert's freedom or for my reputation as an abolitionist." Birney allowed himself a rare smile. He looked his usual austere self, with fine, clear eyes, though his sideburns showed gray.

"Well done," Tappan said. "You have not forgotten how to act as a slaveholder, I take it?" he chortled, but Birney dropped his smile, and the joke fell flat.

"Brother Thomas!" Birney said. "Do you recognize Robert? He comes from Huntsville, if you can believe it. He was Frederick Barnes's slave. Did you ever meet him?"

For a moment Nichols stared. So seldom did anything link him to his past that he had almost forgotten his origins. Neither brother Martin nor sister Cecilia ever answered his letters.

"So you know my sister, then," Nichols said. "Cecilia Barnes?" Only with an effort did he recall that Frederick Barnes was dead—died of cholera in the great epidemic. And his sister, he had heard (not from her) had remarried a wealthy planter from Greenville, Mississippi. Perhaps that was the reason for this man's escape.

The man said soberly that he indeed knew Mrs. Barnes. His deep, yellowed eyes gave nothing away. "I have seen *you* a few times, Mr. Nichols, when you were a young man. But I don't believe we were ever *introduced.*" They both laughed softly, nervously, at that.

"I am thankful," Birney said in his smooth, patrician way, "that you can now meet on a social basis. However, I have some business in mind. I thought one of you gentlemen"—he glanced at Nichols and Tappan—"might employ Robert. He is a stranger in New York and needs work. I knew him as an intelligent and hardworking individual as a slave, and I am sure he will be more so as a freedman."

There was silence, with Tappan looking into his lap and Nichols blankly pressing his lips together. This was a sticky proposition, perhaps more so than Birney realized. Prejudice was such that customers did not like to see black men in a store, and workers found them revolting as colaborers.

Tappan shook his head dolefully. "I am afraid, Brother James, that I could not employ the best man in New York just now. We have not recovered from the bankruptcy. Yes, certainly, we have paid our debts, or what I *know* of our debts, but my brother, frankly, has made many financial agreements that I would consider *inadvisable.*" He stopped there, his face reddening at the thought of his brother's financial errors. Arthur Tappan had not kept to his own "cash only" policy.

"I will not say any more. As to my personal needs, our family is large, as you know, but just now I am completely occupied going to Hartford and New Haven about the *Amistad.*"

Nichols seized on the subject of the *Amistad,* partly because he preferred a different topic, but also because he was genuinely interested. The newspapers were full of the subject. In August the *Amistad* had been discovered off Long Island, a Spanish ship under the control of wild Africans who had mutinied near Havana. After killing the cook and the captain, they demanded that the surviving crew take them back to Africa. Instead, the Spaniards had sailed in circles for two months, traveling east in the daylight, then turning west again at night. Finally they had arrived off New York. The mutineers, led by a lordly individual named Cinque, had come onshore searching for provisions, terrifying several farmers before the authorities apprehended them.

The fate of the vessel and its slaves was to be decided by a Connecticut court. Should Cinque and the other thirty-eight adult males be tried for murder and piracy? Should salvage rights be granted to those who had first found the ship and sailed it to Connecticut (where slavery was still legal), giving them title to the vessel and its cargo, slaves included? And what should be done with the three little African girls found on board? The trial had begun two days before, and Tappan was deeply involved in the *Amistad* defense.

"I tell you, there has never been a trial like it," Tappan said, his small, tidy face turning almost rapt. "We are not trying theories of slavery, but men, thirty-nine men who were kidnapped out of freedom in their native Africa. In themselves they disprove any theory of slavery as natural. They act like proud *men. They* stood up like *men* and overcame their captors, and now for their courage our courts threaten to send them back to a certain death in Havana."

Soon, though, the discussion veered to the subject of political abolitionism. That was the only subject abolitionists talked about now, it seemed to Nichols. Birney took the view that they would only end slavery through political means. For other abolitionists—for Garrison in particular, but men like Tappan partly agreed—politics would be the end of moral suasion.

"Brother Lewis," Birney said, "you say that this *Amistad* case tries men, not ideas. Have you not noticed, however, that those laws you are arguing in court were written by men, they are judged by men, and they are enforced by men? At some point we must admit that sending petitions to Congress, and publishing newspapers and books, and making speeches do nothing to replace those *men*. Antislavery ideas come to nothing if they do not change the government. If those poor Africans end up enslaved after so bravely fighting for their freedom, it will be because we have the wrong *men* in government."

This seemed inescapably true to Nichols, but Tappan would not readily surrender. "Brother Birney, you are right that the men must change, but I do not admit you are right as to how to change them. Nothing says that Whigs cannot be abolitionists, or Democrats either. But surely if we surrender the priority of *moral appeal* to take up political parties we will soon have to compromise our ideas. The abolitionist cause must be above politics."

"Above, floating in the clouds?"

"Not at all. I am not with our brother Garrison in this matter. I consider it a duty to vote. But as soon as we form a party, then our objective becomes to win elections, and everything else becomes secondary."

Nichols, who was no theorist, naturally gravitated to Birney's side of the argument. In the first years of the society it had been thrilling to make conventions and publish newspapers, but now he was impatient with that. It was patently obvious, as he had said himself from the beginning, that the planters were not going to give up their slaves unless someone made them.

The trouble with moral suasion, he thought, is that it requires the slaveholders to be as good as the abolitionists. Whereas he was sure they were not and would not likely become so. He wondered whether he himself would have had the strength of a James Birney, to free his slaves and leave his good living to become an abolitionist. Or like the Tappans, for that matter, who might have survived the Panic of 1837 if not for the burden of their reputation. Lost in these thoughts, Nichols felt ashamed of himself for putting distance between himself and this office. He thought so highly of himself, for what? For making money?

"Well," Birney said at last, with a sigh, "this is not why I asked you here." They became aware of Robert Barnes then, who sat soberly watching their discussion, not saying a word. They were talking ideas: here was a man.

"I will take him," Nichols said. "I believe I can find him a place."

―――――――――――

Sitting in Nichols's office, they agreed on a new name. Robert Duncan he would be. Nichols got Duncan room and board with a black family that had once boarded Theodore Weld. He warned Duncan about the slave

cacophony. When the work had recommenced to his satisfaction, Nichols went to the storage room and unlocked it.

"It is all right now," he said into the dark interior. "You are safe."

Robert Duncan came out blinking. "You can go back to work," Nichols said. "Mr. McLeod will direct you. No one will harm you."

"Sir, what did you tell them?" Duncan asked.

Nichols did not like the way he said it. He seemed suspicious rather than grateful. "I told them what I told you just now. And that you will be there to assist them."

"I'm to be the monkey man," Duncan said. "Go monkey. Come monkey."

"That's right," Nichols said, irritated. "You are lucky to have a job."

"Yes, sir," Duncan said.

Duncan went back to work, and Nichols, after watching from the gallery for some time, returned to his office. He heard no more about it. He asked his foreman occasionally how Duncan was working, and each time McLeod reported positively. "For a black man he carries himself pretty high," he said after a couple of weeks, "but he is a wise fellow, doesn't say much, and makes himself useful. Doesn't drink, I am sure. Usually he is the first man here in the morning."

The second week in January, Thomas Nichols happened to see Robert Duncan come in to the workroom in the early morning, carrying a large, heavy canvas roll. "Hello, Mr. Duncan," Nichols called out, for no one else had yet arrived except the foreman, who was laying out the tools. "What have you got in your bag?"

It was leather, Duncan explained, which he was using to cut out harness in his after-hours.

"You must save your money to do that," Nichols said.

"Yes, I do, sir. I sell what I make and buy more leather."

Thomas started to offer some friendly advice about where Duncan could sell his harness, but Duncan took on a blank stare. He did not seem to want to discuss his career. Nichols decided not to mind. It was good, he thought, that Duncan had made himself useful. Such a man disproved the theory that slaves, if freed, would be indolent and troublesome.

Nichols was about to walk off into his office when Duncan said, in a soft and private voice, "I do wish I could see Miss Nichols. Catherine, I mean. You remember her well, don't you Mr. Nichols?"

Thomas stopped and looked at Duncan, unable to understand his intent. Duncan bent to his work, laying out tools. "We must talk about Catherine sometime, Mr. Nichols, don't you think? Did you know that she has a child?"

Nichols stood rigidly for a few minutes, expecting more, but Duncan began to whistle as he walked down the table, setting out crimpers. Nichols walked away. When he reached his office he shut the door and stood with his hands leaning on his desk. All he could think was that this black man, whom he had helped, meant to harm him by spreading word that he had once had a black mistress. Why had he mentioned that she had a child?

The words had been insinuatingly imprecise. Certainly Duncan wanted to find Catherine, for what reason Nichols did not know. Or did he even care to find her? Had Duncan perhaps raised her memory simply to get at him?

For most of that day Thomas stayed in his office. It was quite irrational, he told himself, but he did not want to see the runaway.

A week later, as he worked late, he heard footsteps in the workshop. When he went out into the large, chilly space he found a single lantern hung up from a long chain. In the dim, yellow light Duncan was cutting out long strips of leather on the scarred, wooden worktable. He looked up at Nichols as though he had been waiting for his appearance.

"Sir, I could do better if I had enough money to buy the hides in a larger bulk," Duncan said, as though he had been asked. He set down his knife. "It is hard with the money I am making now."

"You must be frugal," Nichols said quietly.

"Yes," Duncan said. "Frugality is a great thing. But it is difficult to save money when you must live from hand to mouth. I really must have more money if I am to save more."

Nichols began to turn away, to go about his business. He reached into his pocket for the key to lock up. "I'm afraid it is time for us to go," he said.

"Before we go," Duncan said, in a louder than necessary tone. "Before we go, let me ask about Catherine. You did not know that she had a child? A boy child, named Thomas. He must have been born after you left Alabama. That would be what, sixteen years ago?"

"Fifteen."

"So I think Tommy would be about fourteen or maybe a little older. Strange you did not know of him."

Nichols stopped, unable to think what to say in reply. He rattled the keys in his pocket.

"Yes, we can go, Mr. Nichols, but please, first, let us talk about Catherine. A fine woman, don't you believe? It is a pity she has not come to see you. She has never come, you say?"

He answered grimly. "No. I don't suppose she knows where I am. I don't know if she is even alive."

"Sir, I have hopes that she is very alive. Catherine knows how to manage in difficult times. I think she is alive, a free woman still, but I wonder that she has not approached you."

"What do you want?"

"Mr. Nichols, I really must have more money if I am to save more. And I do want to save more. I don't want to be dependent on your help."

"Duncan, I have helped you."

"Yes, Mr. Nichols. I am only trying to get on my feet."

"Go ahead and tell people," he said in a fury. "They will see what kind of fellow you are."

"Oh, I wouldn't care to do that. You have helped me quite a lot. I would rather keep on just this way. Where else can a Negro with no friends in this city find help? Only from a good man like you."

There was a long silence before Nichols found his voice. "How much do you need?" he said. "Naturally I want to help you." He knew, certainly, that this would not end the threat. What else could he do, however? He could not sacrifice his reputation. He could not have Ruth know all this, after he had been silent for so long. And it was perfectly right to help a runaway slave.

Chapter 16
1840: Elizabeth Cady Stanton

I AM SURPRISED it is such a quaint old place," Elizabeth Cady Stanton said to her new husband as the carriage swung into the Weld farmyard. All the way from New York she had been wondering how it would seem—the home of the famous Theodore Weld and his notorious lecturing wife, Angelina Grimké. The gate was a pretty sight, even on such a cold day. On either side stood ancient weeping willows, their fresh green bangles whipped almost vertical by the north wind.

"Rather run-down," Henry said disparagingly. "I believe it once belonged to Nathanael Greene, the general." The house was stone, well made, with a wooden annex in back. It looked comfortable, though somewhat seedy, as Henry pointed out. "Theodore has only been here a few weeks," Henry added. "He will need some time to make it trim."

"Let's get in," Elizabeth said, flouncing her skirt and pulling her shawl tightly around her. "I could eat a bear." She was anxious to meet the famous pair and to feel their close examination of dear Henry's young, pretty bride.

She was disappointed, however, when she got inside. Weld turned out to be handsome enough, in a cool way, but he showed no interest in her, only in his old friend Charles Stuart who had come in the carriage with them. The two women, Angelina and her sister Sarah, were thin to the bone, dour, plain. The house was so cold they had wrapped themselves in long winter coats, and Angelina clutched a red-faced, hiccuping baby. A great fuss was made of introducing him to Charles Stuart, his namesake. (Stuart had not seen Weld in years.) And surprisingly, they made no fuss at all over her, though she had just five days before eloped with Henry, against her father's stern warnings!

Elizabeth had been thinking of hot, steaming coffee but was offered only well water. "I suppose thou art hungry," Sarah said while watching her sip at it. "We will eat immediately."

"Oh, that would be marvelous. A cold day like this gives one such an appetite!"

They sat down, however, to an entirely cold meal served on ordinary tin plates: rice with molasses to flavor it, bread—a kind of hard cracker, actually, made of whole grains—milk, turnips, and pumpkin. All of it seemed congealed and flavorless. They had no meat.

"We have found that we save a great deal of time by cooking once a week," Angelina said, with an artificial brightness. She must have noticed that Elizabeth was hardly eating.

"What do you do with the time you save?" Elizabeth asked. She looked around at the bare room, its unadorned plastered walls, its scrubbed floors. Furnishings were scant. She could not imagine what would occupy their time in such a featureless desert.

"There is a great deal of labor," Sarah answered. "We have no servants."

"We leave time for discussion," Theodore said. "By planning our day efficiently we have time for many searching discussions between us in our little family."

"And research, I am sure. I know you invested hours in *American Slavery As It Is*," Henry added.

"I am still not over the labor," said Sarah. "Such countless hours, and it was utterly soul-withering stuff to read. There is, I tell you, no light in a Southern newspaper."

"Not much in a Northern paper either, I would say," Henry put in. He was happily stuffing himself with rice, pouring on molasses and stirring them together into a mush. He had, Elizabeth realized already, no taste in food. "Nor even, dare I say it, in some abolitionist papers. Theodore, tell me what you think of the *Liberator.* I think you still see it though you no longer come to the office."

The national antislavery organization, desperately short on funds, had canceled all its agencies, leaving Theodore without employment. The band that had once run the antislavery office was split up: Weld to his farm, Elizur Wright to edit an anti-Garrisonian paper in Massachusetts, Whittier to whatever Quaker bachelors did.

"Yes, I see the *Liberator*," Theodore said quietly. "We are subscribers. Week by week I open it, hoping to find in it some breath of Christ's Spirit. I long to see a forgetfulness of self, a love for the brethren, and an end of constant egoism."

"Behold, how good and pleasant it is for brethren to dwell together in unity," Stuart said dolefully, quoting the Psalm. "And how utterly wretched when they quarrel. I hoped never to see it among the antislavery brethren."

"Well, it's a sorry pass, I agree," said Henry, "but I think it's inevitable with a character like Garrison's. You have to take his measure, and when you know what kind of man he is you must hit hard, for he will surely hit you."

"Thou forgettest, surely, our Lord's admonition to love thine enemies and to turn the other cheek to those who smite thee," Sarah said.

"I don't mean hit with the hand, dear Sarah," Stanton said, "I mean strike with the truth. At the Massachusetts Antislavery Society meeting last year I asked Garrison, who had prepared that most astonishing annual report—you must have read it in the *Liberator*—whether he believed it was a sin to go to the polls and vote. I knew he had no courage to say it was sin, for most of our people won't tolerate such nonsense. 'Sin for *me!*' he said, dodging the question. He says he will judge no man, yet he writes stuff every week that judges, convicts, and condemns. 'Sin for *me!*'" Stanton harrumphed his contempt. "I told him in front of the whole convention that he had supported Amasa Walker for Congress just five years before. 'It is false!' he shouted out. I pulled out a whole sheaf of *Liberator*s, and he saw that his deceptions would be exposed. They would not let me read them. They shouted me down. Now I ask you, with such a man, what can you do? Sweet reason is nothing to him. Truth is nothing. He wants to rule, and he *will* rule if we allow him."

"Why must any man rule?" Theodore said, but nobody seemed to hear him.

Charles Stuart wanted to know what would happen at the annual meetings of the American Antislavery Society, due to begin in a week. He had seen Lewis Tappan, who expected a colossal fight. "Brother Tappan showed me a constitution he has written for a new society," he said. "He is quite ready to leave his own handiwork, after all he has invested."

"No, Tappan does not expect to win," Stanton said. "They have already transferred the *Emancipator* to the New York society, and sold off the books in stock."

"What? To keep them out of Mr. Garrison's hands?" Angelina said. "Surely that is not honest. The society is not their personal property, to dispose of as they wish."

"They say the debts are great, and they fear they will be held responsible for them. There is nothing to sell but old books, worth very little."

"Why is Mr. Tappan so sure it will come to a break?" Elizabeth wanted to know.

"Surely Brother Lewis can endure sharing leadership with the Boston group," Angelina added. "The creature you describe, Brother Henry, is not the Garrison we knew."

"It is not merely personalities," Theodore said gloomily. "There is the political question, which seems impossible to resolve. For Brother Tappan it is the women's issue. He considers it indecent to have mixed relations, and Garrison will insist on putting women into official capacities. That is where he foresees the breach. I talked with Tappan very lengthily last week. I told him I could not support him in that, and I thought he was wrong to make an issue out of it. But if it is not that, it will be some other reason. Monstrous egos have risen up. No one is interested in the truth."

This doleful pronouncement led to silence. Elizabeth darted her eyes around the table as if to ask, "Won't anyone speak?" She finally spoke herself. "I think that is a silly reason for a quarrel. Why can't women and men serve together? Mr. Tappan should have a greater reason for dividing the organization."

"No, my dear," Charles Stuart spoke, in infinite sadness. "It is not silly. The relations of men and women are and ought to be infinitely tender. We upset those ancient patterns at our peril. They are the very foundation on which our lives and families are built, and cannot be dictated by an argument."

That launched a spirited discussion, in which (Elizabeth was pleased to find) no one else agreed with Stuart. This was surely the most freethinking group she had ever encountered. Her own husband said he had no objection to women's participation, though he pointed out that it would inevitably be seized on by the slave power to prove that abolitionists would destroy all domestic institutions.

The baby stopped the conversation. All through the meal he had hiccuped and fussed, but now he began to wail pitifully, red-faced. Angelina held him and walked with him but could not comfort him. She became more and more agitated, until they stopped talking.

"Go on, go on," she said. "I do not want to interrupt this most interesting talk." Her husband did go on, almost as though he could not hear the baby. The rest of them, however, found it difficult to talk comfortably while the wailing continued.

"Is the child hungry?" Elizabeth asked.

Angelina shot her a glance of blood-red impatience and contempt. "He eats at four o'clock. When children are fed according to their whims they gain an imperious temper. The lessons of self-control, even in infancy, are vital." But the baby, who looked very frail to Elizabeth, would not be comforted, and Angelina went from impatient frustration to pale weakness herself, until she had to sit down and let Sarah take the baby away. "Please do not feed him," Angelina said plaintively as Sarah left the room, holding the wailing child as though he were infected.

When he took Stuart on a tour of the farm in the afternoon, Theodore did not find it so easy to converse with his old friend. He had described him to Angelina as the most perfect of men, and he had really longed for this reunion, but very soon he felt that their intimate friendship was like a pressed flower found in an old book: interesting and nostalgic, but lacking any freshness. It was not so much that Stuart had changed. The difficulty was more that Theodore Weld had changed. He found himself impatient with Stuart's constant outbursts of praise to God. What had once seemed joyous and generous now seemed artificial and irrelevant.

The farm was in poor repair. They had bought fifty acres of good land fronting the Passaic River, but dikes had broken, and the river had flooded much good land. Weld told his plans to rebuild dikes, drain, work the soil. He proudly showed his pruning of the old apple and pear trees, the grape and berry vines. He had plans for the woodlot, and already he had bought a cow and a dozen chickens with money he had borrowed from Lewis Tappan. He talked enthusiastically about his farming, almost as though he were determined to find it interesting.

"How have you found the church in Belleville?" Stuart asked as they were tramping through the thick, soft mud of the vegetable garden.

Weld said he had not had many chances to attend it.

"Oh," Stuart said, "but is there another church in this region?"

"No," Weld said. "Frankly, dear Charles, we have given up hope in the churches. There seems no love of truth in any of them."

"I know that Mrs. Weld and her sisters are Quakers," Stuart said thoughtfully.

"It has nothing to do with their religion," Weld said abruptly. "We are all of the same mind. We find it more profitable to keep our religion alive here at home, with our own private discussions and prayers together. We need truth, Charles, as a thirsty man needs water, and there is no love for truth in the churches."

"But they read the same Bible that you do. They pray to our heavenly Father there, surely."

"Yes, but they refuse to go to the depths of truth. This has come out all too clearly in our discussions of slavery, but it is so of everything. I am afraid the churches have become a hindrance to the truth, Charles."

This distressed Stuart, as Weld had known that it would, but Stuart was no match for Weld's argument. Finally he was reduced to saying, "The church is dreadful in its failures, but are you any less so? Are you called to judge them?"

Theodore said, "I don't judge them. I only judge myself, and I know it is utterly useless for me to go in to those churches. It has been years since I have been able to bear the cant and hypocrisy. I can't be tranquil when I am oppressed by that. Ever since I went to Cincinnati I have been in the colored churches, even though they are no better than the rest, but I wanted to take my stand with the African people. I believe I would do it still, but here there are no colored churches nearby, and I feel no obligation to the rest. Rather I am obliged to the truth, to find it and follow it."

"I would not argue that the churches are deeply flawed," Stuart said, "but I cannot see it so absolutely as you seem to. They lend us their buildings and pulpits, even when every other building is shut to us, and though many ministers have not separated themselves from the sin of slavery, on the whole ministers are a hundred times more likely to be actively against slavery than the ordinary run of men. Will you really not fellowship with the churches, for all their shortcomings? Dear brother, I fear that soon you will not fellowship with *me!*"

Weld stopped in the fields. For a moment he looked dark and blind, staring. Then he threw his arms around his friend and pressed his face into Stuart's large, broad chest, temporarily overcome, and glad for the rush of emotion that told him he was still attached to this dear man.

"No, Charles, dear brother. We must travel different roads. However far apart in our minds, we can keep our fellowship at the foot of God." He stepped back to look into Stuart's red face. "I have kept our covenant, to meet at dawn by the Spirit. Have you?"

"Yes," Stuart said, his strong hands gripping Weld's arms. The cold spring wind whipped at their hair. "Yes, I will always pray for you, and with you."

Elizabeth Stanton meanwhile had joined Sarah in scrubbing the house floors, a chore that evidently had to be done according to schedule whether guests were present or not. It was a novel experience for Elizabeth, who had grown up with servants. Her knees hurt and her back crackled. Sarah, though much older than she, scurried across the floor twice as fast as she could go with her rag and bucket and cake of lye soap.

"Will you soon return to lecturing and writing?" Elizabeth asked, while using two hands to scrub at a corner. "When I was at my cousin Gerrit Smith's house people told me you were a powerful testimony, and they were sorry you had become absent from the public eye."

Sarah did not immediately answer, and then she spoke musingly. "I think, dear one, that my days in public are over. They were a great trial to me, and I only did it because I had a duty, I believed, to accompany my sister. Now she has better company in Mr. Weld."

"But he is retired also."

"Yes, for the present, though we hope that his voice will soon recover. He ought to go out. He is restless here."

"He seems greatly interested in the farm."

"Yes, the farm," Sarah mused. "Yes, Theodore does like farming, I am sure, but he needs some great cause. I think our days of quiet are almost over. I sense it, and I am a great one for sensing."

She heaved a sigh. "Do you know I went to R. D. Frummer, the phrenologist, and he said straight off that the most prominent bump on my whole head was the intuitive bump? When I thought of it, I was quite sure he was right, for I have all my life been able to sense what other people could not. I think a great deal of phrenology. I am sure it is a science that will inevitably transform our understanding of human relations. Suppose a young man and woman, before they were married, were to submit their heads to a phrenologist, would that not prevent many unhappy unions?"

"Oh dear," Elizabeth giggled, "I wish I had seen one before I married my husband. I am sure we have different heads! I suppose it is too late."

Chapter 17
1842: Nichols Returns to Alabama

Dear Brother,
Twice Dear Brother,

I have got religion. Don't you believe in miracles? I cannot tell you how it has happened. It is beyond anything. People don't believe it here, so I don't tell them. I just go to the church and let them see.

I had a slave mistress, I am ashamed to say it, but Jesus has made that all clean now and done his glory by it. She is godly, and one Sunday I woke up and felt so ashamed. I told her I was Methodist. She told me to go. I went and everything was made right by our Precious Savior. I am writing "our" because now you and me are in one family again. I fall on my knees and thank you for writing so many times to try to persuade me. It was not your failing, Tom, but mine.

I want to see you. I wish you could come back home. Everybody would like to see you. Your opinions are not known here. We would make up for lost time, dear brother. Won't you write me and say you are coming.

Martin

Thomas, who had hardly thought of his brother Martin in recent years, received this letter at his manufactory. He walked out onto the workshop floor, saw a young fellow, and thrust the letter in front of his eyes. "This is from my brother, he has found the Savior!"

Through the rest of the working day he left the letter on his desk and occasionally picked it up again, each time reviving the elation in his soul. It was beyond explaining how much this meant to him, that this brother whom he had not seen or written or even thought of had been converted and wished now to see him.

Thomas left early to go home, where he found Ruth in the kitchen plucking a chicken. Ruth had her straw-colored hair pulled back, and down from the bird covered her apron. Thomas brushed the feathers away, kissed her, and without saying a word held out the letter so that she could read it. He felt great pleasure in feeling her thinness pressing against his side, in knowing that she would be pleased. She did not disappoint him, but as she read made rapturous sounds and then threw her arms around him.

"Dear Thomas," she said, "oh, wonderful, you must go. You must!"

He had not even considered that. "Oh, no," he said, "I would need a month, at least, and the manufactory requires constant supervision . . ."

"Dearest Thomas," she said, drawing apart and looking at him very seriously, "he is your brother, and he has asked you to come. How can he ever free his slaves if you do not go there to help him see the way? Do you think it can happen otherwise?"

He knew Martin, he knew Alabama, he knew that the slaves could not be freed. Ruth, who was innocent of all such knowledge, was sure that the slaves must be let go. "If he is truly converted, he cannot live in the same way," she said firmly, as if she were asserting that apples would be ripe in October. She thought Martin wanted Thomas to come help him set his life aright, and pointed out his reference to his slave mistress. "She has prepared the way, I am sure of it. He has been led to God by a slave woman, how can he allow her to remain as she is—or any other of God's creatures?" She was so sure of it that she almost persuaded him.

She spoke of the trip as a duty, a duty to family as well as the cause. Her quiet, bullheaded, Dutch sureness was very hard for him to resist. He began to dream of how it would be to return home. He began to work out how slaves might be made financially independent, how they might form a free black plantation, a model that could transform the mind-set of white Alabamians when they saw blacks and whites working together with dignity.

He did not mention such matters to his brother when he wrote. Rather he recommended various Christian publications Martin might find profitable. He would have sent a packet of books to Huntsville, but by the time he considered this he was making plans to go himself and thought he could take the books with him.

He went to see Lewis Tappan, who had established himself in a small, frugal office just off Wall Street. Tappan kept information on creditors in large, carefully written ledgers. It was a new idea, which Nichols had doubted would succeed: to accumulate a history of various traders and sell subscriptions to the information.

"I would not recommend such a trip," Tappan said sternly. "Have you no thought for your children?"

Nichols was taken aback. "What do you mean?"

"Do you think an abolitionist can be safe in the Southern states just now?"

"My brother writes me that my convictions are unknown to people there," Nichols said.

"Yes, but *he* knows, and didn't you tell me he is a drunkard? Drunkards talk. If anyone should discover the truth, you will be in severe danger."

When he told Ruth what Tappan had said, she turned down the corners of her mouth and said starchily that Lewis Tappan thought he was in danger of murder whenever he left his front door.

"I don't think you do him justice," Thomas said. "At the time of the riots he was as cool as a summer melon. I have found him quite courageous. When the mob wrecked his house he actually joked of it."

With Ruth's urging he went ahead, buying a steamer ticket for New Orleans. The ticket agent even had steamboat schedules that could get him to Huntsville. Thomas packed to go nearly as light as he had left home so many years before. He would need no warm clothing, and he thought the packet of books a sufficient gift for his brother. He tried to conceive of a present for Brady but had no idea what a young man might like from New York. He settled on a French pocketknife with two blades and a bone handle, a gift that would fit in his pocket.

———————

He was feeling this gift, hard and cool in his pocket, as the steamboat drew close to Huntsville. The river was the same familiar sight, brown and sluggish, splayed out across the valley, an endless play of sandbars, islands, snags, trees on the bank in various states of decay. Maybe there were more houses visible from the river nowadays, he could not remember. But the steamboat was certainly a different mode of transport: uniformed officers, private cabins, and a schedule. Unfortunately they were too efficient now to stop off at Triana, so he could not live his old fantasy of arriving from the boat unannounced. He would have to go to town and hire a horse.

His return felt different from what he had imagined. From the day he left, a youthful, hot-tempered soul, he had dreamed of his triumphal return as a man with money. The dream had come true, but looking at this familiar terrain he felt flat, almost despairing. So much guilt and misery had pounded into him here, and was he a different man? He was older, and his temples were graying, but those old ghosts still inhabited the basement of his soul. This was the land where he had learned to sin, to hate, to fight. He could not imagine how his new self would survive in this old place of sin-sickness.

Huntsville had been built far from the river, a considerable inconvenience in this era of river travel. Three wagons stood waiting under the shade of a lonely oak set above the landing. Mules slumped motionless except for their tails, switching relentlessly. Negro drivers were similarly inert, their backs to the tree. They stood when they saw him disembark and walked toward him using a long, limber stride he had not seen since he left.

Nichols pointed at one, sent him onto the boat to get his trunk and grip, and climbed up into the Negro's wagon.

Everything seemed completely unchanged—the Negro's seat on the wagon, with arms held high and head hunkered low, the puddle-pocked road, the everlasting sun. He asked the Negro what his name was and where he came from.

"Rob, master, and I come from around here."

"Where exactly? I know this area pretty well."

Rob cocked an eye at him for a second. "Right now I am rented out to Miss Douglass, the schoolteacher in town. This is her wagon. But my family is all with Mr. Barnes, west of town at Blue Rock Creek, and he is the one who owns me."

Memory stirred. "That's Philip Barnes, or Oranthus?"

Again the cocked eye. "Mr. Barnes is named Oranthus. Philip is his brother I believe."

"Didn't they have another brother?"

"Yes sir, they did. Mr. Frederick, but he died."

"You knew him though?"

"Yes, sir, everybody knows the Barneses."

"Whatever happened to his property when he died?" Nichols asked.

"I don't rightly know, sir," which Nichols knew was a lie.

"Did you ever hear of a black wench named Catherine? Belonged to the Nicholses down at Triana?" He felt a mixture of disappointment and relief when the man said no, sir. She really was gone, then, along with her son. Thomas had given a great deal of thought to Robert Duncan's assertion that Catherine had a son who shared his name. He had even wondered, as he watched the bank from the steamboat, whether he might possibly see the boy, or man as he now would surely be.

"Take me round the square before we go to the livery stable," he said, and they drove slowly up Eustiss in front of the courthouse, north on Franklin, left on Randolph away from the Methodist church, then back by Madison to the beginning point. They passed most of the brick buildings in town, the identical buildings he had left, nearly. He looked carefully and cautiously at the loungers, and he recognized no one.

"A lot of new faces in town," he said quietly.

Rob snorted. "You must have been gone a long time, Master," he said. "They look like the same fellows to me."

"How old are you, Rob?"

"Seventeen, sir, or nearly."

"You must have been just about born the year I left this town for good."

"Brother!"

Martin Nichols came running pell-mell across the yard, dressed in a neat white shirt and black trousers with braces. He seized the bridle of Thomas's horse while Thomas dismounted, then clutched Thomas to his ample torso. Martin was clean-shaven and smelled of sweat, not whiskey. A Negro came out to take the horse into the barn, and two black women came onto the veranda, peering curiously. Thomas wondered which one was the mistress.

"Well," Martin said when they were seated in the old parlor. "You have come home at last. It is hard to believe. Which of us is more the prodigal son?" And at that he laughed heartily.

"Do you want some water?" Martin asked. "There is no more whiskey to be had here, thank God, but you never were a drinker, were you?"

"Oh, I used to drink," Thomas said. "You don't remember? But not since I found the Savior."

"Nor have I! Not a drop! And I never will again. I don't want to!"

Thomas said he would like some water, since he was pretty warm from his ride. Martin sent one of the servants off to get it. "Does the old place seem very different?" he asked. "You left it before Sissy got onto it. She had it gussied up, and I guess I've tried to keep it that way. No doubt *she* would find fault. But she let me back into it when she married in Greenville."

"Yes, no doubt. You wrote about a black mistress. What has happened to her?"

Martin's mouth sagged for an instant. "Well, she is gone, I can assure you."

"Oh, I am sure. But to where?"

"I sent her over to the Popes." This was a prominent Huntsville family. "I sold her for one dollar. They will take care of her I believe."

"You didn't think about freeing her, then?"

"Don't you bring your Yankee ideas." He said it with a smile. "Daddy did it, and you see how much good it brought." He stood up suddenly, as though he found it uncomfortable to sit still. "Why don't we sit out on the veranda?"

Martin was indeed changed. He asked for details about Thomas's family, and about his business, and he listened to the answers with every sign of interest. Thomas was aware, all the same, that his brother had no context to understand his life. No idea of New York could really enter a mind that had never left Huntsville. Even the idea of a manufactory was pure theory to a man whose slaves made, of necessity, all their own tackle and shoes and brooms.

So their conversation moved to the one subject where they made happy and easy contact: religion. Granted that here, too, Martin moved in a narrower context, for the local Methodism was all he knew—he had never even heard of Finney. However, the substance that they cared for was the same. His brother was really and profoundly converted. He had ceased drinking even coffee, had given up his mistress, had become regular in his habits.

When it was time to sleep, Martin led him to the same room where his father had died. For a moment Thomas sat on the bed, wondering whether Martin had put him there deliberately. Something of his life had ended on that night, and something had begun. There was the same window where the rain had pounded on that night. Thomas had very limited memories of his father, as a stern and joyless man, whose religion had produced in him no benevolence. Yet he had freed his slaves. He must have wanted to do good.

Would not the old man be joyed to find his two oldest sons talking happily of their conversion? Thomas thought for a few minutes of this soulful conversation about religion, until he began to think of the slaves, especially the mistress his brother had sold away to break with immorality. Sadness for the woman, for his brother, indeed for this sin-wracked land where he had been born, filled up his body as if water poured in from a spring.

"Have you considered," Thomas asked his brother, "your Christian duty to these people?"

They had stopped their horses to look over the unbroken fields of the plantation, deep green with cotton. Wherever the land dipped and the spring flood had lingered the cotton was weak and struggling, but most of the field was healthy and abundant. When Thomas had left there had been no fields so cleared of forest that you could see a mile unbroken; but the Barnes money had made it possible, and the plantation was now rich. A hundred yards away a work crew was hoeing under the eye of a white man mounted on a horse.

"They are well treated, if that is what you mean," Martin replied. "My overseers don't drink, and I see that the servants get good food. I think I treat them pretty fairly."

"I guess if they were draft animals I would agree, but, Martin, they are men. The Savior tells us to love your neighbor as yourself. Don't you think that slaves want to be free just as you would?"

"I am not so sure that they do, though they probably think that they do. Your children, wouldn't they like to have candy every day?"

"Martin, I would not argue that we simply pronounce freedom and think we have done something. I want to make a new economy in which free laborers can be rewarded for their work. I have ideas about how that can be done here, to make a model for the entire state."

His brother turned on his horse and smiled at him, though there was no warmth in the smile. "You are the same brother I knew. You always had a scheme to change the world."

"Yes, to change the world. Surely that is the meaning of your conversion. God calls us to active benevolence, so that we can build his kingdom on earth. You cannot think that in the millennium there will be slaves."

"Well, brother, why not? There are slaves in the Bible. Pastor says they are told to obey, so they can reap rewards in heaven. And masters are to treat their slaves kindly, as I am trying to do. I can't see any harm in slavery. I am talking about the proper kind of master, not the abusive kind, which I know myself to have been."

"Would you like to be a slave?"

"Well no, but I am not a Negro, I am a white man. We are meant to be free. You know, these blacks do not take to freedom. I never knew one who could manage that trick."

"What about Catherine?"

He had not intended to ask his brother about her, but her name had come out before he thought. Martin, his face darkened, looked away at mention of her name.

"She ran away. Never been seen again. Yes, Catherine made a proof that these people can be free." He spoke sarcastically.

"No, listen, Martin, they cannot be free in these circumstances, but what if we created a free labor plantation? If they profited from the fruit of their labor they would work harder, you would not need overseers to watch them, the plantation would become a happy place. Don't you long to see such an example of God's benevolent reign here, at Triana?"

Rivulets of perspiration were running down their faces, and the flies had found them. "Let's go on," Martin said, and he jerked the reins to follow a trail toward the river. For nearly a mile he rode at a trot. The forest loomed dark as a mountain, impenetrable to their approach. Then they were at the foot of its immensity; then they entered it. The air was cooler under the tall trees, and Martin turned his horse to survey the land. It shone bright and green beyond the shadows.

"There is still good land to clear," Martin said. "This land can still yield more." His jowly face was set. Clearly he did not intend to talk about the free labor plantation. Thomas saw that it would do no good to try, and let the subject go.

Martin could not resist one word, however, when they arrived back at the house. They were ascending the steps to the veranda when he said, "This was our father's land. We almost lost it with his benevolence, as you call it, and I am not going to lose it again. He didn't do those Negroes any good."

"All right," Thomas said, stopping to put a hand on his brother's arm, to make him listen, "you don't accept that you would do them good. Look at it another way. Who has given you the lives of men to command, to buy and sell? God gave them freedom in their native Africa, and some mansteeler came and captured them by violence. Does that give you right to keep them captive, and their children and children's children? Rather than giving you right, it makes you an accessory to robbery."

"You are calling me a thief. By what law am I a thief to inherit property?"

"By the law of God! If you inherit from a thief you are yourself a thief until you return the stolen property."

"Then why, in the Bible, are not slaveholders told this? Why are we told simply to be kind?"

"That slavery was a different institution, something more like indentured servanthood. I could give you a book by Theodore Weld . . ."

"I don't need your books to understand the Bible. The Spirit of God makes it clear enough for me."

"Then what says the Spirit of God to our Lord's command to love your neighbor as yourself?"

"I am doing the best I can by these Negroes. I don't hear they are so well treated in the North either. How do you treat them? Do you give them houses like yours? Do they have fine positions in your manufactory?"

They did not argue for the rest of the week, but they barely spoke. Thomas was depressed in the heavy, hot days. He was caught in the constricted feelings of his youth, years when he had felt as frustrated and helpless as a trussed goose. Something in the angry air and in the gloom of the old house breathed a malarial decay, telling him he was useless and worse than useless. Wherever he looked he saw the scenes he had once lived, the life he had once wasted. Besides, he was upset with himself that he had argued so childishly, not speaking tenderly to his brother from the bowels of Christ, but harshly chiding. When had he ever, this way, changed his brother's mind? Thomas had come so far for only one reason, to call his brother by the love of the Savior to leave sin behind and to offer help in remaking the plantation into a place of heavenly justice. Now the entire possibility was in doubt. Martin avoided him, riding off at dawn and coming late for meals.

On Saturday Thomas waited on the veranda until his brother came riding up, and then asked for a word with him. "I am sorry, Martin," he said, "for my harshness. You have been kind to welcome me, and I have repaid it badly. For the sake of the Savior can you forgive me?"

Martin looked away, out into the bright, gray haze. "No need," he said slowly. "You have strong beliefs, which is perfectly right." He grimaced at the painted planks of the veranda. "Let us go in to eat," he said.

They sat at two corners of the dining room table, eating from china plates. While the meat was brought in neither one of them said anything. The shades had been drawn since the morning, and the room was dark, with soft rectangles of light from the windows reflecting on the painted floor.

"I daresay," Martin said at last, holding a forkful of meat, "that you are quite right about slavery as far as New York is concerned. You were never here to see this place after our daddy gave the slaves their freedom. I tell you, Thomas, we nearly lost the land. It was this near. Only the grace of God— I see it now, it was grace though I never knew it—kept it safe for us."

Thomas tightened his lips slightly, praying inwardly he would know how to answer with gentleness. "I am so glad"—he had to push to get it through his lips, his heart was thumping hard—"that you see God's grace for what it is."

"Of course it is God, how else do you explain it? Everything was gone, Tommy, everything. The Negroes were starving. You cannot imagine what a wreck it all became."

"But dear brother." Thomas was surprised to find himself choking on the words, as he was suddenly filled with pathos. "My dear, dear Martin: the grace must spread, it is not just for the few but for the many. God saved this land for a purpose, surely, to free his people, *all* his people, to enjoy the riches of his goodness. Martin, I did not come to be against you but to share with you the greater grace of God. We can turn this land into a fruitful place, fruitful for all its children."

"Don't start again with the idea of freeing the slaves, Tommy. Daddy did that. You weren't here to see the results."

"I *know* it was a failure. I don't want to repeat that." He heard his voice beginning to strain toward shouting, and stopped.

They ate in silence for a few minutes. Then Thomas tried again, calmly. "Martin, I do not say that the slaves are ready for emancipation. But what might be possible if we began carefully to raise them? What if we began a school to teach them . . ."

"That's against the law."

". . . and taught them step-by-step to raise crops, to care for their land and their home, to live by the fruit of their labor. Suppose we didn't merely grant them freedom but made them into free men, doing unto them as we would have done unto us were we in the same situation. Would not the light from Triana begin to shine, and . . ."

"No!" Martin cut him short, slamming a fist on the table so the china rattled. "You talk as if they were white men. You can treat them any way you like and they still stay black. They're different from you and me, Tommy. It isn't kind to pretend that they are what they aren't."

"I have seen black men with capacity to beat half the white men in this county. It does not have to be."

"I'd bet they have white blood in them."

"And if they do? Would you free all the slaves with white blood in them? How many, do you think, *lack* some white blood?"

Martin smiled ruefully. "Yes, and I reckon you're thinking that I have supplied my share. Well, you did some of that, too, don't forget, before you were saved."

Thomas stopped cold. He had not anticipated that his own sin would come up. Yet he had to keep talking, he thought, to carry this discussion to the end. It was the reason why he had come.

"I am deeply ashamed of my past," he said in a subdued voice. "I have begged God's forgiveness many times."

Martin had pushed his plate away and folded his hands on the table. Thomas could not read his expression, to know whether he had become open or was still adamant.

"When we think of these things," Thomas said soberly, "we must realize that God has drawn no line precisely between black and white. When we speak of the slaves we speak of our own offspring."

He wondered, suddenly, whether Martin might know where Catherine had gone. He had known her after him, had he not? Thomas could not ask that, however, not now and perhaps at no time he could imagine.

"Martin," he said, "you have made the point that I have not lived here for a long time. But let me say honestly that you have never lived anywhere else, and so cannot see that these facts of life, seeming so solid here, can become quite different. In another place, at another time, you might see it quite differently. The difference between the white man and the black man is color . . ."

Martin slammed down his fist on the table, then stood up suddenly. "That's nothing but a lie," he said as he went out. "There's a world of difference," he shouted back at Thomas from the veranda.

Thomas awoke Sunday morning with his bedclothes twisted around him in a sweaty clot. The room, with its faded French paper, its deep blue curtains closed against the already-hot sun, seemed unfamiliar and disturbing. He needed a few minutes to remember where he was and what had happened. Then the memory of yesterday's argument flooded back.

He had prayed last night, kneeling by this bed, that Martin's harsh reaction would prove a sign of inward turmoil—the Spirit of God witnessing to his spirit. Today the long, torpid line of the Sabbath stretched out before them, the day of rest, constant as a cicada's song. Surely they would converse again like brothers, surely today, the Lord's Day, Martin would understand God's call to him regarding the slaves.

Thomas got up and, rather than wait for the servants to bring water, descended to the pump in the yard. He splashed water on himself, rubbed his face with a towel he had carried, combed his hair back and down over his collar. Nothing was stirring in the house yet, so he decided to walk down by the slave cabins. Once they had been cut off from the big house by a screen of trees. The trees were gone now, and without them the cabins were plainly exposed, a weathered row.

Behind the second cabin he found a tall, yellow girl putting sticks on a smoky fire. She stared at him curiously when he came around the corner, and smiled at him with big, gapped teeth. "Morning, Master," she called out.

He would have told her that he was no master, but brother. But he merely nodded and stopped with his hands on his hips. When he was young he would have walked up to her fire with no more hesitation than he would feel walking up to pat a dog, but now he was shy. He wondered if she knew who he was. News could travel fast among the Negroes, he knew that, but he did not know just what news. Were they interested that their master's brother had come back from the North, or was he just to them one more white face?

Ever since he had set his feet in the direction of these cabins he had been thinking about where Catherine had once lived. He did not like to have this girl watch him look at it, but, he thought, what could she know? She was not born when Catherine left this place. So casually he walked over to the door of the cabin. There was not much to see: worn planks, with a deep brown patina all around the latchstring, where a thousand hands had accidentally caressed the wood. His hand had been only one.

Perhaps Robert Duncan had also pulled on this latch. He wondered. Thomas involuntarily took a deep breath and let it out. How deep had been his sin, how worldly his life when he had known no other.

―――――――――――

He went to church with his brother, filling up a buckboard with Negroes and driving off to the nearby crossroads of Bruce, where a Methodist church had begun in a small unelaborate wooden building, a crate with windows and a bell tower. The service was attended by thirty or forty dirt farmers and their families plus a few slaves who worked as farmhands or house servants. His brother was the only person of consequence. People greeted Thomas most cordially, though they acted a little squint-eyed when they heard he came from New York.

The slaves took up benches in back, the youngest children sat on the floor in front; they all but filled the small, low-ceilinged building, which smelled of sweat and soap and sweet pinewood. The singing was impressive: slow, almost tuneless, loud, fundamental. The minister prayed at some length, and so did the elders. Thomas, who had not been in a Methodist service since his boyhood, was surprised to find it so deep and careful. All he recalled was ranting and shouting.

The minister was a man of moderate height, with wide-set, piercing eyes. He nodded in a friendly way to the congregation as he began his sermon, reading the Bible text. It was from Ephesians: "Servants, be obedient to them that are your masters according to the flesh, with fear and trembling, in singleness of your heart, as unto Christ; not with eyeservice, as men-pleasers; but as the servants of Christ, doing the will of God from the heart; with good will doing service, as to the LORD, and not to men: knowing that whatsoever good thing any man doeth, the same shall he receive of the LORD, whether he be bond or free."

"Now this holy text doesn't need any explanation," he said, and proceeded to explain it. "Those of you who are slaves, it says to obey because that is the way a Christian can truly please his Lord. When I tell my Johnny to get me my horse, he jumps to do it because Johnny knows that it isn't me who has told him what to do, it is *Jesus Christ himself.*"

Thomas's hands gripped the bench tightly. Stephen Foster and others of Garrison's disciples disrupted church services in Massachusetts, demanding to speak, and got dragged out bodily. What would they do here?

The minister said that a plague of bad attitudes afflicted the world today: slaves who moved slowly when no one was watching them, slaves who were insolent, slaves who had never lacked for food and wore excellent cotton garments but who were not grateful. When the master's back was turned they were gossiping and slacking. "Do you think that the Lord Christ does not see? Do you consider him blind?" the minister asked. "Are you pleasing him by your humility and servile behavior? Or do you harbor the bitter poison of jealousy and envy?"

The world was in a terrible state, the minister said, and they must turn back to Jesus, give their hearts to him afresh. He called the people to remember the times of their fathers when these lands were at peace, when slave and master could live together in harmony and without fear.

Then he said that the Bible was not written for the black man only but for the white man too. The white man had to obey the Scriptures knowing he too had a master to serve. He had to obey the authorities, and pray for them, and respect them. It was so of the church, most of all. He, Jason Briggs, was God's appointed minister to them, and he was thankful that they honored him the way they should, with no backbiting. The Savior called them to do it. But he found it terrible that the appointed bishop of the whole Methodist

Episcopal Church, Reverend James Andrew, a Georgian who had given his entire life to the church, was being attacked fiercely by Northern abolitionist interests that had infiltrated the church, sneaking in like dogs. This man had inherited slaves through his wife, and for that crime he was likely to be hanged and quartered by the very church that he had served. Oh, where would peace come from if God's people themselves would persecute the righteous among them?

It was all that Thomas could stand, just to listen to the man go on. He did not dare look left or right, for he thought if he could not maintain iron discipline, if for one second he caught another person's eye, he would explode.

But that was not all. The minister, who had begun his talk by staring to the back pews where the Negroes sat, and who then had scattered his eyes to all corners of the room, now put his irises directly on Thomas. He began to talk about the hatred of the North for their Southern way of life. Nat Turner the murdering Negro was a hero to these abolitionists, he said, who longed for the day when the peaceful and neighborly states rich in cotton would witness blood rebellion. They stirred up the peace-loving Negro to hate. He knew from talking to Methodist preachers in Mississippi that Northern troublemakers had planned a rebellion, convincing gullible Negroes to trust them and stirring up misery between the races. It could happen again, right here on the Tennessee River, just as it had in Virginia, just as it had in Mississippi. They must keep their guard. All this time the minister was staring at Thomas. Thomas stared back.

After the service had ended they filed out silently. Thomas had enough sense to know that he was in some danger, but that was not chiefly on his mind. He was thinking what he might say to the pastor, if the minister had courage enough to stand by the door.

He did. He extended his hand. Thomas did not take it. "You are a disgrace," he said in a low voice. "Before God you are found wanting."

"Snake!" the minister said loudly. "Brood of vipers! Who sent you here to disturb us?"

"Come on," Martin said, pushing Thomas from behind, and then seizing his arm and pulling him unwillingly to the door.

The congregation, gathered outside, stared silently while Martin led Thomas to his buckboard, hurriedly freed the reins, backed and turned the horses. Some of his Negroes had been caught unawares and came running after the wagon, calling for him to stop, then jumping in the back, laughing.

Thomas heard a loud, sudden thump, thought at first it was another slave jumping in, and then caught in the corner of his eye the slow, tumbling movement of a potato-sized rock in the wagon bed. One of the Negroes, a woman about twenty years old, Thomas guessed, was holding her arm, silently cradling the pain.

"Giddap," Martin said to the horses, and slapped the reins to make them go.

———————

"What did you say to Pastor?" Martin asked. It was well past midnight, they had been riding toward Decatur for nearly two hours, and he must have decided they were safe from discovery. For the whole afternoon and evening they had sat in the forest with their horses, dead silent. After nightfall they had ridden silently on dark roads.

"I told him he was found wanting."

Martin did what Thomas had never expected. Martin laughed. "I guess you got to him there. It was almost worth it to see the look on his face."

The laugh carried Thomas back to their boyhood, to the cynical, suspicious way in which they had laughed at everyone, especially their father. Thomas did not regret the laugh this time, for it restored some small shred of their brotherhood.

"You really think they might have done me harm?"

"Might. You can't tell."

"Thank you for rescuing me."

His brother laughed again at that. "I wonder if any of them showed up at Triana tonight, and how hard it was to convince them that you were gone."

"Will it cause trouble for you?"

"Not me. I haven't done anything wrong."

"I haven't either."

"But you're a Yankee now, and you get credit for all the things that Yankees do."

They said good-bye within sight of the first house outside Decatur. They could see its outline in the starlight but talked to each other in pure invisibility, from the backs of their horses. In the morning Thomas would catch a steamboat toward New Orleans and be gone.

He could not leave without one more attempt. "Brother Martin, will you not give up slavery? You must know that our Savior calls you to do it, from love to him."

There was such a long silence that he hoped perhaps his words had sunk their hook into his brother's skin. But when the answer growled out of Martin's shadow it was negative. "It ain't the Savior calling me to that, Tommy, it's you. There's no chance I am going to do it."

"Even at the cost of losing your soul? Will you suffer eternal fire for it?"

"That's not in your Bible. Didn't you hear the minister's sermon?"

"You don't believe that, Martin. You can't."

"I believe enough of it, you know. I can read enough to know that the Bible tells slaves to obey and masters to be kind."

Exasperated, Thomas said, "But let me send you a book. Theodore Weld has settled all that magnificently."

"Send me all the books that you like. I've made up my mind on this, and it wasn't hard."

Chapter 18
1843: Call for Revolt

INSTINCTUALLY CATHERINE NICHOLS was averse to moral crusades and abstract theories. "Mind your own business" was as close to philosophy as she got, generally. Schools drew her practically; she wanted advancement for Tommy. When he had reached the limits of free schooling in Cincinnati, she tended north from town to town until reaching Jamestown, New York, where Tommy was allowed to attend the high school. He was the only black and very soon the best student. The teacher, an Oneida graduate, invited him to attend the Congregational Church. It was there they accidentally found themselves abolition heroes.

Catherine generally attended the church nearest her lodgings without much distinguishing the denomination. When Tommy went to the Congregational Church, she went with him and found that she was well treated—that is, was not treated at all, but the minister shook her hand at the door when she left. Prejudice remained inconspicuous, which was good enough for Catherine. She planned her meals for the week during the sermon.

They sat in the balcony because she was accustomed to do so. Tommy, however, soon wanted to move closer to the minister. He had no protest in mind, he merely wanted a better view. He was nineteen, a bit of a dandy, tall and light-skinned. He had never lost his fascination with preachers and preaching.

Catherine had not taught him any idea of servility, and consequently he had no idea what it meant for a black person to wish to sit in the front pews. Nor was she about to teach him. Since he wanted to sit in front, she accompanied him. When they walked down the aisle, however, ushers intercepted them and said that they should sit in the balcony. Catherine asked why. She did not care where she sat, but when someone pushed her, she pushed back. The ushers said that the pews were rented.

She took Tommy back up to the balcony. He chafed against it, but she told him to wait. "We will get a pew down front," she told him. When one of the white families moved west to join cousins in Illinois, she went to Tommy's schoolteacher and gave him three months' rent for their pew. He came back with a receipt. Whether he knew what he was doing she was never quite sure.

On Sunday next she and Tommy marched down to their rented pew. The ushers tried to stop them, but she had her receipt, and that confounded them. These were Yankees: a written receipt could stop a mob. The ushers stared at the piece of paper with its inky scribbles, and they surrendered. Catherine and Tommy sat in their pew.

On Tuesday evening the minister called on her at home and very kindly asked her to sit in the balcony, for the peace of the church. He made it sound as though he were on her side but that for the weaker, prejudiced brethren, she should defer her rights.

"Reverend Hall," she said sweetly, "I would never do this for myself. Please understand. It is for my son, Tommy. He admires you so much. He talks about wanting to be a preacher himself. I feel this way: to go back would discourage him, and he might lose his faith in the Lord. That happens to so many young boys."

Catherine mentioned Jesus' call to "suffer the children to come unto me." Tommy was rather large, at nineteen, to fit this biblical appeal, but she used it shamelessly nonetheless.

Reverend Hall's eyes took on a hard cast, and he told her that the elders had voted to deny her the pew. He had brought her money to give back. He pulled a folded-over envelope from his coat pocket.

"Reverend, thank you, but I am satisfied with the pew as it is. I believe I will keep it and let the church keep my money."

He told her again that the elders had voted to deny her the pew.

"Well, I have the receipt for it," she said. "I suppose if it came to it the courts would recognize my rental."

On Sunday she and Tommy marched down to their pew and found that it had been literally removed, pulled up from the floorboards. You could see, on the yellow pine planks, a virgin unvarnished strip where the pew supports had covered the boards; and dark stains where nails had been yanked out of the floor.

All eyes were on them, watching what they would do. Catherine felt rising anger, the fury that always came when she was denied. She tightened, focusing her mind to a spot as hard and tight as a pinhead. Then, after glancing at Tommy, she led him into the vacant slip where the pew had been, and sat down on the floor. Tommy hesitated, then took a seat cross-legged next to her. They sat there through the service.

The next week they walked down the aisle in the same way. When they reached their slip, however, they found that the floorboards had been ripped out. Where their pew had been, a dank hole dropped into the basement, smelling of darkness and winter. Without a word she and Tommy turned and marched out of the church, never to return. But the antislavery papers heard the story, it was written up, letters to the church authorities were published, other churches in Jamestown made her public offers of a pew. She and Tommy got a measure of local fame. Therefore when the national Negro antislavery convention was announced for Buffalo, Baptists in Jamestown, from civic pride and a desire to shame the Congregationalists, organized to send them.

Based on her Cincinnati experiences, Catherine considered abolitionists to be airy, impractical people, full of theory, but she was curious to see what

Negro abolitionists might be. Besides, she thought it would do Tommy good to see educated men of his race. She fussed that she had no suitable clothes to wear, but ultimately made do by borrowing a dress from her employer, a woman whose husband printed the town newspaper. By the time she had bathed and done her hair up, she considered herself still a handsome woman.

She and Tommy traveled by train, a mode of transport rapidly eclipsing the canal boat even in western New York. Compared to the canal, a train was sooty, noisy, and exhausting; but compared to a trip by wagon or on foot— the most common way in Catherine's experience—trains were extraordinary. To travel by train gave the Nichols an unfamiliar sense of excitement and pride, that they participated in a project larger than their own lives.

In Buffalo they were met by the local committee and conveyed to a boardinghouse. Late into the evening they sat on the veranda with other neat and proper Negroes, bowing and curtsying their way through introductions, trying to outtalk each other. Many of the delegates had read of the Nicholses' travails, and those who had not absorbed the story avidly. Despite herself, Catherine enjoyed it. She tended to scoff at the high-mindedness of the talk, at the fake gentility, but she found herself caught up in the high spirits. Not for a very long time, not since she was a girl attending camp meetings, had she been at such a jamboree.

The other delegates also said it had been long. Since the 1840 quarrel that split the abolitionists in two, nobody could convene an abolitionist meeting without calling it Garrisonian or anti-Garrisonian. That had made a Negro convention impossible, as black people were on both sides of the divide. These blacks, though, were impatient over the divide. How could a controversy over political theory matter to men who were not allowed the vote? Why should a quarrel between white men keep black men apart? Furthermore, abolition had accomplished this: a new generation of young, educated blacks had come to the fore. They had spoken at abolitionist meetings and written in abolitionist newspapers; they had been to schools like Oneida or Oberlin, and they were ready to find their voice.

In the morning the delegates walked from their lodgings to the meeting place, an African church gleaming with a fresh coat of red paint. The sight of so many well-dressed black people drew curious stares along the street, but no hostility. At the church they mingled freely with several score white observers, some of whom walked about the room conspicuously arm in arm with blacks, talking volubly. One minuscule white man, with thick, curly, yellowed hair, seemed impelled to physically embrace every black person whom he met.

Catherine was pleased to see, despite this mixing, that all the presiders were black. The speeches were rather somber until a young, vigorous Presbyterian minister from Troy, Henry Highland Garnet, limped to the podium. Garnet had gone to school at Oneida, was one of the founding members of Lewis Tappan's new antislavery organization, was an enthusiastic booster of the Liberty Party that nominated James Birney for president. Today, however, Garnet did not talk politics. He unfolded his text and glared out over the audience, his face a deep, shining black.

In a powerful voice, deep and guttural like the roar of a lion, Garnet called on slaves to stop living as slaves but to insist that they were free men. Slaves should tell their owners that they wanted liberty, and "if the masters refused it, to tell them, then we shall take it, let the consequence be what it may." Yes, he assured them, there would be violence, such as the slaveholders initiated.

He reminded them of Denmark Vesey, who had launched a slave rebellion in South Carolina; of "patriotic Nathaniel Turner," who led his band to Jerusalem, Virginia. He cited Cinque and the Amistads, as well as the leaders of the *Creole*, another ship whose slaves had mutinied. For an hour and a half he held up before them their murdered sons and prostituted daughters. "Remember," he thundered, "that there can *be* no redemption of sin without the shedding of blood."

"Brethren, arise, arise!" he cried, his full voice building toward a crescendo. "Strike for your lives and liberties. Now is the day and hour. Let every slave throughout the land do this, and the days of slavery are numbered. You cannot be more oppressed than you have been—you cannot suffer greater cruelties than you have already. *Rather die free men than live to be slaves.* Remember that you are four millions."

In the great stirring after Garnet was done, Frederick Douglass got the attention of the chairman. You could never miss Douglass. He was the tallest man in the room, with a face carved out of ebony. At the boarding-house he had dominated them all without trying. When he opened his mouth now he spoke softly, with a voice so deep it seemed like a force of nature. Reverend Garnet said the truth about slavery, Douglass agreed. He knew that truth too well, he had lived in it. He need not elaborate on what Reverend Garnet had said so well. This great evil was all but impossible to bear, let alone to endure with patience.

Nonetheless, he favored trying the moral means a little longer, Douglass said. He would not want to be an agent in any way of a slave insurrection, for surely that would lead to great and bloody destruction. He still hoped that somehow by God's grace freedom might be gained without such slaughter.

After he sat down others backed his point. The delegation from Cincinnati pointed out the great danger an insurrection would bring to free blacks in the border states. Others pleaded not to abandon the tactics of moral suasion. Two wrongs do not make a right, they said, and when could a war that killed ever be right?

Over the dinner table a half dozen lively conversations continued. Tommy and Catherine sat opposite Charles Remond, a Garrisonian who had spoken against the call to arms. Tommy went at him vigorously. "I don't see that a man is obliged to take slave treatment," he said. "If I gave you a kick and told you to hoe my corn, would you do it? Well, I would have just the same right as those slavers do."

Remond said with equanimity that Mr. Nichols was quite correct: the slaveholder had no more right to his slaves than he did to order the Queen of England to brush his boots. The question was not one of right but of how to make right. The slave master had his way through violence; could he be changed through violence?

"I'd just as soon knock him down as change him," Tommy said vehemently.

"Perhaps you ought to care for him," Remond said. "That is the way of Christ, to love your enemies."

"I'll love him if he treats me like a man. Until then, I'll knock him down to get his attention."

Remond stuck his fork into a piece of meat and held it halfway to his mouth, studying Tommy with a look somewhere between curiosity and irritation. He shifted his glance to Catherine. "Mrs. Nichols, were you ever in slavery?"

"Sir, I certainly was."

"And so you can comment on your son's proposal. What would happen to a slave in Virginia who knocked his master down? Would he gain his attention?"

Catherine was quite astonished by her own reaction. She had enjoyed the displays of eloquence at the morning's meeting. Now her eyes unexpectedly filled with tears. "Excuse me, Mr. Remond. I cannot speak of Virginia, but in Alabama I have some experience. Reverend Garnet reminded us that the slaves are four million, but I doubt forty of them could be found to rebel. If they did they would all be dead by the morning."

She looked at Tommy hard, as though reproving him before he could reprove her. Then she turned back to Remond. "I'm not expecting your moral way, as Mr. Douglass called it, to do any good either. White people don't have morals, in my experience."

"Don't you have hope, then, Mrs. Nichols?"

"Not where Alabama is concerned, Mr. Remond. I'm just glad to be quit of slavery myself."

———

Tommy was furious with his mother. He demanded to know whether she had ever been struck by a master, and when she told him she had the scars to prove it, he demanded to see the proof. She refused the impertinence.

"Well, I don't see how someone who has been beaten can say, 'Let's be kind. Let's love them until they change their minds.'"

"I didn't say that," Catherine replied. "I said that if you strike back, you'll be hanged, or worse. It's got nothing to do with love."

"If an uprising had a chance of success would you support it?"

"It won't have a chance of success. You think these ministers and merchants here at this meeting are going to load up their guns and march south? You think the *slaves* are going to rise up? You don't know anything about it if you think that. The masters would kill them before breakfast and not even lose their appetite."

"You sound like you admire them."

"Good night, boy. I was never so glad as the day I crossed the river. I wanted nothing more in life than to get you away from that country."

"You hate it that much, but you won't say, 'Strike against it.'" Tommy had turned cool toward her, in that maddeningly superior way young men have.

"I just want to be done with it."

"But you can't stop thinking of it, because you have to look at me."

She waited for him to go on, and when he didn't, said, "What do you mean by that?"

"Who was my father?" he asked, hostile and suspicious in his manner.

They were sitting in their room, she in a chair, he on the edge of one bed. Catherine was disgusted and dismayed. "Oh, never mind who your father was. Yes, he was a white man, if it matters. You never saw him. I raised you and made you what you are. You are completely my child in your soul, if that is what is worrying you." Catherine did not want to talk about this. She had determined that she never would. She felt that it was a topic that could have no happy conclusion.

"But tell me who he was."

"I'm not going to tell you. Why should it matter? He was just a boy, no older than you."

"Tell me who he was, Mother."

"Why?"

"I'll find him and kill him for you," he said.

She laughed. "Don't talk nonsense. Why would I want that?"

"The man violated you," he said. "Tell me his name."

"I don't want you to kill him," she said peevishly. "That's nonsense. I want you to grow up and never have to think about him." She stared fiercely, determined to eradicate this curiosity from his mind.

"I can't do that, Mother. Mr. Douglass said the slavers will not be happy until they are welcomed and congratulated in every part of the nation. We must fight them, we cannot ignore them."

"Mr. Douglass does not know everything. There are no slaveholders in New York State. We are quit of those people forever." She refused to talk any more on the subject.

Chapter 19

1848: Douglass Meets Brown

FREDERICK DOUGLASS alighted from the train in Springfield, Massachusetts, and went looking for the home of John Brown. Henry Highland Garnet had recommended they meet, saying in his dramatic voice with his eyebrows raised that Brown was perhaps the only white man in the United States who treated you as his equal. Garnet was not a man to praise just anybody, and Douglass had taken note. When out of the blue he received a note from Brown inviting him to discuss "urgent matters," Douglass decided to stop off on his way from Boston to Rochester.

He had a peculiar interest in possible contributors, having just launched his newspaper, *The North Star*. He needed friends, as Garrison and his tribe were provoked that he had made his declaration of independence by starting a rival to *The Liberator*. Douglass owed a great deal to Garrison, who had taken him from shipyard laborer to international lecturer, but he did not think he owed him fealty. About his personal independence Douglass felt strongly, and he resented any implication that a black man ought not, could not, edit a paper.

Besides, Douglass was a practical man, and the American Antislavery Society, dominated by Garrison, seemed to him increasingly weightless. It spent its energy decrying the ambitions of political abolitionists or jeering the churches for their moral hypocrisy. It had occurred to Douglass, though he had not stated it openly, that someday immoral, compromising politicians might actually *do* something about slavery—and before the millennium.

Brown he knew nothing about. The man had no known association with any of the abolitionist factions. He was some sort of wool agent, and in Douglass's mind that would put him in the better part of town, among the finer houses. Douglass walked to that area directly, figuring that he would find the way.

He could not find the street, however. There was no lack of neatly painted street signs, certainly: Springfield was a tight, clean, modern manufacturing town. Yet he wandered until his face was frozen from the wind. Finally he asked a black ragpicker where he might find the address.

"That be south by the river, my fellow," the man said in a friendly way. "Is that a friend of yours?"

"An acquaintance," Douglass said. "A man named John Brown."

"John Brown? The Ohio man? Are you thinking that John Brown lives in a fine house up here? You don't know John Brown if you're thinking so."

Douglass was mortified. He stiffly thanked the man, then turned to go off.

"You can't go wrong with John Brown," the ragpicker sang out cheerfully to his back. "He's a fine, fearless man."

He found the house in a poor street, only a short distance from the brick warehouses and dreary alleyways that lined the river. It was a wood building, single-storied, gray-painted, close to the street. Mrs. Brown came to the door herself and invited him in without the least indication he was anything out of the ordinary. She might have been letting in the cat, though Douglass doubted she would keep a cat—it would be too fancy a taste for her.

In the parlor sat John Brown. He had a grip like a nutcracker. Close-cropped, coarse, grizzled hair grew low on his forehead and seemed to have its own mind as to pattern—it grew like wheat that has been whipped up by a wind. His body was small, tough, and wiry. Brown might have been a fitter working on the docks.

Brown told one of a number of silent, staring children to bring Mr. Douglass a chair, and the boy did it instantly. The dignified assumption of command impressed Douglass, who had not been raised in a family nor had a great deal of experience raising his own children, as he was so frequently gone on lecture tours. Douglass had been in a great many homes where children were indulged. That evidently was not the case with Mr. John Brown.

"Mr. Douglass," Brown said without bothering to ask about his trip, or to make other pleasantries, "I understand that you have bought your freedom."

For a split second Douglass thought he might be referring to the new press he had purchased to publish *The North Star*, it was so much on his mind. But he quickly realized that Brown spoke literally.

"Yes," he said, feeling his way. "Some friends in England put up the money. I don't admit that under the laws of God anything was owed to Hugh Auld, my master according to the laws of Maryland. But it is pretty difficult to be an advertised lecturer, and impossible to carry on a settled business like a newspaper, when at any moment a slave catcher might come along and claim you as stolen property. For the sake of my wife and children, I did the deed, and I must say that since doing it I feel a great deal more security."

Douglass had been sternly criticized by Henry Wright, among others of the more radical Garrisonians, for rewarding slaveholders with a cash payment. It was an alarming precedent, they said, buying back stolen property from a thief. The criticism had contributed to Douglass's disaffection from the Garrisonians. Had they nothing better to do than patrol the outskirts of abolitionist purity?

"I hold no grudge for your doing it," Brown answered with a peculiar intensity. "I hate to see man stealers get any reward for their transgressions. Any reward at all. But you can be assured that the money will get them no satisfaction. They will wish that they had never seen it, for it will confirm judgment against them on that day. God will hold them accountable for every life they have held captive. Their stolen goods will burn like fire in the last days. Jehovah will break their bones and trample them to dust!"

There was a light in John Brown's steel-gray eyes as he spoke. His fist clenched and unclenched.

"In the meantime," Douglass said in his deep, cool voice, "Hugh Auld was happy to get the money, and I was sorry indeed to give it to him. It might have been useful for a great many things."

"Yes," Brown hissed, "but you will be useful for far more. You may be a Moses to lead your people into the promised land. Brother Douglass, I have no use for the fine-sounding theories on how we ought to behave as opposers of slavery. My theory is to bring down the slave power, to smash them utterly and forever. You may be the useful man for such a cause."

To shift the subject, Douglass asked Brown about himself. With nearly the same snare drum cadence, Brown said that he was a tanner by trade, who had been raised by a God-fearing father in Hudson, Ohio. He had always hated slavery but after Elijah Lovejoy was murdered by a proslavery mob had pledged his life to the cause of the slave. "Right now I am an agent of wool growers in the midwestern states," he said, "bringing some system and justice to men who have been sorely abused by the manufacturers. I hold 600,000 pounds of the finest wool, and no one will give me the honest price. They are determined to break me because I threaten their dishonest gain, but I will hold to the true price." He said quite a lot about the grade of wool and the price.

Douglass spoke of their mutual friends, the ministers Henry Highland Garnet and Jermain Loguen, and mentioned other abolitionists he had seen in Boston. He was hoping to locate where Brown stood among the abolitionist factions, but Brown did not seem interested in this kind of talk. He kept alluding to his loathing of the slaveholder.

They sat at a worn pine table in the kitchen. The children crowded around, two of the littlest ones sharing a chair, three others on a bench. Mrs. Brown served a stew, mostly potatoes, which she poured into battered tin bowls. Brown himself cut wide hunks of brown bread with an oversize, black-handled knife, sawing right on the table. The children ate hungrily and silently. It occurred to Douglass that he might easily have been in a black laborer's home, not only in the lack of amenities, but also in the apparent ease with which he was treated. He spoke to Mary Brown with his usual charm, making her smile with her wide-set eyes but not managing to convince her to speak.

The bowls were cleared off as quickly as they had been poured full. The children disappeared. Mary Brown offered a cup of water, and then took the stack of dishes out back, where he could hear her clattering by the pump. Brown sat quietly and tensely in his chair, like a small cougar.

"You were a slave, Mr. Douglass," he said. "I need not tell you that slavery is war against a people, those chosen by the color of their skins for bondage. The man stealers have by blood enthralled a people. Yet they will be caught in their own snare. The house they have built will fall on their heads. There will be no mercy from the Lord of armies, for they have by their iniquities forfeited their right to live. I know, Mr. Douglass, that you escaped the man stealers by devious means, but the slave has *every* right to seek his freedom by *any* means."

Brown spat out this sermon and then stared fiercely at Douglass, as though he expected a rebuttal. After a minute of silence he slowly pushed back his chair, stood up, and left the kitchen. A moment later he returned carrying a long roll of paper tied with string. Painstakingly he untied the knot, picking at it with his broad, flat fingernails, then rolled the paper out on the table. It was a map of the United States. Brown rustled in a cabinet and came back with a salt shaker and two spoons, which he laid on the corners of the map.

Thoughtfully, slowly Brown ran a bony finger along the Allegheny Mountains. "This is the key to breaking the chain of greed," he said softly. "God has placed in these mountains natural forts, rocks and cliffs and canyons allowing one man to defend against the attacks of a hundred. In these deep forests an army can hide undetected. They can strike and disappear. These mountains form a natural corridor of escape, running from deep in the places of bondage right to the farms and villages of a free country.

"I tell you my plan in utter secrecy. It must not be discussed elsewhere. I do not want to start on a large scale, but with twenty-five handpicked men, men of prudence and valor. We will arm them and supply them, and they can infiltrate the mountains, taking up posts in groups of five, spread over twenty-five miles. From there the most eloquent and persuasive of them will go down to the farms and convince the slaves to escape to them. As some men escape, others will gain courage to join them. The women and children can at an opportune time come north. Men of courage will join the mountain army. There will be a new state there, with a government of freedom ready to assume power at the needful time. Soon the value of a slave will plummet, as so many continually run off, the best and strongest first. The man stealers who regard a black man as an economic property, not as a man, will find that these assets have grown worthless. I will begin an irreversible tide washing away slavery forever. From these mountains it will spread throughout all the slaveholding states."

Brown tapped the map with his workingman's finger and seemed to study it for a moment. "The plan will succeed," he said finally. "All it lacks is men. If I have the men I can get the supplies."

Douglass said that Brown might underestimate the resolve of the slaveholders. "They will get bloodhounds and track you into those mountain forts. No one can hide from a bloodhound."

"Yes," Brown said fiercely, "but chances are that we can whip them, and after they have been whipped the next group will come more slowly."

"You aren't concerned with bloodshed?"

"Without the shedding of blood there is no salvation," Brown said in a low voice. "But I would not cause any more violence than the slaveholder insists on. I do not mean to start a widespread insurrection, to see the man stealers die by the thousands. We would make every effort to capture the slaveholders, and when we captured them we would not kill them but hold them as hostages."

"I still have hope that we can turn the slaveholder by peaceful means, by moral persuasion."

Brown looked up sharply. "That can never be," he said. "It is a delusion to think such men, with their proud hearts and their evil minds, can ever repent. God has given them up. Like the Israelites they can only be restored after their own downfall and captivity.

"Mr. Douglass, I am not entirely averse to bloodshed. If it must be, let it come. It will do a great deal of good for your people. I hear you yourself fought a slave breaker with your bare hands and gained your sense of manhood by it. Yes, that is how it is. Men must fight for their freedom, or they can never have self-respect. I want to arm the slave with guns for that very reason, that he may gain his manhood."

Douglass tried to ask for more information about the plans, such as who was supporting them, who had been recruited. Brown waved him off. "It must be secret," he said. "Only the chosen will know, and even they will not know more than they need."

Douglass then perused the map. "Have you consulted Harriet Tubman?" he asked. "She has been in these mountains many times. I am sure you know of her."

Brown would say nothing, not even to admit that he knew Mrs. Tubman. He stood up, rolled the map away, and painstakingly tied the string around it again. Working the knot with his blunt, worn fingers seemed to take forever. "You have heard my plan," he said when he was done. "I can see that you are not prepared to venture all for it. Perhaps you will think more."

"Yes," Douglass said as he stood. "The plan has a great deal to commend it. I must think of it."

"But say nothing!"

"I can keep a secret."

"I will pray," Brown said in a matter-of-fact voice. "I will pray to the Lord of Hosts, Jehovah, whose plans these are, who knows the chosen for the battle. He must winnow them as he did for Gideon. We need no men lacking valor in the day of reckoning!"

When Douglass went to bed late that night, in a strange home after a long and arduous day, he was surprised to find himself so excited that he could not sleep. It was the old man, he recognized, who affected him so.

Others were weighing political strategy or writing newspaper articles on the three-fifths clause of the Constitution. Brown had moved past argument to action. Douglass wanted to believe that this old, Bible-quoting man would strike to cut out slavery's heart. He wanted to think that brave action would suddenly accomplish in a whirlwind what pamphlets and speeches had been unable to do—the freedom of the slaves. He wanted so much to believe it, he realized, that it affected his judgment.

Chapter 20
1848: Free Soil

THOMAS NICHOLS traveled to Buffalo for the Free Soil convention, not because he was enthusiastic about its potential but because he was discouraged. From the sweltering, soot-stained car he watched the bountiful grain fields of New York, still green but fading into heavy-headed gold. He was alone in the midst of convivial and drunken fellow travelers. A constant traffic of leather-lunged, foul-smelling men rubbed past him. He tried but failed to forget that they aimed for the same destination. The contrast grated on him, the glaring clash between the land of rich and innocent splendor and its brutish inhabitants. And these were supposed to be the best, most moral men!

Repeatedly Nichols thought of the early anniversaries of the American Antislavery Society, with their holy, serious milieu. They had pledged their lives to free the slaves, confident—hopeful, anyway—that it would take two years, three, perhaps five, to convert the nation to the cause of righteousness. What foolishness that had been! And yet, how serious and righteous those who believed it. Now Free Soil promised to be far more realistic, full of plain talk about appealing to the interests of the common man. Was it inevitable that a more practical cause must attract the most compromised men, like these drunkards?

After the old antislavery organization fell apart, Nichols had sided with political abolition, working for the Liberty Party. He had joined committees and contributed to funds that would print Liberty literature. Twice James Birney had been their candidate, and he never won a single electoral vote. The most the party could claim—and some of them did actually proudly claim it—was that they had taken enough New York votes from Henry Clay to swing the state to the Democrats, so the slaveholder James Polk got elected president, admitted Texas to the Union as a new slave state, and went to war with Mexico to gain even more land for slavery. Merely thinking of this was enough to make Nichols's mouth twitch.

Why, then, was he going to Buffalo? Ruth had urged him. Joshua Leavitt, his old comrade at the American Antislavery Society, had twisted his arm. Even Lewis Tappan, who had only recently come over to politics, said he ought to go.

No one could hide any longer the slave power's control of both regular parties. Factions had splintered off—the Barnburning Democrats in New York, and the Conscience Whigs in Massachusetts and Ohio. It was an unsettled time, the political stars realigning. From Cincinnati, Birney's old protégé Salmon Chase had organized the call to Buffalo, to unite rebel factions with the Liberty Party and to seek a more attractive candidate for president. Chase would draw together all who hoped the new West would be free soil. They might not end slavery, but they could prevent its extension—and that would be at least a beginning.

Nichols could make the argument as well as anybody. Yet in his heart of hearts he doubted it. He told himself that he had grown too cynical, but there it was nonetheless. He went to Buffalo leaning backward.

———

Arriving at the train station Nichols was struck by the crowding and the filth. It seemed as though he had come just moments after some catastrophe struck the town—an earthquake, perhaps, which had thrown confused men onto the street and dust into the air. All along the platform men hunkered on their haunches, watching over heaps of luggage. Carrying only his single canvas grip, Nichols picked his way through the station to the street, which was even more congested with men in their rough wool, baggy-kneed suits and wide, sweat-stained straw hats. Some of them clustered and talked, but more of them sat alone and staring, as though they planned to outlast whatever might come by simple stubbornness.

The desk at his hotel was surrounded by a ring of men leaning over the counter, by another ring of men leaning against them, and by a third ring trying to squeeze their way into the second ring. They were all trying to catch the attention of one weary clerk, who looked at them with infinite boredom and checked his listings book with the appearance of complete futility. Nichols surveyed the scene, gathered his fight, then plunged in to swim through the rings of men. Surfacing in front of the desk he insisted that he had a reservation. Reluctantly the clerk glanced at his confirming letter, found his name in the book—Nichols, looking upside down, put out a finger to point the line—and gave him a key.

There was no water for washing in the room, and the bed was unmade from the last inhabitant, but Nichols had no stomach for a protest; he was relieved to have a bed at all.

Nichols was not so lucky when he went out to get supper. Starting with his own hotel he found every dining room with its tables filled and more waiting in line. The air was hot with the odor of men and boiling lard. Crowds milled through the streets, kicking up so much dust that the sky had an orange tinge. He glumly wandered to the docks in time to see a steamer come in from Cleveland, its deck crowded with the white disks of more straw hats. In a park not far from the water a vast meadow of rumpled canvas was laid out, with workers pounding in stakes and making tentative ventures in raising what, he was told by knowing onlookers, would be the largest tent in the world.

"There is too many people to fit into any hall," said a man whose red face was split from top to bottom, sharp-chinned, gap-toothed, adze-nosed, who carried on a continuous commentary from a cane chair he had apparently brought to the site. "Too many people. So we got a tent; it had to be the largest tent to fit in the whole. Three parties come together, the Whigs, the Democrats, the Liberty. More Democrat than any other, because of Van Buren. We New Yorkers love our Little Magician, he is our man. *He'll* put the South in her place. They won't bully *him*."

Remembering how Van Buren had treated the Amistads, thinking of him as an Andrew Jackson man from the start, Nichols wanted to spit. Why, the Dutchman wouldn't even end slavery in the District of Columbia, he had made that clear. What was the use?

He walked on around the margin of the park, stopping to listen to a loud discussion of the Wilmot Proviso—an amendment that had failed in the Senate, guaranteeing that slavery would not be contemplated in the territories gained during the Mexican War. "If you've got slavery you've got niggers," a man in western butternut was saying. "The territories of the West should be reserved for free white men. If you let in slave labor the free man will be driven out. I've been in Tennessee, and the free white man in those hills is the poorest white man you will ever find. It's cheaper to use the blacks. They've got to be kept out of the West, or they'll spoil the whole country."

Another man proclaimed that he saw no harm in blacks as long as they were a small part of the population; he said he had grown up with a Negro family who were hard, steady workers and decent people, but that whenever you put a few such families together their stock declined precipitously. There was a good deal of nodding. Nichols was appalled.

He wandered about the streets until the lamps were lit and the temperature cooled. Back at his hotel the hallway was crowded with men still talking. The temperature was stifling. Doorways were open and through them he saw men, coatless, sitting on beds or squatting down on the floor, listening while one or another declaimed. It was an atmosphere of complete absorption, ripe with politics, just the sort of mass emotion they had always hoped abolition would bring. And yes, it was drunken, stupid, racist.

He climbed the stairs—they, too, had been taken over by a debate, so he had to thread his way among men too full of talk to move—to the third story. Nichols wanted to see any familiar face. He walked the length of the hallway and was on his way back to the stairs when a door opened and he heard a familiar voice. It was Joshua Leavitt, standing in the doorway with his coat over his arm, a tall, straight figure with a long white beard, his eyes sunk deep beneath his brows.

"Nichols!" Leavitt cried in a booming bass voice. "So you are here! I wish I had known, I could have put you on the committee. Have you ever dreamed of so many people? Come in to my room and sit down."

The room was crammed with chairs, most of them occupied by men in their shirtsleeves. They, too, were talking politics in utmost seriousness. Leavitt sat him down and took a seat opposite, their knees almost touching. "What do you think?" he asked, looking with eyes as intent as an eagle's.

Nichols was middle-aged now and far more measured than he had been as a copper-haired, hot-tempered youth. Still he spoke what he felt, and he felt he was watching a generation of care and hope fall into the gutter. "I see no future in it," he said. "These are the wrong men. They have no better principles than those who would send Africans back to Africa. They don't want to help the Negro, they want land. When they say 'free soil' they mean 'free for me.'"

Leavitt, who had a scholar's look, drew himself up to his full height. "Yes, Brother Thomas," he said softly, "there are men such as that here. Many of them have not had the benefit of antislavery instruction. The fact is that a democracy is no church; it accomplishes its work through the power of votes, and those who ally the maximum number of votes may do good. We might stay purer and accomplish nothing, or we might mingle with men of limited morality and sway them to our convictions."

"Fine, but when does the swaying start? I heard Van Buren's name a dozen times," Nichols answered.

He saw by the soft blue of Leavitt's eyes that he had hit something hard. "Don't tell me you are ready to fling away Hale for that man-pleasing sop!" Nichols said. "He won't even end slavery in the District of Columbia! He pledged he would not, even if Congress passed a bill! The man is no more against slavery than he is against summer!"

Leavitt reached out a hand to Nichols's shoulder, as though to quiet him. The hesitancy remained in his eyes. "Brother," he said, and stopped.

"Well, go on, tell me why we should consider the man who wanted to send the Amistads back to slavery. Have you given up everything?"

"No, Brother, but there are negotiations going on. I cannot tell you everything because I am pledged to secrecy."

"Secrecy!" Nichols said.

"I believe secrecy is not an unusual condition in sensitive negotiations," Leavitt said, drawing himself tall.

"Well, go on."

"I can tell you that I have almost a pledge that Van Buren will not oppose a move to rid the District of slavery. And in sum: we have not given up everything. By no means. The Democrats seek our support, they have a candidate who is known and may suit our purposes. I will be frank to tell you that we will not support him unless we have our way with the platform." He paused, as though to consider whether he ought to go on. Then he leaned forward again and put his mouth near Nichols's ear. "I *think*," he said, "that we will have our way. Our way entirely."

Nichols was implored to take in other New Yorkers, so his hotel room grew abundant with groaning and thrashing shapes. He hardly slept but was out the door before the bodies, wrapped in bedding like corpses, could come to life and require him to make conversation.

There were plenty of men already out in the hot morning sun, including some who seemed to have slept in their clothes. On the sidewalk a man in a blue suit had a pailful of boiled eggs, which he sold for a nickel each. Nichols bought two, peeling and eating them as he walked, his teeth crunching on specks of eggshell.

Last night he had determined to go home, to leave this sordid moral swamp and give it up. A dozen times he had gone over Leavitt's conversation, growing angrier each time. The man thought himself a political wizard; he thought he could outbargain the Little Magician and his shifty Jacksonian agents. Leavitt, a minister whose experiences in life were mainly editing religious papers!

Fatalism settled over Nichols, and he thought he would stay to see it out. He bought a newspaper from a little boy pulling a stack in his wagon, then settled in the park by the new and vast tent, to see what the day held.

———

Ten thousand, perhaps twenty thousand men met in the big tent, entertained by a series of rousing political speeches while the real work went on in a Universalist meetinghouse nearby. Five hundred delegates, equally representing Democrats, Whigs, and Liberty men, were to propose a platform and a candidate. Every so often the Committee of Conferees, as the select group was called, would send over someone to breathlessly report on their progress. The vast crowd sweated in the crowded tent, cheering or jeering the speakers as though they were viewing an amusement.

At times Nichols managed to enjoy himself. He heard a good many outstanding orators, including Frederick Douglass. As Douglass had been a Garrison man, Nichols had never heard him before. He was a powerful, funny, sarcastic speaker. He tore to shreds any idea of Negro inferiority, for who could be more urbane, intelligent, and manly than he? Nichols thought hearing Douglass almost worth the trip in itself.

Outside and around the tent gathered every species of vendor and confidence man. When a dull speech was on, Nichols could get up and wander the perimeter, watching rubes from all over the nation get fleeced. For twenty-five cents you could buy ice cream—peach, strawberry, plum. There were lemonade and watermelon. After the first day Nichols went back to his hotel feeling almost happy, and wondered at himself.

It is impossible to be in such a throng and not share the elation. This congregation—so vast that across the tent one could not see a face, only an oval dot—seemed to roll out to infinity, vast as the great democracy. Ninety percent of the delegates were small-town men or farmers, who had never seen a gathering of a thousand. Orators assured them that this was the turning point in the nation, that the new constellation of free men, free labor, free land would create something vast and unprecedented—a land, almost a continent, where a man was unfettered in his mind. They were so many! The obsolete forces of European hierarchy, of privilege and ignorance and feudal darkness, must depart.

Late morning of the second day the conferees announced they had resolutions to bring before the multitude. The day had begun with a promise of heat and now was beyond promise. Moist, stifling air filled the tent. After several time-killing speeches the resolutions were read one by one, offering something to please every faction. They would put an end to slavery's expansion. They called for cheap postage, river and harbor improvements, fair tariffs, and free homesteads in the territories. Each resolution was cheered to the skies, and when the whole package was put as a question, men stood, shouting and waving hats and handkerchiefs and yelling so loud that the sound seemed like solidified thunder. Nichols stood with the others, feeling giddy in spite of himself. He tried shouting and discovered that he could not hear his own voice, no matter how much he pushed. He could not verify that he made any sound at all.

That night he caught up with Leavitt in his hotel room. Henry Stanton was there with him, no longer a young man but corpulent, self-important, too busy for more than a distracted handshake. He said he was on his way out and departed immediately with a sheaf of papers tucked into a large green-cloth valise.

Leavitt was tired, his complexion pasty and his graying hair greasy. Yet he smiled on Nichols and offered some grapes that were half devoured, a partial skeleton in a bowl on the table. "Sit down, Brother Nichols" Leavitt said. "Please." When they were both at ease he grew serious. "We got everything we asked for," he said. "The platform is a Liberty platform."

"I didn't hear anything about the rights of Negroes," Nichols said.

"No, but you must understand that a platform is meant to draw the voters to it. It is not a complete description of the party, only a pledge of action that will win the undecided." Leavitt shifted in his seat, uncomfortable and resentful of having to explain himself. From outside the door came sounds of metal heels clicking down the halls, loud voices declaiming or laughing.

"The key, Brother Thomas, is to stop slavery from expanding. It will surely wither and die, as the slaveholders themselves know, if kept to its current place in worn-out soil. It is a parasite that must grow or die. They know that. That explains the fervor with which they demanded Texas, and now the lands beyond."

"Yes, I know all that," Nichols said. "But when I think of it I don't think only of the institution, I think of the humanity. Might we save the nation from slavery and leave the slaves still broken?"

"I don't follow you."

"There are four millions of slaves. A withered slavery will not free them or educate them, it may not even feed them. Slavery cannot be tossed out like an overripe melon. It must be repented. I heard nothing of repentance today, not a word even that a crime or sin has been committed. I cannot imagine that God himself will permit such a sin to be passed over, as though it were merely an institutional arrangement that we can rearrange at our convenience. Surely there must be repentance."

"Brother Thomas, you cannot think that I have forgotten the meaning of repentance. But a political party cannot be built like a church. Surely you know that."

———————

When Nichols returned to New York City he went directly from the train to Lewis Tappan's office. Tappan suggested that they walk down to the Battery, to avoid interruption. They stopped to watch a ferry come in from New Jersey and stood surrounded by the stream of farmers and traders carrying their wares to market.

"Our friend Leavitt was the one to bring the Dutchman's nomination," Nichols said, not disguising his contempt, "I suppose because Leavitt has the reputation for honesty. He was quite a sight, with the long white beard and black coat. Very hot it was, but he never seemed to perspire. The immense crowd was hushed. A lot of them thought Hale would be nominated, they did not know that our Liberty men had gone over to Van Buren like a dog in heat. Leavitt said he was awed by the occasion, he felt that the Spirit of God was there present, and in that fine preacher's voice he called on them to make the nomination unanimous, as it had been in committee. His voice was trembling. He said, 'The Liberty Party has not died, it is *translated.*'"

"Where was Stanton?" Tappan wanted to know.

"Stanton I heard was a chief architect. He had a letter from Hale that was to be kept private, yet he brought it out at the first moment. He was ready to drop Hale before he got there, I believe. I am afraid our friend Stanton has gone over to a temptation and a snare. He seeks patronage. He barely spoke to me when I saw him in Leavitt's room."

Nichols made no attempt to hide his own depression. "I thought all the long way home of what I could do, Lewis. I see no future for me in that immoral mass. They will abandon anything for votes. They will certainly abandon the black people. They are just as interested in appealing to the Negro haters as to those who hate slavery. They say with a wink, 'We will get rid of slavery in the territories, and get *rid of the Negro too*, and we will get you free land.'"

The crowd from the ferry had dwindled and gone on, leaving only the deckhands and a few stragglers. A farmer had a cart full of cabbages. The day was blue and windy; there were whitecaps out on the bay.

"I think of becoming a preacher, Brother Lewis, or an evangelist."

"Really?" Tappan was surprised. "What makes you think of that? You are rather late in life."

"I have made some money; I do not have to continue at that. I fear for the future, Lewis. You remember how Weld used to talk about the fierce judgment we would face for enslaving our brother? I never could see it so clearly as after this Free Soil convention. This is not the foundation for true reform, Brother Lewis. God cannot honor such greed for position. I almost think that Garrison is right. No reform is better than an alliance with Belial."

"So you think of preaching, in order to . . ."

"What has happened to our movement, Brother Lewis? We were so powerfully charged toward righteousness, and all that is gone. Where have the powerful men of faith gone? They have all abandoned the cause, or retired, or even left the faith. We used to think that nothing could break us or make us turn away. Where are they?"

Tappan, who was a literal man, took the question literally. "Weld, you know, is in New Jersey, digging like a common laborer. He has his own version of religion that is no good to anyone. He says he can't be constrained by creeds or movements or institutions, so he has all the freedom to do little but dig and to accomplish nothing."

"And Birney . . . hasn't he grown skeptical? So I heard."

"I do not think so. I had not heard that. Birney is ill. He fell from a horse and is partly affected in the head, you know. He is weak and can no longer travel. But you must know that."

"I was told by someone who knew him that he questioned the Christian doctrines."

"Perhaps so. But you must remember his accident. His mind is not right. He is not the man that he was."

"And Elizur Wright? Where is he?"

Tappan sighed. "Lost to the cause. And to the church, I believe."

"Stanton is entirely skeptical, or beyond that: he has no more interest in religion, unless he is trying to convince some Christians to support his candidacy. All of Garrison's tribe care only for the wildest notions of religion. As soon as they hear that someone is following an orthodox path they rise up in horror to try to cure him of his folly. Only if someone says that God has revealed through marks on a cypress tree that certain women are spirit messengers do the Garrisonians sit up and take notice."

"Garrison never joined a church in the first place," Tappan said.

"No, but he was one of our number. We must admit that. Is there some fault in our organization or our plan that our best members are lost in tangles of speculation, or lost altogether?"

"Let us walk," Tappan said, and without waiting for agreement set out briskly uptown. Tappan's jaw always worked most freely when his feet were in motion.

"Perhaps," Tappan said after a quarter mile or more of cobblestones had passed under them, "we thought more highly of ourselves than we ought to think. Is it not in the nature of the world that temptations should come? You find many warnings in Scripture not to fall short or to be led astray. Perhaps I never noted them sufficiently. There are so many disappointments on the pathway to eternal light."

"The organized churches have been a bitter disappointment to us all," Nichols said while making a conscious effort to lengthen his stride and keep abreast. Tappan was a short man, but his feet moved as rapidly as a machine loom.

"Yes, and I am sure that many have fallen away because orthodox believers have shown no sign of righteousness. But I think you are making the situation worse than it is. I have thought greatly of this. The Seventy whom we sent out throughout the country as antislavery agents—how many of them are continuing in some way to work for the gospel and for the slave?"

"I do not know."

"Most of them. Nearly all of them, in fact. Several are active in the American Missionary Association. The sun may not shine so brightly as we wish, but it does show through the clouds. Perhaps some of our most prominent leaders have fallen, but the soldiers in the army are still fighting. They have carried the message to a thousand churches. The throng you saw in Buffalo, where do you think they came from?"

"From every state, I believe."

"Yes, and many had been infected with the moral idea of slaveholding. They may not come up to the level we want for them, but they do now think of slavery, which they certainly did not in '33. In how many churches and meetinghouses have our soldiers brought the slave question? In thousands upon thousands. The Congress debates the question, the newspapers write of it, the slaveholders can no longer gag it up. The leaven is in the dough, and even if the question is only put in terms of slavery's expansion or free territories, the moral question will not go away. They will have to think of sin as sin. They will have to think of the Negro."

Nichols thought of this while they tramped north of the financial districts and into the residential sections of the city. What had once been pleasant gardens had become pure Irish. Irish children scrambled everywhere now that the famine was sending them in boatloads. One wondered how a country could absorb them and their popery. They, too, were supporters of slavery.

"You make it sound as though the matter is out of our hands now," Nichols said.

"Perhaps it is. Perhaps it never *was* quite in our hands, but the time was right for the Spirit of God to use us in all boldness. We did not begin this movement, I remind you, because we expected a short road to success. Perhaps some of us did think it would be short, but that was not the reason we began. It was a matter of benevolence—God's call of each man and woman to active benevolence. The slave was then and is now the most needy creature on earth. I think we must go on for the slave. I do not think we are given a choice in the matter."

They left the wooden structures of Ireland and crossed into large, stone houses, many of them new. When Nichols first came to New York, this had been farmland. Now, the only sign of farming was the occasional milk cow these wealthy families kept.

On a wide avenue Nichols heard shouts and turned to see behind him a gorgeous green carriage with footmen behind, driven at top speed. Others on the street had turned to stare. Some shouted at the carriage, as though some famous personage were inside.

To Nichols's surprise he saw a boy pick up a rock and shy it at the carriage. It struck one of the fine roan horses, causing it to flinch. As the carriage rattled past, a coarse blond woman just in front of Nichols shouted after it, "Back to prison, Madame Killer!" and laughed. The carriage, blinds drawn, was soon past them and out of sight, though shouts and stares followed it all the way down the street.

"Who was that?" Nichols asked.

"You don't know her?" Tappan answered. "Madame Restell. She has just been released from prison at Blackwell's Island. They say she has made a million dollars preying on innocent mothers and their children. You can see her notices in any of the newspapers."

"What does she do?"

Tappan cleared his throat and blushed, as though intensely embarrassed. "She will kill the infant of a pregnant woman while it is still in her womb."

Nichols thought of himself as a rough-and-tumble businessman, beyond shock, but he felt himself flush. He remembered that he had heard something of this when he first came to New York, but he had never known it to be a reality. "I suppose it is used for cases of scandal?" he mused.

"Yes," Tappan said, "when men have preyed on women they bring them to Madame Restell."

"If people know what she does, how can she continue?"

"She has a great deal of money. And she offers a cure that many powerful men make use of, I suspect."

"Ah. New York," Nichols said, taking a deep breath and letting it out. "To return to the subject of slavery, Brother Lewis, may we talk of Mr. Weld? I believe we all thought him to be the best man, the noblest man, the most selfless man. When you speak of the leaven in the dough, think how much of that is owing to him and the mobs he faced, the abuse he breasted, the storms he endured, and the sheer exhaustion he must have overcome to speak, speak, speak. I thought . . ." Nichols paused here, surprised at his own emotion. "I thought if I had ever seen an angel it was in the shape of Theodore Weld."

Nichols coughed lightly into his fist, looked around him, and then plunged ahead with his speech. "It troubles me deeply to think that he has given up the cause, given up Christian doctrines, even given up reform. Not to make too much of one man, but did you not feel the same? If someone had said ten years ago that Theodore Weld (and Mrs. Weld, for that matter) would be faithless to the cause, faithless even to Christ, could you have believed it?" Nichols paused, glanced at Tappan, then went on. "I might have thought it possible of almost anyone else. And I wonder, How were we wrong, that our very best man has been lost?"

He finally stopped talking, and for a good one hundred yards they continued speechless up Fifth Avenue, dodging around pedestrians and hand-pulled carts, listening to the fine carriages as well as the drays rumble down the avenue.

Nichols finally glanced up at Tappan to see whether he had anything to say. "Brother Tappan," he asked, "what do you think?"

"He is the saddest case," Tappan said firmly. "A pure lost cause, I think. I was very willing for him to recover from the stress of battle, very patient when he seemed unable to find his place after the movement was split apart by the Boston infidels. Enough, however. I must now say he is a Saul. He started well, but he could not continue to the end.

"I think of Lyman Beecher's comment sometimes, made during the Lane Seminary troubles. At the time I thought Weld was all right and Beecher entirely wrong, and I rather think so still today, but Beecher's comment remained with me: 'You can't touch him with a ten-foot pole,' he said of Weld. He thought Weld very proud, putting himself above every human agency, and now I think there must be some truth to it. Weld always had to be the brilliant leader, while protesting all the time if anyone used his name or wanted to put him on a platform. We could never truly make him part of anything. He wouldn't be tied down. He was so much an individual that he finally moved right off the face of the earth."

Nichols chewed on that. "Perhaps that is the price of genius."

"If so, I want no more geniuses around me. I have asked Mr. Weld in a thousand ways and a thousand times to participate in activities, from the humble to the lofty. The only ones, I believe, that he would accept were those where he was not and could not be implicated in any other person's folly. You couldn't touch him, as Beecher said, with a ten-foot pole."

"It may be," Nichols said dolefully. "One might even say it is the same charge made against us: that we are morally proud, that we cannot live together with other Americans who lack our righteous vision."

"If we were morally proud," Tappan said, "we would stand aloof. In reality we have tried in every way to make our appeal. We go everywhere, try anything. We ask only one thing: for repentance."

"How can our democracy know repentance?" Nichols asked. "As you say, we have made slavery the subject of discussion. That leaven is indeed in the dough. Yet at the Buffalo convention I saw no sign of the leaven of repentance. None."

Tappan, a fastidious man, rarely touched another man, so it was quite uncharacteristic of him that he put out one arm to slap Nichols on the back. "We do what we can," he said. "We do what we can and leave it to the dictates of Providence. Only one thing we cannot do. We must not give up hope, for the sake of the slave."

Book IV
The Beginning of Blood

Chapter 21
1849: Is God Dead?

FREDERICK DOUGLASS, cast loose of Garrison now that he had his own paper, had gone over to politics, supporting Martin Van Buren and the Free Soilers in the 1848 election. He had seen, after all, the impressive sight of fifteen thousand white men cheering him, a black man.

When Van Buren received only ten percent of the popular vote, however, it dampened Douglass's political hopes. The Little Magician's campaign was the most broadly appealing possible, the Free Soilers had compromised wherever possible, and yet they could not muster strength to elect anyone.

What could stop the rapacious mouth of slavery? Douglass lectured at a meeting in Salem, Ohio, showing from the way he talked that John Brown's thinking had been working in his mind. Did not the slave have a right to defend himself? Did not the slave, as a *man*, have every right to choose where and when he should work? If a million slaves refused their masters' orders and made every attempt to escape, how could anyone question their justice? And if they did so, how could slavery endure? Surely violence would follow, the slaveholder's violence, yet already there was violence done every day against the slaves. Might deliverance come only through the shedding of blood? Douglass spoke ambivalently of the appeal of violence, as though testing his own thoughts. Yet there was no doubt toward what he was leaning.

Sojourner Truth was an old black woman, with fissured skin, sunken eyes, and a stare that would make a lion back down. She got up from her seat in the rear of the church. Slowly she made her halting way to the front. She fixed her eyes on Douglass.

"Frederick Douglass," she called out. "Frederick Douglass, is God dead?"

For a moment she stared fiercely at him, then turned away and slowly moved to the back of the church, where she sat down again.

Chapter 22
1850: Fugitive Slaves

WITH EIGHT INCHES of snow on the ground and soft, fat flakes dropping heavily in a windless storm, Catherine Nichols scuttled from the Jamestown general store. Looking down the street through a curtain of snowflakes, she saw a group of men standing with their horses near the hotel. Why were they not inside, or moving toward it? One of them looked intently her way, staring almost.

Inside Mrs. Hatchie's door Catherine dusted the snow off her cloak and set down her basket in a corner. She had taken leave from work in order to buy provisions. Mrs. Hatchie, a bony, horse-faced woman with long, braided hair on top of her head, barely looked up as Catherine returned to her seat and picked up the basted shirt she had left in midstitch.

"There's some strange men in town," Catherine said after a dozen quick turns with the needle.

"What do you say?"

"Five or six men, standing out in the snow, and staring."

"What are they doing?"

"I don't know, ma'am. I was thinking maybe you knew."

Twenty or thirty stitches later: "Maisie!"

A girl of fourteen came in, her face marked by volcanic acne.

"Maisie, go down to the hotel and find out who those men are."

Maisie was gone for a very long time, while the two women's thimbles clicked and two shirts inched into being in their hands. The girl came back tracking in snow with her boots, which Mrs. Hatchie got up to sweep out of doors before it melted. Maisie stood with her hands in front of the stove, warming.

"Well?" her mother asked. "Did you find out? Did you even remember to ask?"

"Yes, Mama, I took a long time because they were already in the hotel to stay." This was a long speech for Maisie, and she had to take a deep breath to go on. "Mama, those men come from Alabama."

"My word. It's near Kentucky, isn't it?"

"Yes, Mama, it is a very long way, farther than Kentucky."

"What are they doing here? I never heard of a reason for men to come here from Kentucky."

"They are from Alabama. That's what Mr. Beacham told me." She hesitated. "I heard them ask if he knew of a black man named Obadiah."

"Who is that?"

"I don't know, he didn't say." Now that Maisie was up and going the words came in a rush. "Mr. Beacham told those men he recalled a Dutchman of that name but no black man. I think Mr. Beacham must be thinking of Onesimus who has the mill at Silver Creek. They call him the Dutchman sometimes."

"I don't think I ever heard of any person named Obadiah."

"It's a Bible name, Mama."

"I know that, girl. You, Catherine, do you know somebody by that name? A black?"

Catherine was so busy with her feverish thoughts she barely had the coolness to respond. "I believe I remember somebody of that name, but he didn't come from here." She was thinking frantically because at her house, something over a mile out of town, she had Obadiah Long and his wife, Harriet, not even in hiding because they believed they were beyond the risk of capture.

The curiosity of foreign visitors was enough that the mayor, who owned the dry goods store, went to call on the men. He found them in the hotel parlor by the fire, steam rising from their sodden clothes. There were five of them, two from Alabama who said they had ridden clear across Pennsylvania to reach Jamestown, and three from Olean, two days' ride east. They were all young, leathery men except a heavy, black-whiskered Alabaman who had gray in his temples and lively black eyes. He said his name was Nichols. The mayor suspected they might be gold prospectors and hinted around about that for a while. Rumors had it there was gold in the south mountains, though nobody had ever seen any proof.

"We saw a nigger woman on the street when we were coming in," the bearded man said. "Pretty unusual to see a black this far north, isn't it?"

"Well, it is, but we have a few of the Africans around here," Mayor Galusha said. "Was she a tall lady, rather thin in the ribs?"

"She wasn't a lady," said the other Alabaman, who was young and blond. "She had cotton hair and a black skin."

"Well, sure," the mayor said, not wanting to offend. "But if she was the one I'm thinking that would be Mrs. Nichols." The Alabamans exchanged a glance and a smile. "Same name as you, now isn't that curious. She does sewing and chores for Mrs. Hatchie. She just came back to town a year ago, after leaving us to go up north to farm. It didn't work out, I understand."

"Would her Christian name be Catherine?" the blond Alabaman asked, a teasing, hungry smile licking at his face.

"Yes, sir, I believe that is her name. Do you want to see her? I could send for her, she's just down at Mrs. Hatchie's," he said.

"No, that's all right. We don't want to disturb Mrs. Hatchie's work."

"She could come after."

"No, no." It was the bearded one, speaking firmly. The Olean men had not said a word yet, they merely watched like dogs observing the table set. "Where does she live? We might just go and see her. We knew each other long ago."

"Oh, out of town on the highway to the lake. A short way, but it's back into the trees. In this weather . . . It would be easier to call her down from Mrs. Hatchie's."

"Do you know does she have some people living with her? I'll be frank with you, mister. We are hunting some escaped slaves, and we think they are here."

The mayor, who had been friendly and solicitous, was suddenly uneasy. He had read in the newspapers that slave catchers would come since the Fugitive Slave Law had passed. There had been a considerable hue and cry about it that he had not credited. He had assumed that the whole affair was only for places near to slavery, or on one of the routes to Canada such as Cleveland.

"We don't have any runaways around here," he said. "The routes for them are farther west. Anyway Mrs. Nichols has been in Jamestown for a dozen years, and she is an honest person."

"Oh, we know Catherine Nichols," said Brady Nichols. "We don't want her. We have been following some runaways, named Long, that we think she is sheltering. Also we think she knows the whereabouts of a tall nigger named Robert Barnes. In New York City he called himself Robert Duncan. We just missed him there. He might be called anything now. We are pretty sure that Obadiah Long came here because Catherine had written to them. She does write, doesn't she?"

"She has got some education somewhere," Mayor Galusha admitted. "Her son was one of the best students at the high school."

The men exchanged smiles again. "You let Africans go into your schools?" the blond one asked scornfully, but the older man cut him off with a shake of his head and turned to the mayor.

"Mister, we need your help or someone's in locating that house."

———————————

Catherine Nichols was by that time running out the lake road toward her home. On hearing who the men were she had sat intensely thinking, then suddenly leaped up from her seat, threw her shirting into the basket, and said she had to get home.

"My dear, finish the shirt at least," Mrs. Hatchie had said, but Catherine had already put on her coat and had her hand on the door.

"I've got to go," she said.

"You've forgotten your provisions!"

"Oh." She pondered the basket of foodstuffs by the door. "No, I had better leave that. I'm sorry, Mrs. Hatchie. I can't help it." And she rushed out, stumbling through the fat snow on the stoop.

On the road she tried to think even while she ran. Sled ruts were obscured under the deep blanket of snow, so she sometimes plunged into gullies, falling to her knees and struggling up again. Never, ever, had she entertained this possibility. Obadiah and Harriet had arrived two weeks ago, carried in a wagon under a tarpaulin by a Quaker farmer. For the first days they had crept around the house, always looking out the windows and into the distance. She had laughed and told them to be at ease, they were far from slavery now.

She walked this mile every day, but running in deep snow was a different matter. Not halfway there her lungs began to burn, as though she had breathed in lye. Exhaustion pulled on her to stop. Her feet lost their skill, and she slewed them forward roughly, artlessly, as though they were not alive but merely strapped to her legs. She could taste the blood in her mouth.

She would have to walk. But when she did walk, she could barely toil forward in the knee-deep drifts. The pace was excruciatingly slow, and she stumbled into a run again. Her throat was aflame, she seemed hardly to inch forward over the long, white fields.

If those men came this way they would see her—the cleared farmland offered no hiding place—and the situation would be lost. Even if she reached the house before them, what could she do? She had no near neighbors, no horse on which they could fly.

She made herself go on. Finally she was within sight of the trees surrounding her house; finally she was plunging over the field that led there; finally she was bursting in the door. Her Tommy sat reading on a stool in the corner; Obadiah, his ancient folded face, small as a walnut, stared at the stove. Harriet, she could tell by the smell of biscuits, was in the back kitchen. The two men looked up at her calmly, then stumbled to their feet. Tommy came and began dusting the snow off her; Obadiah snatched a handkerchief and offered it. She batted snow off her hair, then stopped them from dusting her and told as quickly as she could what had happened in town.

Tommy went to the window and looked out. He had become a tall, lanky, light-skinned Negro with a mustache. The farming in North Elba had made him stronger. "Nobody here yet," he said.

Harriet Long came in from the kitchen, rubbing the flour on her hands. Catherine saw that her eyes were locked on Obadiah's, showing tenderness, not quite fear. "What do you gain by gaping?" Catherine snapped. She had not seen a man and woman look that way toward each other in years, and it provoked her.

"Where could we be sheltered?" Obadiah asked quietly. "Any old building out in the woods? Our tracks would soon be covered, and in this storm we might even keep a fire."

Tommy looked at Catherine inquiringly. "Teacher's?" he asked. He was thinking of his teacher's house in town.

"How would they get there without being seen?"

"In the dark."

"It's hours until dark. What in the meantime?"

There was a long silence, all four of them looking toward each other but not quite at each other. It was a tiny room with a low ceiling, built by one of the first settlers in the area. It felt too close for all of them.

"It would be difficult for Harriet to go without shelter," Obadiah said slowly. "She is not accustomed to this climate."

"No," Catherine said, "but we have no near neighbors. Nobody to trust except in town. And you see there is nowhere to hide you here."

"I am going to load my gun," Tommy said, and got to his knees by the bed, reaching a hand blindly underneath and pulling out an old flintlock. He had bought it in North Elba after conversation with John Brown, the obdurate old man who had homesteaded not far from their farm. Catherine watched Tommy stretch on the floor and begin to clean and load the gun.

She could not imagine him using it with any effect, her son who had never fought even with fists.

Far off in the falling snow, out across the fields, a horse neighed.

———————————

"Perfect," Abner Barnes was saying enthusiastically. He and Brady Nichols were walking their horses side by side, followed by two men from town and the three men from Olean, all single file in their track. "The snow is perfect," Abner told Brady. While the others huddled forward over their mounts, he sat up straight and seemed to overflow with animal spirits. "They'll be sitting snug, they won't hear us coming, and whoopee—we'll have them in the bag."

Brady kept quiet. He would have to bag a runaway, not just think about it, before he felt any cheer. He had never seen snow like this, never dreamed it. He had set off on this trip as a lark, expecting to return home in a month with plenty to brag about. So far they had hardly seen a Negro. And no wonder. If the blacks at home knew how life was in the North they would never wish to escape. Brady hated this place, hated its cold and the vicious temper of its people. This Fugitive Slave Law was no good, he knew now. They might write a law saying that the North must help them recover their lost property, but they could not force them to behave rightly.

"Better be quiet," he told Abner. That was when the horse neighed, and he pulled up, looking inquiringly of the men from town. Had the horse smelled food or another horse? Were they near?

These men were another irritation. The national law required any man to cooperate in catching escaped property, but everybody in Jamestown melted away, had excuses, downright refused to show them the route to Catherine Nichols's. These two drunkards insisted on three dollars each before starting out, with a promise of more. They claimed to know the place but now were staring around them as if they had discovered themselves in China.

"It's back there," one of them said, waving vaguely toward a gray line of trees far off the road.

"No it ain't," the other said.

"It's looking different in the snow," the first one said morosely, losing all his starch when contradicted.

Through the snow Brady scanned a sloping field to their left and thought he saw the characteristic dip and run of a lane leading into some trees. It was hard to know with everything under this abominable snow.

"Is there a house back there?" he asked.

The others stared in the direction he had pointed. "I can't see anything," one of the drunkards from town said. A man from Olean, a man of utter silence, grunted agreement. Brady shielded his eyes and tried to see. The snow was falling more thickly.

"Let's go over and see," he said. "If there's nothing we'll go back."

The others seemed cheered by the latter promise. They followed his horse when he pushed it ahead and off the road into the field.

If there was a lane it was old and overgrown. The horses floundered through brush and snow. One minute they thought it was surely a lane, the next considered it impossible. Finally they entered the darkened shelter of oaks, where the snow was not so deep. Immediately Brady saw the house, a small, log cabin—all white on one side where blowing snow had stuck, black as coal (so it seemed in the light) on the other. He could not see smoke from the chimney; it might be abandoned. Indicating with his hand for the men to circle, he waited for them to move past him, then rode up as noisily as he could and dismounted at the door. There was a small porch. Immediately he saw a set of footprints by the door; the footprints had been half filled by snow. Someone was definitely in, he thought.

He knocked. There were sounds, rattlings, then it slowly opened, and he found himself staring at a tall, young mulatto man holding a rifle pointed at his chest.

"I don't think you belong here," the Negro said.

"No, I don't, but I am looking for some people who don't belong here either."

"Who might that be?"

"A runaway slave named Obadiah Long. An old man."

"If I knew him I wouldn't tell you," Tommy Nichols replied. He was no good at poker. The mention of Obadiah had twitched his face.

"The law says you have to help me. Unless you want to be taken to court." Brady heard sounds in back of the house, but Tommy showed no reaction. He was all intent on facing down Brady.

"Let them take me to court," Tommy said. "I'd like to see them."

Brady saw Abner's blond head appear through a hanging curtain. He studiously watched the black man, looking right at his forehead as he did at cards. Just at the second that Abner made a move and grabbed him, Brady stepped to one side. The gun went off with a deafening sound. The men from Olean rushed in and helped Abner subdue Tommy. They found a piece of India cotton cloth and ripped it into strips, then tied his hands and legs.

"Check the outbuildings," Brady said, whereupon Tommy burst out, "My mother!"

"What about your mother?"

"She is in the backhouse," he said sullenly.

"Do I care?" Abner said. "You think I've never seen a black backside?"

"Be careful," Brady said, and the silent, lean men went outside.

They had just escaped the curtain when Brady heard a clear, deep voice, a woman's voice. "What are you doing in my house?" Brady thought at once it must be Catherine Nichols. She had left Alabama when he was a boy, but people still talked about her. They said she never slept with a black man; she always had a white. They said she was rich and dressed like a New Orleans prostitute. They said she had more education than any white man in the county, excepting James Birney, and she would talk law with him.

In the snowy yard the three men from Olean had their guns out, but they were not pointing them at the woman. She stood glaring at them, wrapped only in a thin robe she clutched tight to her. Brady suffered a letdown. She was no beauty. She was a slim, hard-bitten black woman in indifferent clothing, her eye sockets blue-black. She was not beautiful, but she stood with an attitude that told you she might once have been, or thought she had been.

"Hello," Brady said. "I haven't seen you in a long time. I'm Brady Nichols. I think you have got some of my stolen property here."

"If that gunshot hit anything you will surely be sorry," she said hotly. "You're on my property."

"That was the young man's gun. He didn't hit anything."

"Where is Tommy?"

"Tommy, is it?" he smirked. "I wonder who that would be after. Your Tommy is all right. We tied him up so he wouldn't hurt himself." Then it occurred to him, and he half grinned thinking of it, that Tommy must be his nephew.

One of the drunkards from town was relieving himself against the wall of the cottage. "You stop that," Catherine yelled at him. "This is my house. Use the backhouse like decent people." The man looked up sheepishly and buttoned himself.

"You listen now and shut up," Brady said. He was done being curious and now felt irritated to be standing in the snow talking to a black woman. "I want your friends, the Longs. And I want Robert."

Her face, unlike her son's, did not show any knowledge. "Robert?" she asked. "I don't know a Robert. Some Longs I used to know in Huntsville, but I didn't know they had got away. Good for them. Harriet Long, as I recall, is a free woman."

One of the leathery men came up to Brady and said, "There's only a broken up stable and it's empty, nobody has used it forever. I guess she don't have a horse."

"Circle and look for tracks," Brady said, without taking his eyes off Catherine.

"I did that. If they got away an hour ago the snow would have already covered it up. There's no sign."

Brady seized Catherine's arm and pulled her near, then slapped her, just from spite. To come all this way and get nothing.

"Get in the house," he said. They went in and stood around her son, as though he were the centerpiece exhibit. Tommy had ranted so much that Abner had put a gag in his mouth, and still he was making noise. He lay on his backside, wriggling like a fish in a trap.

"Be quiet, Tommy," his mother said to him. "You're not doing anything."

"I want to know where those runaways are," Brady said. "I give you this chance and this chance only."

"You might be forgetting you are not in Alabama here," she fired back. "They actually have laws here that say you can't slam into someone's house and tie him up."

"The law is on my side," Brady roared. "My side! Property law!"

She didn't say anything, just stared at him with the most venomous disdain and hatred.

"I have lost a Negro," he said. "Actually not my Negro, but I have come on behalf of a property holder. He has been stolen, and I have come to recover stolen property. I will tell you what. The old Negro is worth something, but if I can't find him I will take back a young Negro."

Catherine did not show it, but a panicky fear traveled through her. "You can't do that."

"See if I can. Who believes a black man before a white man?"

"There are white men in town," she said, "who know Tommy. Here in the North they don't approve kidnappers."

"They have to catch up with us to have a say in that," he said. "Tell me where your friends are, if you're smart. You know the Nicholses; you know what people we are. Don't fool with me. And this is Frederick Barnes's son." He nodded to Abner. "As mean as his daddy. You remember Frederick Barnes? Come forth, Catherine." He nudged Tommy with his toe. "Tell, or I take this one." Tommy had begun to writhe and grunt again. Brady looked down to notice this and kicked at him sharply. "Stop that."

She would not tell. She would not even say a word. Brady, in a fury because he could not move her, told the others to truss the boy and tie him across a saddle.

Even after they were gone Catherine still sat, unmoving, on the baggy quilt. Only after some time did she get up and go to the window. She could see the small, black figures of the horses, just struggling onto the road back to Jamestown.

She went to the back of the house, opened the door, looked around to be sure that she was unobserved, then walked to the backhouse. It was a tiny, unpainted structure fifty feet from the house. She knocked on the door.

"They're gone," she said. "With Tommy."

There was a sound of scrambling, the door opened slowly, and first Harriet then Obadiah stepped out blinking.

Outside town the slave catchers stopped and, scraping back a patch of snow, built a fire at the base of a sugar maple. Brady and the three men from Olean proceeded into town, leaving Abner and Tommy by the fire. The drunkards they had paid off and left behind to walk.

A purplish dusk had fallen over the town when they got the wagon from the livery stable and took their bags out a back door of the hotel. The street was turned upside down, brighter on the snow than in the darkening sky. The snow had relented, and deep cold was coming on.

Brady paid the men from Olean and sent them on their way. "I want you to get well out of town before you stop for the night," he said. "People might ask you questions, and I don't want any trouble." Brady watched as they rode out east, their horses only dancing shadows. He would go west.

He had not counted on the difficulties a wagon might have in deep snow, however. After reclaiming Abner and his captive, he followed a westerly road covering steep hills and valleys. The wagon got stuck repeatedly. Soon night fell completely. Now the cold seemed to assert itself like a god, rising against them. When they passed a farmhouse, Brady knocked at the door and asked whether they could sleep in the barn.

Brady had feared the farmer would be a hospitable Westerner who would invite them in to spend the night by his fire, but he was more a New Englander who only grudgingly did his Christian duty and let them stay in the barn, warning them to leave his cows alone and not to build a fire. They fed the horses, cut up a loaf of frozen bread, tied Tommy to a post, and bunked down on a heap of straw.

Tommy had stopped resisting. He looked stunned, like a hog that is hit on its head with the back of an ax just before its throat is cut.

———————

"You go with her," Harriet insisted to Obadiah. "They aren't coming back here." Even in her panic Catherine appreciated Harriet's gesture of confidence. Harriet had always fiercely kept Obadiah from the company of another woman, and in the two weeks since they had appeared at Catherine's door, she had been just the same, never trusting Catherine for a moment with her man.

It was all unknown what could be done, but speed was the one element they could control, and it might—might—make the crucial difference. Catherine found terror breaking into her thoughts, but she would not allow it room. They must not think, they must do. She and Obadiah took turns breaking the snow, following another road than the slave catchers'. When they reached town they went straight to Tommy's old teacher. He was a balding strawberry blond, with moles on his face and hands, and his body gone to seed.

"Let's go to Mayor Galusha," the teacher said, already reaching down beside the door for his boots. He led them behind the house, through the alleyway, and up the back steps of the mayor's brick house.

Mayor Evan Galusha had been nursing a sore feeling all day when he thought over his dealings with the men from the South. Like most Northerners he found black people repellent, but it stuck in his craw that Southerners could come and presume to dictate law. He would not probably have done a thing to defend a black man—this Catherine knew of him—but he was ready at a whistle to defend his town. When the teacher told him what had happened, he stood up immediately in the kitchen where he had welcomed them (he was not ready to have Negroes in his parlor) and began to call his children to take messages to other houses in the village. It took less than fifteen minutes to fill his parlor with a mixed lot of mechanics, carpenters, storekeepers, railroad men. Catherine and Obadiah had nothing to do but watch as the men drank coffee and divided into posses to go out on the roads around Jamestown.

Obadiah stopped the teacher as he waddled rapidly through the kitchen. "Can I go with you, Master?" Obadiah said. "An extra man can be a help."

The teacher stopped and looked at Obadiah. "No," he said finally. "We are all right, and I don't believe the other men would be pleased to ride with a black man. They aren't used to Negroes, you know." And he went on, scurrying out the door.

"Well, you are going to try to *save* a black man," Obadiah said softly to himself.

"They don't care two hoots about Tommy," Catherine explained. "What we hear in New York is not rights of the black man but danger of the slave power. They don't care how white people treat their slaves in Alabama, but they won't have them bringing their peculiar institution north. They get resentful that Alabama planters want to rearrange people's life here to suit their life there. The less black people come into it the better, from their point of view."

"Well," said Obadiah after a pause to think, "I don't care too much what they are thinking, so long as they are doing."

———————

Abner woke up so cold his entire concentration focused on wrapping himself tighter in his blanket. He rolled, squirmed, and pulled, trying to make it impossibly longer, warmer. Only after several minutes of blurry, frigid misery did he begin to think of the lantern light that had broken his sleep. He seemed to have felt the warm, yellow beam. Had someone shined a light over him? Was someone here? Or had he only dreamed it?

Abner listened and heard shards of conversation. He needed only seconds to roll over and shake Brady out of sleep, whispering in his ear to be quiet. Brady turned onto his hands and knees, stopped for a moment to listen, then got to his feet. He tiptoed to the barn door and put one eye up to a crack by the doorpost.

"Several men," Brady said in Abner's ear.

They waited in silence interminably. Abner began to tremble from the cold. He stared in the darkness, trying to remember the lay of the barn, hoping to see a way of escape. Surely there was a back door. His eyes fell on the shadow of the black man they had captured. He lay quite still, a dark lump, breathing slowly and audibly. Abner's impulse was to kick at him, the source of this trouble. He did so, the black man gave a sharp grunt and yell, and immediately, before Brady even turned on him, Abner knew he had done something terribly stupid.

Immediately they heard hands on the barn door, pushing against it. "Is somebody in there?"

The black man made all the muffled noise he could, even though Abner kicked him again, harder, in the buttocks.

"Let us in," a voice said. The door was barred.

"What do you want?" Brady yelled.

"We're looking for some men that kidnapped a Negro," the voice said.

Tommy squirmed and made strangled grunts.

"Who is that? Let us in. We want to look around."

"We've got a Negro in here," Brady said, "but he's a runaway. We are on our way back to take him to his proper home."

"That's fine, then, we just want to see him. The Negro we want is a local."

"That's not what we've got here. This one is an Alabama Negro," Brady said. As he said it he pulled Abner's head to him with both hands, put hot breath against Abner's ear, and said, "Let's get out of here. Out the back."

Brady moved in the darkness to the horses' stall, took down a bridle from the wall, and began putting it on his horse. Abner started in on another horse. They were both expert, their hands finding the tackle in the dark as easily as a man may put on his trousers when awakened at midnight. The men outside yelled insistently for them to open. Brady would shout back occasionally, keeping them busy.

"What about the nigger?" Abner whispered.

"We'll leave him," Brady hissed. "You don't want to end up in a Yankee court, now do you?"

They led the horses to the rear of the barn. A low, narrow door, not intended for horses, not often used, opened toward the yard on the side of the farmhouse. If they could reach the shadow of the house they might go undetected and get clean away. Brady began to pull up the latch, when he thought of something.

He went back and rummaged in the wagon again. Taking out a lantern, he sniffed it and spilled its oil onto the straw they had slept on. Then he took a lucifer from the oilskin pouch in his inner coat pocket. Its yellow explosion filled the barn with light. Brady knelt and carefully lit the straw and oil. Flames licked up immediately. The Negro, seeing the flame, began to squirm and cry out anew, fighting against his cords like a man possessed.

Taking his pistol in hand, Brady slowly opened the door and began creeping outward with his horse. He hoped the fire would distract them.

The fools evidently had not thought to cover the rear of the barn. Or perhaps there were not enough of them. For a moment Brady regretted running. What if there were only three men? They could fight them and escape with the wagon and the slave. But he shook off the idea. There was nothing in the barn worth such a risk.

Abner's horse balked at the door. Brady could see it clearly silhouetted against the hot, spreading light inside. Abner pulled hard, the horse reared, and Abner skillfully timed its descent to pull with all his might just before the horse's feet struck the ground. The horse staggered, got its head through, and seeing no fire outside, followed Abner outside. It was impossible to see anything in the darkness because the rectangle of the doorway was now so bright.

Then loud enough to wake the dead, there was a deafening slap of thunder. Brady saw the gun's explosion white-yellow from the corner of one eye. Quickly, he was onto his horse, digging his heels into its side. He pointed his pistol vaguely in the direction of the shot, pulled the trigger, and felt the explosion in his hand. The horse shied. He kicked it into a canter and in a moment was shielded by the side of the farmer's house.

Looking over his shoulder he saw Abner's silhouette just behind him. Brady led the way around the corner of the house, along the back—his horse kicked over a pail that went clattering across the snow—and then turned the corner again. Ahead was the road. He had thought of circling off into the fields, but now he decided: he would run for it. He spurred the horse hard, leaned down over its neck, felt its body hunch up and leap forward. They came clear of the house, and Brady ventured a glance to the barn. Flames had leaped up to an upper loft—it would all go. He did not see his pursuers, only a sled with a team of mules. Then he, and Abner behind him, were on the highway and gone, plunging through snow.

They brought in Tommy, wrapped in a blanket and smelling of smoke. When Catherine held him to her she saw the hairs on the back of his head were singed. She closed her eyes tight and could see the flames around him. "I'm all right, Mama," he said repeatedly as she made over him.

Characteristically, she did not tell him what she had suffered. She quickly turned to justice. "Did they get those men?" she asked.

"They got away." Tommy wanted out of her grasp. Hunched over by the stove, he explained how they had lit the barn on fire and run away, leaving their wagon and him to burn. "Mr. Oden got a shot at them, and thought he might have hit them, but we didn't see any blood. Mr. Oden pulled me out with the roof coming down on my head. Praise God, he has delivered me from the fiery furnace today!" Now that he was talking, Tommy seemed near to tears. He got up, staggered slightly, and slumped down into a chair at the kitchen table.

The mayor's cook made coffee and eggs for the whole posse, who were full of the story. What horrible screams the horses and mules had made! They had chased the slavers for a mile but gave it up as pointless.

Another posse arrived, having gone around the lake and found nothing. They had to hear the full story. The smell of wet wool and coffee and wood smoke mingled in the moist, warm air. Tommy told his part of the story whenever he could get a word in edgewise. Sometime in the third or fourth repetition he was surprised, looking out the window, to see a pale halo on the eastern horizon. They had survived the night.

Some went home to bed, but other men of the town—merchants nobody had thought to summon, or men who had declined to go out on a cold night to rescue a black man—kept arriving to hear the story.

Mayor Galusha came over to the doorway where Obadiah stood, took his hand, and pledged that the town of Jamestown would protect him or any man from these raiding slave catchers. "You are most welcome here," he said grandly. Later on the newspaper editor, a Mr. Sommers, came and took down the story. Tommy proudly showed him his sizzled hair and the rope burns on his wrists. The mayor repeated his pledge.

Then the teacher hitched up his wagon to take them home. Despite the sun, which had taken over the sky completely, they were bitterly cold in the open. Still it seemed a relief to be in the quiet open air, with only the crunch of wheels and hooves on the crusting snow to compete with their voices. From far away they saw a plume of smoke. That would be Harriet's fire. When they saw it, Catherine felt suddenly ashamed that she had not sent word to her. All this time she had been waiting in helpless shame and fear, having no idea why they would be so late in coming.

"Won't she be surprised," Tommy said. "Mr. Long, you can stay! You heard Mayor Galusha. He guaranteed protection!"

Obadiah gave a long sigh. "I don't know what, Tommy, but I have never thought to hear a white man talk like that."

"It is a remarkable thing," Catherine said. "They never thought anything of us before this law. Now they say they will fight for us."

Chapter 23
1851: The Christian Antislavery Convention

LEWIS TAPPAN and Thomas Nichols traveled together to Chicago, three days on the rails with a day's stopover in Pittsburgh to rest on the Sabbath. Nichols tremendously enjoyed the days of languid conversation on the train, for Tappan saw everything through a relentless optimism, good medicine for Nichols's despondency. Tappan had retired from his Mercantile Agency now, but he was more active than ever, trying to persuade churches and philanthropic agencies to break off relations with slaveholders. He also visited black churches and Sunday schools, offered tracts to sailors on the New York docks, conducted services in prison, wrote letters and articles by the dozen and, in sum, seemed never to pause.

Tappan must have made a small fortune, yet he traveled frugally, staying in small boardinghouses rather than the grand hotels that had been thrown up in every city the railroads visited. In Pittsburgh they were forced to share a room with two young colporteurs representing Harper and Brothers. Rather than resenting the crowding, Tappan seemed pleased that he had negotiated a lower rate on the room. He plunged into conversation with the young men, asking about the rural villages they visited, particularly what kinds of books farmers and tradesmen purchased. He asked a hundred questions about people's sentiments on slavery.

"I was surprised that you were even reading Mrs. Stowe's story," Nichols said to Tappan in their car the next day, as it rumbled out of Pittsburgh. Tappan had recommended to their roommates the new fiction being serialized in the *National Era.* "I did not think that you were a reader of frivolous fictions."

"Ordinarily I am not. Mr. Bailey suggested that I read the first numbers, which he said were more true than newspaper reporting. I find to my astonishment that it is so. Bailey writes me that there is even more remarkable drama to come, in which Mrs. Stowe may manage to help her readers feel real sympathy for the slave. I was surprised to find Mrs. Stowe such a strong narrator. Harriet was always a quiet little mouse on the few times I saw her with her family."

"Well, who wouldn't be quiet growing up in *that* family?"

"Yes. Her brother Henry is making a loud noise in Brooklyn, isn't he?" Henry Ward Beecher had become the most famous preacher in New York, and he was actively antislavery. The whole Beecher family had turned out better than expected, considering the father's equivocations at Lane Seminary.

Nichols and Tappan agreed with each other that the Fugitive Slave Law had awakened many. The newspapers were full of narrow escapes, heroic rescues, tragic remandings. For the first time in American history black people were cast as active heroes in a moral drama, rather than as troublesome, ignorant obstacles in a moral riddle.

"You know, people who never thought twice about slavery when it was done to John in Louisiana, have had to think about it a good deal more when it is done to Old Ned on Haverhill Green," Nichols said. He told Tappan about the reactions other businessmen had made when his brother Brady came looking for the runaway slave Robert. "They were very curious about my feelings, you know, because they knew me as an abolitionist, yet this was my brother, too. A lot of them did not like Robert, because he was a Negro, and they liked it even less that he did well at his business. But when my brother came knocking on their door and demanding that they hand him over, they felt a little more sympathy for Robert, I think. I don't believe Brady found them very cooperative."

"That was last year, wasn't it?" Tappan asked. "Where is the man now? Still in hiding?"

"Robert Duncan? He has gone to Canada. He felt it was unsafe to stay in New York. I encouraged him to go. He has no family here, for they were all left behind in Alabama." Nichols did not mention it, but he had given Robert money for the move. He was just as glad to have him gone away, taking with him any revelations of Nichols's past.

They talked of Garrison. Tappan said that he had actually hedged his nonviolence, allowing that true abolitionists would defend the slave with their lives.

"Of course he has always said that it is absurd to hold the slave to a different standard of morality from our forefathers'," Nichols said. "If Washington was right to rebel against King George, the poor beaten slave is surely right to rebel against the lash. Garrison has often said that."

"Well, yes, but he never admitted that Washington was right. When he says that abolitionists must defend the slave with their lives, he seems to encourage action that will surely lead to bloodshed."

Nichols smiled with a catlike grin. "But he is too good to say so. Garrison has been so consistently pure that I can almost predict he will continue to find himself to be so. What do you think—will he like our Christian convention?"

"The man still spends more time assassinating Christians and assaulting the Constitution than he does attacking slaveholders," Tappan said through tight lips, with a little shake of his head. "Do you still read him? He will be sure to find our convention fatally compromised. 'We find,' he will say, 'sectarians too often more loyal to their creeds than to the rights of their colored neighbors.' He will say that we are too delicate to assault those who, by his lights, coddle the slaveholder. In short, he will charge that we are not Garrisonians."

"True enough," Nichols said, not wanting to stir up Tappan on this subject.

The train had by now reached the softly rolling green on the border of

Ohio. Nichols looked out the window to observe a thick flock of sheep herded by two small, barefoot boys. Two or three miles across the fields a dark line of wood, abrupt and solid as a storm cloud, ran along the brow of a ridge. Nichols rarely left the city—he was an urban creature through and through now, with an expanding waist and legs that hardly knew a horse's flanks—but whenever he saw country like this he felt some deep drawing from his innards. Old men, he knew, often talked nostalgically about their boyhoods.

"Incidentally," Tappan said, "we are to hear from a black man who shares your name. Thomas Nichols. Have you heard of him?"

Thomas shook his head, no.

"He is a young Oberlin student who was nearly kidnapped and taken into slavery, but some ordinary townspeople, not even abolitionists, rescued him and drove the kidnappers off. It happened in the western part of New York, late last year. I only remember the case because for an instant I thought it was you who would speak, when I first saw the name."

"Well, you can rest assured it is not me," Nichols said, making light. "I have not been mistaken for a black man in some time. My skin is quite pale in the first place, and nowadays I rarely get out of my office."

The Christian Antislavery Convention was plagued by mosquitoes, which swarmed out of the dank swamps along Lake Michigan, clouding the heavy air. The delegates found some relief on the lakefront, where a series of long piers extended from the mucky shore into the cold blue water, and where on the first two nights a slight breeze troubled the attacking host. In the daytime, however, delegates were bottled up in a hot church, 250 men and women from almost every free state in the Union, breathing together the rank miasma with its scent of rotting scum, fanning away the insects that keened a high song around their ears.

For all that, the atmosphere was invigorated. So many of the finest abolitionists were present, well dressed, splendid, sober-minded people: men with their high silk hats gripped firmly in two hands as they bobbed their heads pleasantly in conversation; women sweeping graciously along in full, blossoming skirts; black people, well dressed and sweet smelling, mingling politely. Charles Finney sat on the platform, seeming oblivious to the eyes that studied his own great, staring orbs. He was still slender and angular, with poking knees and awkward elbows. He had grown a thin beard, and his hair hung to his collar.

"Congratulations, Mr. President," Nichols said with a friendly grin when they shook hands. Finney looked blank. "You have been named president of Oberlin, I understand," Nichols continued.

"Oh." Finney seemed to just remember. "I have been in England, so I scarcely know what is going on." Finney fixed his stare on Nichols. "And you, Mr. Nichols, I have not seen you in so many years. How have you carried on the cause that Christ has given to us? Have you conquered over sin?" Nichols began to stammer out an answer, but before he got to it, another man seized Finney's arm and took him away. Nichols was left marveling that Finney could still instantly terrorize his soul as though he were a child.

A hand clapped his shoulder, and he turned to find a tall, handsome face in a fine silk hat. He was some time remembering Jonathan Blanchard, whom he had not seen since the famous meetings of the Seventy in New York City. Then Blanchard had been threadbare and poor, a theological student turned into a fire-eating antislavery agent, but now he was resplendent in a well-made frock coat. He informed Nichols that he had been named president of Knox College in Illinois.

So it went. Many of Nichols's old friends were now ministers in respectable churches; a few were merchants or college professors. Their respectability struck Nichols powerfully, and not altogether happily. He himself had chosen a conservative line in business, had made money, had not spent himself in the cause of Christ as he might have, but he had always taken some pleasure in participating in the disreputable cause of abolition, abhorred by men of good standing. Now the cause had gained standing, as distrust of the slave power had spread through the Yankee states. The wild men did not seem so wild.

On the second afternoon, the black Thomas Nichols was called to the platform. Nichols watched closely, broodingly, from the back of the sanctuary. He could not see the man closely, only that he was thin as a nail and light-skinned. He had a light, youthful voice and spoke with considerable elegance of style, his sardonic wit reminding faintly of Frederick Douglass. "Oh, how wicked of the Negro to steal! To plunder from innocent Southern men and women the very source of their welfare! To rob plantations of the labor which enables the slaveholder to drink French brandy and smoke cigars from Havana! To take—oh, shame!—the very bodies treated so tenderly by their Southern owners! Think of it, dear people, how very evil—that the Negro should steal himself!"

With considerable relish the young man told of his capture and deliverance, describing his captors as *"gentlemen,* in the way they commonly describe gentlemen in the Southern states, as those who perform cannibalism with knife and fork and napkin, or practice barbarous acts while wearing excellent clothes and quoting Shakespeare."

It was not the man's ability with words that kept Nichols fastened on his distant figure. Nichols's imagination was running full of remembered words of Catherine Nichols. He thought he could hear her voice, like a reverberation behind the young man's swaggering cadence and tone. Did he dream it? It had been, after all, nearly thirty years since he had heard the woman. Surely all he heard were the tones of Southern Negroes. Nichols summoned all the reasons for dismissing the vocal resemblance between this man and a woman who, for all he knew, could be dead, but while he was listening the conviction was irresistible that a direct line ran from this voice to the young, lithe dark woman he remembered.

He had previously figured that Catherine's son, if he lived, would be in his middle twenties. This man who bore his name was surely in about that range.

When the meeting was over, the heat seemed to close heavily around Nichols's head. He avoided contact with anybody but walked out alone through the streets until he came to the lake. Sitting on a stack of lumber he watched the slow swells rise and fall on the pilings of the pier.

What ran up the back of his neck was fear, the elementary reformer's fear that he will be discovered to be a sham and hoisted to ignominy by his own principles. He ought to go and ask the man. He would quickly know the truth from the answer to a few innocent questions, such as where the man had been born. He ought to ask simply to set his mind at ease. The name was common enough, and he had no other real indication that this Thomas Nichols might be related to him. He did not even know what the woman had called her son.

What if it was his son? What then? What would he do? What would his responsibilities be? What if Garrison or his allies got hold of the facts and publicized them? Surely they would make sport of their enemy.

Not far from his mind was the fear of revealing to Ruth the life he had lived so long ago, a life long gone except that he had renewed it year by year in keeping the secret. If only he had told her long ago, then it would be an old and dead former life. Now if she knew she would surely ask why he had never told her. How had he lived a false life for so many years? He could imagine the way her lips would purse open and closed as she took in the news. It was impossible, simply impossible, to think it.

Eventually he took his supper with the rest of the reformers, who were staying together in one of the raw-timbered hotels just south of the Chicago River, rough-sawn structures that jutted over the street. The meal was crowded and uproarious.

"Are you ill?" Lewis Tappan asked him abruptly, looking up from a plate of potatoes and pot liquor. "You are pale. A fever I suppose. The fevers rise out of this swamp. The air is not good."

"I have no fever yet," Nichols said vaguely. "I think I must go to bed."

He saw that the best thing would be to let the matter pass. For twenty-five years life had gone on smoothly, and there was no reason to change that. It seemed very unlikely that this Thomas Nichols was any kin to him. Regardless, the young man was doing well without encountering a long-lost and very awkward relation. Nichols thought this out over breakfast, facing a fresh day after a heavy, overnight rain had cooled the air. He felt a renewed appetite and ate two large bowls of corn mush with cream. He had only to proceed as usual, and the four days of conventioneering would quickly pass. Very likely he would have no call to meet the young Thomas Nichols.

He took his time getting to the morning meeting, arriving after the first speech had begun and taking a seat near the back. Only slowly did he gather from the speaker's cues what motion was being debated. It had to do with the Baptist Mission Society and whether it had sufficiently condemned slavery as sin.

Nichols felt someone slide and rustle into the pew directly behind him. He did not glance to see who it might be, but he was suddenly again unable to attend to the speaker. Nichols remembered what he and his brothers had believed when they were boys attending church: that if you stared hard enough at the back of someone's head, that person would have to turn. He felt surely someone was staring that way at him. Of course it was just his nerves. He had still not entirely recovered from yesterday's shock.

Then a hand touched his shoulder. He turned and looked into the face of a black woman, a severe, thin face with wrinkled eyes and standout neck cords. The woman's hair was pulled back and covered over with an elaborate hat.

"Tommy," the woman said cordially. "Tommy Nichols."

"Do I know you, ma'am?"

A hard, skeptical glimmer of a smile passed over her face and disappeared beneath its surface. "You did. You did, Tommy Nichols, a very long time ago. And here you are, and here I am. I always wondered if we might meet again someday."

"Excuse me, ma'am, where did we meet?"

"Stop it," she said, annoyed. "You know who I am. I saw you watching Tommy yesterday."

He could not say anything. He stared at her.

"I remember the day you left Triana," she said. "All full of plans to be the great man and come back to rule the world, or Alabama at least. It looks like you did pretty well, but you never came back."

He stared at her for a moment longer, then all at once gave up his pretense. "I went back once," he admitted, with a strong sense of sliding heavily into the unknown. "After you had gone. But I found an abolitionist couldn't be tolerated."

"Sooner you than me," she said.

Nichols was suddenly afraid of the sight they made, a black woman and he talking while the meeting went on. "We must talk later," he said. "This is not the time."

"We could go out now," Catherine said.

"No, no, that would not do. Sometime private."

Again a glimmer of laughter slid across her face. "At our time of life, a man and a woman don't need privacy. We can talk on the middle of Madison Street."

Nichols glanced around. "We can meet tonight. After nine o'clock. I will meet you in the front of my hotel, on Water Street."

"Why not inside?"

"It will be more comfortable outside, for any colored person."

She laughed silently, opening her mouth to show her teeth, still good. "All right," she said. She spoke no more, though Nichols continued to feel her eyes on the back of his head. When the speech was over, and he could decently move about, Nichols got up without a backward glance and went out of the church.

———————————

Though she had laughed, Catherine's anger ground at her. These people professed to love the slave, and yet they could not contemplate the meeting of a black woman with a white man. The man knew that, undoubtedly. He would know the limits of the white man's liberality. She had never yet met a white man who was true, or a white woman either.

Her son, meanwhile, swirled before her. He had the happy, bustling appearance of someone who has found his milieu. All day people stopped him to congratulate him, to shake hands and inquire about his studies, to ask whether he was available to come to other cities and tell of his experiences. He loved the acclaim from respectable people. Catherine said nothing to him about his father.

That night when it was time to meet the man, she left Tommy in the lobby of their hotel, a seedy place for colored people. Tommy was seated in the lobby with a half dozen of the men, preachers or businessmen, talking energetically of the need for the Negro to be industrious. Catherine laughed to herself when she was out the door. He was ludicrous, a boy still at twenty-five, she thought, but she was extremely proud of him, of his learning, of the way he could speak to such people. Of course he could give a speech on industry, having never stuck at a job in his life.

Puffs of wind had blown up from the south, and a drizzle had begun spitting down. The energy of Chicago was marvelous to her. *In this city*, she thought, *you don't have to be out of cover ever, for there are tops to the sidewalks.* She enjoyed the short walk to the hotel, through streets still clogged with traffic despite the hour and the mist. Wagons and carriages and carts surged along like boats in a river of hurrying people.

She was surprised to discover that Nichols stayed in a small, three-story wooden hotel just better than a boardinghouse and not much different from the place where she and her son put up. She hesitated at the door, thinking to march in and request him at the desk. But he was waiting on the veranda, almost hidden in the dusk. He called her, then immediately set out down the front steps.

"Where are you going?" she asked from just behind him. "It is raining."

"We can't stay here."

"Why not? They don't allow coloreds on the veranda?"

"I would like something more private."

He was halfway down the steps. The light from the hotel's porch lanterns was on him, and Catherine saw under the paunchy, buttoned-up exterior that he was the same boy who had once introduced her to the world. He still had the pale complexion, the same way of holding himself high. For a moment she felt almost tender to him.

"Please come," he said tightly. "I can't talk with you here."

She gave in—why not?—and walked down the stairs. He did not offer his arm but walked quickly, a step apart from her, to the street. Only when he was there did he put out a hand to sample the rain.

"What do you want?" he asked her, and she heard with astonishment that he sounded impatient. "Will this take long?"

"Mr. Nichols, you said to meet here, not I. I have nothing to communicate. I thought it would be interesting to talk together after a great many years."

"Yes," he said. He took out his watch and looked at it. "Yes, well, I didn't expect the rain. I thought we could walk."

"I don't mind."

"No, but it may increase."

"That's all right. I've seen rain." Why did she say this, why not simply leave? But she had come this far.

They walked but had not gone far before the rain did begin to fall in plump drops. She had her umbrella and invited Thomas to share it with her. He did but evidently did not like the arm-to-arm, hip-to-hip proximity. He stopped under a greengrocer's awning.

"Let us go to the church," he said suddenly.

"It will be quite dark inside." She had no great desire to sit inside a church on a dark night.

"I have some matches," he said.

They found the great door unlocked. Thomas was a few minutes lighting one of the lamps and finding two chairs in the front narthex. He sat down and looked at her as though *she* should direct the conversation, and by that time she was out of the mood to do anything for him.

"I'm sure you think I'm a fool," he said at last.

"It is hard to know what to think," Catherine said. "This is the strangest business. You would think we were planning to blow up the bank."

"I never thought about the rain," he said.

"We could have talked in a coffeehouse or somewhere."

Thomas glanced at her for a moment before returning his gaze to the high, dark spaces where the lamp did not penetrate. She could never understand what a reputation meant, he reminded himself. His fear would be quite beyond her.

"You go by Nichols?" he asked.

"Yes."

"Mrs. Nichols, I apologize, but I do not want my past life known. It was before my salvation. Even my wife does not know, and I do not want her to have to suffer for it. I do not want my children to know." He said it firmly.

"All right," she said. "I wasn't going to tell anybody. I have no fond memories of my life as your concubine."

The word almost cut him in two. He looked at her sharply, appealed to her with his eyes, and saw that he could expect no help.

Despite the irrational terror rising up like a scream between his ears, he went on. He must complete his business. "I want to give you an address," he said. He pulled a piece of paper out of his pocket. "It is an address for Robert Duncan. Robert Barnes, when you knew him in Huntsville a long time ago. He is in Canada now. I know he will want to see you."

"Who is this Robert?" she asked skeptically, imperiously.

"The Robert who was Frederick Barnes's slave," he said. "A tall, thin man with very dark skin. Surely you remember him? He has asked me about you. He asks anybody. I never thought I would be able to bring you two together."

"Robert," she said, remembering the figure. "That man is asking about me? How did he find you?"

"After he ran away Mr. Birney found him at his father's estate in Kentucky. It was purely by chance, I believe. Mr. Birney smuggled him to New York, and, knowing that I was from Alabama, called on me. I was able to help him establish his business. Robert asked me about you right off."

"Robert," she said, as though speaking a foreign name. She was unmistakably intrigued. "How has he done this long time?"

"He has done very well. But when the slave catching increased last year he decided to move on to Ontario. He has written me from there. He has settled in and continued his trade."

The sweet, long-off dream of marriage flickered in her mind. Once Robert had asked her, had he not? Or he had wanted to, and she had put him off. She could not quite remember. It had been a very long time since she had thought of such things. Everything had been Tommy.

"I thank you," she said, putting the paper into a pocket of her dress.

"Is there an address where he can write to you?"

She thought of it for a moment. There was no harm that she could see. "He can write me at Jamestown, New York."

"He will be glad to know that," Thomas said. He sat still for a few minutes, then got up from his chair. "Your son made a fine address yesterday," he said.

"He is *your* son." She was angry again, but not quite so angry as before. Nevertheless, her answer seemed to deflate Nichols. What, she wondered, had he thought? Had he been in any doubt about the boy?

"My son," Thomas said. "Yes. Does he know?"

"No."

"Will you tell him?"

"Why would I tell him? He doesn't need to know of a father who can't even talk to his mother on a Chicago street."

Thomas took the rebuke. He was as proud as anyone, but he had greater things in mind than the comments of this woman. "You are quite right," he said. "It will do him no good. It will do no one any good to know our history. It happened long ago, and there I hope we can leave it. God has passed over all that, I hope."

He sat down again, and for the first time looked steadily at Catherine. "Mrs. Nichols, I am not the boy I was when we knew each other. I am a man who carries a heavy load of responsibility. I think you see what I want. I want to leave this past quite buried. I do not want to give the enemy opportunity. My question of you is, What do you want?"

"You don't even want to meet him?" she asked.

"Who?"

"Tommy," she said. "You're not wanting to see him?"

"Not at the cost of opening up the past. I have seen enough to know that he is a fine young man."

"All right," she said, standing up slowly.

"If you have any material needs . . ."

She flared up. "I don't want anything. Let's go now."

Chapter 24
1853: Father and Son

THOMAS NICHOLS smelled the letter as soon as he stepped into the dark foyer of his home. A thin reek of perfume stained the air.

"Good evening, Mr. Nichols," said Elizabeth, a plump, huge-eyed girl in a white pinafore, taking his hat and coat. "A cold evening?"

Already he was looking toward the mail shelf, careful to move languorously, to show no hurry. Riffling through several letters he found it: a sealed sheet on heavy linen paper, the handwriting neat and schoolboyish except for long, showy tails sprouting from each word. Nichols had studied this peculiar handwriting considerably, searching for clues to the personality behind it. He looked carelessly through the other letters, then tossed them all onto his desk as he passed it in the hallway on the way to the kitchen.

"Good evening, Mrs. Nichols," he said to Ruth, who was perspiring heavily in the warm and damp atmosphere, thick with the gluey smell of boiled meat. She would not keep a cook. Nichols only barely persuaded her to keep a girl.

"Good evening, Mr. Nichols," she said with a smile, pushing back the hair from her forehead. "A fine day?"

"All right," he said. The firm was a healthy trade but by now predictable. He envied Lewis Tappan, who could spend all his hours on causes. But the manufacturing of lanterns had not proved as lucrative as the manufacturing of credit assessments. Nichols did not see any way to escape to retirement, so long as he had a household to support. His son Lewis was now at the seminary in Auburn, Rebecca studying at the Brooklyn Female Academy, the younger two children still at home.

"What news from the town?" Ruth happily asked him, as she did every night. She seemed to have shrunk smaller as she grew older and now stood only to his chest. Lately they had rekindled the affection of their earliest years. Ruth had time, with the children independent, to listen to his talk about the world. They sat up every evening when he was home.

After five minutes of chat, Thomas slouched out the hallway to his desk, lit a lamp, and carefully unsealed the letter. It was a large sheet, in the same neat but showy hand that had addressed it. He read, *Dear Mr. Nichols,* and felt a flood of relief. Every time he feared it would begin, *Dear Father.* But so far the young man had maintained propriety.

The letters had begun shortly after the Christian Antislavery Convention. The scented envelope and the flourishing hand had posed a pleasant mystery until he read the first line: *My mother, Mrs. Catherine Nichols, informs me that you are my father.*

In that first letter Tommy maintained a formal, ornate tone, like one of Tappan's agents assessing a credit risk. He told something about his studies and asked for nothing more than the favor of a reply, the very last thing that Nichols wanted to give. How did he know where his letter might be displayed?

"The secret histories of certain abolitionists," he could imagine Garrison writing, *"may go far to explain their calculated, compromised and we dare to say hypocritical alliances with the slave power."*

Yet it was more dangerous not to reply. He finally resolved to write a careful, oblique letter that would frankly request, for personal reasons, that their relationship remain a private matter. *My children and my wife know only that I was raised in a slaveholding family,* he wrote, *which I left when I was barely in my majority. They know nothing of my boyhood involvement in the cruelty and immorality of that institution so long ago. I have hoped to spare them the embarrassment and emotional shock of such knowledge, which I judge to be a quite unnecessary affliction for them. My guilt is my own, long ago brought to the feet of the Savior.* With some dread Nichols made a general offer of assistance. He did not expect to wait long for a financial request.

Such a request had not come, however. Instead his son wrote long disquisitions on the state of the Union, on Oberlin, on the theology of perfection (Finney's hobbyhorse). When Nichols showed any hint of polite interest in a subject, he would receive a detailed answer by the earliest mail.

Tommy assured him that he had no wish to make their relationship public. *I only want to have the intimate correspondence that any son might wish with his father, even a father who has been unfortunately absent for twenty-five years.*

At first Nichols carried on the correspondence because he feared what might happen if he should fail to answer. Gradually something else was added to fear: he found himself flattered. It was something unusual for a man over fifty to hear so frequently from a younger man and to gain insight into life at Oberlin. Lewis did not write so often or so personably from the seminary. And as Thomas realized increasingly, Thomas Nichols was his son. This young man was his own blood, as fully as Lewis.

To Ruth he said only that the letters were from a young black student. He even read aloud some of the young man's thoughts and observations. He was very careful, however, to burn each letter after he had read it, and as he watched the flames lick the paper and the pages curl and puff into flame, he felt his own conscience sorely. Only his pride insisted on keeping this secret, pride and his fear of punishment. He was not a good man.

At times he felt that he must bare all, braving the consequences. He was ready to submit his life to the cold stare of judgment. Then he would reflect, and dread would seize him, and he would know that he must surely keep the silence.

Now as he sat down and began to read this latest letter, after the first rush of relief was past, he felt a mixture of furtive anxiety and delicious pleasure. He had asked Tommy about the impact of the Fugitive Slave Law on the town of Oberlin. *They say with pride here,* Tommy wrote, *that no Negro has ever been taken away unwillingly, and so far no blood shed. Yet they would shed blood, their own blood, to keep men from the hands of the slave catchers, if need be. It is not only black citizens who swear so but many white. Such is the influence of godliness on this place.*

Nichols became so involved in the letter that, looking up to reflect, he was momentarily surprised by his own desk.

It was unfortunate, he felt, that Finney's perfectionistic ideas had made him outcast in many Christian circles. Nichols did not care about perfection—could not even begin to understand it—but he still trusted Finney. He had begun to feel identified with Finney all over again simply because his son—his secret Negro son—studied with him. Oberlin he perceived as an example of Finney's godly influence, an earnest of hope. This defense of Negroes was a perfect case in point.

> *I am often called on to testify about my own kidnapping, as everyone here knows of those dramatic circumstances. I have been asked to account for my bravery under such circumstances (for I tell them that I felt no concern for my own welfare, being sure that God would provide for my rescue). I answer them that any courage I demonstrate has been not to my credit but to a mother who carried me out of slavery, under grave risk of life. I tell them that there is no greater model of courage than an escaping slave. I also give credit to the heroes who built this institution and fought the earliest battles for the slave, when it could mean life to speak for his cause. Yesterday I was speaking on this line with a group of students in Tappan Hall, and I said that my own father, though a vicious slaveholder at the time of my conception, has become a genuine abolitionist, though I am pledged never to reveal his identity. I hope you will understand that I spoke so in great excitement, and that afterwards though I was urged to reveal your name I completely refused, as a matter of trust. How I do long, however, for my fellows to know the*

full picture of your personal courage. I am sure they were intrigued and impressed at the little I told them.

"My goodness," Nichols said aloud, and then looked up, afraid that Ruth might hear. He put the letter under a stack of papers. Standing and rubbing his hands together, he wondered what he could do. The secret was leaking out, he thought. It seemed to him that his entire, carefully wrought life might come apart.

The train from Cleveland into Oberlin ran straight over flat and featureless farmland, but a mile east of the town shuddered through a long S curve to cross Plum Creek. From the rearmost car Thomas Nichols could see the engine ahead on the curve, pluming cinders and smoke into the pristine sky. Beyond, above the bright green of high trees, a square church tower poked its head. So he had arrived, after the long journey. His eyes filled with the town he had thought of so much but never seen. The train began to slow as they passed the first houses, neat, picket-fenced homes, for all the world like those of a New England village except that the terrain was so extraordinarily flat. With a screeching of brakes and a slamming of couplings, the train eased into Oberlin.

He waited a few minutes before he got off the train, and then marched straight ahead down the platform, deflecting the eyes of the slackers who watched from a bench at the ticket office. Nichols had tried to think who in Oberlin he knew, but there was only Finney, and he thought it unlikely that he would accidentally meet the great man. Yet Oberlin was too much a center for Christian reform for Nichols to be confident of anonymity. He was prepared, should he encounter an acquaintance, to let it be known that he had come to see a student whom he supported. That far he would go.

He had tried to write several times and ended up burning every letter. If he wrote subtly, he was too subtle. If he wrote frankly, the letter was further incrimination. He feared that Tommy would be offended, would show the letter and might even ultimately, out of spite, let it be published. Such things had happened. A private meeting would leave no evidence and would allow him to judge Tommy's temper. It was a long journey, an extreme journey. He saw that, but he saw even more clearly that he must keep the secrets.

Nichols walked up the Main Street, picking his way along the margins where bright house gardens sank into the street's black gunk. He passed a saddlery, two dry goods stores, a shoe factory, and a cooperage. Men sat on the porches, talking, observing. It was almost, Nichols thought, like being in Alabama again, he saw so many black people on the street.

A hundred yards from the rails a sign on a side street read "BED." The establishment, a gray-painted wooden structure, looked a cut below his usual hotel. Loungers on the boardwalk were throwing a bowie knife at a chunk of firewood. The proprietor, a Mr. Wack, was a small, waspish man who told him, without prompting, "I don't care what your business is here. That's your take-up, not mine. You've got to pay in advance." He did, gladly, being sure that he would not encounter any of his reform-minded friends here.

After he had eaten a dreadful dinner—one cold chop, swimming in a greasy soup with scraps of cabbage, and cold, hard biscuits—he went out to walk through the town. He had been told that at certain hours you could hear the students praying in their rooms like a great humming swarm of bees. He heard no sound like that, however. Just north of the commercial sector was Tappan Square, a large, fenced-in sward of grass planted with young spruce. The college buildings were scattered around it, large, ordinary buildings. The young men he saw walking with their great black Bibles seemed conventional, serious. There were, astonishingly, many of them. Oberlin was the largest school in Ohio, he had heard, and now the full significance of this fact became clear. If all these became reform men, what a force they would be! For some reason this thought put him at ease, tension eased out of his arms and shoulders, and for the first time he allowed himself some hope that his errand would succeed.

When he returned to his room, Nichols penned a short note to Tommy, asking him to meet in the dining room of Wack's. He gave it to the porter and then, after stretching on his bed for a decent interval, descended to the room where meals were served. He had a newspaper that he held in front of himself, pretending to be absorbed as he waited for his son. The clatter of cutlery as the tables were set made him jump.

"Mr. Nichols, this is not a decent place." Tommy sat gingerly in his chair, pulling on his thin line of mustache. "Palmer's is where people stay, right by the college."

"I don't want to be seen where people stay," Nichols said flatly though not, he hoped, unkindly. "I came for one purpose: to assure that my identity would not be revealed."

Even as he said that, earnestly and calmly, he felt lost as to his reasons. He had actually found himself trembling as he waited for Tommy to come. Now he gazed at this slender, handsome, light-skinned man, well dressed and respectful, whom he would not have recognized at all except that he wore a tie and jacket, while all the other black men who entered Wack's were evidently laborers. Looking at him, Thomas felt an unexpected inner pleasure, a feeling like the flow of honey—thick and slow and sweet. His feelings were a jumble.

Oblivious, Tommy leaned forward in concentrated thought. "Father . . . may I call you Father?"

That sent a shock through his spine. "Mr. Nichols would be better, much better."

Tommy seemed to take it in with barely a ripple. "I think you are wrongly worried, Mr. Nichols. I never told the students your name, and they could never guess it. But I am very glad, very honored, that you have come. I have dreamed of it."

Nichols stared at him and thought, *I must stick to the subject*. He could not afford to be swept into sentiment, he must finish the business. "Do not be sure. Many people know that I came from Alabama and was a slaveholder. We share the same name. I believe even . . ." He stopped for a moment before going on. "I believe we even share some physical likenesses."

The young man had large brown eyes, hooded like his mother's. His skin was a light coffee color, and his hair almost straight. He had seemed to stiffen slightly as Nichols spoke.

"If you wish our relation kept secret," Tommy said, "it will be so. You may be sure of it."

"I cannot have hints thrown around," Nichols added firmly, feeling that he was gaining control. "No more discussion, at all."

"I said it will be so. I am a man of my word." Tommy had his head tipped back, his nostrils flared.

"How is your mother?" Nichols asked, to change the topic. He might have stood, shaken hands, walked away. The business was done, at least superficially. Yet he wanted to linger. *Your son,* he was thinking. Perhaps they might never meet again.

"She is well," Tommy said coolly. "She writes me often from Jamestown." Then, while Nichols watched it happen on his face, Tommy dived again toward intimacy. "Is it true," he asked, with love and vulnerability showing in his eyes, "that you taught her how to write?"

"Yes," Nichols said, hesitant but thinking that the boy deserved an answer to his questions. "It was illegal, but I did teach her. I am thankful that something I did in those days of ignorance and sin has been beneficial."

"But why did you teach her?"

Nichols stopped momentarily, trying to remember. "She wanted to learn," he said, "and I believe I found it pleasant to teach her."

"So even then, in those days of sin, you showed the divine spark. The Holy God was at work in your soul, even then. She was yours to command, you had no need to teach her, she had to obey on pain of death . . ."

Nichols almost smiled. His son had got his ideas of slaves and masters from reading abolitionist pamphlets, probably. Undoubtedly Mrs.

Stowe's book, with its lurid portrait of Uncle Tom's death, played a part. He sometimes wondered whether a subtler portrait would serve the cause better. Every slaveholder vehemently denied the abolitionist picture of cruelty, and their sense of offended truth made it impossible to reach them. Perhaps a subtler portrait . . . but they would not listen anyway, that was certain. Nichols thought of his own brother, a professing Christian.

He smiled at his son, warmly. "You left the slave states when you were very young, didn't you? You don't remember much, I suppose, but you have heard dreadful things, all true, I don't doubt. I have witnessed terrible things myself. But you should understand that those incidents are not everything. Living together, a master and slave can sometimes grow very fond of each other. I was fond of your mother, I thought her very lovely . . ." He stopped for a moment, groping for words.

To his own great surprise, he began to weep. "Even now when I see you I am ashamed," he said in a whisper. He tried to go on but could not. Tommy extended a hand across the table and wrapped his dark fingers around his father's hand. It took Nichols a moment to think how this might appear, and then he pulled his hand away. He felt inside an absolute chaos caught between love and repulsion, between natural affection for his own blood and horror that it could be seen mixed with coffee skin and African features. He was simultaneously humiliated by his own reaction, for he had tried to be free from racial views and had sometimes prided himself on his naturalness with blacks.

"You are my son," he said, gaining some control of his voice, pulling back and sitting up straight, "and you may properly expect my support. But not recognition. That can never be. I must tell you that I cannot continue our correspondence. I have expected too much to think that you can keep it completely covert. I am done with answering your letters, even though they have been very respectful, and I have read them with great interest. I am sure the time is right to cease. We can go no further without doing harm. I would like to make arrangements for money to be deposited to your account, on a monthly basis if you like, or twice a year, or whatever you wish. I want to be generous and fair to you. I appreciate that you have not asked for this. I want to give it to you."

He could not immediately interpret the look on the young man's face. Tommy's mouth seemed to tighten into a square knot. At first Nichols thought the metallic eyes were angry, so angry that the man might strike him. Then he saw the boy's mouth trembling, twitching, as though he wanted to cry. Tommy stood up, scraping his chair noisily on the floor. He stood for a moment as though about to spit out something, then turned and walked quickly out of the dining room. Even though he said no words, his movements were so hasty and large they attracted the attention of the dozen or so men loitering at their tables.

Thomas did not pursue his son. He raised his eyebrows as though to say, for everyone's consumption, that there was no understanding some people. He put his napkin carelessly on the table, and, doing his best to act so that his secret would not be exposed to anyone's curiosity, walked gracefully out of the room.

Chapter 25
1855: Rifles for Kansas

Thomas Nichols was surprised, when he saw the elegant lobby of Albany's Central Hotel, that Tappan would stay at such a splendorous place. Giant Turkish carpets and brass fixtures were strewn about the place like dandelions. Tappan he found seated in an overstuffed chair, his hands on his knees, a happy and almost childlike expression in his eyes. His appearance startled Nichols; age seemed to have come on the man as suddenly as a drop into a ditch.

"This is a luxurious place," Nichols said as they shook hands, simply to have something to say. "There is a pump on each hall, I understand?" He noticed Tappan's skin had become thin as paper. Small white hairs stuck out from his cheeks.

"Not a pump, a tap," Tappan corrected. He was always interested in naming things correctly. "A steam pump lifts the water onto the roof, into a reservoir. One turns a screw, and out the water comes."

"What a marvelous age we live in."

Tappan tottered slightly from side to side as he made his way with Nichols down the hallway. Nichols had looked forward to the time they might spend together on the way to Syracuse. Instead he felt his spirits drop, seeing this good man so old and this new rock pile so careless and luxurious. A man could be good, yes, but it made no resistance to evil, he thought, no more than butter to a hot knife. Tappan was near the end of his life, and what had he accomplished, really? The world ran on.

When they spoke of the new antislavery organization, Tappan surprised Nichols with his circumspection. "I told them not to count on me for much," Tappan said. "What I have I mostly give to the American Missionary Association."

"Then, why, Brother Lewis, have you been asking me to join in the cause? I thought you were enthusiastic." Tappan's diffidence was also a surprise, and it distressed Nichols powerfully. Tappan, Gerrit Smith, and William Goodell, a newspaper editor, had formed the American Abolition Society as a middle ground, somewhere between the moral indifference of the Republicans, who had taken up where the Free Labor Party left off, and the high-minded Pharisaism of the Garrisonians. In principle, the new organization was right, Nichols thought, but it looked to be a collection of the same old well-respected abolitionists, which was like saying well-respected cranks. Nichols was sick of such small beer. What difference had this group ever made? Tappan had talked him into coming, and why?

Tappan made a little smile at Nichols's question. "I have no illusions that we will win the great masses over, Brother Thomas. We would have gotten nowhere all this time if we tried to measure our popularity."

"And have we gotten somewhere?" As soon as the question was out of his lips Nichols doubted whether he should have said it. In other company he could be quite cynical, but with Tappan it made him feel ashamed. Yet it was not really cynical, it was the question that plagued him.

"Yes, I think we have gotten somewhere," Tappan said with a sigh. "Though I admit the end of the race is certainly not in sight. As the apostle says, we must press on toward the mark." He said it so lightly that Nichols could not respond; he would as soon tell a man who had seen an angel that there was no such thing.

On entering the church Thomas Nichols immediately spotted a tall, dignified black man with silver mustache and goatee, Robert Duncan.

They had not seen each other since Brady had come looking to steal Duncan back to Alabama. Nichols went up to Duncan immediately, anxious to hear news, perhaps to escape from the depression he felt.

"Pretty cold there in Canada, isn't it?" Nichols asked him after they said hello.

Duncan let a smile pass through his mouth. "I don't find it much colder than New York, and in Canada my manhood is not in doubt."

Nichols nodded, though the answer irritated him. Since the Fugitive Slave Law thousands of blacks had fled to Canada, and some wrote to the newspapers that they would never return to the United States. The unthinkable had come, that black leaders had taken up colonization, saying that the Negro could never be treated fairly in the United States. Henry Highland Garnet, of all people, had gone to Liberia. Nichols was of the opinion that they all showed an unsteady face and played into the propaganda of the slave power.

"What brings you to this meeting, then, which I understand to be quite an American business?"

"I only came because Mr. Douglass invited me."

"Oh? You know Douglass?"

"Yes, I know him," Duncan said quietly. "We were introduced by our mutual friend."

"*Our* mutual friend? Do you mean Miss Nichols?" Nichols asked. "You met her then?"

Duncan smiled enigmatically. "Yes, I did meet her." The sentence was left hanging in the air.

"I assume she wrote to you after I gave her your address," Nichols said. "I am glad that I could bring the two of you together. I remembered that you had asked about her, from the first moment I saw you."

"She told me about your meeting."

"Did she?" Nichols felt the warning in Duncan's tone.

"She said you were ashamed to be seen with her." Duncan's voice was calm, though a ray of malice ran just under the surface. The large sanctuary hummed with conversation. Nichols concentrated on Duncan's face, which seemed oddly maniacal, a little smile playing on his lips. The blackness of the skin, the way the nostrils flared, the yellowy whites of the eyes—all the aspects of negritude seemed overwhelmingly repulsive just now.

"I was not ashamed to be seen with her; it was the question of my past. You know I have never been ashamed to be seen with an African person."

"I have no wish to shame you," Duncan said softly. He suddenly sat up tall, as though drawing back from hostilities. "She is a woman who makes a very great impact on a man," he said. "I won't hide from you that when I met her, I had in mind that we might still marry, even at our ages. I went down to Jamestown to see her, after she had responded encouragingly to my letters, I thought."

Nichols required a moment to realize that Duncan had, kindly, changed the subject away from Nichols's vulnerability to his own. "But she was not interested?" Nichols asked.

"She was not interested. Or perhaps she was at first, but then her heart hardened against me. At any rate it was no good. Our time has passed by."

"You must have been profoundly disappointed."

Duncan bowed his head slightly, in assent.

"She has no other?"

That brought a smile. "Only her son, I believe." He said it coolly, but Nichols felt a great wave of sadness behind the smile.

Oddly, that sadness seemed to rekindle the shame Nichols felt—general, groundless, foggy shame kindled by his past, by this black man and his memories and his disappointments. He felt for a moment the kind of desperate unease that made him wish to flee out of his own skin, to leave himself, so to speak, standing behind as his soul escaped into unknowingness.

The convention went off cheerfully, the old familiars asserting themselves smoothly. More than four thousand dollars was pledged to the cause, and the various duties were assigned. Yet as the business meetings progressed, Nichols found himself more befuddled and discouraged. He felt they kept busily talking and planning to avoid facing the truth, that it was a pointless exercise. They had preached the message for twenty years, and their only harvest was the Republican Party, which sought to make the West a white man's paradise.

Garrison celebrates the Fourth of July by burning the Constitution, Nichols thought, *and thousands of abolitionists shout Amen. Federal troops rule Boston and drag a captured black man to the South on behalf of the Land of Liberty. Freed slaves give up all hope in America and push to Canada, or Haiti, or Africa. Our old friends Stanton and Chase and Giddings pursue the votes of men stained with immorality. We go on with these tidy conventions.*

On the second day he ate a gloomy dinner with Lewis Tappan and Charles Stuart. Stuart brought awful tales of the famine in Ireland. Now he had married—married! the perennial bachelor!—and settled in Canada.

Nichols had always liked him—he was a sweet, unearthly man—and had many questions to ask regarding England and Ireland, but Stuart kept bending toward the one thought on his mind, Theodore Weld. Nichols had not heard Weld mentioned in years, but Stuart continued in correspondence. Weld, he said, had given up farming and started a school as part of a communal experiment on the New Jersey shore. Stuart reached into his coat pocket and produced the school's plan of learning. It was a single printed sheet, dense with type.

"All the grand classical subjects," Stuart said softly. "Science, art, geography, and not one word of the Bible. Theodore, my Theodore! Where are they to find the truth to judge all things? He will bring up these children to be artful deceivers." Stuart seemed to lapse into purest gloom. "Theodore, even his name is tender to me. Theodore is the finest, most angelic man, my dearest friend beyond all friends, but my heart stares into the infinite darkness with terror. He has lost the golden key of understanding, the only truth that can govern the unruly and hell-bound thoughts of man."

Tappan was looking grumpily down at his potatoes, as though willing them to dance on his plate. He cleared his throat and spoke without lifting his eyes. "Weld got lost long before he gained such opinions," he said. "In more than a decade he has done not one thing for temperance or abolition or any other benevolent cause. First he was going to become a farmer. That was all his soul could contemplate, the life of the soil. Then he became a teacher of Shakespeare. I lost patience with him then. I tell you frankly, Brother Charles, I gave up on him. I confess that I no longer share your idea that he is a near angel."

"Was it his marriage?" Nichols asked. "Mrs. Weld and her sister being Quaker could not have been orthodox in the faith."

"Nay," Stuart broke in, "when I visited them we had the most blessed times of prayer. I never saw a more beautiful spirit of submission. Nay, Theodore cannot be conceived of as one led astray, even if the sisters were from hell itself. Even today, if the world were filled with Theodores, it would be the most peaceable place, and perhaps that is what deceives him. He sees everything through his own blessedness and thinks it can substitute for the mind of Christ. *I* have never had that temptation, for to see the world through my natural eyes I see darkness and hellishness everywhere. But Theodore . . ."

"Is it true," Tappan asked, "that James Birney has joined him there at Raritan Bay?" That was the name of the experimental community, which occupied a single, large stone building near Perth Amboy.

"Yes, and I have written Birney," Stuart said sadly. "He seems to have regained some of his health. Birney is no help, however, for he cannot think with the same clarity he used to have. He has lost interest in doctrines, he says, and wants only to see how men and women live."

"They think so highly of themselves that they cannot imagine themselves led astray," Tappan said, as dryly as though he were stating the accounts of his company.

"What can I do," Stuart said, as though in fearful desperation, "but bring my oldest and most cherished friend before God's throne? I would almost give up my own place in God's grace to have him there in my place. I know better now what the apostle wrote, regarding his praying without ceasing. At all hours a prayer goes up from my heart for Theodore, and indeed for all those children he would lead astray."

That night while Tappan slept, laboring with breath as loudly as a steam engine, Nichols sat at the table with a candle, trying to write to Ruth but finding no way to describe the chasms he saw. Such disintegration, that the greatest of friends were separated, that these men who had once been so hopeful and confident were reduced to flat and sorrowful commentaries. Nichols wrestled with his collar to loosen a button. The air of the room seemed to be exhaled from some tepid swamp. Only with the greatest of efforts did he calm himself.

Speeches and motions and reports were parading toward their inevitable conclusions, while Nichols sat in a glum daze, unable to care about the particulars. A grizzled, gray-headed man came down the central aisle, *a local farmer*, Nichols thought. He was dressed in ill-fitting clothes, he reeked of horse, and his face had an ineradicable hardness to it, like the toughness of saddle leather that has been left to the destruction of rain and sun. He was some backwoods character, the kind that was always wandering into abolitionist meetings. Nichols watched him idly, his mind far off from the speech someone was making.

The man was looking for something, peering down the rows of participants. Then, having found his target, he began hissing loudly. Gerrit Smith, the lanky giant, stood up and walked into the aisle, and, in full view of everyone, the farmer began talking to him in a normal speaking voice. It was as if he had no idea a report was being presented from the platform, almost as if he positively intended to disrupt.

Frederick Douglass, sitting on the platform, suddenly jumped up and asked for the podium. "Mr. Brown, would you come up here?" he said in his thunder-filled voice, and the farmer turned and walked up to the platform without a trace of surprise. "I hope the speaker will pardon my interruption," Douglass said in that voice that carried through walls. "I would like to introduce to you a man who has had a profound influence on my own mind, being one who has no guile and no prejudice, who would treat a black man exactly as he would a white man, that is, as a human being. I know he would without question give his life for the slave, and there are not many men, black or white, of whom I might say such a thing. Mr. John Brown, please come and tell us your thoughts on the present crisis."

Brown seemed to take this as utterly in his normal day. Without even a pause or a word of thanks to Douglass, he began talking in a plain western accent. "I have got five sons in Kansas, five of my seed who have gone there to create a haven of liberty," he said, exactly in that laconic voice that a western farmer will use to complain about the price of wheat. "I have twenty children all together. These five are not particular to me, but the land they settle is, as it must be for all who love freedom and hate the devil. They are settling in to the eastern part of the state, where they have the ambition to farm and raise their families in the fear of God and of no man."

Brown paused to look over his audience, looking like a schoolmaster much in doubt whether his students have the capacity to grasp the subject he offers. After passing his hard eyes across the well-dressed men and women in the room, he went on. "They write me—" He paused and reached into his jacket to pull out a paper, which he held up for them to see. "They tell me Kansas is a good country where any man who fears God and not hard work can raise food and plenty for his family. Now I have heard from these boys of mine, and I come to ask for your help. I am on my way to them as soon as I can go. They write and plead with me for guns to protect the liberty and the peace. They need rifles and cartridges and revolvers. They tell me that the great proportion of settlers are freedom-loving men, but they are greatly afraid of the man stealers who come in from Missouri. Every slaveholding state in the Union is sending money or men or guns to those slaveholders to keep the freedom-loving free men from the polls. They will have that country another foul sink of their hatred for their fellowman. They will have it a seat of slavery, another step in taking the free states so-called and making them slave. They come over from Missouri with plenty of ruffians, armed, and have put the free settlers in a state of great fear. There is no answering them with arguments; they don't care about an argument. They are ready to shoot because they are godless men. Now I am asking you all, won't you give so that the settlers who are pledged for the slave may have the wherewithal to defend themselves? They need guns or they need money, and money is probably better. I want to take up a collection. I am planning to go straight there with everything I can get to help them. The sons of Belial are at the gate, and there is no time for discussion."

Nichols was aware of Tappan moving restlessly in his pew. Nichols glanced over to see his lips twitching and his face intent.

The whole room seemed stirred, if you judged by the desert silence. Nichols himself felt quite attracted to Brown's simplicity. This was no speechmaker but a plain Yankee who meant business. What flashed into Nichols's mind was Theodore Weld. Years back Weld had always been saying that he was a western man who could not fit in the city with refined people. Now Weld was teaching Shakespeare in New Jersey. Here was a real western man, as plain as his own name. He talked like somebody who saw God's judgment hanging over the nation as surely as he saw his face in the mirror.

The meeting lurched off its plan. Gerrit Smith was called up to read the letters that Brown had brandished. They were plain, unpreachy letters, such as a farmer or mechanic would write describing the weather, the quality of timber available for building, the plows being used to break ground. It seemed that the sons hated slavery as much as their father.

After Smith stepped down, one of the AMA missionaries in Canada asked for the floor. He was an excitable, strapping redhead, who worked with the colonies of blacks who had fled over the border. He moved that they take up a collection for Brown's work.

Tappan became audibly disturbed. At first he only mumbled. Then he stood at his seat, waiting for the floor. His cheeks were scrubbed their ordinary red, but the rest of his skin looked deathly white. He looked old, deathly old.

"How can it be?" he asked when he was recognized "that we will send instruments of war to Kansas?" He seemed to bubble with frustration that the matter was even considered, but his voice was not strong. "We who have always forsworn violence or coercion in our cause. We who have always held that immorality cannot be corrected by immoral means. I do not take issue with the description that Brother John Brown's sons have given, nor the proposition that we ought to help them. But what help should we send? Weapons of war? Will Kansas be a better country if it has more guns? I ask you to reconsider. I have been with this movement as long or longer than any of you, but I have never heard such a suggestion as this. When Amos Dresser was beaten in Nashville, did we raise funds to buy revolvers? When our tracts were burned by postal authorities, did we purchase rifles? When our lecturers were stoned and their halls burned down, their lives threatened . . ."

Tappan stopped in midsentence. The audience listened grudgingly, Nichols thought. For all that he respected Tappan, he himself felt impatient with this speech. It had become clear what the audience thought of Brown: they were for him.

Tappan was not an orator, to move the unyielding. He glanced around the hall for a moment, and then settled on the most powerful symbol he could think of.

"Would not one Uncle Tom, with his loving submission to God, do more good than a hundred men with the force of bullets?"

Nichols, who loved the man, thought sorrowfully of the irony. Tappan appealed to a fictional character, an idea, because no flesh and blood example existed. Those who had been the bright candles, the Welds and the Stantons, had burned down to nothing. Those who had been patient were no longer happy to turn the cheek. They had no optimism that the truth would change anything.

You could not forever defer hope. Douglass, Smith, and even Charles Stuart supported the motion. The guns were for defense, at any rate, to keep the peace, not break it. Tappan listened to these men with a face of flint. Nichols remembered that Arthur Tappan himself had handed out guns to defend his store and thought of raising the point. There was no need, however. The real issue was not guns, but the solidity and clarity of a different kind of man, John Brown. They took the collection.

Afterward quite a huddle of men surrounded Brown. Nichols stood on the periphery for a time, noting the man's stiff, wild hair. His face looked as if he had never smiled. Brown was quoting the Bible, chapter and verse. Without the shedding of blood there is no redemption from sin, he said. He spoke fiercely of the wages of sin piled up by the slaveholding states, the wages awaiting payment.

As Nichols walked back to the hotel his excitement drained away. It was a warm, green afternoon. They had collected sixty dollars for Brown. What would that money do? Buy one rifle? Two? And when that rifle reached Kansas, what would it do? For just an instant he saw in his mind's eye a lead slug burying into soft gut tissue. He decided to think of other things. His mind returned to Robert Duncan and their conversation, but that was not much better. He still felt raw and anxious.

When he reached the hotel Lewis Tappan was at the desk in their room, writing neatly and fast on a large sheet of paper. He said it was a report for a New York newspaper—he did not say which one. Nichols stood watching him scribble for a few minutes. Two old men he had seen today, each with an energy he had to admire, each with a kind of purity going in a different direction. Once Tappan had been at the forefront of reform, but today he seemed merely old. The world was surely approaching closer to Mr. Brown's conviction, to his single-minded and practical fervor. And he, Thomas Nichols, was ready for it, he felt seized by that conviction suddenly. Let Mr. Brown have the day now, they had done it mildly and temperately long enough.

"It is a new day, Brother Lewis. The scene rushes on." He meant it kindly.

Tappan paused for a moment at his pen, looked up with his small, round face, and then went back to writing. "It is an old story," he said without lifting his head. "As old as Cain."

Chapter 26
1856: Pottawatomie

Later on, when they were giving court testimony, everybody who had seen John Brown in Kansas described him as an old man. In reality he was just fifty-six and hard as an oak limb. It shows how young they all were, to call him old.

The settlers had come to Kansas mainly for the land. They left debt-ridden, rock-sprung acres in the eastern hills for mere rumors of deep-soiled, flat, treeless, and rock-free Kansas—country already cleared for farming by God himself. Kansas drew in those who would risk everything or had nothing to risk, or else those who were pulled to a fight like a bull to a red flag.

John Brown, with six sons and one married daughter, settled along a creek near the Marais de Cygnes, south of Lawrence. In no time there was bad blood with their slave-state neighbors, some of whom vowed they would sooner shoot a Brown in the head than kill a rattlesnake. A lot of it was bluff, but not all of it. Along every cottonwood creek men were choosing captains and counting guns and giving themselves military names. (The Browns helped to start up the Pottawatomie Rifles.)

They had the telegraph now, which meant that even while they were on the frontier, living in tents and dugouts, eating salt pork out of barrels, Washington knew every bowie-knife tavern fight. The commentary that senators in Washington made over a Kansas fistfight was in the papers and talked in the Kansas general stores and taverns the very next day, or two at the most.

On May 19, Charles Sumner, senator from Massachusetts, began a sensational two-day speech on "The Crime Against Kansas." Kansas settlers read in their newspapers how he referred to the proslavery ruffians as "hirelings picked from the drunken spew and vomit of an uneasy civilization." He named all the Democrats who had swung the Kansas-Nebraska Act, using language that was bound to inspire less elegant words along muddy creeks and rutted wagon roads. Even Republicans were taken aback by the heat of his words.

Next day on the Marais de Cygnes, riders came down the California road, spreading alarm. A Missouri army, they told John Brown and his neighbors, was advancing with five cannon to pillage Lawrence. Surely this was the fight long threatened. John Brown and his sons and the other free-state men—thirty-four in all—gathered at Weiner's Store and trooped off for Lawrence.

A series of messengers met them on the road. The first said they were too late, the town was not to be defended. A second reported that Missourians had burned the Lawrence hotel and ransacked the newspapers, without opposition. A third said that U.S. Army troops had taken control of the town and broken up the fighting.

Confused, the Pottawatomie Rifles stopped and camped. Should they go on, or go back home? Nobody wanted to be called a coward, but their wives and children were unguarded at home.

The old man had been talking, talking, talking, not always on the subject at hand, mixing up Bible quotations with his raw, blank hatred of slavery. At the campfire he ranted about blood for blood. A repayment was due to the slavehounds, life for life, limb for limb. He said he had a plan, that he would lead a band of volunteers. He demanded to know who would go. Who would fight for the Lord? The other men sat around and listened to him, shifting their boots in and out of the fire's warmth. One by one they went off to sleep, leaving Brown and his raging voice.

Next morning they dragged out of their blanket rolls, kicked up the fire for coffee, and stood silent and inert, stiff and unhappy. Brown was still talking, carrying on as though he had never stopped to sleep.

They heard hooves and a creak of saddle leather, then saw the gray shape of a horse and rider coming out of the fog. They asked news of Lawrence.

"Cup of coffee be good," the rider said. They got him a mug and beat on him for news of the battle. All that he said on that was stale, but he seemed to want to tell something about Sumner. Finally they hushed down the questions about Lawrence, and he said it. Charles Sumner of Massachusetts had been beaten near to death on the Senate floor, before the eyes of numerous senators. Congressman Preston Brooks used a cane to repeatedly strike Sumner while he writhed helplessly on the floor, covered with blood. Sumner might die soon.

"Fact is, Brooks has already been congratulated by Southern senators," the horseman said. "They consider it a great day for the honor of the South. It's all on the telegraph today."

Brown exploded, raging against the poisonous vermin of slavehounds. He swore he would neither be a slave nor live in a slave land. Was it not better that a hundred slavehounds die than that a single free-state settler be driven out of Kansas?

After he had stalked about for a time, barking at anyone who would stand still, Brown called them all together, bullying them to come in around the fire. He had a secret plan, he said, and he asked for volunteers. He pushed them hard and eventually got four of his sons, a son-in-law, and two other men to go with him. One had a wagon. By the afternoon they were ready, packed into it and setting off. They had a few guns and a quantity of heavy iron broadswords etched with an eagle.

Ten o'clock the next evening, the sky having purpled off into black, the stars fully blossomed, Brown's army of eight set out from the copse of timber where they had camped all day in hiding. They had a lantern, but Brown ordered it covered up. Nobody could be out at such a time, but they must proceed with an absolute caution.

The old man had not told them what they would do, except that they must "clean out" the proslavery men on the creek. There would be, he said, some killing. Stumbling along in the dark they crossed the California road and groped their way over Mosquito Creek. Ahead was the Doyle cabin. Doyle was a scornful proslavery man with three big sons.

Brown stopped them a hundred yards off. Up the slope they could see the cabin's dark shape against the star-strewn sky. "We shall deliver Israel from the Philistines," he said in a fierce, low whisper. "Not by might but by my Spirit, saith the Lord."

Instantly after those words they heard the rush of dogs, like some demonic, yelping spirits from out of the devil's darkness, two furious hounds that were on them forthwith. Every prairie man feared his neighbor's dogs, for there was no dodging from a dog, or talking sense. They never had time even to yell. Frederick Brown took several wild cuts at a dog that was leaping and snarling in a fury around him, and then somewhat accidentally hit the dog with his broadsword. The dog's soprano cry leaped up into the heavy, damp air of the night. The dog fell down and tried to get up and walk with one leg. Frederick dispatched it with a slamming blow to the back. He then cut at the other dog, which lost its courage and ran off into the shadows.

"Watch out, the cur may attack again," the old man said, and they waited at the ready for some time before deciding they were safe.

Something about victory over the dogs quickened them, producing a giddy sense of invincibility. They went forward rapidly now, as though to act before thinking. When they entered the deep shadow of the cabin, however, where they could not see even a door or a window, they stalled a little. The old man pushed past them and beat on the door.

A Tennessee drawl answered. "Who is it?"

"Can you show us the way to Wilkinson's place?" Brown asked.

The door creaked open, and instantly Brown pushed through. The boys crowded in behind their father. By the dim light of a fire in one large room they recognized Doyle. Brown was brandishing his sword at Doyle's throat. "You must surrender!" Brown shouted. "The Northern army is here!" There was a good deal of shouting.

A woman appeared in a sleeping gown, weeping and telling Doyle she had warned him, that he should have known he would get it if he kept on. "Hush, Mother," Doyle said, keeping his eyes brightly on Brown. His three sons, skinny and dressed in dirty homespun, appeared from a corner, their eyes blinking with sleep and their hair tousled. The cabin smelled of burned potato and of sour human scent. A little girl in an oversize camp dress came up and clung to her mother.

Brown no more looked at the woman or the girl than he would have looked at a chicken. "You are my prisoners," he said fiercely to Doyle. "I want you and the three."

The woman pleaded with Brown that he not take the youngest. She approached right up to Brown as though she saw no sword, her hands straining to lift mercy from the air he breathed. "He is a boy," she said. "He has no part in this."

"All right," Brown said after he listened to her. "The youngest I will leave with you. The other three must go now."

Coming out of the cabin the night air smelled fresh, of fertile earth. The pregnant, moist wind was blowing through the grasses, sweetly promising summer. A hundred yards down the road Brown paused. They could smell the keen bitterness of life about to come out of the ground. "Now," said Brown to his sons. "Go ahead."

It was surprisingly quiet: only one deep groan when the sword struck the oldest boy, who was twenty or twenty two, and he sank down so quickly a second blow missed him. One boy ran but was already hurt and did not get far. It was impossible to see the wounds because of the darkness, but the three lay on the ground no longer moving. Brown asked the lantern to be brought. He took a revolver and put it to the back of Doyle's head. The explosion made them all jump.

"They are devoured by the sword," the old man said, "and the judgment of God is on them. Never again can they disturb the living."

Half a mile down the road they got into Allen Wilkinson's cabin by much the same means, except that Wilkinson was too crafty to open up, and they had to threaten to beat the door down. Inside Mrs. Wilkinson lay in bed, sick with the measles. She had two small children in bed with her.

"The wife," Wilkinson said. "I can't leave her." He, too, had a Tennessee drawl. He lit a lamp to show her face lit up with fever and ugly with red splotches. She might have been out of her mind the way she pleaded not to be left, though Brown watched her with suspicious eyes from under his broken straw hat. She was said to be a fine Southern woman, whom Wilkinson beat.

"Let me get someone to stay with her," Wilkinson said.

"We can't do that," Brown said to Wilkinson as calmly as he would discuss the trading of a mule. "We can't have the publicity."

"Leave me here," Wilkinson said. "Just leave me, and by my word on the Bible I will not flee but will be here in the morning. Only let me see her through to the light."

The old man looked at Mrs. Wilkinson and the two children with his stony eyes and his undeviating mouth. "You have some neighbors?" he asked the woman.

"Yes, but they are not here," she said. "I can't go to get them." Her voice was quavering.

"No matter," said Brown. "Let us go," he said to Wilkinson and pushed him to the door.

"My boots," the man said, gesturing in the direction of the bed. They looked down for the first time to see long, yellow stockings on his feet.

"No matter," the old man said. "Your feet will not suffer the dew."

This time Henry Thompson, Brown's son-in-law, struck with the broadsword against the shadow before him. He struck Wilkinson full in the side. Wilkinson cried out, throwing an arm up in self-defense, but the sound had barely begun to come from his mouth before it was cut off by another blow. The youngest son, Oliver, leaned over Wilkinson as he lay, and sawed his blade across his throat.

"The sword of the Lord," Brown said. "So be it on their heads, as they have treated the Lord's chosen."

They did not speak as they continued in the darkness toward Dutch Henry's tavern, where a proslavery court had met a few months before. They seemed to hear singing, as though cicadas had entered their heads and were making a high sawing sound from within. It was a moment as holy as revival. Nothing had ever felt so solemn. Oliver and Salmon lagged behind, so full of the sensation it was hard to concentrate to walk, until the old man barked at them to keep up. Only his voice could cut through their transformed sensations.

They wasted no time in palaver but broke into James Harris's cabin, near the tavern. It was past midnight, everyone inside was asleep, and the door yielded so quickly they caught them still in bed. Harris was lying under a quilt with his wife and child. Three men were also staying over, laid out under an Indian blanket with their feet beneath a plank table. One was William Sherman, a German immigrant who with his brother Henry had settled the place where the Pottawatomie Creek was crossed by the California road.

"Think not of resistance," Brown shouted fiercely, over the din and cry when they broke in. "It is the Northern army, and you must surrender."

They took the men out one at a time, where in the blustering wind Brown questioned them.

"Did you ever aid slave hounds in coming to this territory?"

"Were you at hand during the recent troubles in Lawrence?"

"Did you ever harm the free-state party?"

They all denied it except Sherman, and there was no point in his claiming anything but the truth. They knew him. The old man escorted him the short distance to the creek. The water gurgled placidly, glinting faintly through the willows. "By God's name what do you want with me? Are you going to murder me, you vermin?" Sherman still spoke with a thick, harsh accent.

Brown did not answer him. "Go on, boys," he said impatiently. Theodore Weiner swung with both hands full of strength and cut Sherman's skull open. The man collapsed to the ground with the heavy softness of a meal bag.

They walked back to the cabin and, taking two guns and a saddle, left without any explanation. Mrs. Harris stared at them with the expectant dim expression of a rodent. The children were already asleep in the bed, peaceful. The wind blew and slapped a tree limb against the back wall, making the boys jump whenever it hit smartly. The night was otherwise still but not peaceful. The souls of men slain were in the wind.

Brown told his boys to wash off their swords in the creek. They were done with the Lord's work for that night, he said.

Chapter 27
1856: Nichols's Breakdown

JUNE 13, Thomas Nichols woke up unable to move his right hand. He was aware of no pain, no symptoms of disease, only a paralyzing weight that seemed to press down on his chest. He poked at his right hand with his left, lifted it up, and put it down lifeless again. It had the normal sensations. It gave off no prickles or pain. Yet his attempts to move it yielded nothing. It lay on his stomach like a beached fish.

Of late, in the aftermath of the blood at Pottawatomie, he had been pressed down by exhaustion, barely dragging himself from bed each day. Today he did not even attempt to rise. He lay under the bedclothes while squares of sun from two windows warmed the bed, while flies stunned in the night chill came to loud, buzzing life.

He wanted, not to die, but simply not to have to continue. He would gladly have stopped moving, stopped thinking. Yet sensations and observations continued heavily and painfully in and out of mind, and he received them helplessly.

Oddly, his discovery that he was paralyzed seemed to lift his burden slightly. To call it a relief would be a mistake. Nothing was a relief. It did, however, give him credibility. He was sick. He would not have to endure the suspicion he felt lurking just under Ruth's brisk care.

"Ruth!" he cried, not too loudly. "Ruth!"

He heard her climbing the stairs, her footsteps still light and quick after all these years. She did not believe him, or perhaps she did not understand him, when he said he could not move his hand. She wore the look of forced patience she put on when interrupted in some duty. "Let me adjust your pillow," she said, and lifted his head with surprising strength. Then, hesitating a moment, pushing her straw-blond hair out of her face, she seemed to reconsider. Sitting down slowly on the edge of the bed, she took his hand in hers and began to massage it. How soft and cool her fingers felt! He was surprised by the pleasure of the sensation. He closed his eyes.

The sensations of weight had begun on the day he received Martin's letter. Thomas remembered finding Martin's sheet heavy in his fingers, the coarse paper itself seeming to weigh pounds. His brother rarely wrote, had not written in years. "That was a knock-down argument!" Martin wrote in rageful triumph of Sumner's beating and turned to blaming Thomas for the blood in Kansas. "I had warned you that your abolitionist extremism could only lead to one result, that of bloodshed," the letter said. "How can this be the Lord's holiness?" For days the newspapers had been filled with reports of Southern legislatures congratulating Brooks for his noble deed, with excerpts from Southern newspapers editorializing on the need for a thousand Brooks if the Congress were to become again a fit vessel for Southern honor. Sumner lay in a hospital, struggling for life.

Nichols bought five or six newspapers each day and read them in his office, sometimes to the detriment of his affairs. He could not say, when Ruth asked him, what he looked for so fervidly. He was as likely to become more misinformed as less for all the reading. The news was of Kansas, bloody Kansas, a war with no battle lines and a baffling and transient cast of characters. Captain Brown, Indian Joe, Senator Atchison, Dutch Henry Sherman, any of the vivid players might turn up in the stories for a day or a week and then disappear again, apparently forever.

He found himself unable to sleep. He thought it was the stale, warm air that hung over the city in late May, but when nights turned gray and cool again he still lay listening to the clocks strike the hour, feeling the fatigue and the weight on his chest. His arms turned to heavy flab, and his shoulders became hundred-pound sacks of flour.

Now, struck down by paralysis, he simply lay in bed. Ruth came and massaged his hand twice a day. Sometimes she sang to him in a sweet, rusty alto, but she seldom spoke. He was glad. He could not bear her questions. Even her presence seemed to pose a doubt. He rose almost to a condition of contentment only when her mouth was filled with song and her pliant cool fingers worked his hand.

In a week the paralysis had spread to his right shoulder, while his left hand was also growing weak and limp. When he rose from bed to totter to the chamber pot he clutched his right hand in his left, to keep it from swinging, but now the left hand was so weak the right broke free. He let both hands hang and walked more slowly. He felt no wish to cry. He was not afraid. It occurred to him to feel pity for Ruth, and for the children (whom he rarely saw, and they always whispered when they went by outside his room). Yet that was theoretical pity. In reality he felt nothing more than the persistent dragging wish that he should not have to go on with the next moment of life. He imagined a whirlpool, languorously, greedily slurping his unstruggling body into the bubbling darkness. Whirled once around, twice, falling deeper into the center, then gone.

Ruth called in the doctor, who prescribed a quantity of blue calomel pills and put a leech on Nichols's right hand, just at the wrist. Nichols had never seen one so closely, soft and dully glistening. He watched the dark creature closely, as its ridges and corrugations smoothed into supple fatness. When it was plump with his blood and plucked off, only a tiny red mark was left on the white inner skin of his wrist. This mark bled freely onto a wad of sheep's wool, tied to his skin by a cord. He felt no better but slept the night. Once he woke in panic, sure that his sheet was drenched in blood. It was only his perspiration. The weather had turned warm once again.

He did not mind the doctor's visits, the proddings and examinations. He felt like a horse up for auction and had the horse's neutrality, not caring where he was taken or what was done so long as it was not painful. Ruth, however, watched the visitations with an eye to results. Nichols heard her ask the doctor what he expected. The doctor, a broad-chested man with a wide spade of beard, looked at her with annoyance—he did not seem to like her; perhaps he did not like women generally—and said that such cases were entirely beyond the powers of science to predict.

Next morning Ruth woke Thomas early, pulling back the draperies to let in light. "I asked Reverend Morris to visit," she said briskly. "He has brought some of the elders." A few minutes later half a dozen men in business attire came in, talking with lowered voices. Morris, a young and cheerful Scotsman built low to the ground like a badger, with a thick black stubble of freshly shaved beard, had brought a small vial of olive oil that he said came from ancient trees on the Mount of Olives. The thought flitted across Nichols's mind that there was something Roman Catholic in this, but he had no energy even to consider reproval. James's admonition to pray for the sick was read, a spot of oil was pressed on his wounded hand, prayers were said.

"I trust you will be feeling better, Brother Thomas," the pastor said with cheerful solicitude. "We shall persevere in prayer." He pressed his hand warmly against Thomas's.

This, however, produced no better results. After two days of watching warily, testing his health with her eye, Ruth asked whether he would consider the water cure.

He said nothing, having lost any sense of needing to speak.

"Lizzy Brewington has a cousin who had the treatments at Orange Mountain," Ruth said. "She was helped tremendously. It is a very *scientific* technique, rigorously applied, nothing like the fashion of the mineral spas."

She waited for him to respond, and when he still simply stared, went on. "One must go for several weeks, perhaps even for months. I could not attend you, but I thought Rebecca might go. She needs to be about."

Thomas understood: perhaps Rebecca might meet a marriageable man. She had grown up as a tall, straight girl, with a pockmarked face and high cheekbones. At twenty-three she had a hesitation in her speech, a doubt in her look. Ruth was impatient with her.

The next morning Ruth brought in a strong, young cabman, smelling of onions, to help Thomas down the stairs. She had wanted to dress him in a suit, but he balked, shaking his head. A suit seemed very scratchy to him now. She let him go out in his nightshirt with a robe and slippers. It was a fine June day. Somewhere at the back of his consciousness he felt that he was slipping away from a life precious to him, but he could not bring himself to feel it. He went easily to Orange Mountain.

"And this must be Mr. Nichols?"

Four women stood clustered by a low gray-stone wall, overlooking a spreading valley filled with trees. The women did not face him directly, but at angles, cool but interested in the company he might offer. All four wore supple white dresses. They were young but not too young, well dressed but not quite fashionable, with faces that were not beautiful but interesting.

He merely stared, dull as an ox. Rebecca said, "Yes, this is Mr. Nichols. I am his daughter." She shook all of their hands.

At Orange Mountain, creamy frame buildings fronted one large stretch of grass, which a population of three fat sheep kept clipped to an even green carpet. A sanded trail led to the bathhouses, peeled-log rectangles open to the sky under the maple and oak forest, one house for females and the other (smaller) for males. Every morning Nichols was taken there promptly at 7:00 by a heavyset, red-faced attendant whose most prominent feature was a spreading sandy mustache covering his mouth. It occurred to Nichols to wonder just what Evans's teeth were like, and whether he had deliberately obscured them from sight. Fortunately the man did not talk like some of the callow female attendants whose conversation Nichols overheard. Evans showed less curiosity for Nichols than Nichols showed for him. His concerns were dominated by a stern desire that Nichols follow the strict regimen of the establishment.

That began with Evans wrapping him tightly as a papoose in wet wool blankets. Evans insisted on punctuality at the bathhouse, partly, he said, because the good blankets were used up if you dallied on the way. Certain blankets, which Evans recognized by sight (a frayed binding, a discolored edge) were more effective in creating the desired crisis and purging the system of bodily poisons.

The blankets gave off a strong, sour odor like sauerkraut. Though clammy and chill at first, they soon warmed on Nichols's body, and a powerful itching sensation ensued. This grew stronger on each successive day as a violent red and pus-filled rash spread across his chest and thighs. He perspired profusely in the blankets, sometimes feeling a frightening sense of constriction and suffocation. Evans would reprove him with muttered words like, "Hold up, Master," and "Be faithful." When Nichols was nearly at his wits' end, Evans would bodily lift him like a wrapped package and plunge him, feet first, into the cold of a bath.

Quickly Evans would unwrap him, letting the icy water numb his inflamed skin. The poisons would rush out and congeal on the surface of the water, a collagenous film that had the same sour smell as the blankets. When the cold had penetrated, Evans would lift him out of the water, limp as a newborn lamb, and rub him with rough, stinging linen, then wrap his shivering body in a dry woolen blanket and lead him stumbling back to his room. He would be made to drink down two quarts of the healthful waters and be put into bed. Nearly always he would fall asleep, utterly dreamless until his daughter Rebecca came in with the morning tea.

Yes, he had backslidden into tea. Ruth would be disturbed if she knew he drank it, but she seemed so far distant that he could not concern himself with her views. He found it a relief to be apart from her and from everything and everyone that he knew. Nothing broke into the monotony of the day except his baths, three times a day, the prescribed long promenades through the woods, and periodic, sluggish strolls across the grass to fill his jug with spring water. Evans watched his intake closely, and Nichols did not resist. Monotony was the diet he craved. The water treatment, with its regular and mechanical application of duty, matched his torpid state of mind. Nichols had no desire to speak, to see, to move at all, but he was content to follow directions. He saw no newspaper.

For the first weeks he stayed alone, unable to bear the sight of anyone other than Rebecca and Evans. Change came gradually. He saw that Rebecca longed for a more social existence, and after a time he went with her to join the other patients in the open-air dining room. Instead of taking tea in his bed he began to walk to the veranda where tea was brought out on a cart. He stood by Rebecca while she shyly joined the claque of women talking of their crises, recommending particular vistas for their promenades, sharing their symptoms, and encouraging each other to see hopeful signs of their recovery.

It was a flavor of conversation he hardly knew—more private and less pointed than anything he had encountered in business or benevolence. To Thomas it was like a new music: sinuous, lovely, but outside his powers to emulate. He never spoke. He merely listened, and found the conversation, both form and substance, restful. There was, besides talk of health, a great deal of interest in handwork, in children's education, in music, and virtually none in politics. Nothing that a newspaper concerned itself with made much space in their talk.

Nichols felt peaceable, but his arms remained paralyzed. Doctor Von Rensler, who operated the clinic, would venture no opinion. He said only that the case was difficult and would bear close watching.

The women at Orange Mountain had developed an intelligent consensus that eruptive crises, when the skin boiled and heaved in patches of red and gray and yellow, and strong fevers alternated with chills, were the surest sign of approaching health. They were extremely interested in Nichols's case and looked at him with a certain fond regard, as if he were their pet project. They were quietly sure in their conversations with Rebecca that he had become too anxious about the Kansas debate, a worthy concern certainly, but one that should not be allowed to endanger health.

"One owes a duty to his children," a Mrs. Trout said, her lips puckering with the importance of the thought. "One must gain self-mastery over thoughts that distract one from duty."

He felt, then, a tiny drop of pride when Rebecca was able to speak of his increased rashes, the fits of itching that tormented him at night, the dreadful diseased quality of his skin on the chest and shoulders, demonstrating most certainly that a great deal of internal toxin wanted to pass out through his dermis. They thought for a time that he was on the verge of the healing crisis. Each day the ladies asked Rebecca how her father did (they never addressed him directly but looked at him indulgently). As the days passed and the turning point did not come, she spoke more confusedly, as though flustered.

After four weeks at Orange Mountain, Rebecca began fretting. "How long will we stay here?" she asked her father one day, "if the treatment brings no relief?" She stared at him as though expecting a reply, and when he made none she turned away with a jerk of her neck.

He felt vaguely sorry that she was unhappy, but he could not help it or understand it. What could he do? He seemed to hang in time like a Chinaman's paper lantern. She became more demanding when she fed him his meals (everything had to be spooned into him), putting the next mouthful up to his lips before he had quite finished the previous one. He had felt the silence between them as fond and comfortable. Relations now became unpleasantly tight.

Then, on a Tuesday, Rebecca refused to go to the lawn for tea. Nichols pointed mutely to his watch to indicate that the hour had arrived. "I cannot," she said, tears starting in her eyes. "You will have to go by yourself."

Of course he could not go alone, so he lay down on his bed and pretended to sleep. He felt quite sorry for himself, thinking at first that his failure to heal was prompting her refusal. She was frustrated with him, and he could not help it. Then, however, he considered the possibility of another cause. Had someone offended her?

He observed Rebecca while she spooned him his noon meal. She seemed veiled in sadness, a plain cipher, her face red and rough, remote from him as he was from her. He would have liked to know what had happened, but he could no more ask than he could fly.

He required two days of watching to work it out, not because it was so difficult a deduction but because his mind had reverted to wandering through vacant spaces. Then from nowhere, as if in a vision appearing out of those blurred vistas, his memory scanned a young man, dull and serious and slight. A young man who wore his collar up. The vision was fragmentary but quite clear. He could see the collar and the wisping beard, though not the eyes. Where had he seen this young man? What was his name? Orange Mountain attracted a few men, usually for short visits. He believed he had seen the man at their teas. Surely Rebecca had hoped to attract him. Perhaps they had even spoken, perhaps he had given her some hope.

As soon as Nichols reached this conclusion, he was sure of it and appalled. He could not remember the man's name, nor even his face, but he despised him for smug and cruel behavior. Poor child Rebecca, attaching her hopes to any stick figure who happened to wear pants.

He could not sustain the effort of grief, however. For only a very short time her little sadness could affect him. Then the weight on his chest seemed to come down like an elephant's foot, making it too difficult to think of her anymore.

The rash had been excellent from the beginning, but now a fever began to brew up at night, making him tremble and sweat through all the dark hours and leaving him flimsy as paper. These were considered more hopeful signs of a crisis. He was a spectator to it. He watched himself go down into the night and emerge fluttering like a leaf in the morning light. As the fever increased he did not sleep at night nor really awaken in the day; he endured the hours in a stupor. When he opened his eyes Rebecca was near, holding a cup of water that she wanted him to drink. The purging of poisons required that he take in vast quantities of pure water from this cup with its metallic scent and a burr on its lip.

Each time he surfaced from insensibility Rebecca seemed higher above him, as though he looked up at her from a well. Through his stupor he saw that she was agitated. He dreamed of her weeping, shaking, sobbing.

Did she do these things in reality? He did not know. He could not divide his dreams from truth. He felt something like regret that she should suffer, and something like curiosity that she should prove so fragile, yet he could not even reach his hand to hers in comfort. He had become, in his sickness, almost a wraith. He wondered whether he was about to die. The possibility did not frighten him or fill him with dismay. He only thought, *Let's go on with whatever must be.*

———————————

For Rebecca, benevolent organizations and church activities had never been enough. She had a romantic character caught in a plain, dull covering. Outside she was so uninteresting that no man ever looked at her twice. Inside she teemed with reckless love. Marriage would have been best for her, so she could work out her spirit through the drama of family. But she was not going to marry, it seemed. She was too plain and her tongue too thick to charm a man's interest. And now she was too old, as well. The day might come when she could find a suitable role in helping to raise her brother's children, whenever he married and had a home to share. In the meantime she took solace from the reading of novels. They were her gateway to a full life.

A friend supplied the books. Her family did not know and certainly would not have approved. The books were remarkably pious, but for her and her kin, living still under the shadow of Jonathan Edwards, they smelled of Vanity Fair. They would not make you consider your death; they made you think of your life.

The publication of *Uncle Tom's Cabin*, clever, lively, sentimental, and Christian all at the same time, disturbed these barriers a little. The secret and guilty life Rebecca had cultivated, the life of romantic imagination, unexpectedly bumped into her parents' religious world. One might be an abolitionist, a Christian, and a novelist, all at once! Yet shy and clumsy as she was, Rebecca found no real avenues for exploring this possibility.

That was why she responded avidly to the society of women she met at Orange Mountain. They had intense and rich lives. They could speak with astonishing frankness of themselves. They gathered Rebecca into their conversations and urged her on in her creative spirit. She wrote in her diary, "I have come to see that I contain in my inner self the possibility of spiritual energy, to animate those of like spirit."

Then *he* came. His name was Netherton and was obscurely related to the famous Congregational preacher; he was a neat, proper gentleman who wore his collars high and looked at her, as at everything, like a cat staring at a spider. He never said why he was taking the cure. There seemed nothing wrong with him.

She did not believe her own eyes at first, that he was looking especially at her. It roiled her spirit. She might never have believed what she saw in his eyes, except that Mrs. Staples, a round and motherly woman who had once visited Paris, began to smile at her knowingly whenever *he* approached. Rebecca blushed with annoyance and let Mrs. Staples see she was extremely vexed, but the lady continued to smile until one day Rebecca could bear it no more.

"Mrs. Staples, whatever are you smiling at when you smile at me so often?" She asked it privately, while they were taking a long promenade along Sue Creek.

"Oh, my dear, I am sure you know."

Rebecca was quiet, mulling over this answer while they walked. Mrs. Staples pointed with her walking stick at several pretty scenes of the brook, but Rebecca made no sign of response. It took her considerable courage to speak again.

"I really do not know why you smile, Mrs. Staples."

Mrs. Staples was kind enough not to laugh at her. She looked at her fondly, studying her face. "Miss Nichols, I see a young man spending much of his time watching your eyes. It is a pleasant sight, so I smile. I thought you might also find it pleasant."

They said no more about it, but continued their walk with Rebecca's mind tumbling in confusion and her face patched with red. She parted from Mrs. Staples at the blue bridge, continuing her walk up the unmarked pathway to the top of Feather Ridge. An outcrop of rock made a seat there, with a view down the green valley, dark forest framing the seam of the creek with a quilting of long grass meadows and farms.

The more she thought, the more agitated she became, until she gave up the effort of reaching serenity. He watched her eyes! She wondered whether this was the precise moment when one's true destiny is revealed, the moment that afterward seems to contain one's heaven and earth, seed-like and ready to grow.

Of course she said nothing to her father or to anyone else, least of all Mr. Netherton. She made no mistake after that, however. He was looking at her.

A few days later he called her name, as she was walking to the cottage with the water jug. She stopped. He offered to accompany her across the few yards of grass.

"I don't need any help, thank you," she said quickly, from embarrass-ment, and turned her head away.

She had not taken three steps before she realized what she had done. Yet she could not turn and undo it. If she were to turn back to him, what would he think? She went indoors and sat down, staring, in a straight wooden chair by the door. She was terror stricken. Had she hurt his tender heart? Had she ruined her destiny of love? Fortunately she saw him at tea, and he smiled at her again.

Sometimes in the conversations over tea he would ask her opinions. She never had any satisfying answer, though afterward at night, or while she was spooning dinner into her father, she would think of a thousand good responses. Mr. Netherton spoke to her again one evening when she was standing at the front door of the cottage. Her father had begun to fever, and it meant little sleep for her. She was facing another exhausting night and had stepped outside for momentary peace, looking over the yellowing grass leading up to the main hall.

"Miss Nichols."

He had come up behind her and was standing near, startlingly so. She almost threw her face into her hands, but she controlled her impulse and clenched her fingers at her side. "Mr. Netherton," she managed to say.

"Is your father ill, Miss Nichols? I thought he did not look well."

"Yes, he has a fever in the evenings."

"Perhaps it is the beginnings of a crisis."

She was dumb; she could not think what she could say. She sucked on her cheeks, and then realized that it was an ugly habit and stopped it, but still had nothing pleasant to say.

"Miss Nichols, it would be a joy to you, I am sure, if your father recovered, but a trial to the rest of us."

"Why, Mr. Netherton?"

"Because you would go and leave us, and perhaps we would never see you again."

She was so confused that she excused herself and went inside. She never thought about the impression she must have made on him; she could only think what she had heard. Her ears roared with the sound of his last sentence, and her mind shouted the signs of destiny.

She did not see Mr. Netherton the following day, but thought nothing of it because she was occupied with her father's increasing illness. The second day she was prepared for Mr. Netherton, however, ready to smile steadily at him. He was not there. He did not appear at dinner. He did not appear at afternoon tea. She was afraid to ask about him, to seem forward or unladylike. He might be ill. Any number of reasons might explain his absence.

Then after two more days had passed she could not ask because it would seem so odd, to inquire four days after his disappearance. Yet he was gone. Unquestionably, he was gone.

Why had she been so foolish and cold? She berated herself, bitterly. She had turned away when he spoke. She had not given him an instant's encouragement. Who could blame him for departing? Now apparently she would never know where he had gone. The ladies said nothing of him. They assumed, perhaps, that she understood the cause of his leaving.

She thought of this constantly while she tended her father. He was suffering the fevers, looking at her with his watery, cold eyes. She could not bear to look at him, to face his contempt. Her father, she thought, had never cared about her fate. He would not care now. He only wanted a nurse. His fever kept her awake at night, and she grew more and more weary. Finally, one night, she began to tremble and could not stop. A pitcher fell accidentally out of her hand and shattered, and when she knelt down to pick up the shards she could not even grip them, her hands shook so furiously. She dropped the few bits of pottery she held in her palm and went out, without even searching out a sweater.

Thomas woke from his fever dizzy and confused, feeling an instant panic yet unable to say why until he realized that the space around his head was vacant. He cast his eyes about and discovered only the smooth plaster. He was quite alone in his room. Only one picture decorated the wall, a pen drawing of President Washington. That old, stolid, dull face looked down on him, a vaguely disapproving stare. He drifted asleep to dream of a meeting of presidents, decrepit, stern men who muttered disapproval.

Again he awoke, hot with fever, and panicky. He opened his eyes thinking he would still be alone. But over him he found a dark face.

As a child he had always been tended by his nurse, Black Mary. The face of a black woman remained the most consoling sight he knew in sickness. He did not even think who this woman might be, he merely felt comforted, nursed. He closed his eyes and rested. When he opened them again he saw that the woman was Catherine Nichols. Just as he recognized her and tried to speak, she turned away, and his mind traveled also to other thoughts. He fell asleep again, dreaming.

Apparently her face remained in his mind, however, even as he slept.

He dreamed of armies, uniformed and marching ranks, which, when they came close and raised their guns, were revealed as black men, their faces darker than a hole in a barn, reflecting no light. The armies lifted off the earth to fly above it, sweeping its surface like hawks on the hunt. The ground was seared beneath them, tongues of fire from their eyes setting the grasses on fire.

He woke and found the room vacant again. The dream seemed still to march in his brain. Frightened, he cried out. The sound of his voice was strange to him, he had heard it so little lately. It seemed like that of an old man, hoarse and ragged. Yes, he heard it again, and the voice was his own.

Catherine Nichols came into the room, frowning at him.

"Where is my daughter?" Thomas demanded, surprising himself again with that unfamiliar rasping voice. "Where is Rebecca?" He felt shaky, dreamy, unsettled by Catherine's ghostly presence.

"She is resting," Catherine said, sliding a practiced hand onto his forehead.

"Where is she? Why did she leave me?" He was still frightened. His dream was too close, and he was not sure if he was dreaming still.

"She was weary," Catherine said. "Rest now yourself. She has worn herself to a frazzle."

"Are you really Catherine?"

She glanced at him with a jaded smile he seemed to remember well, but she did not answer.

"Why are you here?" he asked.

"I am a guest at the water cure," she said, pressing her lips together. "I found your daughter nerve-racked and came to nurse you in her place."

"A guest?"

"Yes, a guest of Mrs. Fosters of Rochester. You know her?"

He shook his head.

"A very distinguished lady." Catherine lowered the blinds on her eyes, as though daring him to doubt her. "Now hush. You have passed the crisis, but care is needed."

Catherine Nichols had come to Orange Mountain as companion and nurse to Mrs. Fosters, a widow from Rochester who supported Frederick Douglass's paper. Catherine had moved to Rochester specifically to help Douglass with his affairs. He had invited her assistance, and she was weary of sewing shirts and cooking meals. Working on a paper would be more interesting, she believed.

She soon realized that Douglass's *North Star* was too poor to support her. Douglass had, in any case, an Englishwoman working with him who made it plain she had no intention of sharing his attentions. Douglass, always resourceful, introduced Catherine to Mrs. Fosters, who enjoyed shocking people by living with a black companion. Catherine had no work to do for Mrs. Fosters, except to live a life of ease and carry on conversation.

Mrs. Fosters had come to Orange Mountain to take the cure, though Catherine possessed no idea just what Mrs. Fosters considered to be in need of repair. The lady seemed perfectly healthy to her. None of the patients at Orange Mountain appeared truly sick. She commented on it, and Mrs. Fosters pointed out Rebecca one afternoon, stalking gloomily to the spring with a pitcher in her grip. The young lady's father, Mrs. Fosters understood, was paralyzed in the hands. The doctors were mystified, and the water cure was his only hope.

"The young lady would seem to require a cure herself," Catherine had said. "I never saw a sight so dismal."

She discovered the daughter two nights later, when out walking under a moon. Hearing Rebecca's soft shushing weeping, Catherine explored the shadows until she found her folded up in a dark corner of the main building, half behind a chimney, where no one might have seen her all night. The young woman was trembling. Her dark hair hung in her eyes as though she were mad. She could speak nothing, could not even stammer out her name. Catherine led her gently to Mrs. Fosters. Together they tucked her into Catherine's bed. Then Mrs. Fosters suggested that

Catherine go to see to the young lady's father. "He is quite sick, I understand," she said. "He may need some assistance. At least he ought to know that we have her safe in bed here."

Catherine went in and saw the patient, sleeping fitfully in a narrow bed by the window. Even before she felt his skin she knew he was quite ill. The smell of fever was there, a scent she forever associated with the death of her master, the old man Nichols, so long ago. When she lightly touched the skin on the man's neck she felt it burning. His figure twitched, shrinking away from her touch. Someone needed to watch him.

She took up the lantern, intending to go for help, then hesitated a moment. She held the lamp up over the man, trying to think what she had overlooked. Disturbed by the light, perhaps, he flopped over in her direction. She saw in an instant the strong delicate features, the gray hair. Thomas Nichols. After she was done with the shock, she laughed.

"You can't keep away from me, no matter how you try," she said to herself, smiling. She thought that if he awoke and found her he might well die of the surprise. Although he had treated her shabbily she felt no real rancor for the man. He meant no harm, she thought; he was just terrified of his past.

She settled down in a chair to watch him. That was how Thomas Nichols found her in the morning, when the fever began to break.

"Look," Thomas said to Rebecca, his voice flush with joy. "Look, I can move." On his right hand he lifted the first three fingers and set them down again.

Rebecca was instantly weeping. "Oh! How? When did you . . ."

"I don't know. I forgot my sickness this morning and reached out for my cup."

"Let us thank God," she said. "Really, we *must* thank him."

Tears welled up in Thomas's own eyes, and he lay back in bed, blinking them away. The physical change was infinitesimal, but what freedom of action it promised! He jiggled the fingers again. It was the easiest thing in the world to decide to move them and to have it so.

The next day he could rub his fingers together. A day after that he lifted his entire right arm from the bed and held it tremblingly aloft for a few seconds. He broke down and wept at that and was weak from emotion during the entire afternoon. The healing had begun. His flesh was weak yet renewed in motion. Restoration! Somehow, he felt, he would now live a different life, nevermore dull and fearful. The presence of Catherine Nichols moving freely in and out of his room, his old hidden shame unburied, made a part of that new hope.

He had to endure visits from everyone when they heard of the cure. All of Rebecca's acquaintances gaggled in, more to say they had seen him than because they cared to talk with him. Doctor Von Rensler would not allow him to move too much; he said that he must beware a relapse. His hands were still weak; he must write with a pen with each hand for half an hour a day, to strengthen and restore the nervous tissue. Of course the water cures that had done the miracle must continue. (Von Rensler insisted that Rebecca not refer to the cure as a miracle, however. The matter was science, he said.)

Meanwhile, Rebecca became acquainted with Mrs. Fosters and with Catherine. She found their association quite stimulating and romantic. Every time she heard them talk with their astounding naturalness, behaving as equals though black and white, she felt as though she had stumbled into an exotic world. Even Mrs. Stowe had never imagined such a thing, Rebecca thought.

That one awful night had washed Mr. Netherton completely out of Rebecca. She felt an occasional pang when she thought of him, but mostly because of the foolish way she had reacted to her disappointment. No one seemed to blame her.

Mrs. Fosters perceived that Thomas and Catherine had some past acquaintance. Their way was too familiar for anything else. "You must admit," she insisted during one of their long afternoon promenades, "that you know each other from very long ago."

They did not contradict her, so she went on. "Catherine, you never told me you had ever lived in New York City. What ever did you do there?"

"I have never set foot in that place, Livia," Catherine maintained. "Mr. Nichols and I are acquainted from the Christian Antislavery Convention, where my son was a principal speaker."

This satisfied Mrs. Fosters for a time, but a few days later she was working on her suspicions again. She asked Catherine—innocently, it seemed—about her escape from slavery. Catherine said she had been given her freedom when her owner died. As a free black woman she had been driven from place to place, trying to provide for her son. Finally she had come to the North at Cincinnati.

"But where was your home in the South?" Mrs. Fosters asked.

"It was in the state of Alabama," Catherine said carelessly. "That is the real cotton South. When a slave is sold to Alabama, he says good-bye to his life."

"A terrible and cruel place for a slave, no doubt," Mrs. Fosters said.

"Papa," Rebecca said, "did you see such terrible things when you were a boy?" For of course she knew that he had come to New York from Alabama.

Then Mrs. Fosters put together the facts, that they shared a name, that they came from the same state. She was able to worm out of Thomas that Catherine had been his father's slave. They had grown up together on the same plot of land, he admitted. At this revelation Mrs. Fosters was as jubilant as a child. To think, she said, that the master and his slave had now arrived at Orange Mountain as friends and equals.

Thomas saw that Catherine would remain reticent. Of course she did not want the detailed past known any more than he did. Besides, other guests at Orange Mountain seemed a great deal less interested than did Mrs. Fosters and Rebecca. The subject was distasteful to them; they would not talk much of it when Mrs. Fosters raised it in conversation.

Thomas had not counted on his daughter's moral curiosity, however. One evening, while she was rubbing salve on his shoulders, Rebecca asked him why he had never invited Catherine to their home.

"I only met her one time, in Chicago, and then very briefly," he said. "She was not near. She lives in the western part of the state, you know."

"You never mentioned her, either," Rebecca said. "I am sure I would have remembered if you had."

"Well, I do not mention many people whom I meet. How many men and women do you think I encounter?"

Then he recognized her drift. She spoke from fear that he was prejudiced. She thought that he had kept Catherine secret because Catherine was black. She believed that he had not wanted to associate with a Negro.

"My dear," he said. He extended one still-weak hand to touch her shoulder. "Do you think that this is because I am ashamed of Mrs. Nichols? It is because I am ashamed of myself. I took part in the most inhumane treatment of fellow persons. I not only approved, I encouraged it. I have never wanted to speak of such terrible sins."

"But that was before you were converted!"

"Yes. Yet it is still very painful to me today. I am a new creature in Christ, and I want to put to death everything of that old man. I do not mind speaking of these memories with you, but I hope you will never mention them in other circles, even at our home. Let this be our private subject. I do not want your mother to know of it. It would be too painful for her to think of me in that light."

She looked at him wide-eyed. "Do you mean we could talk of these matters with Mrs. Nichols?"

He hesitated, considering. "If you like you may," he said. "Only do not pry. She may find the memories difficult as well."

"Oh, of course. To think, she was once a slave!"

"There was nothing romantic about it," he warned.

So Rebecca did ask, and one warm afternoon on the veranda he and Catherine spoke of their past. At first they were both reticent, but then began taking some open pleasure in remembering characters they had known together. Black Mary was discussed; so was James Birney and the day he had read the will freeing the Triana slaves. For Thomas, that was a powerfully moving conversation. He was a far different man from the one who once sulked over the loss of human chattel. He could remember his brother's fury, his demand that all the celebrating slaves be beaten. Today, he thought, I would be one with those in the celebration.

He wondered whether Catherine still remembered the way he had come to her and used her. Perhaps she had all but forgotten about *him* on that day.

Mrs. Fosters thought it the most marvelously interesting discussion she had ever heard and said they ought to write it in the *North Star*. But Thomas sternly begged her not to talk about it at all. Rebecca, taking pleasure in a secret, assured her father she would never tell.

Chapter 28
1857: Confession

THOMAS NICHOLS found it hard to return to the world. He tried to read only one newspaper and to purge his mind of its contents afterward, so he would not dwell on the outrages poisoning the country. He feared that the heaviness—the weight that had lifted from his arms and shoulders—would crush down on him again. Yet he could not avoid the subject of slavery. It was the one constant note of the time.

Old Judge Taney, an arrogant, doddering soul, determined that he would at one stroke solve the slave dilemma by writing a wide opinion regarding *Dred Scott*. In March he presented the Supreme Court decision that no Negro could be a citizen of the United States, that blacks could have "no rights which a white man was bound to respect." Furthermore, Taney said that the Constitution gave the government no right to ban slavery in the territories.

People predicted the Union could not survive. Their great nation, the home of democracy, would be smashed up like crockery. It seemed inevitable, and yet it had not happened so far, and they waited as if helpless.

Thomas knew he had never done enough to end slavery, because he had worked harder at his manufactory than at abolition. He also knew that no matter what he or anyone might have done, it was all in vain. He was both culpable and helpless, so it seemed. He thought, in this regard, of the old gibe against the Calvinists: "You can and you can't, you will and you won't, you're damned if you do and damned if you don't." It seemed to apply to abolition.

Toward the end of the summer a large insurance company failed, shaking the markets. Since Thomas's business was old and predictable, he paid little attention to the panic until, in September, he had a large order returned to his factory. Next day, having done quick calculations of inventory, Thomas closed his factory until the first of October. His workers dragged past the pay window, getting their last take-home. Most of them were too young to remember 1837, Thomas thought, so how did they know to be despondent?

October came, and he did not reopen. One heard daily rumors of the collapse of land prices. A clipper went down off South America bearing $20 million in gold from San Francisco. No one would do any business.

On October 7, Thomas was in his office when his chief clerk rapped on the glass. Jacob was a tiny, balding, middle-aged man. "You ought to come out," he said in a high, excited voice. "Men are running in the street. They say they are throwing the market away. I thought you would like to know." He turned and disappeared down the stairway.

Thomas descended to stand in the front door of the building. At first the street seemed its ordinary gray self. Then a young man with yellow hair came pounding around the corner, ran past them with a grim expression printed on his pale face, and disappeared, swinging himself around the next corner by a lamppost. A few minutes later two men on horseback, bareheaded and dressed in black suits, galloped down the street by the same route.

A squad of top-hatted, black-suited, sober men—seven or eight of them—came up the street in the opposite direction, all of them talking wildly. One was laughing and pushing the others' backs. "The world has gone mad," one of them cried out to Thomas and the clerk.

"What has happened?"

"Mobs and mobs trying to sell pieces of paper, and no one to buy."

Within days all banks stopped paying in coin. "There is nothing but paper trading hands," Thomas told his daughter Rebecca when he came home. "Worthless paper flying around in the wind. No one will buy. All the hard money has disappeared."

He grew silent. He knew, because people mentioned it. When he opened his mouth it seemed to take longer for words to come out. Rebecca brought him tea when he came home each evening. (Ruth would not touch the substance.) She was a comfortable presence, who did not ask for too much.

"Surely it is punishment for our national sins," Rebecca said when he told her of the crash. "How many of these concerns have their fingers in the profits of slavery?"

"It ruins us all," he said. "Pure or impure." He meant the market crash, but as he spoke he realized his words could refer to slavery as well. He felt the weight bearing on his chest and took a deep breath to try to loosen it.

"For every evil there is some good," Rebecca said shyly. "Have you heard of the prayer meeting at the Fulton Street Church?"

"That is Reverend Lanphier's," he said. Over the summer Lanphier had come to the Old Dutch Church in connection with the visitation of poor families—a plan that Rebecca was involved with through the New York Sunday School Union. In the spring she and another young woman had gone door by door through a poor neighborhood. Every month they went back to visit the families. She liked to tell him their complicated stories.

"I heard a man say the gathering was so solemn it sent chills down his back," Rebecca said.

He *had* heard of the meeting and wondered now why he felt no impulse to attend. Really, he was doing almost nothing at his place of business. They did no manufacturing and almost no sales. He could calculate his finances four or five times a day if he liked, in more or less elaborate detail, but he had no vital energy to do anything in response, and at any rate what could he do?

Lewis Tappan came by his office one afternoon to talk of the same prayer meeting. Tappan's hair was quite silvered and his hand unsteady. He said daily prayer meetings were springing to life all over the city.

Nichols went to see on the very next day.

Arriving at the Old Dutch Church at a quarter till twelve, his first impression was that he was in the wrong place, for the prayer meeting had more the look of a bank run. A solid phalanx of black-coated, top-hatted men surrounded the door, waiting their turns to enter. More rushed up behind at every minute. Nichols recognized not a single soul.

Inside the sanctuary, young men scurried down the aisles to get a good seat. Nichols watched in astonishment as men poured in ceaselessly behind him, filling every pew, and then gushed in yet more, to fill up the platform and the choir and the steps. Finally the aisles were jammed up, and still men pushed their way forward. The steeple clock struck the hour, and before the first loud bell had sounded, complete staring silence fell over the building. The twelve chimes slowly rang in the hour, as though signaling that the multitude had assembled for the world's last night.

From the back of the auditorium a single tenor voice began to sing, and in two beats the whole meaty throng had joined in, a deep, slow, shuddering Old Hundredth:

> *All people that on earth do dwell,*
> *Sing to the Lord with cheerful voice;*
> *Him serve with mirth; his praise forth tell,*
> *Come ye before him and rejoice.*

All four verses were sung in the same way, vibrating up through the floor into Nichols's backbone. Then silence reigned again, a watchful silence. One voice rose from the balcony, a voice deep and somber, reading from Holy Scripture the words of Isaiah:

Behold, the nations are as a drop of a bucket, and are counted as the small dust of the balance: behold, he taketh up the isles as a very little thing. And Lebanon is not sufficient to burn, nor the beasts thereof sufficient for a burnt offering. All nations before him are as nothing; and they are counted to him less than nothing, and vanity.

Again silence, until a little man just in front of Thomas stood up and asked to pray. He led them with a plaintive, sharp voice, like the sound of a key dropping on a wood floor. He prayed for little children afraid that their fathers would come home inebriated, for mothers who had no food in the cupboard and were afraid of hunger, for fathers who were frightened by the terrible violence in this modern Sodom. Nichols lost the thread. His thoughts drifted elsewhere. Then he heard a bell, one sharp, high *ting* from the front of the hall. The little man wrapped up his prayer quite hurriedly, and there was silence again.

That was the procedure, Nichols remembered. These meetings had no leadership except the bell, which marked five minutes. No statement was permitted to go longer.

For the whole hour there were prayers, songs, Scriptures, and exhortations, all punctuated by expectant silence. Nichols wandered out of the building, carrying this silence inside him. The presence of those thousand men, shoulder to shoulder, voice to voice, was almost mesmerizing.

After that he went every day. The weight on his heart felt no less heavy, but he attended to it less. He listened as others spoke of a great work of God, and to whom else could it be attributed? The meetings had no leader, no preacher like Finney or Edwards. Some power beyond human agency was driving them forward. They heard that prayer meetings had spread throughout New York, up and down the coast to all the great cities (even Boston), to Chicago and Pittsburgh and St. Louis. The whole nation of men had, it seemed, an overwhelming urge to wait on God.

Politics was not permitted at the meetings, especially the politics of slavery, yet certainly it was their national strangulation that required such prayer.

That besides the financial panic. For one hour everything that divided them or paralyzed them was gone. They were as one, a single organism, deep and brooding.

Outside the church, streets were now full of nomadic bands, unemployed toughs who would ride others off the sidewalks or lob a stone through a window. On one afternoon a mob of them broke into a large bakery near Wall Street and passed out flour to anyone who came with a pan or a bag to put it in. As he walked to the ferry, Thomas saw the raiders, their clothing dusted with white. Some carried flour home in their shirtfront.

Another day the customhouse was mobbed. Troops were called out, and they beat into the crowds ferociously, protecting millions in gold held in the house's safe. The mob was blamed on the Democrats; it was blamed on the black Republicans; it was blamed on the Catholic cabal. Many of the Nicholses' neighbors talked of following in the steps of France and its republicans.

Nichols felt anxiety, but somehow it was now one inch removed from his heart. His attention had turned to the prayer meetings. For days and weeks he forgot about himself, forgot about the weight, concentrated as he was on seeing what might appear from the hand of God through their prayers.

On the first of November this hopeful expectation turned inside out on itself. Somehow his attention, which had been all goggle-eyed outward, turned unexpectedly to his own soul.

The idea appeared in his mind, full grown and out of nowhere, that he should confess. His secrets held so long and so close he should release to this large crowd—pour them out like water to God and to the world. From there, he suddenly grasped, must begin the healing miracle. He himself would be somehow the cure.

He was at the prayer meeting when this came to him. He was instantly filled with fright, terrified. The prayers went on as usual, but his ears had changed so that he did not hear them, but heard the long and ragged gaps between. Confession was not particularly a feature of the prayer meetings, though it did occasionally occur that a man would stand and, weeping or stammering, tell of his sins. Nichols had never considered it, even for a second. But now he seemed to hear, as though a command from heaven, his need to spill out. The silences rubbed this into him, saying, *Now. Stand and speak. I will testify with your spirit. Now.* It was so insistent that he could not even argue against it.

Yet each time the silence lasted long and the tension grew too great for him to bear, just as he was ready to break and stand trembling to speak, from somewhere else in the congregation a voice would begin praying, or speaking, or singing, and his mind would rest for another period, until the raw, blank silence came again and he heard the urgent voice again: *Now.*

At last it came that silence lasted, that no one spoke or sang. The quiet seemed to stretch into minutes. His heart hammered. The thought, almost audible, thundered inside: *Now. Stand. I have made them to wait for you.* At last he slid into a standing position, and as soon as he reached his feet and opened his mouth (it seemed to him that everyone watched him agape for his words) an extraordinary calm passed through him. He had not known how his soul chattered like a monkey in a cage, had not understood how noisy and disrupted it was, until that moment when quiet came over him for the first time in, what, ever? He went almost limp. It was so easy to speak he scarcely knew what he said, or how he said it.

How strange his voice sounded! To hear himself saying, before this vast throng, the very words he had strangled shut for so many years. For thirty years, his voice said out loud, he had held a secret sin that wormed at his conscience. (It was now so easy to speak his heart was lightsome.) He had been born a slaveholder in Alabama, raised to join the blue bloods, and he had held a black woman in concubinage. He had a son by this woman, a son whom he knew today but had never acknowledged. God forgive him, he had never spoken of this sin, he had carried it as a heavy burden these many years. His own beloved family had no idea. He pledged today to make it right, toward his family and toward his sable son. He confessed the deed now before men, before angels, before God himself.

Then he sat down. It was so simple. He had spoken.

Not until Nichols was on the ferry to Brooklyn did he begin to realize fully what he had done. He was seated in the crowded cabin, thick with cigar smoke and the hot, sour smell of unwashed bodies; he even had in his lap a newspaper with the latest Congressional debate on Kansas, but the paper went unread, and his eyes did not focus on his surroundings. The engine made a deep, hollow, familiar throb behind his back. He was mesmerized by the scene he could feel and see already, of his entering his hallway and finding Ruth in the kitchen.

He must tell her what he had told at the prayer meeting. He could barely breathe, the idea so terrified him. Yet he could not avoid it. The news would travel to her, very soon.

It is a strange thing how frightened a man can be of a woman, particularly a gentle, modest woman. He thought briefly of madness. That is, he felt the possibility of submitting to the weight again, of letting it paralyze him, of descending into Orange Mountain and the endless baths. He might not continue living, but let living occur.

He was thinking so intensely that he seemed to view the scene in front of him through a window. The boat docked, and he shuffled with the crowd onto the docks, smelling the warm horses, pipe smoke, some potatoes puffing in a fire by the customhouse. Up the street he walked, beginning to hum and then forgetting the song in midtune. Everything with Ruth had been straightforward and routine for a very long time. Now he had thrown everything open, and why? Ruth would ask him exactly that, why? And who was he, the man who had lied for so many years and now had confessed to a room of strangers? Who was he?

Just as this inward dialogue grew most intense, a hand fell on his arm. Nichols let out a bark, jerking away in fright. He had been too concentrated to hear footsteps. A man in a heavy, well-made coat was next to him, his lips smiling, his hands raised as though to say, "No offense intended."

"I am sorry to startle you," the man said. They were in a narrow street back from the dock. "I am Robert McClellan. I was there at the prayer meeting today." He left this phrase hanging significantly.

"Ah," Nichols said warily. His heart still pounded vigorously from the fright. Now that he saw he would not be physically assaulted, he still braced for a verbal attack.

Yet the man was well dressed and evidently a gentleman. "Brother," he said. "Dear brother in Christ, I saw you on the boat. I wanted to thank you for walking in the light. What a statement you made today." The man gripped Nichols's arm and spoke more urgently. "It is our only hope, to confess our sins one to another and be healed. After you spoke, the place where I sat was moved by the Holy Ghost."

"Oh," Nichols said. He took a deep breath and extended an arm in the direction that he was going. "Can you walk along with me?" As soon as he got over his panic he felt relieved by the interruption. He had been too fearful, forgetting the marvelous God-soaked reality of the prayer meeting. "I felt that God impelled me," he added shyly, "or I would never have spoken."

"Of course! Oh, that was obvious, that you spoke by the power of God. He will use your words! You have seen nothing yet."

"I hope I have seen the last of *my* confession." Nichols said. "There are no more secrets to tell."

"I was thinking," McClellan continued, "could you come to my church on this Wednesday and confess there also? Perhaps we might stir up the Third Person of the Holy Trinity to lie with power on the souls of this sin-sick city."

Nichols felt slightly confused, and he became more so as the man continued talking. McClellan was very enthused about what he might stir up by talking elsewhere. He kept referring to a bonfire of truth. Nichols had no wish to confess his sins elsewhere. He tried to demur, but the man now had a firm hand on his arm.

"Brother, where is your home? Can I accompany you there? I would like to talk more of the things of God."

"No, please," Nichols said. "I would rather be alone. Here . . ." He fished in one pocket of his coat and found a card. The man tried to read it by the light of the streetlight, and while he was peering at it Nichols attempted to walk on.

"Wait!" McClellan said. "I will go with you. No, I understand." He stopped and pulled on Nichols's coat to make him stop with him. "I am sorry. You wish to be in prayer. I will walk silently by your side."

Uneasily Nichols went forward. McClellan, true to his word, kept silent. In fact he had folded his hands in front of his chest and walked with his head down as though he, too, was in prayer. He kept this up for a hundred yards, and then began peering at the card Nichols had given him, trying to make it out despite the darkness. He walked straight into a lamppost. The impact was audible. Nichols was obliged to stop and provide a steadying hand.

"I am so sorry, Brother, I have done a foolish thing, I know you wish to pray. But let me walk with you, to strengthen you in whatever trials you face before the Lord. You remember how our Savior asked his disciples to watch with him in the garden? If even he needed the attendance of his friends, I suppose we all do."

Nichols must have sighed, for McClellan said hurriedly, "I will just be quiet," and set himself to studying Nichols's card again as he walked alongside him. They proceeded side by side up the long hill below Nichols's house. The narrow street was unlit. Stars shone coldly from the corridor of sky caught between the buildings lining the street. On the corner a watchman in a long military coat squatted over a fire. He made an elaborate bow as they passed. "Evening, gentlemen," he said.

Two streets ahead, shielded from the street by spruce trees, was Nichols's tall and narrow brick house. What if McClellan wanted to come in? He could not bring this man to his house. The man would want to tell Ruth about the marvel of his confession, and she would look coolly and say, "What are we talking of?" Nichols thought wildly of telling the man to go, shooing him off, and he might have done so if the man had not been so beautifully dressed. Nichols could not be rude to a gentleman.

On the corner was a grocery store, oil lamps bright in the window. "Excuse me, I need to nip in here for something," Nichols said. "Just wait here for me, please." Without hesitation he went in the door and then waited while Mrs. McGriff came in from the back room. The store smelled of dust and potatoes and the smoking fat of her dinner.

He had never looked at Mrs. McGriff, though they did enough trade here to have credit. He looked at her now, a serious young woman with a snub nose and nothing but business on her mind. "Mrs. McGriff," he said tentatively, "it may seem an odd request, but do you have a way out the back?"

"Of course I do. Do you think I can have my children racing through the store every time they go out?"

"No, no." He had often found Mrs. McGriff rubbing each can with a cloth, wearing off its label and making it prematurely shopworn. She would not allow children in, certainly.

"I would like to go out your back door, if you would allow me. And if you don't mind, there is a gentleman who will come after me. He's a fine man, no real trouble I assure you, but I would rather you didn't tell him just where I live, if he should ask."

"Not a bill collector, I hope, Mr. Nichols." Mrs. McGriff spoke swiftly, with the genuine alarm of a shopkeeper who has been stuck with bills.

"No, no, nothing like that. Only someone who might disturb Mrs. Nichols."

"Oh?" She cocked her head a little sideways.

He was making more troubles for himself, but he could not have that man at home tonight. Or any night, really. "Mrs. McGriff, I assure you there is nothing untoward in it at all. Merely a matter of personalities. He is not the sort that Mrs. Nichols would want to know. I just met him this evening." He looked at the woman pleadingly, and then said, "Now, may I go out?"

"Please yourself," she said, and opened the little half-door that protected her till from intruders.

In a moment he had bolted through the door to her kitchen, with its steamy atmosphere of cabbage and fatty salt pork. He stooped through a low door, clattered down some wooden steps, and was in the cold dark of an alleyway behind the building.

So he came in the back door, right into Ruth's kitchen where she sat with knife in hand in front of a table strewn with apple peelings. "Thomas!" she said. "What is with you?"

His first thought was astonishment, that his confession had reached her already. "I came as quickly as I could," he said.

"Quickly for what?" she asked. "You can come as quickly through the front door of the house as through the servants' entrance, surely."

"Yes," he said, hesitating in confusion. "Are you angry with me?"

"Why should I be angry? You can come in any door that you like. Only I have never known you to walk in that kitchen door."

Then he realized she had only been surprised by his entrance. No word of his confession could have reached her. He began to explain about Mr. McClellan, but soon realized that he could not unravel that mystery without going into the prayer meeting.

When he came to it, when he looked at her unsmiling face, at her white hands poised to put the knife into another apple, he was panic-stricken. It was harder to tell her the truth than it had been to confess before a thousand unknown men. That was surely because he loved her, for all the difference that his sickness had brought between them; he loved her and feared for what a confession might do to them both.

"Are you well?" she asked. "You are looking so strangely."

He gathered a breath and plunged into it, like a swimmer dropping off the slimy bank and into the deep green water. "I must tell you something, Ruth, something that I have hidden from you during our entire married life. Today, Ruth,"—he took another breath but still felt short on air—"today the Savior has done a great thing in me, he has set me free from the pride that has bound me all these years. Today at the prayer meeting I made my confession. I am sorry"—he raised his eyes to look at her face but found it stony and so looked away again—"sorry that I did not speak first to you. I had never thought that I could bring this out to anyone, after so many years of hiding my sin within me. Today—I believe the Savior spoke to me and gave me orders to speak."

She seemed to look him over like a market hen. "What did you say?" she asked.

"May I sit down?" He felt suddenly light-headed. Ruth put down her knife and sat very still, her hands folded quietly on the scarred table between them.

"It was long before I knew you," he said. "Before I knew the Savior. When I grew up as a slaveholder. I had a concubine, a black." Involuntarily he glanced into Ruth's eyes, but they remained calm, revealing nothing. "She was a slave of my father's, and she was set free when he died. I left her then and came north. Later I heard that my brother had her.

"Ruth, when I think of the iniquity I cannot believe it was I. I ask myself, did I know better? I think I did, at least I had been taught better. My father was a believing man, and I think my mother was devout before she died."

"Why did you never tell me?" she asked. Her tone was killingly neutral.

"Because it seemed so different from my Christian self. It seemed to me that Thomas Nichols had become a different man. So I told myself. And really, Ruth, after my conversion those sins seemed to have been done by another man entirely. And I was so ashamed. I knew you could never accept me if you knew my filthy past. Yet God has shown me that everything hidden must be revealed. It was only pride that made me keep this secret."

"Where is this woman now?" Ruth asked, her tone still even and her blue eyes cool and expressionless. "You said she was set free." When she saw that he hesitated, she pursued further. "Did you see her when you visited your brother?"

"No," he said. "She left Alabama long ago."

For a moment Thomas thought that he had escaped a full revelation. Perhaps she would press no more. In an instant, however, he saw that he must plunge all the way. He must let go of all support.

"But I have seen her," he said, and even though he had not previously thought of this as the crucial revelation, he instantly recognized that it was. "We met at the Christian Antislavery convention in Chicago."

"Five . . . six years ago?" Ruth could not sustain her neutrality. She seemed to rise up five inches taller, even though she did not move.

"Yes. And Ruth, she was present at the Orange Mountain. Purely by a coincidence. I assure you there is no unseemly connection. None in any way."

"At Orange Mountain? Yet you never told me."

Now in her voice he heard a hollow, bruised tone, a sound of resignation and winter. He dropped his eyes onto the table. "Ruth," he said, appealing to that name. "Ruth, how can I say what I felt? I thought of sparing you. I knew you could never understand the depravity of my upbringing."

"Never understand, no." Ruth said it flatly.

"That old evil is gone, quite gone. Our Savior washed it clean long ago. Believe me when I say that there is nothing but the memories of shared people between us. Rebecca met her, in fact, and grew fond of her, though she only knew her as an old slave of my father's. She was charmed."

He stopped when he realized that Ruth's expression had changed. He understood why: he had introduced their daughter to his harlot.

"I could not help it. I was sick, Rebecca was nursing me, Rebecca grew frantic, and Catherine came to her aid. I had not even known she was there."

"Catherine?"

"Catherine Nichols," he said. "She is unmarried but lives as a lady's companion in Rochester."

Ruth's face bulged, as though a subterranean pressure worked from within. She slapped two red hands across her eyes and held them there like bandages.

"There is no need," he said, trying to grasp an elbow. "She is nothing to me."

She took off her hands from her eyes and faced him ferociously. "My own daughter meets my husband's mistress, dallies with his former slave, and it is nothing to me who is not told. Who is only the wife and mother."

He could not even lower his eyes to avoid the swollen, angry, scarlet face of his wife. The full enormity of his plunge reached him, and he wished that he could disappear. "Please," he said. "Please forgive me. I know I was wrong, all wrong. Please forgive me." She did not answer but lowered her face into her hands again. He listened to her sobs until he was abstracted, almost bored. What could he do? Nothing, now.

Then with a terrifying pulse he realized he must still go further.

"Ruth," he said quietly. "Ruth, I have a son. Another son, I mean. A black son."

Ruth had buried her head into the crook of her arm on the table. She stopped her sobs. She was utterly soundless now, except for the quiet rattle of breath in and out of her slender chest. He wondered whether she had heard. Then she rose up slowly and looked at him. Something in the slow way she did it was terrible past words.

"What is his name?" she asked.

"Thomas," he said.

"Thomas," she said, rolling the word over her tongue. "Thomas. And he is how old?"

"Since I left Alabama," he said. "I never saw him. That would make him thirty-one, thirty-two." He was silent for a moment, wondering whether to go on. "I have seen him once since he is a man. At Oberlin." He recognized like death yet another confession he must make. He had not even realized, himself, how many secrets he had kept from her. "I helped to pay his expenses for the college."

"Where is he now?"

"His mother told me that he is minister to a church. In Troy, she said."

"But you have not seen him?"

"Not since several years ago when he was at Oberlin. I had seen him once before at the Christian Antislavery conference, but I had not made myself known to him. We exchanged a number of letters before we met at Oberlin. You remember those letters."

"And his mother, Catherine, she is a lady's companion. Though she is an African woman."

"Yes. Quite black."

"She has got an education?"

He hesitated. "Not from schools. When she was a girl I taught her to read. That was a part of our attachment."

Ruth closed her eyes, as though bearing a headache. She took a short breath and blew it out, and she looked at Thomas, all business. She blew out another breath. Obviously she found it hard to speak. "If you have a son I must meet him. I must welcome him into my home as his mother, if he will come."

"No, Ruth," he said. "That is not needful. He is a grown man."

"If he is your child, I must meet him," she said, raising her voice. "And even his mother, if that can be done."

"Ruth," he said. "It was all long ago."

"Yes," she answered, "but he is living today. I will meet him and help him if we can. It is only right that we should invite him to be in our family."

He could only stare at her. She had a concentration in her eyes so great that she barely saw him, or the room, he thought, but then she moved her eyes his way and a crooked smile pursed her lips. She put a hand on his, patting it as she would a boy's. "Oh, Thomas," she said, as though the word contained almost infinite depths of sadness.

"Can you forgive me?"

She made no effort to brush the tears away, nor did she respond to his question. He thought she was too distracted to have heard. Then still not looking at him, she said, "Yes." He sat still and looked at her. He wondered whether he understood her correctly. At one time, when they were newly married, he had marveled at how tiny she was, but now he marveled at how out of character her delicate body was, for she seemed to him quite massive in spirit, as solid as a mountain.

"You forgive me?" he asked.

"Yes, yes," she said. Then he got up and moved around the table to hold her. The smell of apples was all over her. For quite a long time he held her, his eyes shut. Never before, even at his conversion, had he known the full terror of condemnation. The weight on his heart, he realized, was gone, and he was light as a cloud.

The visit of Catherine Nichols and her son Thomas to the home of Mr. and Mrs. Thomas Nichols of Brooklyn was not reported in any abolitionist paper. That would have been considered indelicate by some, and making too much of an ordinary thing to others. Even so, a great many people commented on the event in private, for such a thing had never happened before.

The most liberal abolitionists, such as those following Garrison or Wendell Phillips, said that religious antislavery must have advanced further than they had expected. They had never thought that a man who made such a point of his religious orthodoxy as Mr. Nichols would ever contemplate his own black son. But since he had only done what any one of them would have been obliged to do, they did not want to overpraise it by remarking on it in the papers.

More conservative abolitionists had a different reason for keeping the matter private: they were extremely aware that it might play into the hands of Southern sympathizers, who were always, even yet, complaining that the aim of abolition was miscegenation. One of the reasons abolitionists were, in the main, unimpressed by the new Republican Party was that its leaders were so anxious to let it be known that they could not stand the company of Negroes, that they were against slavery only because it was detrimental to white men and to America. But abolitionists were themselves sensitive to publicity on this point.

Lewis Tappan fell into neither camp. He made a point of coming to the Nicholses' home while Catherine and Thomas were visiting, and he cheerfully shook hands all around and made the conversation flow with his memories of the early days of abolition. Thomas Nichols was fairly certain that neither his son nor Catherine had any idea how famous an abolitionist they were meeting, and this did not seem to occur to Tappan either. He talked as though they all knew the famous old names and would not let them be too gloomy about the prospects of antislavery. Tappan reminded them that despite everything a Democratic administration had done, Kansas was on the way to becoming a free state. He asked the young black Thomas Nichols many questions about the state of the church in Troy, even inquiring whether he saw any untoward results from the city's mobbing of Theodore Weld in 1836. When he learned that Tommy had never heard of the mobs, or of Theodore Weld, he was cheerfully astonished.

Apart from that brief, pleasant afternoon conference, the four-day visit of black Nichols with white Nichols was cordial but somewhat constrained. Tommy dressed in the neatest outfit of clothes that his father had ever imagined and made a point of his education by talking in grand, freighted sentences. Catherine and Ruth circled each other warily, though Ruth was in the kitchen much of the time because her chief girl had been let go the day that the visitors arrived. Sent to offer spiced hot cider, she came back to the kitchen saying that she wasn't going to serve niggers. Ruth put her out the door immediately.

So Ruth was busy, and more so because she would not allow Catherine to help in preparing food. She thought Catherine ought to be treated like a guest, and consequently did not treat her like a friend. But perhaps this was deliberate. She needed all her nerve to get through the days. Too many questions about the past, too much conversation might have made it impossible for her. She did not want to know much.

Still they were seen together, the two families, as they walked out on one fine, snowy day, and again when they shared a pew at Sunday services. If it was a show it was one with fair intentions.

Because Ruth was occupied in the kitchen, Thomas and Rebecca did a good deal of the sitting and conversing. Rebecca entertained on the piano and looked with particular interest and shyness at her half brother, who appeared to her grandly elegant. She was too reticent to ask questions about slave days, however. No one had really told her any details of her father's former relation to Catherine Nichols, but she knew enough to be embarrassed by it.

Even though the conversation was artificial, an effort at making a show even for themselves, Thomas felt a continuous wellspring of joy. Sometimes he felt as though he could start laughing, for nothing. He could feel his freedom in the healing of his hands, which moved freely as old harness. He was sure, quite certain, that he would never again be paralyzed.

He felt that his life had come full circle, that the loose ends were tied. Everything secret had been revealed and had found not condemnation but love. The superabundant goodness of God was very evident to him, so that the whole time he jabbered with his son (incredible, was he really conversing with his black son?) a smile was threatening to break out on his face.

When the visitors had left at last, Thomas buried himself in his newspapers for some hours, feeling blank and somehow disappointed. Ruth came through bearing a basket of linens and he stopped her, asking her to sit down and talk to him.

"I thank you," he said to her when she did. "Not only have you forgiven me, you have redeemed the years."

"It wasn't much of a visit," she said, running her hand over his neck. "What will you do now?"

"What do you mean?" he asked.

"What will you do with your son, now that you have begun?"

"I don't know. He is a grown man. And since he has grown up without me, I suspect he will live well enough without me."

"No doubt," Ruth said.

"The truth is I don't much feel he is my son. My son by blood, I acknowledge."

"There is some resemblance."

"Yet by spirit he is someone else's."

"Whose?" Ruth asked.

"I don't mean anybody's. I mean not mine, since I never saw him before he was grown."

"I see," Ruth said.

"Even so I am glad that we had them come," Thomas said. "I am glad you insisted on it. It was not an intimate visit, but how could it be when we are separated by so much? We share blood and the same God, but we are divided by everything else. It was only a first step."

"A first step for what?" Ruth said. "That is what I wonder, for what? Will we ever see them again? Will we grow closer to your son?"

"Oh, yes, surely we will. Slavery will end, someday, my dear, and then we will be together without difference. Someday in this land black and white will visit together without the slightest celebrity."

"I cannot imagine it," Ruth said.

"But that is because you never lived with Negroes, as I did," Thomas said. "The gulf between us is not so great as you imagine it."

She looked skeptical. "And when will slavery end?"

"Perhaps sooner than we think," Thomas sighed. But the question took all the optimism out of him.

Chapter 29
1859: Harpers Ferry

JOHN BROWN led twenty-two men, and left three outside the town, ready to arm those who would surely join them from Maryland and Pennsylvania and Virginia. Black Thomas Nichols was one of those to keep watch, disappointed bitterly but scared enough not to protest over his role outside the fighting. Nineteen men, then, to take the little town sunk deep in the valley where the Potomoc and the Shenandoah Rivers meet.

They left the farmhouse where they had hidden and marched in the chill, misty night, their rifles on their shoulders, behind a wagon loaded with heavy iron pikes. These they would hand out for weapons to the freed slaves who had never fired a rifle.

Only a handful of watchmen protected the bridges into town, and they put up no resistance at all, having never considered that anyone in the whole world might attack a sleepy, inland place like Harpers Ferry. The federal armory, too, set near the point of land where the two rivers converged, below the town, which stair-stepped a steep hill, was easily, almost effortlessly controlled. They ought to have sensed it was too simple, sensed that it was a trap not planned by men but sealed by fate from all eternity.

They put out sentries and sent a raiding party into the surrounding country. It came back at midnight with a wagon load of confused slaves and a few prisoners, including a local planter distantly related to George Washington. News would spread, they knew, and soon they would be receiving the joyous, overspilling crowds of men coming to fight for freedom. They had struck the blow and now waited, scared and excited and shivering in the misty chill, for the army to come to battle.

They provoked a different reaction, however. In the streets above the armory, white citizens gathered with whatever weapons they had, shouting questions, shouting rumors, scattering at the sound of a shot. The Lutheran church began to ring its bell, crying Rebellion, Rebellion, into the night. Men drank. A few brave or foolish or drunk enough sneaked down near the armory and ran away with bullets chasing them. Townsfolk connected their bits of information and lies and rumors to arrive at the conclusion that they were under attack, that slaves were rising up. The telegraph lines had been cut. It was the South's nightmare, Nat Turner risen from the grave.

In the early morning hours the train from Wheeling came into town. After a few hours of waiting in the darkness and confusion the train crossed the bridge headed into Maryland, and John Brown let it go. Soon it had reached a town with live telegraph wires, and spread the word of a slave rebellion. Troops were sent from Washington.

Others ran or rode with the message down all the surrounding roads. Every farmer with a shotgun, every merchant with a squirrel rifle, every white mechanic or teacher who could shoot and had a gun came at a run to Harpers Ferry. By midmorning a constant withering fire came down on the armory from the houses and trees on the ridge above. The mob was drunk and excited.

John Brown, his men, and his prisoners, including the few frightened slaves he had freed, retreated into one small, well-built engine house, where fire equipment was stored. They burrowed holes in the brick walls so they could shoot out and waited for their help to come. Bleak and iron-gray ridges above the town showed only dimly and occasionally through a cold gray mist.

Several of Brown's men, out on various missions, were shot, captured, or killed. One died in the street, was snatched up out of fire by brave citizens, and had his ears cut off for souvenirs. Another, captured, was dragged to the river and shot in the head with a revolver. His body lay in the shallow water, target practice for the rest of the day. Several townsmen, including the mayor, were shot and killed by Brown's men.

Brown sent out two parties with a white flag. They were promptly shot down. Two of Brown's sons were mortally wounded. One lay in the engine house screaming for his father to shoot him, to end the pain. Brown told him to die like a man and barely seemed to notice when he did. A few of Brown's men tried to escape in the fog and confusion, and made it; a few were killed. By afternoon Brown's men knew, though no one said so, that the free blacks and the rebellious slaves and the whites who yearned to fight for liberty were not coming.

Firing slowed to an occasional shot at nightfall. There was talk of escape, but Brown seemed not to hear. He seemed still to wait for something, as though his ear was attuned to some sound of approaching rescue that no one else could detect.

In the night the United States Marines arrived and dug in around the engine house. At dawn Brevet Colonel Robert E. Lee sent a note to Brown, carried by Lieutenant J. E. B. Stuart. Brown cracked the door and took the note, which demanded his surrender. Through the door Brown told Stuart he would never surrender; he must be allowed to escape.

At that, Stuart jumped out of harm's way and troops, on signal, raced up with a long, heavy ladder to assault the doors to the engine house. In a short time they had pounded their way inside. All raiders were killed or captured. John Brown, though severely injured, survived.

During that same night Thomas Nichols, who had watched from the trees beside the Maryland road while farmers and mechanics, then ragged militia, then finally federal troops hurried their way toward the town, decided that he should flee. Nineteen men, he was wise enough to know, could not match these troops. He began walking into Maryland, having little idea where to go and no money to support his journey. He only knew to go north, as his mother once had done.

The white-haired old man did what he did best: talk. He was unrepentant, articulate, fiery in admitting what he had done (though he denied intending violence—he said he only wanted to free slaves) and in condemning slavery as the great evil that justified him. His words cast a dominating spell even on the slaveholders who heard him. The Virginians, who admired nobility even in their sworn enemies, were perplexed and amazed that a violent abolitionist, their worst nightmare, could be a man of evident principle. John Brown's words were taken down and reported in every newspaper in the land.

The trial was done in two weeks. It took the jury forty-five minutes to convict John Brown. At his sentencing he was asked if he had anything to say.

"I see a book kissed," he sang out in a loud, clear voice, "which I suppose to be the Bible, or at least the New Testament, which teaches me that all things whatsoever I would that men should do to me, I should do to them. It teaches me further to remember them that are in bonds, as bound with them. I endeavored to act up to that instruction. I say I am yet too young to understand that God is any respecter of persons. I believe that to have interfered as I have done in behalf of his despised poor, is no wrong, but right. Now, if it is deemed necessary that I should forfeit my life for the furtherance of the ends of justice, and mingle my blood with the blood of millions in this slave country whose rights are disregarded by wicked, cruel, and unjust enactments, I say let it be done."

The nation heard him through its newspapers and stood transfixed, the North in admiration, the South in astonished hatred (and hatred for the North, which admired this vicious man).

On December 2, Brown was marched out to be hanged. He made no resistance. He seemed rather to want to be hanged. He had written to his wife, "I have been *whipped* as the saying is, but I am sure I can recover all the lost capital occasioned by that disaster; by only hanging a few minutes by the neck." Finally, the old man had found his calling. He told everyone that he felt the powerful presence of God with him in the cell. He spent many long hours writing letters.

Just before the soldiers came, he wrote out one last message:

> *I, John Brown, am now quite* certain *that the crimes of this* guilty, land: *will never be purged* away; *but with Blood. I had* as I now think: vainly *flattered myself that without* very much *bloodshed; it might be done.*

———————

At the end of the year, on the very eve of New Year's, Thomas Nichols knocked on his mother's door. He had walked, worked, borrowed money, begged wagon rides, moving and hiding from any hint of the law all these hundreds of miles until he reached Rochester. Certain he was a hunted man, he had kept his identity a secret from all but the most trusted abolitionists. He had thought of going to his own father in New York but could not feel confident to do so.

"Oh," his mother cried when she opened the door and saw him. "Oh my God. You are alive." She knew, or had an inkling, that he had gone with Brown, and she had thought he was dead.

"Yes," he said, "alive. Alive to fight another day."

Chapter 30
1861: War

THOMAS NICHOLS was not a tall man, and as the square was jam-packed from one corner to the other, he could see little more than a forest of hats, like black stumps. You could hear it better than you could see it, he thought, hear it and feel it, the jubilation like a prison whose walls have fallen down. All the way down Park Avenue a spirit of giddy celebration had been visible, in flag-waving matrons, in spring smiles, in boys marching in troops like army men, stamping their feet. It seemed they had life again, after dwelling in Sheol. It seemed they had a *country*.

Nichols stood shoulder to shoulder with his son Lewis, now a Congregational minister at a free church in Long Island. They were listening to a speech from one of the New York members of Congress, denouncing the rebellious aggression of the secession. The platform was decorated with flags; from many buildings flags waved. Two days before, the Southerners had fired the first shots, had pounded Fort Sumter into submission, had lowered Old Glory and replaced it with another flag of their invention. Yesterday President Lincoln had called for volunteer troops from all the states to put down this assault on the Republic for which their fathers had died.

For so long they had been all doubt and gloom and indecision. They had feared the Southern threats, worrying day to day that they would do what they had so long threatened: break up the Union because they had lost the election. Mayor Fernando Wood had, in January, proposed that New York City join the secession, linking its commerce unequivocally to the cotton trade. Where was the mayor today?

Suddenly everything was clear. They would fight for the right.

The square echoed with shouts. A band played, and when the audience applauded the brass bleated and trumpeted. "They have said," the congressman shouted, his voice raw with the effort, "the men of this rebellion have said they reserve the right of revolution, as did our forefathers who founded this nation. But what do they share with Washington? What do they share with Jefferson? The shot fired at Lexington was fired for freedom; the shot fired at Sumter for slavery. The patriots at Bunker Hill shed their blood for democracy; these men will fight for aristocracy and privilege. They do not fight in the spirit of 1776, they have *betrayed* it." (Cheers and loud cheers. Just ahead of Thomas Nichols a child appeared out of nowhere, lifted up onto his father's shoulders.)

It was a good speech but Nichols looked at his son, wishing to read his expression. Lewis had become a cold and cerebral man, far different from the warmhearted child. *Despite the chalk-white skin he is not like me, not like his mother either. Who is he like?*

The speaker finished, and the band struck up some rousing Republican tune. Men threw their hats into the air.

The next speaker read out Lincoln's appeal for troops. "The president has called for 75,000 militia to put down an insurrection," he shouted in a clear, high-pitched voice. There were cheers for the president's call. "The rebels will very likely come to greater wisdom when they feel the point of a bayonet." (Great cheers.) "They are like the bully boys who want to fight you if you don't give them your penny, and then, when it comes to it, have no stomach for the blows. Since the days of Andrew Jackson they have complained they can only control half the government, or two-thirds. Now they say that they will break up the only home of liberty unless we allow slavery to be blessed on every square inch of our nation. They say it is not enough that we let them have their way at home; they must have their way in *our* homes. They say they are ready to fight. We shall see if they are ready to fight!"

The crowd broke into a demonstration, chanting, "War! War! War!" Nichols did not join in this, but he smiled nonetheless at the happy enthusiasm. It had been a long time since anyone had been able to provoke such delight in a New York crowd.

"The president says that he wants 75,000. What say we give him 100,000? Two hundred thousand? What say we send a message to Mr. Jeff Davis, that if he would like to fire on American property, if he wishes to tear down our flag from over the harbor of Charleston, where it has flown for eighty years, then he will have to fight all of us."

Hats flew up into the air, like a snowstorm of heavy, black flakes. The cheer reverberated from the brick walls around the square.

"What have we here, right here, on this spot? One hundred thousand men? More?" The speaker paused, listening to a dozen shouted possibilities. "Mr. Robinson on the platform behind me assures me there are 125,000 men in this plaza. Right here we could fill Mr. Lincoln's need. What say the city of New York prove its mettle?"

They had set up tables at the front, and they wanted volunteers to come forward. "Now!" he said. "Let us do it now, while the blood is hot! Come forward with a good heart to fight for your country!"

Nichols felt a shove from behind. A short, blond man was pushing his way forward. "I'm going up," the man said, repeating himself every time he pushed someone aside. "I'm going up."

The whole jam-packed crowd was now alive with cries of "Make way! Clear a way!" Men were pushing up to the tables. The speaker's voice was overwhelmed by the stirring, the muttering, the shouting, as the crowd came to life.

Thomas looked at his son. "Go on," he said in his ear. "Go on and sign up. I wish I were your age again. I would do it in a moment."

Lewis shook his head, however.

"Why won't you go? You will miss your chance and regret it the rest of your life. Go on!"

Lewis looked at him sidelong, as though he were the stupidest man in New York.

"I wish I understood my son," Nichols said. He had found Lewis Tappan at his ledger in the American Missionary Association offices. Though he no longer played a leading role in the organization (which was much expanded, sending out scores of missionaries), Tappan's habit was to come every day to work on the accounts. Nichols seldom saw the old man, but it was comforting to know where he could be found.

"I don't see that there is so much to understand," Tappan said. He had gained a substantial stomach, while paradoxically growing more birdlike and frail. "He doesn't want to fight. What he feels personally, I feel more generally. My whole life I have hoped we could avoid this fight."

"Of course, no one wants war," Nichols replied, "but if we must fight, then what a cause to fight for! For the Union! Against slavery! When I was that age I would fight like a rooster."

"I was never a fighter," Tappan said. "Perhaps I lacked courage."

"You?" Nichols gently scoffed. "Not when I met you. No, give yourself credit. You never backed off from a conflict."

Tappan smiled and seemed to muse on that. His room had no exterior windows, receiving its only light through an air shaft, so it had a gloomy and retired atmosphere. "I never thought of it as courage," he said. "You would never find your way into reform unless you were prepared to sacrifice everything. It is different now. The younger men think they can build a career in reform, and I suppose they can." He stopped and mused again. "At any rate, Thomas, do not be too hard on your son. I don't think it is wise to be too enthusiastic about fighting our brothers in the South."

"Brother Lewis, you know my Thomas, a minister like my Lewis. He has been writing me asking do I know someone in the administration or in the army. He wants to form a black regiment and fight. He says it would be the greatest deed of his life, to die for the end of slavery."

Tappan lifted his bushy eyebrows, as though he had just heard a doubtful application for a loan. "Is that what this fight will do? What did they say today? Are we fighting to free the slaves?"

"No, of course not. They say we are fighting for the Union. To save the only free and democratic place on earth. But I think of it the way the president told us when he was here last year. The Union must ultimately be all slave or all free; it cannot be both forever. This fight is the beginning of the end for slavery, or else for our country."

"Well, perhaps so. Forgive me if I lack your enthusiasm. I have been against violence for so long it is a habit. I opposed giving John Brown rifles in Kansas, you remember, when all my comrades were for it."

Nichols smiled wryly. "Yes, but I think I remember guarding the door of a certain silk establishment, when rioters threatened to loot it. With a gun, I guarded it."

"That was defensive. I have never been a peace man as Mr. Garrison describes it."

"Surely this fight is also defensive, since the attack was made by rebels."

Tappan waved the thought away like a fly. "I don't deny it. I do not see that they have given Mr. Lincoln any alternative but the sword. If they had I am sure he would squinch out of it. Yet I can sympathize with your son Lewis."

Nichols felt a rush of gratitude for Tappan, who was his true father more than his blood father had ever been. He had seen the man impetuous, angry, ill-tempered, and naive, but the basic direction was sound. He was as true as gold coin.

"What do you think of Mr. Lincoln?" he asked, to camouflage his embarrassment at these thoughts. "He has been remarkably prudent, I think."

Tappan sighed. "Prudent, I suppose. I did not vote for him. After Fremont I vowed never again to support a man who was not thoroughgoing in his beliefs. Too often, I think, in our lust for popular approval we have been willing to compromise. That is why to this day I contend I was right to steer clear of the Free Soil. We needed a moral alternative, not a political alternative."

"You are saying that Mr. Garrison was right?" Nichols had to work to keep his face straight in asking the question.

"Never! Mr. Garrison was violent and extreme. He would gleefully attack the only possible source of moral purity, the church of Jesus Christ, because it failed to come up to his standard, and in so doing he damaged the only force that might have brought the slaveholders to their knees. I can never quite forgive him for wrecking our movement." He stopped, lost in thought.

"You were talking about Lincoln."

"Yes. I think he is an honest man, so far as that goes, but he has made no commitment to godliness. Mr. Lincoln belongs to no church. On slavery, he has said it is wrong to hold another human being as property, but he has not said he will exterminate the wrong, even in the District of Columbia where he has the power. I believe he is more a man of politics than of principle."

"But if he were too much a man of principle, he could never be elected."

Tappan nodded sagely. "That is so. Possibly we abolitionists are a different tribe from those who seek office. At any rate I would not say of Lincoln what Wendell Phillips has said, that he is a slavehound from Illinois because he will not do away with the Fugitive Slave Law. Let me just say: he is a politician. I never have hoped too much from political coercion, and I hope for less than ever now."

By now the whole bracing invigoration of the rally was gone from Nichols. *I am too passionate a man,* he thought to himself, *too eager to shout hallelujah, and too quick to discouragement.* He picked up his hat from Tappan's desk and began to stand. Tappan, however, was not done. He signaled for Nichols to sit down a minute longer.

When Tappan spoke it was as much to the ceiling as to Nichols. "This fight will take its course. It is beyond the control of a president. The Lord's purposes must be discovered, the hard but just ways of the Lord.

"We hoped and we worked, you and I, for a better way. We wanted a way of peace based on true repentance. Repentance never came; rather, hardening of heart. And now the way of the Lord must be found through darkness and blood. I pray that it will not be too hard."

The words hung in the air until Nichols said, "At the meeting they predicted a short conflict. They said the South would have no stomach when it came to blows."

Tappan shrugged. "Even so, I would not be too quick to urge my sons to fight. I admire your courage, Brother Thomas. You have always been quick to the mark when the struggle was on. But this struggle, who can tell its path?" His hazel eyes were dark in the gloomy office, his pale skin the color of a ghost moon.

"When you think of it, really, Brother Thomas, how many slaves have felt the lash cut their back? How many mothers have clawed at their captors while their own children were carried away? How many husbands have witnessed helplessly their wives sold off to a bidder? How many pints of blood have been shed, through violence done by people who called themselves Christian? Could such sins ever be swiftly undone? I fear not."

Chapter 31
1863: Emancipation

AT NEW YORK'S Cooper Union was planned an Emancipation Jubilee, to celebrate the slaves set free by Abraham Lincoln's wartime proclamation. The nation remained in the grip of a long and bloody war, with no end in sight, and the actual outcome for those slaves remained very doubtful. Yet opinion in the North had changed. The shift was subtle, but there was no question of it. The idea of free Negroes seemed less frightening, and the appeal of a moral war fought for their freedom seemed more ennobling. There also seemed some prospect that the proclamation might set off the black insurrections that John Brown had once hoped for and hasten the end of the war. By now, with hundreds of thousands of men streaming back to their homes forever crippled, and with hundreds of thousands of others dead and never to return at all, no one spoke of a short and easy conflict.

Thomas Nichols had arranged to drive Lewis Tappan in his carriage, because he had a carriage now (Tappan remained too frugal) and because it seemed proper that the two of them, old comrades, and now some of the few in New York who could tell the old stories of abolition, should be together for the ceremonies. He had arranged to meet Tappan at the AMA offices, to have a private supper together, and then to go to the meetings.

They had not seen each other in more than a year, and Nichols felt a slight alarm, when he saw Tappan come hobbling out of the offices, that the old man was in poor health. But not so. Tappan seemed more hale than ever.

He complained that he had sprained an ankle while dandling a grandchild.

When they had settled in a coffeehouse and made their order, Tappan asked immediately for news of Nichols's sons. Nichols smiled at the plural. Tappan was the only man he knew who reflexively referred to Thomas as one of his children.

"Thomas writes that he will join a regiment they are getting up in Boston. An all black regiment, though the officers will be white. Strange to think, he will be better educated than many of the men who command him."

"Yes," Tappan mused. "I am very glad. It is scandalous that the administration has been so slow to use the black man to fight for himself. The African will never really have liberty until he has the ballot and the musket. And Lewis? My namesake? I believe I heard that he had a command."

"Yes. He is a captain, at Washington City. He complains that they drill and drill in the mud but never fight. Between you and me, I think he may be secretly happy they do not. He never wanted to fight."

"I remember."

Their chops arrived, and they fell to eating. For a while they chewed in silence. Tappan sat back, heaved a sigh, took another bite, heaved another sigh. "It is a great day," he said. "A day I dreamed of but never fully believed would come."

"Yes," Nichols said, suddenly sober. "A great day. Three millions of slaves, freed at midnight."

"If I were a drinking man," Tappan said with a wink, "I would propose a toast."

———————————

At Cooper Union a throng poured into the large downstairs auditorium, where every prominent New York politician had held forth, indeed where Lincoln had first, a lifetime ago, unforgettably laid out his view of the national crisis.

Henry Highland Garnet, the elegant, deep-voiced black preacher, greeted them all in large, round tones and read Lincoln's proclamation aloud. He led them in three cheers for Mr. Lincoln, each cheer gaining in momentum until the last was a belly-splitter. The room was close and crowded, and the sound was live off the plaster.

Lewis Tappan was introduced for a few remarks. He limped forward on the platform and stood for a moment, looking around at the large and interested audience before he ventured to speak. To Nichols he looked unspeakably frail, a small candle a draft might extinguish. Tappan was what, seventy-five years old? He looked it. Nichols worried for a moment that Brother Tappan was not up to it and that the men and women who had gathered, knowing little about Lewis Tappan except the name, would never understand the debt they owed him. He wanted Tappan to shine.

"I have in my hand," Tappan said, brandishing a paper, "a letter dated March 9, 1841, written by John Quincy Adams, the former president. In it Mr. Adams informs me that the Supreme Court of the United States has freed the Amistad captives—a group of some seventy Africans who had taken possession of their captors' ship and steered it to the shores of Long Island. For that they were imprisoned in Connecticut, and I along with other abolitionists set out to save them."

At that time, Tappan said, the government of Martin Van Buren was entirely of the view that these Africans ought to be returned to their captors as slaves. The citizens of Connecticut and of New York, Tappan thought, had tended to the same opinion. "We were very unpopular in this city then," Tappan said with a smile, "more unpopular than I suppose you can imagine. At times we were threatened by riots, riots conducted with the full blessing of the city administration. It is difficult, I daresay, for many of you to think how unpopular our cause was."

That day when the Amistads were freed, Tappan said, was perhaps the happiest of his life, for on that day some seventy slaves had been actually freed. He was a businessman, interested in profits, and that had been a handsome profit.

"Today, however, today . . . surely it is a greater profit, and a greater happiness, for we free three millions. Think of it, three millions of human beings who have never, perhaps, known the meaning of possessing themselves."

He said he was not unaware of the deficiencies of the Proclamation. It was not as sweeping as he would have liked, did not free slaves in the border states, for example, but he was not going to quibble over those matters tonight. "Surely this jubilee of freedom, which we celebrate, is the first harvest of a general overthrow of slavery, to occur not in some distant time but quite soon. I think I will live to see slavery entirely abolished in these United States, and I remind you that I am a very old man."

He hesitated and smiled at the audience broadly. "Some people," he said, hesitating, "have called into question whether the Negro is capable of conducting himself well in freedom, whether he can take his place with his fellow free men in a dignified way, and not give us reason ever to regret this jubilee. I believe I can answer that question in the affirmative. Yes, the black man can. Indeed, he will. The capacity is certainly there. All the black man needs is the opportunity.

"In fact"—and now he smiled so broadly that Nichols was piqued, wondering what he had up his sleeve—"in fact, the esteemed Sir John Bowring told me once that the Negro is actually superior to the white man, both in intelligence and in physique." Tappan paused and let that sink in to nervous titters in the audience. "With all respect for Sir Bowring I am not so sure." He paused, wiggled his torso, gave one quick smile before putting on a serious face. "I believe," he said, "that a white man is as good as a black man, if he behaves himself."

The hall swelled with laughter and cheers, an appreciative clamor.

Tappan closed with a poem:

> *Judge not of virtue by the name,*
> *Or think to read it on the skin;*
> *Honor in white and black the same—*
> *The stamp of glory is within.*

For Further Reading

On Lewis Tappan:
Wyatt-Brown, Bertram. *Lewis Tappan and the Evangelical War Against Slavery*. The Press of Case Western Reserve University, Cleveland, 1969. Reissued by Louisiana State University Press, Baton Rouge and London, 1997.

On Theodore Weld:
Abzug, Robert H. *Passionate Liberator: Theodore Dwight Weld and the Dilemma of Reform*. Oxford University Press, New York and Oxford, 1980.
Thomas, Benjamin P. *Theodore Weld: Crusader for Freedom*. Farrar, Straus and Giroux, New York, 1973.
Barnes, Gilbert H., Dwight Dumond, and Peter Smith, eds. *Letters of Theodore Dwight Weld, Angelina Grimké Weld and Sarah Grimké, 1822–1844*. Peter Smith, Gloucester, Mass., 1965.

On Angelina Grimké:
Lerner, Gerda. *The Grimké Sisters from South Carolina: Pioneers for Woman's Rights and Abolition*. Schocken Books, New York, 1967.

On Charles Stuart:
Barker, Anthony J. *Captain Charles Stuart: Anglo-American Abolitionist*. Louisiana State University Press, Baton Rouge and London, 1986.

On Frederick Douglass:
Douglass, Frederick. *My Bondage and My Freedom*. Miller, Orton, and

Mulligan, New York and Auburn, 1855. Reissued in numerous editions.

On John Brown:

Oates, Stephen B. *To Purge This Land with Blood.* University of Massachusetts Press, Amhurst, 1970.

On James Birney:

Fladeland, Betty. *James G. Birney.* Cornell University Press, Ithaca, 1955.

On the Lane Rebels:

Lesick, Lawrence Thomas. *The Lane Rebels: Evangelicalism and Antislavery in Antebellum America.* The Scarecrow Press, Methuchen, N.J., and S. London, 1980.